Other Books by Howard Losness

Honor Thy Father
In Between
        A Dangerous Mind
        The Secret
        Escaped!
        The Columbian
        The Trick
        Damaged Goods
        Suicide Cliff
        Lost Woman
        Cross Check
        The Messenger
        A Pocket Full of Pebbles (Short Stories)
        The Plot
        A Dangerous Mind
        The Mark

Young Adult Books
        Little Eagle and the Sacred Waterfall
        The Secret

Illustrated Children's Books
        The Scarecrow and Farmer Rabbit
        It's Fun to be Small
        Humphrey Gets Lost
        The Boy who Lived Beneath the Sea

MY JOURNEY

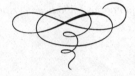

—————— HOWARD LOSNESS ——————

iUniverse, Inc.
New York   Bloomington

My Journey

iUniverse books may be ordered through booksellers or by contacting:

iUniverse
1663 Liberty Drive
Bloomington, IN 47403
www.iuniverse.com
1-800-Authors (1-800-288-4677)

ISBN: 978-1-4401-6654-9 (pbk)
ISBN: 978-1-4401-6655-6 (ebook)

Printed in the United States of America

iUniverse rev. date: 8/17/09

Dedication

This work is dedicated to my Mother, Lillian Agnes Johnson-Losness and my Father, Hans Trygve Losness. (I don't know why, but he always hated his middle name). Somewhere in time, while I was still a in the sprit form, long before my soul was transformed into the physical body that I now possess, I don't know how I could have been wise enough to have chosen to be born of the family that I eventually developed into, but I'm eternally grateful for the opportunity to have experienced the times that we had together, first as a child growing up, developing and forming the personality that I now have, and then as a young adult. The sum of their upbringing, molding and developing me into myself as I am today, which I hope to set forth in this manuscript.

Additionally, I'm eternally grateful to have the relationship with my younger sister, Janice. She is a living angel walking amongst us. A wonderful wife to Bob, whom I'm sure he will agree, an outstanding mother to Julie and Jeff and an equally gracious person to all her grandchildren, Ethan and Kellon Akers, and Hannah and Avery Haney and a gift to society as a whole. She leaves her mark on everyone wherever she goes. She is a dedicated soul to her church. I hope they realize how lucky they are to have her as a member of their congregation. We always look forward to our get together every year in Palm Springs. The time we have together is always too short, but the relationship is cherished.

You're the greatest, Ja Ja.

Brother Larry and I have had an outstanding relationship going back as far as I can remember when I used to take him hunting with me when I was in high school and he was but a wee lad of eight or nine years old. He was my best friend then and still is. We've been partners in business for years and never, that I can recall, have a single cross word ever passed between us.

Thanks for the friendship and the memories, brother.

I was blessed with three find boys, Larry, Aaron and Christian Losness, each with their own individual imprints. I only hope that I have left as profound, positive impression on their lives and my parents did no mine.

You have been a blessing beyond words, guys.

Last, but by no means least, I'm grateful for having found my wife, Myrna during a time in my life when my hour was in its darkest stage. Her laughter and loving way has been a source of inspiration and joy, filling my life. I could not have been more blessed.

I Love you.

In Memory of Brandi

Brandi: We love you and miss you more than I ever thought possible. The fourteen years that you graced our lives will never be forgotten. I look forward to meeting you again in the next life. You will always hold a place dear to our hearts for as long as we live.

My Journey

My Journey

BOOK ONE

BOOK ONE

The Beginning

A wise man once said that we are the sum of experiences of our past. I think that that is a little understated. It has been proven without a doubt that our lives have been and continue to be influenced by our gene pool. For example, in one way or another all of my mother's children, Janice, Larry and I, have been and/or are interested in music. We get this from our mother who inherited it from her father, John Johnson. Brother Larry played the baritone horn in the high school band, Janice played the piano, and I played the tuba in both high school and college and then again for a short period with the U.S. Army band when I got drafted, but more about that later.

Mother liked to sing and play the guitar. Apparently, all of Grandpa Johnson's children possessed the music gene as well. I can recall that Uncle Albert, mom's older brother, was very talented, being able to play the piano without reading music and playing the guitar as well. On the Losness side of the family – grandpa and our father - as far as I can tell, was tone deft and couldn't carry a tune in a bucket. Thanks for the music gene, Grandpa Johnson.

I have only a limited memory of Grandma and Grandpa Johnson, my mother's parents. John Johnson and his wife, Johanna migrated from Norway during the great depression and settled down on a small farm in Bottineau, North Dakota. He was a tall, erect man possessing no nonsense piercing blue eyes. As a young man he had blond hair and fine sculptured facial features. Strong but not overpowering. I recall my mother telling me that he was a musician in the sense that he could play any instrument, but favored the piano and guitar; hence the transfer of music to his offspring's gene pool. From what I can gather, aside from what little he earned teaching music to his pupils, he and his family lived off the land. They raised chickens and pigs and had a garden from which they raised most of their food. I can recall my mother saying that she used to hate it when, in the middle of winter, she and her sister, Emma, would have to go out in the middle of winter and dig carrots from the frozen ground.

Mt memory of Grandma Johnson is just about as vague. She was a kindly lady with soft Norwegian features, quiet spoken who always wore a pastel floral dress and played the part of a dutiful, devoted wife and housekeeper. She was soft spoken and I never heard a harsh word come from her lips. Not much of a memory, but that was about it. They had four children, three girls and one boy, Albert, now all deceased.

Mom's favorite sibling was Emma, who was a little older than mom. If there is such a thing as a pair of soul sisters, they were it. They were like two peas in a pod, as close as they could be both in word and deed and in looks as well. Then, one day, Emma and Herm, that's Emma's husband, suffered a major, emotional setback in their lives that would come to affect the entire family. Their six year old daughter, Jeannie, had been outside ridding her tricycle on the sidewalk when a cement truck working on the house next door, accidentally back over her, killing her instantly.

I can recall mom's reaction the moment she received the telephone call from Emma. We were living in Hermiston, Oregon at the time and it was like someone threw a shroud over the house and everyone in it. I had only met Jeannie once that I can remember, but could visualize the image of little Jeannie in my mind's eye at the time. She was the spitting image of her mother, only smaller, of course. A kind and gentle child of God with her mother's smile, eyes and disposition.

The construction firm had offered a considerable cash settlement to the family, but they refused, saying that to take the money would be like taking blood money and they would never be able to enjoy a penny of it.

Shortly after that, Emma contracted cancer, and before anyone knew it, she had passed away. Everyone thought that her illness had been the result of little Jeannie's sudden death. In any case, she never recovered from the pain of the loss of her daughter.

Olie and Gjertina Losness, grandfather and grandmother Losness, came over from Norway and settled in Fargo, North Dakota. He became an engineer on a train. Which line I don't recall, that enabled him to travel free of charge around the country. As a result, he came to visit us from time to time at Hermiston, Oregon which is where we moved after living seven years in Irrigon, Oregon. I can remember that I was a junior in high school when he first came to visit us in Hermiston, along with grandma Losness.

Like all of the Losness men, he wasn't much of a talker. He would sit on the couch with his arms folded in front of him like a grand Buddha, close his eyes and wait for someone to say something, from which, without opening his eyes, he would respond with the shortest sentences possible.

Grandma had this way about her, grandmotherly, would be the correct way to describe her, I guess. She would say, "Now, Howard. Do you smoke?"

To which I would reply, "No,"

She would then grab my hand and inspect my fingers to see if there were any signs of tobacco. Yellow fingers. Satisfied that I wasn't a smoker, she rewarded me with a hug and a kiss. Dad used to tell us that he had started smoking at the ripe old age of twelve and I guess that she knew it.

In Fargo where they lived, they must have lived somewhere near the railroad tracks because hobos would periodically knock on her door, asking to trade work – chopping wood, mowing the lawn, pulling weeds, or washing windows - for a handout. Whether she had work for them or not, grandma Losness always had something to eat for the poor fellow and he and his fellow travelers knew it. For some reason, they only came to her door, not the house next door nor the one across the street. Just grandma Losness' house. Turns out that that they had a way of marking her fence so that every time that a hobo came by, he knew which house was friendly and which was not.

Speaking of railroad tracks in Fargo ran next to a lake somewhere, because dad used to laugh when he told us the story that he and his brother Fritz used to go swimming nude in the lake and when the passenger train came by, they would float on their backs with their little wing-dings sticking out of the water, trying to shock the ladies in the train.

Then there was the time that he and Fritz decided to paint graffiti on a neighbor's barn. They got caught of course and had to repaint the whole barn. I guess they were full of spirit!

Growing Up

My earliest memory is but a short snippet that took place in Fargo, North Dakota which is where I was born. I don't know how old I was, but I know that I was ambulatory, so I may have been somewhere around two years of age. It was winter time, and I can recall opening the front door of our house and seeing snow piled way over my head. Then, there is something about playing in an attic, opening a truck and exploring the contents, but that's about it.

The next memory kicks in at Sun Valley, Idaho where dad worked as a cook at the lodge. I can recall ice skating on the rink outside the lodge where he worked. Put a pair of skates on me now and I'll fall flat on my butt, but I guess back then, I could skate. I can recall one evening going to an event out doors where a famous red headed man by the name of Author Godfrey, a comedian, had been master of ceremonies. He was drunk and was slurring his words.

Then, later, I can recall a little store and a gas station that apparently dad owned and operated. Perhaps that is where the seed of my self employment derived. I don't recall this, but I have pictures of me riding a little tricycle around the one glass gas pump that he had outside the store. There were pictures of me riding a pony too, but apparently I wasn't too enthralled with the whole experience 'cause I was crying.

That's about it until I reached the age of twelve when, for all intents and purposes, my life began. I was in the fifth grade. We had just moved from a little town called North Bonneville, Washington to Irrigon, Oregon population 236, which was located on the Columbia River.

Irrigon had one paved street running through town – the highway in and out of town - and there were no stop lights. If you blinked while driving through, running or biking, you would have missed the whole forgettable experience. Aside from a set of train tracks that paralleled the highway, everything else was dirt and gravel. If the streets had names, it was a well kept secret. Everyone went by, 'Down by McCoy's', or 'Over by the culvert at Kenny's place,' or 'Near Fannie's Market,' or 'Down by the river.' The grave yard was an eerie, unkempt place down by the river that no one ever went near. As far as I know, no one was ever buried there, at least not during the five years we lived there. Aside from its existence, it is not worth mentioning.

Irrigon was a great place to be from. As an adult, I wouldn't want to live there now, but as a kid, it was a great place to grow up. Whether you liked it or not, independence was almost forced on you. Everyone my age, despite any diminished skills they may or not possess, participated in one way or another in some school activity, be it music, athletics or the school paper. If you were a total klutz, they made you a team manager, thereby elevating your status from a nobody to someone important, even if your only job was to carry towels and fetch water and then clean up after everyone else.

As one might expect for a small town, everyone knew everyone else and everyone else's business. The local gossip machine was this elderly woman who everyone simply knew as 'Ruth'. She specialized in snooping around and reporting her findings to the *Hermiston Herald*, a paper that devoted a couple of inches every Wednesday to our little berg. Tantalizing news such as:

> *The Hayes family went over to Umikers for a Saturday brunch where they were served fried chicken, or Harm Smith and family drove to Ukiah for a family reunion. Present were ....*
>
> Everyone looked forward to the Wednesday paper to see if there name appeared in print, thereby giving you the status of celebrity, at least for the week.

For telephones, everyone had party lines with two or three parties per line. If your phone rang, it rang once for you, twice for the Smith residence and three times for Harry's place. Chances are, if it rang once, both Smith and Harry would pick up the line and listen in. It wasn't difficult to memorize everyone's telephone number, as each number had only three digits. Ours was 324. As I said, there were few secrets in town. When the Henry J's came out (this was an automobile for those not old enough to realize what a Henry J was), old man Kenny bought one, and before he even drove into his driveway, everyone in town knew the color and how much he had paid for it. When he ran it into the ditch, everyone knew where and why before it had been towed to the garage where the repairman, Orie Thompson advised him that it would cost more to fix than buy a new one.

In the unlikely event any of my friends had the luxury of owning a television set, I wasn't aware of it. Aside for church socials and friends gathering to play cards, radio was the main source of entertainment for adults. The closest movie theatre was six miles away, way too far to consider driving to, and they changed the film every Saturday. I think in the five years we lived in Irrigon, I went to the movies three times.

My first teacher in Irrigon, the fifth grade, and most memorable instructor was Dorothy Hayes, a kindly elderly woman with grey hair and glasses and a perpetual smile. My folks got to know them through church, one of the only two in town. Our church was a Baptist church pastured by Reverend Mel Smith, a man who would come to make a lasting impression on my life, and the other, a Seven Day Adventist Church. I was invited to attend the Seven Day Adventist church one Sunday by one of our neighbor's girls. I accepted and it was one of the most frightening experiences I've ever had. In our church, people sat quietly and listened to the sermon. Except for the choir singing, one of the voices of which was mom's (I could always hear her voice, no matter how many people were singing), people were pretty sedate. The Sunday that I attended the Seven Day Adventist Church, people were waiving their arms, getting down in the isles and carrying on to the point that I thought I was in a cult or someone has spiked the grape juice. I promised God that if he would let me survive that I would amend by wicked ways, such as they were, and never waver from the straight and narrow. Needless to say, once I was out in the clean, fresh air, I never went back.

We lived in a two bedroom house that couldn't have been more than a few hundred square feet. Our bedroom where the three of us slept was so small that with a pair of bunk beds on one wall where Larry and I slept and a single bed on the other side where Janice slept, there was barely enough room to walk from the kitchen to the bathroom.

We were poor as church mice, but as kids, we didn't know the difference. The whole town was poor. That's why they lived there. Our property included two large adjacent lots. I don't recall how one figured out where one lot ended and another began, but in town that size, who cares? We didn't even have an address as far as I can tell, just a post office box. And there was no such thing as a regular sized lot. Houses were situated helter-skelter like random pieces of wheat thrown across the land on a windy day.

Every spring we, dad and I, turned the soil by hand and planted a garden. We had rows upon rows of potatoes, corn, onions and every vegetable known to man that would grow in that climate. The soil was sandy and loose and in the summer's heat, everything grew fast and large. What we didn't eat, mom canned or froze for the winter. Several fruit trees lined the perimeter of our property, one of which produced the largest, most delicious peaches I've ever eaten. For the most part, we grew or raised everything that we ate. We purchased milk from a farmer down the road in quart containers that had four inches of cream floating at the top.

Every year Dad would order a hundred baby chicks from Sears in Portland. We were advised that our shipment would arrive by rail in a large cardboard box. Every morning at six o'clock I went down to the spot where the train slowed down enough to drop off deliveries until our package finally arrived. By the time they arrived in a large square cardboard box, invariably, three or four of the little yellow fuzzy creatures would have been trampled to death by the others, trying to keep warm. I would discard the dead chicks and then would balance the square box on the handlebars of my bike and then ride home with the little creatures peeping with excitement.

Dad had built a chicken coop on the back of the property to house the chicks. It was one of my chores to make sure that they had enough chicken feed everyday, so, as one might suspect, I became their best friend. Whenever I came near the chicken coop, they'd run towards me like a long lost buddy. Thankfully, when it came time separate their heads from their bodies, dad performed that task. Once they were killed and cleaned, I got stuck with the unpleasant job of dunking them in hot water and plucking their feathers. If you've never smelt hot chicken feathers fresh off the chicken, you're missing something you don't ever want to experience.

Aside from raising chickens, we raised a pig every year as well. Invariably, the pig would figure out how to dig a hole under his pen and would escape. We'd have to track him down and then herd him back home again. Fortunately, he was big and fat and never got very far, but by the time we got him back in the pen, he was usually huffing and puffing so hard we thought he might have a heart attack!

Ever since I can remember both mom and dad worked. For the first few years, they worked at a place simply called The Ordinance. The Ordinance was a government facility consisting of countless cement igloos wherein chemicals and munitions from past wars were stored. I never became clear what exactly dad did, but it was my understanding that they kept moving the munitions from one igloo to another. To what end, I have no clue. Mom's job was to make an accounting of what went where. She was called a checker.

Every morning around five-thirty or six they would get up, make their lunch and drive the ten miles or so to the ordinance. And every evening around six they would arrive back home, dead tired. My favorite picture is one that I took with my little Kodak Brownie camera of them laying in each others arms, sleeping on the couch, dead tired after a long day's work. That single picture said everything about our life, their devotion to each other and to the family.

Mom would later get a job in the school cafeteria and then eventually get hired as a sales clerk at a department store in Hermiston, the place that we moved to when I was a junior in high school. She became so good at her job that she was promoted to a buyer where she would travel to the big cities like Portland and Seattle to buy all the clothes for the store for the upcoming season. That single promotion would give her a new lease on life.

The fifth grade in Irrigon came to be a very significant year in the development of my character. I got my first job and was exposed to my first experience in team sports – basketball.

The janitor of our school, Mr. Henry, had a small farm outside of town. In our town, with the exception of a few houses and businesses, everything was out of town. When it became known that he was looking for a lad to irrigate his land once a week, I jumped at the opportunity. Getting out of school every Tuesday had nothing to do with my decision, nor did making twenty-five cents an hour. It was the opportunity to build character.

You're not buying this are you?

So it was agreed. Every Tuesday at noon, I was excused from school to ride my bike down to his farm. The job was simple. Open the irrigation gates and let the water flood the crops. When the water reached the end of the lot, I was to insert the gate into the opening and then open another gate onto the next lot until everything was irrigated.

Mr. Henry grew corn and vegetables on one lot with the balance of his farm had been planted in alfalfa. The crops were watered by irrigation ditches. I would simply open the gate, diverting the water onto the area to be watered. And then wait. I would stand on the canal bank and watch as the water slowly made its way down the earth. The ground seemed to come alive as the water edged its way down the earth as grasshoppers, ants and other wildlife scurried to escape the weekly flood. From the time I opened the gate until the lot was fully drenched took the better part of forty-five minutes. There wasn't much to do in between except watch the water trickle down which is like watching grass grow or paint drying so, being the nosey kid that I was, I set about exploring the rest of the farm.

There was this old barn which, just to look at it, was fascinating. Inside Mr. Henry had stored all his old farming gear: pitchforks, wagon parts and, of course, lots of dried hay. The chickens were allowed to run loose and roam about the grounds freely. They had become acquainted with humans, so my presence didn't seem to bother them in the least. They would flap their wings and screech, getting out of the way as I walked through the yard.

I sat on the tractor and pretended to race down the farm, making roaring noises. That got tiresome after a few minutes. That left the fenced in pasture where Joey, the Billy goat lived. I had been cautioned by my employer not to enter the pen, as Joey apparently didn't cotton to strangers and he didn't want me to get hurt.

As I stood outside the fence looking at the goat, Joey roamed over to where I stood and stared at me, causally chewing on a piece of grass. His jaws swayed back and forth as his teeth ground the grass into a pulp. Apparently he was sizing me up. When I placed my hand on the post he immediately charged and butted at it, ramming his horns in to the fence, clearly setting the tone as to whose domain this was. It wasn't until that moment that I realized the force that a pair of horns on an animal the size of Joey.

He had my attention!

Horns or no horns, not one to be intimidated by a caged-in animal, I taunted him by putting my tennis shoe against the fence. A moment later I picked myself off the ground.

I eyed Joey with renewed interest.

A new game was afoot!

I looked around for anything that was harder than my body to taunt him. A rotted four-by-four post lay on the ground a few feet away. I picked it up and placed it on the fence. Sure enough, Joey charged and butted it with his horns. The impact scared the daylights out of me. As I picked the slivers out of my hand, I had a renewed respect for him and his territory, but not enough to let well enough alone.

About that time I heard the honking of a horn. Mr. Henry had come to check up on me.

"How're all doin'?" he inquired, looking at the patch of alfalfa that was flooded.

"Just fine. I was just lookin' for a shovel."

"You ain't botherin' Joey, there are ya? 'Cause he's an ornery one, he is. I don't trust him a lick. He'd soon as knock ya into next Sunday as look at ya."

"I can see that he can bear some watchin' alright."

"You stay outta that pen, ya hear?"

"Yes, sir!"

"Ya can go home now. I'll finish up. Next Tuesday?"

"Next Tuesday."

Every waking hour, my mind was preoccupied with the question of how was I going to outsmart Joey the next time we met.

The answer came the following Tuesday afternoon, when it came time for me to peddle my Schwinn bike down to the farm where I knew Joey was waiting for me. I turned off the well-worn gravel road and onto Henry's property, my heart anticipating the contest that was inevitable. A contest which I, the superior thinker, would undoubtedly win.

As I rode onto the property, the water was already churning at the top of the ditch bank, aching to get out. I slid to a halt, letting my bike crash into the dirt, and ran to the culvert where I released the water onto the alfalfa patch. Grasshoppers, ants and assorted bugs scampered to get out the way of Noah's weekly flood. I stood there for a moment, surveying the lot and then turned my attention to the pasture next to the barn. I had forty-five minutes before it was time to change the water again. Plenty of time to psych Joey out.

I approached the pasture cautiously, tiptoeing with my back to the barn, trying to be as quiet as possible. At the corner, I peered around, searching the pasture for Joey. At first glance, I didn't see him. My heart rate increased as I visualized him behind me. I spun around, but no Joey. My imagination was clearly working overtime. I stepped out from behind the barn and met Joey's eyes. He had been standing next to the barn too, waiting for me, as if playing hide and seek.

Now that we knew where each other were, it was time that we established the pecking order, with me in charge, of course. I rattled the fence, attempting to taunt him, but he wasn't biting. Instead, he simply turned his back and slowly made his way to the middle of the pasture where he stood, looking in the opposite direction.

If he wasn't going to play my game, I thought, I figured that I would frustrate him by invading his territory. The fence was only about five feet tall, and even at age twelve, I was tall for my age. Scaling a five foot fence offered no challenge. A moment later I stood on Joey's turf.

Still, he ignored me.

I made threatening noises, and when that failed to get his attention, I picked up a small stone and hurled at him. It fell short, bouncing past him and coming to rest well within his visual range. At least I had his attention.

Still, he ignored me.

I looked for another pebble. The only one of any size in sight lay ten feet inside the pen. Still, a good thirty feet from where Joey continued standing, facing the opposite direction.

I measured the distance with my eye, thinking that even if he were to charge, I had plenty of time to retreat and climb over the fence. I silently walked over and retrieved the rock.

As I bent over to pick it up, unbeknownst to be, Joey had turned and was now silently regarding me. By the time I had picked up the stone and had refocused on Joey's hindquarters, he was well on his way to charging me.

Without hesitation, I dropped the rock and sprinted for the fence. The sound of Joey's hooves were getting louder and closer. I quickly assessed the fact that there was no time to climb over the fence. I had only one chance, and that was to hurdle the five foot obstacle on a dead run. I ran the high hurdles in track, but they were only thirty inches tall and the fence was double that. I had no choice!

I could almost feel Joey's breath on my back. My heart was beating double the rate. I wondered what old man Henry would say when he returned home that evening and found my trampled body in Joey's pen, and what he would tell my mother.

I was within three feet of the fence now. It was now or never. I gave it everything I had! I pushed off my right foot and sailed through the air. It was clear that I wasn't going to make it, but maybe I'd get enough momentum to at least reach the top of the fence, and from there I could simply fall over.

Joey had other plans.

Just as I reached the pinnacle of my jump, Joey's horns reached me. The combination of his horns catching me by the seat of my pants combined with my forward-upward motion, propelled me over the top of the fence like a rocket.

I lay sprawled out on the ground on the other side for a moment. Safe. It was time to assess the damage. My legs moved okay and I didn't feel the pain of anything broken. The only damage suffered was my ego, and with only myself and Joey knowing the difference, that would pass.

Joey stood on the other side of the fence, glaring at me. He knew that he was the king of his domain, and now, I knew it, too. I never bothered him again.

Sports

My first introduction to team sports was fifth grade basketball. I had never shot hoops before and took to the game like a duck takes to water. Dad soon got caught up in the sport too, erecting a free standing basketball hoop on a hard dirt area that was located in the back yard between our house and the chicken coop. On those days when dad came home and wasn't dead tired, and on weekends, we'd practice shooting hoops. He introduced me to games such as around the world, where you got one shot from a given point of a semi-circle perimeter and, if you made it, moved onto the next spot. If the shooter missed, he could either stay at that position and wait for another turn, or he could 'chance-it'. If the shooter made it, he could continue on around the horn, but if the shooter 'chanced-it' and missed, he had to go back to the beginning and wait his turn and then start the process all over again.

Twenty-one was a game where you simply made a shot from the free-throw line and if you made it, would then retrieve your own ball and shoot a lay-in for a total of three points. If the shooter missed, he lost his turn. If he made both shots, he continued shooting until he missed. The first one to twenty-one, won. That game was eventually embellished to moving the first shot back five yards to the top of the court for a three-pointer, much like basketball today, except in those days, there was no such thing as a three-point shot.

Then, there was the game of Horse. The first one to shoot could shoot from anywhere, and in any manner, and if he made it, the other player had to make the same shot, the same way. Say I attempted a under my legs left-handed lay-up, and made it, dad would have to make the same shot. Each time a player missed the shot that the previous player had made, he would add an additional letter, until he eventually spelled 'Horse', at which time the other player won the game.

And, of course, there was one-on-one. Just plain basketball. Dad was in his late thirties then, and being young and in shape, I had a decided advantage, conditioning-wise, so we usually only played one game to, say eleven before reverting back to the less strenuous games.

About the time that I was getting pretty good at making baskets and winning at least half of the time, Dad decided to sweetened the pot. "Let's make it interesting. What do you say?" he said, looking me in the eye.

I was game for anything. "Sure. What do you have in mind?"

"Let's play for doing the dishes," he would challenge.

I might mention here that Dad had a far out way of shooting that didn't inspire confidence in his ability to outshoot me. He stood flat-footed, squarely facing the basket and shoot every shot two-handed, be it a lay in, a free-throw, or a shot from anywhere in the field. Two-handed with each hand placed evenly on either side of the ball. I was always amazed how deadly he was.

Not one to turn down a chance to beat him, not to mention the chance to get out of doing the dishes, I readily accepted the challenge. This was my first introduction to learning that how conniving my father was. I was amazed how his game had suddenly sharpened up as he easily made his free-throws, winning at twenty-one.

"How about we add weeding the garden, double or nothing," I would add, thinking how much I hated doing the dishes.

"Okay. I'll go first."

Ten minutes later I was sentenced to not only doing the dishes, but weeding the garden as well. I'm not sure at what point I finally learned my lesson, that I had been had, but I think it was somewhere around my twentieth birthday!

That wasn't the only sneaky trick that he had up his sleeves. I'm embarrassed to tell you the rest, but for the sake of teaching your children to avoid such traps, I'll relay a couple of simple examples.

Dad was a great cook. In his younger days, before we moved to Oregon, as I mentioned previously, he used to be a cook at the famous ski resort of Sun Valley, Idaho. He reportedly knew Bing Crosby, the Marks Brothers and other movie stars. I think when he said that he 'knew' them, he meant that he had actually seen them around the premises and may have even cooked for them.

Anyway, one of my favorite dishes that dad had cooked was vegetable soup, made from fresh garden vegetables. We all loved it. You gotta know that in the Losness household, you don't eat soup without crackers -- buttered crackers. Most people butter their crackers as they use them, one at a time. Me, I like to butter a whole stack of them at once, so when it's time to eat my soup, I don't have to take the time to let my soup cool down while I butter each and every cracker. Also, you get to keep the eating rhythm when you don't have to stop to butter every cracker.

While everyone is consuming their soup, I'm feverously concentrating on buttering a stack of crackers. I figure about ten to twelve should do the trick. Conger up the image of a twelve-year-old stacking his dozen buttered crackers next to his bowl of soup and then picking up his spoon. Now I'm, ready! Spoon in one hand and a buttered cracker in the other. Right about now, I'm the envy of everyone at the table.

"Say, isn't that Bobby Holden riding up on our lawn?" Dad says, pointing to the window behind me.

That should have been my first clue, because the window behind me led to our garden and the basketball court, and no one ever came that way. I look around anyway, expecting to see the smiling face of my little toothless friend. I say toothless because Bobbie had these false front teeth that had a habit of falling out whenever he laughed. And I loved making him laugh.

"Where?" I inquire, straining to see him. "I don't see anything."

"Oh, I must have been mistaken," my father replied as my brother and sister tried to contain themselves from giggling.

Mom is giving Dad a stern look, but has an impish smile on her face at the same time.

I don't have a clue what has come over my family. Well, back to my soup and …. My crackers! They're gone! The stack of crackers that I spend the better part of the evening buttering had disappeared. Meanwhile, I notice that Dad has suddenly come into a cache of neatly stacked, buttered crackers.

It took me until my senior year -- of college -- to learn my lesson on that one.

Now, periodically Mom made a killer chocolate cake with chocolate frosting that was to die for! On those rare occasions when she would bake one, for reasons that I'll relay later, we were usually served our portions after dinner. I like a cold glass of milk with my cake. I also like to savor the best for last, so I'd surgically separate the top frosting from the rest of the cake and set it aside. I'd no sooner finish the cake and get ready to taste the remaining delicacy when my father would say, "Say, isn't that Bobby Holden riding up on our lawn?"

I must have been dumb as a post. I never did learn that lesson.

Somewhere along the line, Dad got wind that the town had a basketball team and was looking for another player. I'd previously asked dad if he played basketball in the high school that he attended, in Fargo North Dakota. He had said yes, and then proceeded to drag out his year book, a smallish book entitled *Oak Leaves, 1933*, consisting of no more than a couple dozen pages of photos and jokes and an equal amount of pages devoted to advertisement such as the Viking Hotel, Chris Losness – his uncle, my great uncle, the owner.

Sure enough, there in the sports section was a group of eight guys standing; wearing what looked like white muscle shirts. At a height of six feet, with his reddish blond hair combed straight back, our dad was indeed a member of the team. The caption under the photograph read:

> "Captain Losness was Oak Grove's all-around man. He
> was a fast player and helped the Grovers through many
> scraps with his sure shooting."

The year book bragged about how he had been the high point man and how valuable he had been to the team.

In the humor section of the year book, he had his role too:

Okerlund: "Don't you think, Hans, that you out to brush up a bit with a dictionary? Use big words; they lend dignity to your themes."

Hans: "Perhaps you're right, but while eschewing mediocrity of expression through platitudinous phraseology, it behooves one to beware of ponderosity, and to be mindful that pedantry being indicatory of an inherent megalomania frustrates its own aim and results merely in obnubliation."

It was fun, looking at him there, the same age as I, his hair combed back the same as it was now that he was older , except there was less of it to comb. Oak Grove was a private Lutheran school. Apparently, when it came time for him to go from the lower grades into high school, instead of registering at the public school, he walked over to Oak Grove and registered himself as a student there. That surprised me a little, as I didn't ever think of my father as a studious person. I had seen pictures of him as a young man, standing by an old Plymouth, one foot on the fender, holding a rifle, with a cocky look on his face, not unlike Bonnie and Clyde. I wondered if we might have been friends had we been born at the same time.

"Things were different back then," he said, a faraway look in his eye, still talking about basketball.

"How's that?"

"For starters, after every basket, both teams went back to the center of the gym and we had a jump ball."

"After *every* point?" I exclaimed, visualizing him shooting his two handed shots.

"After every point."

"So if you were a tall guy, you really had the advantage."

He smiled. "Guess so."

Back then, a six foot guy was considered tall. I stand six-feet-two inches and am by no means considered tall in light of the fact that most basketball players now are a minimum of six-six and upwards into seven footers.

Now, I had seen dad shoot baskets behind the house, using his unorthodox two-handed shot, even on lay-ups and was curious to see how he played in a team atmosphere, so I attended their first team meeting. It consisted on two guys, brothers, who had graduated from high school the year before, aged nineteen, a farmer, somewhere in the mid-twenties, an overweight guy that I had never seen before, a guy they called 'Swede", and dad, the oldest guy out there -- somewhere in his mid-thirties. Everyone brought a basketball except dad. The only ball we had was an old leather ball, worn thin from playing outside in all types of weather. I'm not even sure that it was round. I do know that it had a slow leak and had to be pumped up every so often.

They introduced themselves, shook hands and commenced to warm up by shooting baskets. I noticed right off that dad was the only guy out there that was shooting two handed. I also noted that he was making better than fifty percent of his shots. Swede and the two recent high school graduate brothers were in the best shape.

There were only six men, so five on five was out of the question. To start things out, they chose up sides, the two brothers became self appointed captains. Once sides were chosen, they started playing a game. It only took five minutes of running around to realize that half of the men were so out of shape that playing full court was out of the question. Dad, the older farmer and the unknown guy were all standing around with the hands on their knees, wheezing. After that, they played half court.

The two brothers said that they should maybe work on a couple of plays. Swede was six-two, the tallest of the six men, so he was designated center. The two brothers were quick and good shots, and it was only natural that they be guards. That left dad and the other two guys as forwards. They ran a few plays, practiced screens, shot around a while and after an hour decided to call it a night.

Dad sat down on one of the wooden bleachers to catch his breath. He was sweating profusely which was accompanied by intermittent wheezing. I suggested that he might consider giving up smoking. That brought a harsh look followed by, "Hand me my shirt, will you?"

We had no sooner stepped out into the cold fall air when he lit up an unfiltered Camel cigarette. We drove home in our 1942 green, four-door, Studebaker sedan.

The first game was the following Friday night at six o 'clock. It was scheduled as the preliminary game before the high school varsity team took the floor, all eleven of them. The gymnasium was small, with hard, wooden bleachers that had been built on one side of the gym. Four rows. The opposite wall had high windows and at the end opposite of the entrance was a small stage. As the game started, no more than a handful of spectators were present, mostly wives, or girl friends of the players. I sat there in attendance, by myself, representing the family.

The opposition was from a neighboring town. They were a rough looking bunch, unskilled and unpolished ball players. Eight players in all, day labors for the most part. I could tell by the way that they handled themselves and the way that they shot and dribbled the ball that it was going to be a long night.

Swede took the tip off right of the bat and passed the ball to one of the guards who dribbled around until the team was set up. They passed the ball to Dad who pivoted and with both hands evenly spaced on the ball, shot a high arched ball that caught all net and went in for their first two points. I jumped off the bench, yelling at the top of my lungs. When the game was over, dad's team collapsed on the floor, wheezing and coughing. They had won the game 26 to 14.

Dad played just the one season and never returned to the boards as we called the gym, probably because work and making a living interfered with the game. I just remember how proud I was to see him out there playing with his family cheering him on. I wondered if, when I grew up and had a family, if I would ever play on a team and if my kids would show up and cheer me on and be as proud of me as I was of my dad. I wish that video cameras had been invented by then so I could have had a film of him playing to look back on. As it was, I wouldn't get my first Kodak Brownie until I was a sophomore in high school.

Music

There were three things that consumed my life from the from the fifth grade to my senior year of high school. Sports, music and work. Let me begin with music.

I have no idea what prompted me to join the band when I was in the fifth grade. To the best of my knowledge, I had no musical ability, but something inside me urged me on towards the music department, which was located in the gym. I didn't have a clue what a note was, nor how to count, as in one-two-three-four, two-two-three-four, etc., nor did I know the difference of playing softly from fortissimos, nor the difference of Strauss's waltz from John Phillip's *Stars and Strips for Ever*, and I certainly couldn't read a note.

Mom loved the Hawaiian steel guitar. That's where you sit on a chair with the guitar on your lap and run this round, steel bar over the frets instead of using your fingers, as we're used to seeing on TV. In time, I tried to learn how to play the steel guitar and was eventually able to play, *I only Have Eyes For You*, and a couple other sappy songs. My heart really wasn't into it. Anyway, one day I asked the band director, Mr. Reed, an elderly man who reeked of cheap cologne, sported well oiled white hair and a pencil thin white mustache, what instrument was available to play in the band. Without hesitation, he said, "Bass drum or tuba." The bass drum didn't sound too enticing, so I chose the tuba. He led me to the corner of the room where, in a large closet, lay this huge round array of plumbing that he called the tuba. I picked it up, slung it around my neck and blew into the mouthpiece, emitting a large bellowing sound, not unlike an elephant that just had his trunk stepped on by another elephant. Thus began a long love affair with the instrument in particular and music in general.

There were two of us that played the tuba in the band that year, and we soon became creative, improvising everything that we played. Forget what the music said. We created our own music. It got to the point that when Mr. Reed handed out new pieces of music, we simply followed along enough to be sure we were on the same page at the same time with the rest of the band, but aside from that, we were on a tear! You have to understand that the role of a tuba instrument is to more or less fill in bass background, and that's about it. Basically, to be seen and barely heard. We made sure that we were heard, loud and clear!

Every year the band went to the state music contest held in Pendleton, Oregon and every year the tuba section was given special accolades by the judges. The two of us were like twins, like minded. We knew when a run was appropriate, be it written into the music or not, and we played it in unison.

Every year the band put on a school concert for the parents and anyone else who felt they could suffer through our music. It was held in the only place that could hold both the band and an audience; the gymnasium. Usually, the concert consists of a couple of marches to get the audience revved up, followed by an Overture or two, just to prove that we could actually play something serious. Somewhere along the middle of the concert, one of the more gifted members of the band was usually selected to play a solo, usually first chair clarinet or trumpet. Rarely ever a trombone and never a tuba.

Except in my sophomore year, I was selected to be the soloist. Why, I don't have a clue. I figured that Mr. Reed had to have been using vodka for a mouthwash when he made that decision, because no way ....

I chose Nancy Graybeal to be my piano accompanist. She had been my accompanist when I played a solo for the state contest in Pendleton the previous year where I had taken first place, so I knew that I could rely on her to get me through this. To this day, sixty years later, I still have that piece of music and a photograph of me standing in front of the band, playing, with Nancy in the background thumping on the piano. How I did during the solo, I haven't a clue. All I can remember was getting up with my horn wrapped around my neck and then bowing when it was all over. Nancy says that I did well, but then she's a good friend. I could have forgotten my mouthpiece and farted on cue and she would have said that I did okay.

When I got home, my father wasn't speaking to me and mother hugged me and told me that she was proud, so there you have it. I either embarrassed the family or my father didn't want to be associated with a tuba player. Either way, that was my one and only tuba solo I ever played in front of the band, let alone the whole town.

When the state music competition came around, Mr. Reed encouraged everyone to enter the individual competition which was to follow the band competition. Again, I don't know what force drove me to such torture, but every year I entered the competition. I must have been a glutton for punishment, because who wants to voluntarily stand in front of an auditorium full of critical strangers and make a fool of ones self?

I recall this one year, Nancy Graybeal had played the introduction to a particularly difficult piece entitled *Universal Judgment* that I had chosen, and then waited for me to wade in. No sound came from my horn. I just sat there in a complete panic. I had completely forgotten every note! You see, it was considered good form to have memorized the piece of music you had chosen to play. I had played the piece so many times, not to mention mentally playing it through my mind both awake and asleep, but when it came to actually perform in public, in front of the judges and all, I developed a complete mental block. I couldn't remember a single note!

I glanced over at Nancy who was intimating that maybe we should make a run for it when one of the judges suggested that I look at the music. Nancy handed me the sheet of music and after one glance it all came back to me. I pried Nancy from behind the curtains where she had decided it was safer to hide, and we carried on. The judges must have felt mercy for me that day, because they awarded me the top grade, a 'one'.

Whenever we played in a parade, marches were always the theme of the day. The only problem was, we actually had to march and play at the same time. That was actually the easy part. The difficult part was keeping a straight line, read your music and dodge the horse pies that were scattered every ten feet in front of you like land mines.

The worse parade to march in was the Pendleton Round-Up. Every year people from fourteen states came to Oregon for the Pendleton Round-Up to ride, rope and tackle bulls, and every year the round-up was preceded by a big parade whereby every school in the county was invited to march. Aside from those members marching in the band, everyone wore their best and worst cowboy and cowgirl outfits. And everyone had cowboy boots and hats. After the parade, those of us in the band stacked our instruments back on the bus and were allowed to enter the arena to watch the round-up.

I know that sounds interesting, but after a couple years of watching cowboys jump from speeding horses onto eight hundred pounds of moving feet and horns, or steering their horse around wine barrels, or roping a calf and then jumping off his horse to see how fast he could get a rope around the calf's feet simply looses interest. I preferred to wander downtown and sit on a bench on Main Street and watch the cowboys and cowgirls strut their stuff. There is no greater entertainment that watching a herd of half-oiled cowboys and cowgirls trying to out impress one another with smooth talk and watching them in their god-awful cowboy garb.

Nine Lives

The school in Irrigon had but one tennis court and I was on it every chance I could get. I played with Kenny Edwards, Glenn Coy and Norman Burnette, but the kid that gave me the most trouble was a little guy two years younger than me by the name of Clifford Ballard. He lived up the street with his single mom. When I wasn't playing some other sport, or working, he and I were on the tennis court. We'd play until the last possible moment until it got too dark to see or when we had to be home for chores or dinner.

We usually rode our bikes to school which was about a mile away from home to the school. We didn't make tennis dates like one might do now, we just showed up and whoever showed up, played. On this particular day, I was practicing my serve alone. It was near fall and the days were short, so the sun was setting around six or so. I knew that the folks would be getting home soon and that they'd be expecting the family to be there for supper.

As I mentioned previously, we had no paved roads. The road from my house to the school was one straight shot with the single exception that I had to made a short jog to the right past Umikers place to get to our house. To get home, I had to cross this one road that exited off the highway, across the railroad tracks and was used regularly to access other side roads in town. If the road had a name, I never knew it, just like every other road in town. This road was known as the main road down by Wilson's Place.

Anyway, this particular day I came zooming down the road on my Schwinn bike as I usually did, hitting the main access road – the road by Wilson's Place - going about twenty miles per hour. I no sooner entered the intersection when Danny Hill driving in his pickup came down the hill on his way home. He was probably late too, and was clocking forty mph, a good pace for such a small, unpaved road, leaving a cloud of dust in his trail.

You guessed it! The irresistible force – his pickup - collided with the movable object – me on my bike - and he nailed me. It wasn't until I was sailing twenty feet in the air, that I realized what had happened. I landed in the ditch on the other side of the road, still astride my bike.

Danny Hill skidded to a stop, backed his pickup back to the spot where I lay on the ground. He was sure that he had killed me.

"Hey, Danny! How's it goin'?"

He skidded to a stop and jumped out. His eyes were glazed. Thinking back on it he must have been in shock. "You're alive!"

"Sure. I'm okay, but I think my bike has had it!"

He had hit me just past that part of the frame where the sprocket for the peddle was attached. My feet must have been parallel to each other; otherwise he would have hit my leg and would have snapped it in half for sure.

He looked at my bike and then back at me, amazed that, one, I was alive, and two, that I wasn't hurt.

He grabbed the bike and flung it in the back of his pickup. "Get in! I'll take you home."

Not being one to want to have him go out of his way, I shrugged my shoulders. "It's okay, I can walk."

He gave me a look that conveyed the fact that I was getting a ride whether I wanted it or not.

The moment my folks opened the door to him, he was apologetic as could be. "I didn't see him! He just shot out in front of me!" he apologized before anyone could get a word out   sideways. "I didn't have time …."

My folks assured him that I seemed to be okay and he kept insisting that they should drive me to Umatilla to see a doctor. In the end they shook hands and while they were talking, I went to the frig to see if there was anything to eat. Ashen white and shaking, Danny turned to go, assuring them that his insurance would pay for the bike.

****

As I mentioned, we lived only a few hundred yards from the Columbia River. The river afforded a place to go fishing, swimming and exploring. There was this island, Sand Island it was called, just up river a mile or so, and legend had it that it was once an Indian burial ground. If you could use your imagination, you could actually see the mounds where they had been buried. Actually, it was just places where the sand had blown against a tumbleweed or some rock, forming a mound, but we didn't know that.

The island was accessible only by wading through a slew that was four or five feet deep. We used to take off our tennis shoes and wade across the slew to get to the island where we would look for arrow heads or anything that had to do with the Indians. Over the course of several years we actually found several arrow heads. Legend had it if you dug up one of their graves that the Indian's spirit would haunt you for the rest of your days, so we never attempted to dig up any graves, not that there were any to begin with.

We usually brought our .22 rifles along to target practice, or shoot at rabbits or for protection in case one of the Indian spirits decided to get frisky. I can remember this one time, walking barefoot across the slew to the island. Someone had apparently broken bottle of coke and it had settled to the bottom of the watery ravine. In the process of wading from the mainland to the island, I had stepped on it. It made a four inch gash in the bottom of my foot and bled like a stuck pig. To this day, whenever I think about it, it sends shivers down my spine. Obviously, I still have the jagged scar as a constant reminder of the incident.

The river can be entertaining, beautiful and dangerous all at the same time. On the surface it looks calm and serene, but beneath the surface flows a deep, powerful current. All one has to do is cast a line with a fairly large sinker out into the river and watch as the current takes the weight several yards down stream.

As boys from Tom Sawyer's day to the current time are prone to do, rafts were made to explore the river. We were no exception, only we didn't float down the river. Our raft consisted of four logs in varying lengths strapped together with twine. Our paddles were two broken fence pieces that we had found washed up on the river bank. We confined our venture to the slew and Sand Island.

This particular day Bobbie Holden and I had our fishing poles and weren't particularly paying attention to the fact that we were floating towards the tip of the island, the outer boundaries that we had set for ourselves. We were in the current before we knew it and scrambled to paddle back towards the slew. In our haste, and within the small confines of our raft, one of us knocked my tennis shoes off into the river. I tried to scramble to retrieve them, but we were moving pretty fast by then and drifting further away from shore. They simultaneously floated away and sank beneath the surface, too fast to retrieve. I gave a momentary thought to jumping in after them, but soon vacated that as idiotic.

About a thousand yards down river from Sand Island was this area where the river ran swift and deep. Some say that there were large boulders under this particular spot, and some say that it was the place where the town founder had drowned years ago and periodically, his spirit arouse in defiance of his untimely death. In either case, periodically, for no apparent reason, a vicious whirlpool would start up.

Just as we approached that area, just like clockwork, the whirlpool started to act up. We were in the outer rings of the current, but caught up in it nonetheless. Bobbie and I looked at each other, horrified. We had no choice but to ride it out. There was no swimming away from it and there was no one in sight to rescue us, although we screamed our lungs out.

We were goners and we knew it.

Then, just as suddenly as it had started, it stopped.

Bobbie and I paddled towards shore as if we were trying out for the Olympic rowing team. When we got close enough to shore, we grabbed our fishing poles and dove off the raft and swam to shore. Bobbie had his shoes on, so he didn't have to walk home barefooted, but I was condemned to hot foot it through the hot sand, thistles and all, to get home. Fortunately, our house was fairly close to where we had jumped off the raft so it wasn't too long of a walk.

The problem was, I only had one pair of tennis shoes. My only other pair of shoes was my go-to-church-on-Sunday shoes. It was Thursday and I knew I had to get another pair of shoes by the weekend or face the consequences. I could fake it for a day or so, hoping that no one noticed that I was barefooted. The tricky part would be delivering my papers, two paper routes in the morning and one in the evening.

I had a savings account at the bank in Umatilla, money that I had earned delivering papers and working for old man Henry, but once I got there, because I was under age, it required my mother to sign. I had just gotten my learner's permit, and knew how to drive. The plan was, to steal the car while the folks were at work, drive to Umatilla, forge my mother's name on a withdrawal receipt, buy a pair of shoes and then drive back home again before anyone saw me.

I had never driven on the highway before, and never driven more than twenty miles per hour, so this was going to be an experience, but it had to be done. Umatilla was seven miles away, a distance that seemed an eternity then, on a small, well traveled – well, there was some traffic - on a two lane road all the way.

I had practiced mom's signature and thought I had it down pat – well, close enough for government work. I had about sixty dollars in the bank and was asking for ten of it back. The instant the teller saw me and compared the signatures, she knew something was fishy. After several minutes of fast talking I walked out of the bank with my ten dollars, not thinking of what mom was going to say when she found out, nor how I was going to explain how I got there in the first place.

Forty-five minutes later I was home with my new tennis shoes which I now had to dirty-up to make them old looking. I got away with it for about one week until mom realized that the soles of my shoes were brand new. I tried to dance around the issue, but in the end had to tell her the truth about everything except taking the car. Although he didn't know it, Bobbie Holden became the hero there.

Sports

The mother of my children once told me that I was good at only two things: making money and playing ball. I must admit that playing sports has played a major role in my life. How it affected my marriage, well, we'll talk about that later.

By the time I was a freshman in high school, I stood-six-feet-two inches and weighed one hundred fifty-five pounds. I was so thin that I actually disappeared when I turned sideways – but I was strong as an ox. Every summer I tossed sixty pounds of bailed of hay over my head onto a truck and threw tons of watermelons onto trucks whose racks were over my head.

At our school, when a freshman entered high school, the first thing he's faced with is the choice of playing football or not. Unless you have zero athletic skills, or are as round as a tire, in a school the size of Irrigon, you get involved in sports, one way or another. I had never been banged around much, so the thought of two hundred pounds on the hoof bearing down on me with the intent of knocking me ass-over-tea kettle was less than enticing. But I went out for football anyway.

I remember Donald Leighton, a varsity junior, telling me that the first two weeks of football practice was pure hell. He said that your body was going to feel like it had been run over by a steam roller and you walked as if you had a pitchfork stuck up your ass, but at the end of that period of time, all the pain would eventually disappear and your body would be feeling lean and mean. I had no idea what he was talking about, but was soon to find out.

Coach Rucker was a NFL wannabe from Idaho State who couldn't cut it as a pro, so he turned to coaching high school ball. He was a husky man with eyes that were cold as a midwinter breeze off the Columbia River, and his mouth was formed in a perpetual frown. His hair was jet black and kept falling over his eyes. He would brush it aside, but a moment later, it was back over his eyes again. I don't think I ever saw Coach Rucker smile.

It was through sports that I would get a glimpse of the personality that dwelled within this lean body. Unbeknownst to me, I had passive-aggressive personality that would get me into more trouble than I bargained for. And, I didn't even know what the word passive-aggressive meant!

One of the jobs I had in the summer was harvesting wheat -- thousand of acres of the stuff. There was a tradition that when the crew made the final cut, finishing off a field, when the jack rabbit ran out of the last place to hide -- and there was always a jackrabbit -- tradition dictated that the youngest and fastest man to catch him. That was me.

Now, when you're in the middle of a thousand acres of freshly cut wheat and you're a rabbit, there siply isn't any place to hide. The stubble is roughly eight inches tall, and the rabbit, ears and all, stands about eighteen inches. So, there you have it, the rabbit and I, running, darting, cutting through the stubble until he hesitates and I make a dive to catch him. Once, I dove for a rabbit and a piece of freshly cut stubble impaled me, piercing my side. To this day I still have the scare on my right side from that incident. And yes, I caught the rabbit.

"What do you do with the poor rabbit once you catch it?" one might inquire.

Turn him loose. By this time the poor thing is breathing so hard that he thinks he's having a heart attack.

This is all to say that I was fast on my feet. It didn't take Coach Rucker long to figure this out, so me made me a running back. Sometimes I was an end, sometimes a running back, but in either case, the plays were designed for me to get the ball and pretend that the goal was a rabbit and go for it. Usually, if I was able to break into the opponent's backfield, I was gone. Remember, when you live in a town the size of Irrigon, you're lucky to have a little more than a dozen guys turn out for football. I think we had sixteen, freshman to seniors.

By the time we had our first game, I knew that I had made the team. I could run and knew which goal was mine and I had passing grades. That was the basic requirement. Anything else was gravy. I was told that I would be starting half-back on the offensive line.

I couldn't wait to get into a real game! At this point, I should mention that I had never even seen a real football game in my life. By real, I mean a college game or a pro game. We had no TV and in a town our size, the only game we saw was our own school, which until my freshman year, I hadn't been too interested in.

By the way, we didn't play standard eleven man football. As you might have gathered, we didn't have enough guys. We played six man football. We didn't have enough men to field a full offensive and defensive team, so most of us played both offense and defense.

I don't know if it was because of my height or my speed, but whenever I carried the ball, everyone kept tackling me around the neck. Maybe that's the reason I have a degenerated neck disc today. Plus every one of my front teeth are cracked in at least one place from gritting them while running with the ball. Teeth guards would have been great, but then we still had leather helmets, so if I appear to be a bit brain dead, you now know the reason.

After football came baseball. We barely had enough men to field a team, but we never had to forfeit a game due to lack of players, although one game, one of the guys fell off his bike or something and his mom kept him home. We were allowed to play without a shortstop that particular game.

I tried pitching. Everyone did, but I couldn't throw straight and hard to save my soul, so I stuck to playing first base. I was right handed, so I wasn't a natural first baseman. Most of the pros are left handed, but I did okay. I loved batting more than anything and couldn't wait for my turn to come up.

My true love was basketball. Again, being tall was an asset. Next to a guy named Jerry Ross who was six-four, I was the tallest guy in school. Jerry was a year ahead of me and although he was taller, he had the propensity to run down the floor shaking his head from side to side whenever he made a mistake, which was often. No matter what Coach

Rucker said to him, he couldn't stop berating himself. Consequently, by the time he made it down the floor after shaking his head from side to side, the other team had shot and made a basket and he had to run back up the floor again, again shaking his head. Then there was a kid in the eighth grade, Joe Mann, who would eventually be taller than both of us.

Back to the present. In our first game, Coach Rucker started me as a forward. The first game I was so charged up that by the beginning of the fourth quarter I had fouled out. Aggressive play and fouling became one of my downfalls. More than once I fouled out of a game.

I had two shots. A turnaround jumper and a hook shot. Both were effective and, when I was on, they were unstoppable. We practiced every day after school, showered and walked home in the freezing air. Our home was about a mile from school and in the winter time, it was not unusual for the temperature to drop below zero. One year it got down to thirty degrees below zero and even the Columbia River froze over. Anyway, by the time I got home, my hair was usually frozen stiff.

I remember this one evening, during practice, it was late and my hands were sweaty. Coach Rucker's normal belligerent attitude had gone even further south. He was growling at everyone. I had muffed a couple of passes and he yelled at me, "What's the matter Losness, no hands?"

He grabbed the ball from the guard and flung it at me, hard.

I caught the ball and flung it back, showing that I not only had hands, but that I could catch and throw as well.

He stepped back and again, hurled a forward football-like pass at me as hard as he could.

The force of the basketball knocked me against the back of the wall, but I caught the ball. The game was on. Suddenly, I felt outright defiance and self propelled aggression. I responded by flinging the ball back at him so hard that he muffed it. He took a couple of steps backward and, retrieving the ball, again flung it at me as hard as he could.

By now, everyone in the gym was in shock, looking at this skinny kid trading blows with God, knowing that today was my last day on the team, if not earth. They parted like the Red Sea and stood silently watching and as David and Goliath did battle.

Finally, the captain of the team, a red head by the name of Bill Kelly, stepped forward and the two combatants came back to reality. I, realizing that there were actually other people in the gym and that indeed, today I wasn't going to die, and Coach Rucker, realizing that in trying to kill one of his kids, may have overstepped his bounds.

"Twenty laps," Rucker barked and disappeared through the double doors at the end of the gym. Everyone took off, led by Bill Kelly. By the end of our run, everyone collapsed downstairs to the showers, some elbowing me and smiling in approval, and others punching me on the shoulder asking if I had lost my marbles. No one saw Rucker that evening. I think he either decided to leave the premises before he said or did something that he would later regret, or left in shame, hoping that none of the players would tell their parents of the outburst. I know I didn't. And even if they did, in those days the coach was God, and no argues with God and wins!

This was not to be the only time that Coach Rucker and I hit heads. Another time, during practice, I had missed a break-away lay-up. He immediately went into one of his tirades.

"Losness! Get your good-fer-nothin' butt to the other end of the gym and shoot lay-ups until you've hit fifty buckets in a row without missing. Kelly, you go and be sure that he does. I don't care if he's here until midnight!"

So, Bill Kelly ushered me to the other end of the gym where I proceeded to do lay-ups, hook shots and jumpers, invariably missing one somewhere around the count of forty.

Kelly would look nervously down the floor at Coach Rucker, hoping that he didn't see that I had missed and had to start over again. Kelly was a straight arrow guy and wasn't about to fudge the count on account of me. I not only respected that, but appreciated it as well. Frankly, my dear, I didn't give a shit if I was there until morning. I finally shot the fifty without missing, for Bill's sake, because I knew he was getting nervous and was as scared of Rucker as anyone. The funny thing was, Coach Rucker and his wife were good friends of my folks and often came over to play pinochle with them. I would usually wander in late, and there they would be, the four of them, sitting around the kitchen table in a fog of smoke, playing cards, Rucker smoking his cigar and the folks smoking cigarettes. I guess Rucker had a wife, although I can't recall her face to save my soul.

When I finally wandered in, usually ten or fifteen minutes later than his announced curfew, he paid me no more attention that a dog taking a dump on the side of the road. I often wondered if they talked about me while I was out, carousing around when I should have been in bed, resting. They probably knew that in a town the size of Irrigon there wasn't anywhere to go and really nothing to do. I had no car and didn't drink and smoke. How else was I going to get in trouble?

When we went on a road trip, it was usually an hour or two bus ride, as in our rural area, most of the schools were miles and miles apart. Some of the gymnasiums we played in were no more than elaborate outhouses.

I recall this one gym.

We had to dress in the men's locker room and then run outside, through the snow and slush into an unheated building that held no more than fifty people on one side of the floor. The building was so small that the basket was literally two feet from the wall. If you had a break away lay-up, you had a decision to make. Make the lay-up and smack into the wall, or stop short and hit a jumper.

We had a good basketball team my sophomore year and were invited to the state tournament. As I said, I was the only sophomore on the team. The upper classmen decided that for the tournament, everyone would get a Mohawk haircut. I've never been a conformist, and I certainly wasn't going to start now. Besides, I knew the wrath that Coach Rucker would rein down on the team when he saw everyone sporting a Mohawk at a state basketball tournament. That wasn't the half of it! Mr. Golden, the school's principal was there too. He came unglued when everyone showed up on the floor, representing the school, with their outrageous haircuts.

Looking back on it and looking at the school's pictures that I have, I may have been the one that looked out of place with just my crew-cut. We got a lot of attention in the newspapers, too.

Then the girls thought it was so cute that a dozen or more of them cut their hair like a Dick Tracy character, called Crewie-Lou. Crewie-Lou wore her hair with the top of the head in a crew-cut with the sides left long. The girl's hair really looked dorky when it started to grow out. If you can visualize a limp, long crew-cut with long, straight hair growing on the sides, you've got the image. I got the pictures to prove it!

In order to earn your letterman's letter, a player had to have made the varsity and had to play in at least three games. I lettered in every sport both my freshman and sophomore year. To this day, I still have them tucked away in a metal ammunition box that my dad gave me. When it came time to have pictures taken for the Letterman Club, I always had to borrow a letterman's sweater from one of the girls, because I didn't have a sweater of my own. I simply couldn't afford one.

At the end of every year the Letterman Club elects new officers. At the end of my sophomore year someone offered my name as a candidate, and five minutes later I was elected president of the Letterman's club for the upcoming year. I mention this only because at the end of the summer, my folks delivered the worse news that a jock in high school could receive. "We're moving!"

The Big Move

The folks had purchased a house in a town fourteen miles away, which was on the other side of the universe as far as I was concerned. The moment everyone in school heard the news that I was moving, I was ridiculed for abandoning them as if I had anything to say about it. I was as pissed as they were. My team leader and hero, Bill Kelly, even offered to drive me to and from school everyday if I'd agree to stay. We both knew that this wouldn't work, but I appreciated the offer anyway.

My Junior year in Hermiston started while we still lived in our little two bedroom house in Irrigon. I used that fact to try to negotiate a deal to start school at Irrigon, but my folks knew that once I was enrolled, it would be like pulling rusty nails to get me to move, so they said that I would be starting school in Hermiston. Dad purchased a 1942 four door Desoto sedan for seventy-five dollars, informing me that this was to be my transportation until we made the move. It was the ugliest car I had ever seen. "You'll drive back and forth in this until we close the deal," he had said.

So every day I got in my piece of shit-wrapped-in-cellophane car and drove two towns away to my new school. The high school had more people in it than our whole town and, whereas in my old school everyone stayed in the same room from the first period to the last class -- actually we had two classes per room, frosh and sophomore class in one room and junior and senior class in another. In my new school, every period was a new room and a new teacher. In Irrigon, while the teacher taught one grade, the other grade studied. At the new school, at the end of every class, the hallways looked like an ant hill. I, of course, being the new kid in school, was an aberration. They didn't know me and displayed no desire to do so. I was taller than 98% of the people, so when they passed me in the hallway, they just turned to check out the new guy.

In scheduling my classes, the first order of the day was to discover when and where band period had been scheduled. It was first period, I was told, so, at eight o'clock, I found my way to the band room and introduced myself to Mr. Marshal, the band director. Mr. Marshal stood all of five-feet-four inches tall and combed his jet black hair straight back. A pencil thin mustache accented his stoic face. His fierce eyes were dark brown and unforgiving. In retrospect, he looked like Hitler with out the brush mustache!

"What instrument do you play?" he demanded over the noise of the band that was warming up.

"Tuba," I said, looking at the three tuba players stationed at the rear of the room.

"What school did you come from?"

"Irrigon."

"Were you first chair?"

"We didn't have first chair," I responded. "We were both equal."

He wasn't satisfied with that answer. I got my first taste of his short temper. "Were you first chair?" he demanded to know again.

I repeated my answer to which he vehemently repeated the question. It was clear that he wasn't going to accept my response that Tom and I were equal tuba players and there was no first chair. Where we sat had no bearing on our playing ability.

After repeating the question for the third time, I realized that I had better give him the answer that he was looking for or suffer dire circumstances. "First chair," I said under my breath.

This seemed to satisfy him. "There's a tuba in the backroom," he said, pointing to a door at the side of the room. Tuba players never own their own tuba's. For one thing they're god awful large and expensive and one would never pack it home every night, unlike a clarinet or trumpet.

"Get your horn and take a place there between Don and Lowell. You'll start out as third chair until you can work your way up." Then, he proceeded to explain the challenge system. "You can challenge one chair up at a time," he explained. "I expect you to challenge Darrell there before the month is out," he said with a flash in his eyes. Darrell was first chair and played what was called a recording bass, a hand held horn as opposed to the type that wraps around your shoulders that I was used to playing. I had never seen a hand held tuba before and knew at that moment, that I had to have the coveted first chair and posses that horn.

I went to the back room and found the only remaining tuba, a beat-up silver thing that looked like it had been the object of a rock throwing contest. By the time that I had returned, Don, a blond haired kid with overly large teeth, had moved over and had made room for me between himself and Lowell, the second chair. I smiled and shook hands with Don whose place I had just taken and had just demoted from third to fourth chair, although he didn't seem to mind a bit.

Lowell was a nice looking, dark complected boy who warmly shook my hand. Darrell on the other hand regarded me with overt hostility and refused to take my hand. At that moment, I knew that game was on and it was only a matter of time until I not only had his chair, but his horn as well.

Mr. Marshall introduced me to the band as the well known first chair tuba player from Irrigon and Hermiston's newest band member. Everyone looked at me and clapped. I later learned that I had a reputation, well actually which both Tom and I had a reputation, which had emanated from prior state band contests.

Mr. Marshall tuned up the band with the usual b-flat note, and then told us to bring up a particular sheet of music. This would be the first time that I had played along with anyone aside from Tom. The sound that came out of Don's tuba sounded like a wounded bull. I now knew why Mr. Marshall had put me ahead of him. Lowell had a nice tone and could articulate his notes well. I was impressed. I knew that if Lowell sounded this good, that Darrell must be really good.

I didn't wait for a month to pass before I challenged Lowell for the second chair. Challenges work like this: The band director, Mr. Marshall, takes the players one at a time, and places them in one of the practice rooms that are located just off the band room while the other contestant is asked to wait outside the band room where he can't hear what is going on. Then the person being challenged is given a piece of music that he has never seen before and is asked to play it while Mr. Marshall and two members of the band, usually first chairs of another section, are stationed next door. They listen and grade the performance

You play and they listen.

Only Mr. Marshall knows the identity of the player so there can be no favoritism given by the other two band members. Once the first person has played, the second one enters the room and plays the same piece all over again. The winner is simply that person who played best, considering accuracy, tone and delivery.

After my first challenge, I was awarded second chair. Lowell accepted this like the gentleman that he was, and Darrell became even more hostile. He knew that I was after his spot in the band and more importantly, his horn. And I knew that for him to lose not only his position as first chair, but his horn and be demoted to second chair would be humiliating.

About this time, I noticed that I was getting looks from the girls in first and second chair clarinet section. First chair was a cute little blond girl that went by the name of BJ. She wore her hair short and had big dimples on her cheeks. Her eyes sparkled when she talked and smiled. She was cute as a bug's ear and I knew that anyone fortunate enough to have her affection would a lucky boy indeed.

The other girl, Jeanette, although a year younger, was much more mature looking. She had a dark complexion, big dark eyes and was built like Venus with arms. She was like no one that I had ever seen before. I was immediately taken in by her appearance. But then, I was the new boy on campus and I chalked up their interest in me as mere curiosity of the new boy in the band and nothing more.

The following month I challenged Darrell for first chair. He met my challenge with an icy stare and defiance. The piece that was given for me to play had several tempo changes combined with runs and such. I muffed the first go around and Darrell retained first chair.

In preparation for the next challenge, I hit the practice room every lunch period. I was determined that nothing was going to keep me from defeating Darrell and taking first chair. One afternoon, after I had just entered the room and started warming up, I heard a light tap on the door. It was Jeanette, the dark haired beauty that occupied second chair clarinet.

"I thought that sounded like you," she said, peeking her head around the door.

"You mean I have a distinctive sound? I thought all tubas sounded the same." I knew better, but that was the only intelligent thing I could come up with.

"No. I could tell it was you."

Usually, when one thinks of a tuba playing, one thinks of a brash, toneless, umpa-umpa, or a tuba in a German polka. Being a tuba player, I know the difference. Contrary to popular opinion, a tuba can actually sound quite melodic.

"How could you tell?"

"I was one of the judges on your last challenge. Even though I couldn't see you, I knew which one you were. You'll get him next time," she added, as if apologizing.

"How did Marshal happen to pick you as a judge?"

"He usually picks first chair, but BJ wasn't available, so he asked me. Hope you don't mind."

"Why should I mind? If I didn't cut it, I shouldn't have won. I know I'm better that Darrell. I'll get him next time."

"I know you will."

That was the beginning of what was to be a two year long relationship – my real first love interest. She was magnificent. After that day, we saw each other every noon period. Sometimes we practiced our horns, and sometimes not. Usually, not.

The rule was, you had to wait thirty days before you could challenge the same chair again. One month to the day I delivered a written challenge to Mr. Marshall who received it with a smile. The following week the challenge took place after which I was awarded first chair. I took over first chair and the recording bass and Darrell quit the band.

The U.S. Navy Band came to town and every first chair was invited to sit in on their concert. For the first time in my life, I sat in awe of what I thought were the finest musicians in the world. Their tuba section was so awesome that I was embarrassed to even play. Little did I know that six years later, I would be part of the U.S. Army band myself.

At the beginning of my senior year I was elected president of the band. As president, during our annual concert, it was my duty, my pleasure, to present our director with a gift to show our appreciation. We bought him a silver baton which he seemed to appreciate. What else do you buy a band director?

The Challenge

I guess this happens in every school when a new kid moves in. It's called a pecking order. I had never experienced if before. I noticed right away that there was this one little kid that kept bumping into me in the hallway. His name was Pee Wee. At first I paid no attention to him, attributing his errant walking to drugs or alcohol, but it persisted until one day he outright pushed me on the kneecap. I knew right then and there that he was challenging me in front of all the rest of the kids.

It made sense. The shortest kid trying to make a name for himself at the new kid's expense. I suppose this happens in prison all the time, but this wasn't prison. The only other time in my life when I had been confronted to the point that it required a response was back in my old school. I had three paper routes: two in the morning -- *the Oregonian* and the *Walla Walla Bulletin* -- and one in the evening, when the *Hermiston Herald* that needed delivering. This particular event took place one evening on a weekend. I had just picked up the papers from the train depot. I had never known the train to stop except for the time that it had hit Principal Houghton's car while he was crossing the track, apparently, without looking both ways.

The train killed him instantly. It had converted his car into a half-donut shape and had pushed his car a mile down the track, past the school where every kid with access to a window had witnessed the tragedy.

Whenever the train had a delivery to make, it simple slowed down enough to drop whatever it was delivering on the ground, like the time dad ordered a hundred chicks from Sears and Roebuck. In the event something needed picking up, a sack was hauled up a pole and someone on the train grabbed it with a hook while the train whizzed by. When it came to dropping off the newspapers, someone simply flung them from the train and it was my job to find them.

Anyway, this one Saturday, these three guys, guys I knew from school, were bored and had decided to have a little sport with me and my papers. They laid waiting for me at the top of the hill, just after I had picked up the papers and had folded them and had put them into my paper bag which hung over the front of my handle bars of my Schwinn bicycle.

As I peaked the hill they were there, waiting. At first I thought they were just kidding around, trying to give me a bad time, but when one of them shoved me off my bike and began throwing my papers around, I knew they meant business. Two of them were brothers, and the third was the tallest and meanest of the three. It was him that I decided to take on.

I hit him with a full below-the-waist tackle driving him hard into the ground. There we tumbled and rolled down the hill towards the rail road tracks. I don't remember smashing him much, more like getting him in a head lock and squeezing the air out of him. He began to cry and muttered "Uncle", the universal kid's language for, 'I give up!' I let him go and he ran towards his home which was the only restaurant in town, across the tracks, wailing at the top of his lungs.

The brothers looked shocked as I stood there, legs apart, waiting for the next customer. I have no doubt that the two of them could have beaten the tar out of me, but once their leader was beaten, they simply shrugged their shoulders and walked away. The following week nothing was said about the incident and no one ever bothered me again.

Anyway, here I am, standing in the hallway with this guy they call Pee Wee, kicking me in the chins and threatening my knee caps. I knew that whatever happened the next few minutes would dictate my fate for the next two years.

I knelt down to his level with my hands on my knees and looked him in the eye. "Look Pee Wee," I said quietly. "We can do this one of two ways. We can either be friends or enemies, but either way, you're not going to intimidate me. Understand?" I looked him in the eyes. "I have little guys like you for breakfast." I paused. "You're choice." I had hoped that I had defused the situation. I extended my hand.

He looked around and decided that this was one battle he wasn't going to win. In order to save face, he nodded and weakly took my hand. I never had any trouble with him or anyone else after that.

Football season was upon us and I made my way down to the dressing room where I inquired as to the process of checking in, getting my gear and such. With an obvious smirk painted on his face, the coach looked me over and told me to strip down to my skivvies. I thought this was an odd request, but did as he requested. When I was standing there, all but buck naked, he called his assistant over.

"Hey, Hagen, check out the new guy!"

I stood there, self conscious, as the coach, assistant coach and now several guys of the varsity squad checked me out. Everyone except Assistant Coach Hagen smiled. Apparently, he wasn't amused like everyone else, an act that I never forgot and one that endured me to the man for the following two years. I'm sure they thought, here is this human toothpick, wanting to go out for the team.

"We got a full squad," the coach said, smiling as he winked to one of the other guys, a husky boy that must have been either a fullback or tackle or both. "You can check out the JV's if you want. That practice at the other end of the field."

I got the point. For a split moment there, the passive-aggressive personality tried to edge its way out of my body, and defiantly refuse to go. I could show them that I could run like the wind and in order for anyone to tackle me, they'd have to catch me first. And, I may be skinny, but I was tough as nails! Instead, I dressed and drove home in my old shit-wrapped-in-cellophane Desoto.

"You're home early," mom said, looking at the clock that registered 3:30. She was expecting me to show up around five or six, after practice.

"I decided not to go out for football," I said and let it go at that.

She could tell that I was irritated as hell, but knowing mom as I did, she let me handle my own affairs.

"You got homework?"

"Na."

"What are those books for, then?"

"I got no place else to leave them," I lied, and let it go at that. For the next two years I would carry an armful of books home and never crack a cover. That's probably why I got a 'C' in Latin and German. Why would any normal kid willingly take Latin and German you ask? I was planning on going to medical school and thought that Latin and German were required languages, so I may as well start learning them now.

When basketball season came around, the varsity gathered in one room and the junior varsity in another. I was a junior, and figured that I was definitely varsity material, so I turned out for the varsity. As luck would have it, the same coach that coached football, coached varsity basketball. It took about ten minutes to figure out that he didn't like me.

"Hey, beanpole, where did you learn to shoot like that?" he demanded as I banked a ten-foot hook shot off the glass and into the basket.

I looked around to see who he was talking to.

"Where did you go to school before you came here?"

Although he knew the answer to his own question, I told him.

"Who the hell was your coach?" he demanded with his hands on his hips.

By now all action on the floor had ceased and he had everyone's attention. That's what he wanted. And I knew it.

Look out! Here comes passive-aggressive attitude and this time I'm not retreating. "Coach Rucker!" I announced with pride. I wanted to add, 'and he can beat the tar out of you any day,' but I didn't

"Did he teach you how to shoot like that?" he demanded.

As you may have surmised, there was no love lost between me and Coach Rucker, but I was damned if I was going to stand there and let this redneck run roughshod over me and my old school.

"I taught myself," I responded, defiantly.

The game was on.

"Well, around here ...."

I have no clue what was said after that, because I saw red and went on auto-pilot. The next thing I knew, I was playing for Coach Hagan who I not only liked, but respected, and the feeling was mutual. The whole season I was humiliated though, being demoted to junior varsity when I had just come from a school where I played starting forward on the varsity for the past two years.

Baseball season came around and I expected to see the same coach, but breathed a sigh of relief when a small man that everyone called 'Sparrow' (not to his face, you understand), called the team together.

"What position do you play?" he inquired of me, the new guy. He had obviously seen me or had heard about me.

"First base," was my reply.

He nodded towards a tall redheaded kid.

"We have a first baseman." Then he nodded towards another kid who was Pee Wee's brother. "And a back-up."

I was beginning to get the picture. A new kid at this school wasn't going to break into the chain. I decided to stick it out, but after a weeks practice with no chance of playing at any position, anytime, I flicked it in.

Track and tennis season was upon us and I knew that if I could catch a rabbit, I could probably outrun ninety-nine percent of these dudes, so I tried out. I tried the hundred yard dash, the 220 yard dash, the 120 yard high hurdles and the 220 low hurdles. In the hurdles I flashed by everyone, but in the hundred yard dash and the 220 I came in second. I decided that the hurdles were my choice. The coach didn't seem to care where I had gone to school, or even what my name was for that matter. I soon came to be known as 'Loose', short for -- well you know. As the year progressed, I took first place in most of the races. Then came the county tryouts for the state invitational track meet. I came in first place in both the 120 high hurdles and the 220 low hurdles and earned a place in the state tournament to be held in Corvallis, Oregon. It was there that I met my match, but at least I had competed and proven to myself and the other coaches that 'Loose' couldn't be kept down.

Same deal in tennis. I took second place in county singles and first in doubles and went to state tennis tournament two years in a row. Again, I met my match at the state, but I felt good for having gone that far.

My senior year I turned out for basketball again. Being a senior, if I made the team, they had to keep me on the varsity, like me or not, and he didn't. I kept my attitude to myself and due to my height and ability to make a shot every now and again, I played most of the time. It wasn't a memorable season, but I got through it. After one remarkable game where I scored twice as many points as anyone else on the team, the coach even made a half-assed attempt to apologize for his attitude. I simply smiled and walked away.

There wasn't a day that went by that I didn't hate that school. If weren't for playing in the band, Tennis and track, and the dark haired girl playing second chair clarinet, who knows what trouble I might have gotten into.

Now, I play tennis on a regular basis with guys on the city courts and my youngest and middle son, Christian and Aaron played racket ball together whenever we got the chance. I've since had to hang up the racquetball game due to my knees, but tennis gets my attention every Monday, Wednesday and Friday for three hours each day. I enjoy competitive sports and I guess I always will.

Sometime during my senior year, between spots, I fell in with a group of guys that had nothing better to do with their time than work on old cars. I loved working on cars and somewhere along the line I got the hair-brained idea that it would be fun to make a car that would have all the parts from other cars. A sort of an all American car.

We went down to the local car wrecking yard where the owner, a guy we affectionately called Trash, owned the place. I scraped up thirty-five dollars and bought the chassis and motor of a 1942 Plymouth. The motor ran and the chassis had two sets of seats attached to the frame. This, I asserted, would be the foundation of our new car. To that chassis, in the wrecking yard we found and attached a discarded body of a '39 Studebaker.

"How Much?" I asked.

"Two dollars," was the reply.

To that we added a Cadillac La Sale hood and front fenders and an old Ford front bumper. The rear fenders were from a '39 Chevy, and for good looks, we added a continental kit from a '49 Ford.

When my father discovered where I was going every afternoon, he was thankful that I hadn't fallen into the clutches of a gang, and said he would bet me a hundred dollars that we wouldn't finish the job. In the event I lost, where I would get a hundred dollars I had no clue, but on the other hand, I knew that he wouldn't pay up if we won anyway, so the wager was on.

The *Hermiston Herald* got wind of our venture and came out to take pictures of our ill fated project one day. On Valentine's day, February 14, 1954, a quarter page section of the paper was dedicated to our story and a picture of the other three guys who happened to be there when the photographer showed up and the story of my father's bet. The headline of the article read, *Hermiston Teenager Would Make 'Rod to Win Wager from Dad*. It described our intention of building a car with parts of every major motor industry represented on the body and explained that because of the uniqueness of the automobile that a special license would have to be obtained from the department of motor vehicles in order for it to be legal on the road. The article was accompanied with a large picture of our creation to date, which was no more that a stripped down car with stuff hanging on it and the three guys building it. Having lived on the opposite part of the town, I was no where to be found when the picture was taken. Probably just as well.

That weekend half the town drove by to look at our ridiculous venture and pointed fingers at us and laughed. Three weeks later, after driving the car around the block and getting stopped by the police for driving without a license, violating the noise ordinance, endangering children and pets, we sold the car back to Trash for twenty-five dollars.

I was full of ideas when it came to making money. By now I had traded in the old Desoto and had purchased a '46 Ford Coupe. It was nearing Christmas and both Larry and I loved hunting. Goose and pheasant hunting. But to hunt you need shells and a license. Well, at least shells. Who needs a license?

I had this hair-brained idea to rent a trailer, hook it up to the little Ford coupe and then drive up into the mountains and cut Christmas trees, and then sell them front the front yard of our house which fronted on a major road out of town.

We drive fifty miles up into the mountains where we found dirt roads on what we assumed was public land (we assumed that any land that didn't have a structure on it was public). By noon we had the trailer packed so full of trees that we had to tie them down with rope to keep them from falling off the trailer.

All went well until we started down a steep dirt incline road on our way home. The weight of our load was more than my little coupe could handle and, despite the fact that I was standing on the brake, we were being pushed, skidding down the hill at an alarming rate.

At the bottom of the hill was a sharp right hand turn. We didn't make the turn. Instead, the force of our load pushed our little coupe into a rather large pine tree at the bottom of the hill. The result of which was all of our trees went spilling out over the landscape and the trailer tipped over. The worst of the damage was that the quarter panel of my little Ford coupe where a rather large sized dent the size of a boulder was displayed.

After assessing the situation, we righted the trailer, reloaded the trees and continued on our way home. We managed to make it home without further mishap, unloading the trees on our front lawn. We clearly had the nicest trees in town and at half the price, so we sold them all in a matter of a week.

I turned my claim into the insurance company, which was way over five hundred dollars, the same amount that they placed as the value of car. "The car is a total wreck," the advised me.

"So what happens to the car?" I inquired.

"We sell it for junk."

"How much?"

"Twenty-five dollars."

"I'll buy it!."

They cut me a check for five hundred dollars less the amount they wanted for the totaled Ford and we went out separate ways.

Dad had this piece of rail road track that we called an anvil. That and a sludge hammer and thirty pounds of bondo car putty, and a week later, and my little Ford was as good as new. It did tend to list a little to the side when it went down the road, due to all that bondo, but otherwise no one was to the wiser. I put the car up for sale and a week later sold it for five hundred dollars.

Education

I don't know why, but I always knew that I was going to be a doctor. No one in our family has ever been a physician and no one ever talked to me about being one. And I didn't know anyone who was or has been a doctor, so go figure. From the age of twelve, I just knew that that was going to be my vocation. Hence, I took German and Latin in high school, as previously mentioned.

Sometime during my senior year I started sending out applications to colleges. One of the applications I sent was to a small Presbyterian school in Portland, Oregon, called Lewis and Clark College. I had heard that all the state colleges - University of Oregon and Oregon State - were party schools with fraternities and sororities popping out of the ground at ever turn. I had made up my mind that I was going to be a serious student for the first time in my life, and had predetermined that large colleges were not my cup of tea. I obviously hadn't completely plugged in the financial consideration when I made that decision, as you will soon see.

In addition to seeking admission, I requested information regarding scholarships. I knew that my grades were not up to par, so requesting a scholastic scholarship would be an exercise in futility, not to mention that I'm sure that the faculty would get a big laugh out of my academic transcripts when they saw them. Aside from track and tennis, I hadn't excelled in any major sport my last two years that was worthy of mention, thus I determined that my only chance at getting financial aid was in music. I was a damned good tuba player, so I thought I would give it a shot.

A short time after my request for admission to Lewis and Clark College and a music scholarship, I received a reply giving me a date to take the entrance exam which was to be followed up by an audition for a music scholarship. I was informed that I was to bring my own tuba. The dates that the entrance exam was given to corresponded with winter break – both theirs and ours.

Shortly after Christmas, dad and I loaded up my tuba in the back seat of his '47 Pontiac and we started off early one morning for Portland, a little over a four hour drive up the Columbia Gorge.

Dad's heater was acting up, or to put it another way, wasn't working at all. By the time we reached the campus of Lewis and Clark College we were both frozen popsicles. We located the auditorium where the placement tests were to be given. It appeared to be a room that had been used for chemistry classes as element charts hung from the wall and chemical equations were still left on the blackboards. The room was large with a descending seating arrangement with the last row of seats a good twenty feet from ground level with the podium. It was unlike any classroom that I had previously been in. I settled in one of the individual wooden desks in the middle of the room along with fifty or so other kids, excited with the prospects of being a part of this new academic life! I finished the test about the same time that most of the kids finished, and took my time to go over my answers, changing some of them.

After the test, Dad and I had just enough time to grab a sandwich and a soda before my music audition. By now my system was pumping adrenalin like a broken sprinkler. I walked into the music department, cradling my tuba under my arm. I was shown a room and given a piece of music to play. I blew into my horn to warm it up and tried the valves. Much to my horror, I found that the valves were frozen stiff!

I tried to unscrew them, thinking that they would loosen up once they were out of their cylinder, but they weren't coming out. I blew hot air into the mouthpiece, in a vein attempt to thaw them out, but they were frozen metal-to-metal and weren't about to budge. I explained to the man that my horn had apparently been frozen on the way up here and asked for a short continuance.

He was impatient and said that he had other auditions to perform and was on a tight schedule. If I was unable to perform now, perhaps I could reapply at another time, he explained and then dismissed me.

Dejected, I returned to the car where dad sat sipping on a mug of hot coffee and smoking a cigarette to keep warm. The ride home was the longest ride of my life. The good news was I passed the entrance exam and was admitted to Lewis and Clark College. The bad news was, I had to find a way to pay for my room and board, tuition and books. I had enough saved money from my summer jobs to get me through three-quarters of the first year. Tuition, room and board was thirteen hundred dollars and change (that was a lot of money in 1955), and I had somewhere in the vicinity of eight hundred dollars in the bank. I knew that eventually I would have to find a job. It never entered my mind to ask my parents for money. I had never asked them for a dime in my life and wasn't about to start now. Anyway, they both worked hard just to make ends meet. I was no longer their responsibility and they still had two kids home to raise.

To start of the first fall semester in Lewis and Clark College in 1955, Mom drove me back to Portland, to the men's dorm, Platt Hall, the only men's dormitory on campus. This was to be my home for the next two years. Platt hall was a three story brick structure with two wings. A recreation room had been built in the middle of the dormitory on one level and a reception area on the other. Parking, for those that had cars, was off to the side. The rooms were small and very efficient with a bed that pulled out that doubled as a couch. It adjoined a built-in desk on one side of the room that looked out onto the large ravine where a bridge and a cobblestone path that led to the campus. A built-in dresser had been built on the other wall. There were two guys assigned per room. Living in a dormitory with a pre-assigned roommate and a hundred other guys of all ages and walks of life was a new experience for me. I was excited!

I remember that Mom wanted to come in and view the accommodations that her son was going to have for at least the next nine months. I didn't see any other guys walking around with their mothers and in essence gave her the impression that I could handle things from here. Afterwards I felt badly that I hadn't taken the time to explore the campus with her. After all, she had driven four hours up the Columbia Gorge to deliver me there. The least I could do was spend some time with her, but no, I was concerned about my ego, worried that the guys might think I was a momma's boy.

I soon learned that the dormitory was been divided into two diverse groups. Freshmen and sophomores were delegated to the north wing with the freshmen being assigned to the bottom floor and the sophomores the second floor. Juniors and seniors occupied in the south wing. The south wing was further divided into subgroups.

Fraternities.

What amazed me was, although the guys from various fraternities acknowledged one another, they didn't seem to socialize with each other. It was like there was a social stratification power struggle going on. Now, I've never been a joiner and the fact that when one joined one fraternity, one simply didn't fraternize with guys from the other fraternity seemed ridiculous. Personally, I liked all of the guys.

The plan was, the fraternities would size up the freshman. By the time they were sophomores they had agreed amongst themselves who they wanted in their little group. Some fraternities specialized in jocks while others seem to gravitate towards the more scholastic guys and others just wanted to party and have a good time. As you might imagine, there was competition for some of the more popular guys such as the class president and jocks or some of the more outgoing social types.

By the time the potential candidates were sophomores the fraternity brothers had their want list made up. Now, they begin 'rushing' them -- inviting them to their parties, with the idea in mind to convince them to join their little social group. Personally, I couldn't see breaking up a friendship with all the guys that I had formed my freshman year and then be forced to make choices as to which group of guys I was going to socialize with the remainder of my college days. Subsequently, I decided to become an 'Independent'. Little did I know at the time that guys like me, independents, who refused to conform, i.e. join a fraternity, were, for all intents and purposes, ostracized because they didn't belong to social group. In a way it was like forming a third political party, doomed to fail before it was even formed.

And it was especially true with girls. Whenever a guy met a girl at a social function or in the coffee shop or just walking on campus, the very first thing they did was look at your lapel for a fraternity pin, and if you didn't have one on, they would ask, "What fraternity do you belong to?" Your answer depended upon how you were going to spend the next chunk of time with this person. In other words, your social life depended upon the answer. It was like a cast system. Once you belonged to this certain bunch of guys, you were identified with them and were expected to act like them. If you were a Delt for example, just the fact that you were a Delt told everyone who your friends were, where you lived and the sort of reputation that you had to live up to. One fraternity for example was known, as in the movie by the same name, as the Animal House! In short, that was your life until death or graduation did you part.

Once you had made a choice about rushing a particular fraternity, and had been accepted, there was what they called, 'Hell Week'. Hell Week is where the members initiate you. In short, for the next week your ass is theirs to do with whatever they chose. I heard stories of embarrassment and abuse that made me throw up. There was no way that I was going to subject myself to such gross humility.

Frankly, to this day, after all this time, I wouldn't have changed a thing.

As I said, there was just one men's dorm and three women's dormitories. The men's dormitories were located on one side of the ravine and the women's on the other side. Three-to- one odds sounded great! The rest of the campus was a delightful setting with cobblestone pathways, and antique glassed buildings that had once been used as horse stables. I would later learn that the campus used to be the Frank Estate of Meyers and Frank, the department store chain. The bricks from the administration building, used to be the main house that looked over a large reflection pool and rose garden with Mount Hood in the background and had been apparently shipped over from England. In short, the campus was a magnificent setting.

After registration and when everyone had settled in, there was a freshman orientation mixer one Friday night. I've never been big on dancing or mixers for that matter, but everyone was going, so I put on a clean shirt and pressed pants and went. As usually, the guys seemed to gather on one side of the floor and the girls on the other. Then the music started and the mixing began. I was standing near the punch bowl and snack table, fortifying myself when I heard this soft voice behind me.

"Care to dance?"

I turned to face this girl with a cherub looking face, smiling from ear-to-ear. She had short, curly auburn hair, brown eyes and looked to be a twin to the Campbell Soup girl.

"I'm not much of a dancer," I offered, stuffing a cracker in my mouth.

She reached for my hand and said, "I'll teach you."

We danced around the floor for fifteen minutes or so, knocking anyone aside that got in the way. I decided that we should adjourn to a table before I got into a fist fight with some overly aggressive girl.

During our tour around the dance floor which appropriately had been held on the tennis court, through subtle interrogation I had learned that her name was Carole with an 'e' and that she was an education major who planned on rushing a sorority at her earliest opportunity.

"Which fraternity do you plan of joining?" she inquired.

At that point I had no idea even what a fraternity was, let alone consider joining one, so I simply replied, "I don't know."

After the dance she asked if I would walk her home to her dormitory, Atkins Hall, which was just across the ravine from Platt Hall. I said yes and that began what would turn out to be a two year relationship.

As I reflect back on those days, I can't recall for the life of me what happened to my relationship with Jeanette back in Hermiston. I can only assume that time and distance had taken care of that matter. Besides, I was here to study and get an education. I didn't have time for women.

Carole had other plans.

I later learned that the sole reason she and her friend were at college wasn't to just get an education, it was to pick out a husband. Little did I know that after just one night on the dance floor, I had become her choice. Her friend aimed a little higher and put her sights on the star freshman basketball player. She got him too! As for me, read on.

My roommate turned out to be the freshman basketball whiz, Hall Ness. He was a 6'6" blond, really thin guy with a quick smile and easy demeanor. The sportswriters of *The Oregonian* paper would later unmercifully crucify him by calling him the walking toothpick.

I registered as a pre-med student and was given Zoology, Math, Chemistry as my electives and Civilization and Humanities as classes that all Freshmen were required to take, like it or not. My first set of classes added up to eighteen hours of solids. As if that wasn't enough, I decided to try out for the track team. I figured the track team could use another hurdler. Little did I know that I'd be running against the conference champion, a black guy, 6'4" by the name of Duke who looked like a young Nate King Cole. The only race he didn't win was when he was disqualified for jumping the gun twice. I never won a race against him.

The next order of business was to find a job. Through the placement office, I was referred to a new restaurant that was just opening on Barbour Boulevard called *Devault's Chuck Wagon*, an all you can eat place. I was interviewed by the owner who informed me that he had inspirations of running for Governor of the state of Oregon. I was hired on the spot.

My job was to park cars, for which I was paid a dollar-fifty an hour and all the tips I could get which was usually a quarter per car. And I got to eat one meal for free. I arrived at work at six, in time for the evening dinner meal and left at ten, about the time that most of the customers were through eating for the evening. By the second year I had been promoted to the inside. The restaurant was buffet style. I wore a large chef's hat and white jacket and stood at the end of the line where the meat was. It was my job to cut roast beef, ham and turkey for the customers. It was warmer inside and I got to smile at the girls.

The plates were mammoth in size -- eighteen inches across. When I ate, I filled that sucker to the brim, four inches high.

"If your friends eat like you, don't bring them here," Mr. Devault advised me when he saw how much I ate. "I don't want to go broke."

Working twenty hours a week, running track after school and studying every evening until one a.m. took its obvious toll on my grades. I knew that in order to get in med school I needed to have at least a 3.5 grade average, a B+. I was about a grade below that and lucky to be there.

Then something happened that would change the course of my

life. It happened during the latter part of my sophomore year. As if eighteen hours wasn't enough, I decided that a doctor should have a little knowledge of psychology, so I signed up for psych 101. It was the latter part of the semester when the professor decided to bring in a guest speaker. A hypnotist. He informed the class that he was going to do a mass hypnosis and that everyone in the room would be going under. It wouldn't hurt, he explained, and when we woke up, we would remember everything. Well almost everything.

I was seated at the back of the class. The professor proceeded to set the stage of hypnotizing everyone. He instructed us to close our eyes and imagine that we were on an elevator and that the elevator was slowly descending. It would take us deeper and deeper into our subconscious. He said that we would feel warm and fuzzy and that there was nothing to fear.

I tried to cooperate and go under, but for the life of me, I couldn't. Too dense, I guess. Anyway, when I finally realized that I wasn't going to go under, I simply gave up and watched.

When everyone was under he told the class to imagine that their arms were tied to a red balloon and that the balloon would take their arms high into the air and that their arms would float effortlessly. I watched as a sea of floated arms sailed about the room like limbs on a tree. When he was through with them he gave them a post hypnotic suggestion. "When you awaken, you will feel great and will have no ill affects from being hypnotized. When you awaken, your right index finger will remain stiff as a board however, and no matter how much you try, you will not be able to bend it until I give you the post-hypnotic word, 'match'! At that time, your finger will go back to normal.

"I'll start counting from five back to one now, and when I reach one, you will all be awake. Ready? Five, four ....."

Once everyone had been revived, the psychologist asked what everyone thought.

"I remember everything," one student said. "I wasn't under." His voice had the sound of disappointment.

"Same here," chimed in another. I don't think I was under. I remember everything."

"Hey, I can't bend my finger!" a voice said from the middle of the room."

All of a sudden everyone seemed to panic. "Me neither!"

While everyone tried bending their right fore-finger, the psychologist let everyone fret for a moment before calling attention to the fact that he had given everyone a post-hypnotic suggestion. He then said the magic word, "Match!" and everyone's finger went limp. What a relief!

Everyone except a guy in the back of the room. "Hey! I still can't bend mine!"

The psychologist re-hypnotized him and the problem was solved. The psychologist used that experiment to demonstrate the power of the mind and its unlimited potential. From that moment on I was hooked! That day I changed my major from Pre-med to Psychology.

Religion

As I mentioned previously, at Lewis and Clark College, freshmen and sophomores are required to take two classes each semester, for the full year: *Civilization and Humanities*. *Humanities* is simply the study and appreciation of the arts and music as they evolved throughout the ages. *Civilization* is the historical study of mankind and his environment. They start you out with Cro-Magnon man and by the time you reach the end of your second year, you're into the present time. The study includes everything in civilization that relates to man including but not limited to government, wars and religion.

Somewhere during the latter part of our sophomore year, small groups of people start to huddle in their dorm rooms, discussing something that has suddenly hit them. They've all had their faith in God shaken and it concerned them.

Bear in mind that this is a Protestant College where every Wednesday at three o'clock there is chapel and the place is filled to the brim with students. The school makes no bones about the fact that it is a Christian college and worship is a common everyday affair. It is more common than not to see a student or a table of students at lunch time, bowing their heads to say grace. But, what has happened, is that during the course of studying civilization and religion, the instructors have very meticulously, methodically and sneakily undermined everyone's so-called 'Sunday school' faith, to the point that now they are not only questioning their own faith, but in many cases, have in fact began to seriously doubt the existence of God. The idea, I later learned, is that this was done on purpose. The intent was to have the student's immature, childish faith destroyed and then rebuilt into a mature faith the following year, their junior year, when everyone took the required course, Religion!

Guess who wasn't going to return to Lewis and Clark College next year?

Prior to this time, frankly, I had never given much thought to my faith or my religion! It's always been there for me and, like an old pair of tennis shoes, it fit just fine without any adjustments, thank you. I was comfortable with it, and certainly never questioned my belief in the Almighty.

Ever since I could remember, as kids mom dressed us in our finest and marched us off to Sunday school where we learned about God and Jesus and memorized passages in the bible. We were taught the stories in the bible, participated in little plays about biblical times and then after Sunday school, we went to church. Not a great source of excitement for a kid, considering that I could have just as well been on the river fishing or out in the desert shooting tin cans or hunting for rabbits. Nonetheless, I went.

At Christmas, we celebrated Christ's birth and everyone took turns being a shepherd, or a wise man, or some other character depicting the birth of Christ. Christmas, we learned was not just about receiving and giving physical gifts from our parents, but it was the gift of Christ given to us from God. We learned that and accepted it as gospel.

On Easter, we learned about the crucifixion of Christ and the fact that Christ rose on the third day from the dead and ascended into heaven which is where we were all going when we die if we were good and followed God's commandments.

No question.

Along the way, over the years, as kids, we stood in front of the church and recited Bible verses. We prayed before every meal and at night before we went to sleep asked God to protect us and if we died before we were awake, to take our soul. And that was the way it was. I was comfortable in my faith and didn't question it. Our faith was like our parents. They were there and they took care of you. No questions.

Same as God. He was there and took care of you. There was nothing to question and nothing to challenge.

Life was good!

We learned at an early age that God didn't always give us what we wanted in life, but then if we weren't allowed to suffer once in a while, how would we appreciate what we had?

Now, along comes this college curriculum that feels that it is their duty to destroy our simple beliefs for a more mature religion. What right do they have to do that, I demand? As you read this you're probably asking yourself, how weak can he be to allow such a thing to have happened in the first place?

You have to remember that this event was designed to occur by minds much more futile than mine and by men who had more time on their hands than money.

So, there we were, sitting around in little groups wondering what it was all about. Some of these kids were guys that had planned on becoming ministers. Others, like myself, never really took our religion seriously in the vein that was anything more than an integral part of our lives. Now, all of the sudden, we're faced with the question, is there really such a thing as a God and if so, are there more than one God? I mean, we have learned that Christianity is the youngest of the religions and man has been worshiping one god or another ever since the wind blew through a cave man's hair and he saw the sun rise and set. So now, considering that since the beginning of man, and considering that our religion is the youngest one on the block, hence the newest on the block, is it real? In short, cutting to the chase, what happens when you die?

Do you just turn into dust and that's the end of your existence? That thought alone is disconcerting. For the rest of eternity you're nothing. No mind, no body, no nothing. Dust! When you have life it's easy to shrug your shoulders and say, if that's the way it is, then that's the way it is. Then have someone put a gun to your head and say, "Time's up, pal," and suddenly your perspective changes. It may be a poor analogy, but the end result is the same. You're about to be gone. Blown out of existence. No more sunshine, no more walks in the park, no more soup and crackers, no more friends or friendship.

Nothing.

When you dwell on the prospect that you're going to cease to exist, really dwell on it, without the promise of going to heaven, or any form of after life, things change. Your attitude about life changes. Why be good? Why be moral? Why not take everything that you can and everyone else be damned? Unless you've had a strong faith, or at least a faith that you believed in, and then have it jerked from under you like a ladder with a noose around your neck, it's difficult to appreciate the mind set.

It concerned me to the point that I had the beginning of a nice, well developed peptic ulcer. And this is from a guy who rarely worries about anything. I'd find myself at night, walking alone outside under the stars, looking up at the vast heavens, contemplating the vastness of eternity and my potential nonexistence. I have to tell you friends, it was frightening.

As if accentuating the matter, I had just read James Joyce's, *A Portrait of an Artist as a Young Man*, wherein there is this scene where he, Stephen, the main character of the story, and the rest of the boys from a parochial school are out on a retreat. The rector is giving them a sermon and is explaining about eternity. To paraphrase, the passage goes something like this:

> Imagine a mountain of sand a million miles high and a million miles wide, and at the end of every year a little bird would fly to the mountain and pick up a grain of that sand and fly away with it. And he would do this until the mountain finally disappeared, and then he would repeat the process as often as there were stars in the sky, leaves on the trees and grains of sand on the ocean. At the end of that unimaginable period of time, eternity would have scarcely have begun.

Although I couldn't, in my wildest imagination, fathom that period of time, I could imagine, or tried to imagine such a thing as a non-existence. To imagine myself dead without any existence after death was so completely unacceptable to me I found myself dwelling on it to the point that I felt I was going to lose my mind.

And then one night, while I was standing in the middle of a field by myself, asking God to give me a sign, to set my mind at ease, to set me straight, I felt a force the likes of which I have never felt before. A force grabbed me and literally squeeze the breath and life out of me. I felt like a sponge in the hands of an unseen giant squeezing the water (life) out of me. And it held me paralyzed until I realized that it was God telling me that He was tired of my whining and disbelief questioning whether or not that He existed. At that moment of realization He released me and I collapsed on the ground, gasping for breath. I can honestly say that that was the most profound experience of my life. After that, one would think that I would have snapped back in place and would have picked up my faith where I left off, but even after that experience I still faltered and questioned my faith.

Now, many years later, I'm finally comfortable with my faith and feel that I have a relationship with the Almighty that admittedly is much more mature than my Sunday School belief, but I'm still not convinced that I'm better off than I was with my previous simplistic belief. I guess the main thing is that one does have a relationship with the Almighty, because after all is said and done at the end of the day, or our life, there are only two choices: eternity with God or nothingness. Personally, I'll take eternity any day.

Then, there is reincarnation, but that's a topic for another day.

Oh, what the hell, as long as I mentioned it, I'll tell you a story. Years after I graduated from college, I really became interested in reincarnation and the afterlife. I read almost every book that I could lay my hands on, including Sylvia Brown a nationally known psychic. But I get ahead of myself.

I was in Lake Tahoe, this was when I was in my mid-thirties, taking a few days off from whatever. I happen to pass by an art festival taking place in one of the parks, so, being interested in art, I stopped to gander at the various artists works. I was about to leave when I noticed this one artist who had been located out in the corner of the lot who had bronze mental sculpture pieces sitting on the grass that he had created.

I wasn't a great proponent of metal art at the time, and after a glance around, started to leave. Then my eye caught this piece standing in the far corner. It was a sculpture piece, standing approximately forty inches tall, of a trapper wearing buckskins, holding a rifle over one shoulder and a cache of traps in the other. Obviously, a trapper.

The moment I saw it I was attracted to that piece like a magnet. I couldn't understand the attraction, but I couldn't take my eyes off of it. I asked the artist what he was asking for it, and he said that it wasn't for sale, that it had been sold to a movie actor, one who had played in a series called, *Lonesome Dove*. I knew the series and the actor, because I had seen it and had enjoyed it very much. I knew that had the sculpture piece been for sale, I would have bought it, no matter what the cost, which I later learned was $7,500.00, a lot of money in those days.

I never got the image and my attraction of that piece out of my mind. Anyway, a few years pass when I learn that Sylvia Brown, the psychic, had an office herein San Jose, so I call and make an appointment to have a consultation with her. After a few moments of conversation, she looks at me intently and says, you know, in your past life, you were a loner. You lived in the woods by yourself and you were a trapper!

I nearly fell off my chair.

Back to College

After attending Lewis and Clark for two years, I came to the realization of two facts: one, I wasn't going to make it into medical school with the grades that I had been getting, and what the hell, I was going to be a Psychologist anyway, and two I could no longer afford to go to Lewis and Lark College, as much as I loved the school, the campus and the students. I had simply run out of money and had to look to alternative choices. I knew that if I was going to continue with my education, I needed to reassess my options.

One door closes and another opens.

During this period of time, Uncle Fritz, Dad's younger brother, owned a tavern downtown Broadway called *Smilie's Tavern*. During the course of business, coming in contact with so many people, Uncle Fritz had somehow contracted tuberculosis and had to be hospitalized for an extended period of time, at least a year the doctor had said. Inez and Fritz were my favorite uncle and aunt and they owned this little motel in Vancouver called the *Hill Top Motel*, across the river from Portland. I can't recall how the arrangement came to be, but I ended up staying with them for the year that Fritz was in the hospital, helping Aunt Inez around the place and helping with their two kids, Paul and Chuck. To this day I remain impressed with Inez's strength. Not once did I see her break down or get depressed, although I'm sure that in the privacy of her bedroom, late at night, she must have had her moments.

If anything, it was her faith in God that gave her the strength to hang on and get through the ordeal.

That year, I signed up for night school at the Portland State University, taking fifteen hours -- a class every night. I loved taking night classes. Everyone in class was either a teacher fulfilling the advanced educational requirements, or kids going to college whose grades were suffering - like me, or people who had to work during the day – like me.

There was this little restaurant down the way from the motel called the *Totem Pole.* A thirty foot totem pole had been erected in front of the restaurant and they specialized in Kentucky fried chicken. I applied for and got a job as chief cook and bottle washer. It was my job first thing in the morning to get a crate of chickens out of the refrigerator that had been delivered earlier that morning, cut them up into the proper pieces with a band saw, wash them and then dunk them into milk and then, while they were wet, dunk them into this special Kentucky Fried Chicken spice and finally, put them into one of five pressure cookers where they cooked for a specific period of time.

Did this for a year.

The good news is, I got to eat all the chicken I wanted. The bad news was, all they had was chicken. When my workday was done, I dashed off to Portland State College which was located downtown, Portland to further my education.

I didn't get to see Carole (remember from Lewis & Clark College) much that year. I recall this one evening after I had gotten home from school, there was a knock on the door. I opened it up to find a woman standing there with a Cheshire grin on her face.

"Yes?" I inquired.

It turned out to be Carole, but I was so damned tired from work and school I didn't even recognize her. That was the beginning of the end of that relationship.

Our family was always poor as church mice and I always remembered whenever Inez and Fritz came to visit us in eastern Oregon, Fritz would always manage to pull me aside and slip me five bucks. He'd wink and say, "Buy your girl a milk shake," and then give that little nervous laugh that he had. I loved that guy!

Dad used to tell stories about when he and Fritz were kids, like floating down the river on their backs, nude, with their little wing-dings sticking out of the water and waving to the passengers on the train that ran parallel to the river as it whizzed by, registering shocked looks on the ladies faces, or when they'd redecorate some farmer's barn and get caught and have to paint it all over again. They were my kind of guys! Dad used to tell me that Fritz was a pro golfer and that he used to caddie for him. A couple of times Fritz would take me out to a cow pasture and tell me where to stand with a bucket. He would then back up several hundred yards and proceed to tee golf balls off in my direction. I never got hit once, and usually the balls fell within ten feet of where I stood. I was impressed!

Big Ambitions

The city of Portland is surrounded by water. You can't go much more than a mile or two in any direction without hitting a river, a stream, a lake, a waterfall or some large mud puddle. Plus, it rains, sleets, snows or drizzles, or you get hit by an errant water hose some 360 days out of the year, so if you don't like water, don't go to the northwest. They don't call the University of Oregon the *Oregon Ducks* or Oregon State, the *Beavers* for nothing. I don't know for sure when the idea of having a floating restaurant entered my mind, but the germ was probably planted when I was working at *Devault's Chuck Wagon* parking cars. Between collecting a quarter for parking some dude's Caddy and standing around in the old night air, trying to stomp my way to warmth, the idea came to me.

The concept was a floating restaurant located in the form of a real Chinese Junk! I visualized the junk being large enough to accommodate at least sixty paying guests, some sitting at tables on the deck decorated with colorful Chinese lanterns with Chinese string instrument music being piped through the sound system. Below deck, would be dining tables as well with each table having access to its own private port hole.

I conceived that from five o'clock to six o'clock the customers would board the junk which would have been tied to a dock on the Willamette River, just below the city. They would have time to freely roam about the ship, taking pictures getting a pre-dinner drink or simply enjoy the ambiance of the vessel floating on the water. At precisely six o'clock the crew would haul in the gang plank and the junk would commence floating down the river.

Patrons who had called in for reservations would be served according to their advanced reserved diner time, while those who had a later dinner reservation might enjoy the ride, have a drink or take a spin around the dance floor located on the designated place at the ship's aft. The junk would drift down river for an hour and a half, then make a slow U-turn and then make its way back up river to its dock, arriving three and one-half hours from departure.

The dinner guests would depart and after they had all left the ship, the second wave of guests would make their way up the gang plank for the eight to midnight dinner cruse, arriving back home around one a.m.

I actually thought about this concept for several months, going to the extent of seeking how much and how one might have to pay to get a Chinese Junk from China to the good old U S of A. The first place I started at was the Building Department where I was met with many snickers, strange looks and then giving the sound advice to, "Forget it!"

"Once you manage to get a ship here, which means floating through international waters and high seas, and then going through customs which will not be a cake walk in itself, then the health department will have ago at you to be sure that the ship contains no infestation from the point of origin – namely China, you will need to bring the ship up to local building-aquatic codes." He took a deep breath which allowed me to ask how long this might take?

"I'd guess two years," was his reply.

"And the cost?"

He just smiled at my young face and inquired if this was a school project.

I decided to put that project on hold and go on to my next idea which was to open a night club that offered a floor show with shapely, well conditioned young dancers performing to a well designed choreographed scripted that I would oversee. That project require money too, and I figured at twenty-five cents a car and my hourly wage of a buck twenty-five, I might be forced to put my idea on hold until my pocket book got more flush that the three dollars that it now held.

The University of Oregon

The following year Fritz was discharged from the hospital and I decided to go back to school on a full time basis. Portland State was too austere for me, more like a prison than a campus. I applied to and was accepted at the University of Oregon in Eugene. While attending Lewis and Clark, I had met a couple with whom I had became great friends, Dave and Laura. They had decided to attend the University of Oregon the same year that I did, so Dave and I decided to become roommates.

We rented the basement of this house near the campus and settled into our usual routine. We cooked our own food which was a terrific savings. We had cereal for breakfast and spaghetti, soup or baked potatoes and pot pies for dinner. Our routine was to make enough food to last two or three days. Whenever we had pot pies and baked potatoes, we would put them in the oven and go play tennis for an hour. When we got back, dinner was ready.

You can imagine how surprised we were when we got our first rain. The basement had bunk beds. Dave took the top and I had the bottom. That morning the alarm went off as usual and we jumped out of bed -- into four inches of water! Our shoes, books and clothes were floating around the room like a surrealistic Dali painting. It took the better part of the morning to clean up the mess and attempt to dry our books in the oven. Needless to say, we had a heart-to-heart conversation with our landlord, who sheepishly lied, saying that he had simply forgotten to mention the rain-flood problem. Yeah! Sure!

After a semester of living in the basement we heard that there was this fraternity house that was looking for renters. We drove by to check it out. Apparently the old fraternity house had burned down a year or so ago and, without a house, they were hard pressed to get pledges, so they were looking for renters to fill the beds. By beds, they meant beds in the sleeping porch. The first thing that we had to understand was that this was their house and we were expected to conform to their way of doing things. For example, at mealtime, if a member violated table manners, such as passing the salt with the wrong hand, or putting one's elbows on the table, or farting, the offender was put on the block and the other fraternity members were allowed to bid on him. The winning bidder was given a wooden paddle with holes drilled in it and the offending person had to bend over and grasp hold of his ankles and grit his teeth while the guy with the paddle swung away. As one might imagine, that was one painful experience, and everyone learned their table manners real quick. Not being members, Dave and I were exempt from bidding, and being bid on. Nonetheless, we conformed to their rules.

I recall that there was this one obnoxious member, George, who would walk the halls at night, after study period was over, challenging anyone to exchange paddle blows with him.

You can tell what's coming, can't you?

Sure enough, one evening as he was walking down the hallway shouting out challenges, when I stepped out in the hallway and challenged him. Shock registered on his face, but he readily accepted my challenge.

"You go first," I offered, bending over and grabbing my ankles. By this time a small herd of the brothers had gathered, hoping that George the bully would get his comeuppance.

George grinned and said, "Okay! You asked for it."

With a mighty swing, a loud 'whoop' sounded as he hit me. I quickly got up, with no pain registering on my face and said, "Okay, my turn."

George was stunned that, not only did I not pick myself off the floor and was still able to walk, but that I actually had a smile on my face. Reluctantly, he bent over and grabbed his ankles. I quickly dealt my blow, one that nearly lifted him off the floor. I then handed him his paddle and then retreated to our room, followed by Dave.

"You were taking a chance out there," he said as he closed the door.

"I know, but it was worth it, wasn't it?" We both laughed so hard that tears rolled down our cheeks as I removed the bath towel from inside my pants.

"Did it hurt much?" he asked once we stopped laughing.

"Didn't feel a thing!" I lied.

From that day forward, word spread about my joisting with brother George and we gained new respect amongst the brothers. More than once did they try to convert us to their brotherhood, but Dave and I stood pat as independents.

Sleeping in a sleeping porch in the middle of winter for those of you who have never done so, is definitely a chilling experience. The room is large enough to accommodate everyone in the house. Everyone sleeps in bunk beds. The room had been designed with three solid walls and one heavy louvered wall exposed to the outdoors. By louvers I mean three inch gaps per slat with chicken wire on the inside to keep birds and creators of prey out. Winter nights in Oregon dip down zero degrees Fahrenheit and below.

Cold!

All I had to keep me warm were two thin blankets and an old coat. Thank God for Dave! He went home at his earliest convenience and brought back two sleeping bags and extra blankets. We had so much stuff on top of us that we woke up in the morning tired just from the weight of the blankets covering us.

How I Spent My Summers

For me, summer vacation has always been the same ever since I could remember. As soon as school was out, I went to work in the *Pendleton Pea Cannery*, working in the cold room. The cold room is this large warehouse type of room where the temperature is kept at a constant thirty degrees below zero. The peas are harvested, washed and then put into these little boxes and shipped to the cold room where they were fast frozen. My job was to keep the machinery moving and make sure everything went as planned. That is to say, that the trays moved from fresh peas at the top to frozen peas at the bottom. In other words, the pea trays were stacked and then rotated to the bottom, one gigantic tray at a time. After they reached the bottom, fast frozen, they were boxed into individual packages and then shipped out to market, usually under the label of *Bird's Eye*.

The rule was, a worker was only supposed to stay in the cold room forty-five minutes at a time and then we were supposed to get out for fifteen minutes to thaw out. Needless to say, we bundled up pretty good. It seemed odd, dressing up in a heavy coat with sweaters underneath, boots with wool hats, socks and gloves. Odd because the temperature outside was nearly a hundred degrees. The two contrasts were ideal conditions for contracting a cold. I know, you only get colds from a virus, nonetheless…

When everyone else left the room, I made it a point to stay in there and think. I was amazed how fast the brain cells would operate at thirty degrees below zero. It was great! What did I think about? I honestly can't recall, I just remember that I was impressed how fast my brain worked and loved thinking of problems and then solving them

Anyway, the pea cannery season went on for two months, but like clockwork, within thirty days from when I had started, I was forced to give notice, because wheat harvest was starting and I had a job driving a D-6 Caterpillar pulling a combine. Every year it was the same. I'd submit my application to the pea canner and Rig Red, as he was known, would read my name and then frown. "You're one of the Losness boys, aren't you?" By now, both Larry and I were working in the pea cannery. "Every year you work for thirty days and then quit. You gonna quit this year?"

"No, sir?"

"Humph! Well, see to it that you don't. If you quit this year, next year I won't be hiring you back. Understood?"

"Yes, sir."

Next year the same conversation took place.

When you sign on to go harvesting, you know up front it's not an eight-to-five job. It's sunrise to sunset, nonstop except for lunch which is brought out in the field on a flat bed truck. You don't get paid by the hour; you get paid a lump sum at the end of the job, a predetermined fee, agreed upon before harvest starts.

The nice thing about harvest is that Dad always worked with me. He would have vacation time coming from the government job at the ordinance where he worked and every harvest season he and I would go harvesting together. He drove a truck. When the wheat bin on the harvester was full, it was his job to pull alongside the moving harvester until the operator emptied all the wheat onto the truck, and then he would drive off to the grain elevator where the load would be weighed and then dumped. My job was driving the caterpillar that pulled the combine.

In the morning, breakfast was a large meal consisting of everything from ham, sausage, fried potatoes and eggs, to pancakes, coffee and orange juice. It was a real man's breakfast. For lunch, the women made an equally large feast and drove it out to us in a flat bed truck or a pickup. The wheat field was usually several miles from the farm house and consisted of several thousand acres, so large that when we started harvesting one field, it might take a whole day just to go around once. In the evening, the machines were left where they stood, and we would service them by greasing and oiling them in preparation for the following day.

By that time we were done for the day we were covered with several layers of dust. The old timers wore long sleeved shirts with their collars rolled up and hats pulled over their ears to keep the dust out. Me, I wore a pair of shorts and no shirt. By the time we had gone fifteen minutes I was covered with dust anyway which kept me cooler than my older counterparts. I never got burnt because the dust acted as a sunscreen.

Driving the cat was the most god-awful boring job that there was. You basically went one speed. It was my job to be sure that I kept the cutting part of the combine so that it took a full swath every time. The drive in the morning wasn't too bad. Usually there was little wind and you had just had a good night sleep so you were fresh. After lunch, when your belly was full and the sun cast a glow off the golden wheat field, it was near impossible to stay awake. One might think, what with the squeaking and clanking of the metal tracks and the loud combine motor whining in your ear, not to mention the diesel motor of the cat, that you would be bright eyed and bushy tailed, but not so. I must have fallen asleep a hundred times a day, every day, but for only a moment, and then I'd wake up and check my bearings and then be lulled back to sleep for another moment. It was torture! And your mind plays tricks on you. In the heat of the day, all you can think of is a large, cold chocolate milkshake, or some other delectable item that is unattainable.

It would be dark when we finally pulled into the bunk house. We'd shower, put on a clean set of cloths and head on down into the main house where another king sized meal had been prepared and was waiting to be consumed. After dinner we would usually sit outside under the stars for an hour or more and talk or just sit and enjoy the evening before retiring to bed. There was no TV, radio or any other form of entertainment.

We didn't work on Sunday's, but then we were stuck way out in the middle of nowhere, fifty miles from civilization without transportation, so everyone pretty much stayed around the bunk and slept or read or wrote letters. This went on for twenty or thirty days until harvest was over. Tanned and ready to go to the next job, I usually left with five or six hundred dollars in my pocket which went directly into my savings account for schooling.

It was during harvest in the year 1959 while I was driving cat on Dave Moore's ranch that I encountered or saw a flying saucer. It was late in the day and we were about half through the field when I noticed this bright silver round object just hanging in the sky, not moving a lick. It stayed there for the better part of half of an hour from the time that I first noticed it. I have no idea how long it had been there before I first saw it. Judging from the size of it, I would say that it was really high up in the sky as it appeared no larger than quarter. Then, in a flash, it cleared the sky in a matter of seconds, a span of miles, and disappeared. Knowing how long of a period it takes commercial airplanes or even fighter jets to clear the sky in the same distance, this thing had to be traveling thousands of miles per hour. Anyway, I kept the sighting to myself, least anyone think that I was loosing it.

My next job, the day after harvest was finished, was bucking bales of hay. The farmer would cut the alfalfa, raking it into rows. When it had dried, a bailing machine would drive over the raked hay and spit out sixty pound bales of hay. It was our job to drive a wagon along side the baled hay and load them onto the truck, eventually throwing and stacking them as much as twelve feet or more above the ground.

When the truck was filled, we would transport the hay to a barn where we would unload the bales and restack them again. The worst thing about flinging bales of hay onto a truck was that you had two hay hooks that you would sink into each end of the baled hay, and they jerk it up onto your knee and then over your head and up onto the truck, all in one motion. When you visualize alfalfa, a picture of soft leafy stems of vegetation emerges. What you don't see beneath the soft vegetation is a nasty weed called a sandbur. When the hay gets baled up, so do the sandburs. Only the soft vegetation has dried, turning unrelenting sticks of straw and sandburs into an unsuspecting torture chamber. Every time you lift a bale of hay and hoist it up with your knee, the likelihood of getting a couple of sandburs stuck into your leg is pretty much guaranteed. I hated that part. The smart ones wore leather chaps, but who was smart, and who could afford leather chaps?

Once, this farmer that I had never heard of before came to our house and asked my folks if I could work for him, to help him bring in his crop. I think Larry and I were the only kids in town that didn't have to go looking for work. It always came to us. Our reputation for giving an honest days work seemed to precede us.

Anyway, this one particular time, this farmer came to the door asking if I could work for him. When my folks said, "Yes," he asked me if I knew how to drive a team of horses.

I thought back to the time that I had ridden a horse on Jimmy Kaiser's ranch once and said, "Sure!" The next morning I rode my bike out to his place.

As it turned out, he had these two old nags, horses that he had hitched up to a ten foot rake. The idea was to drive the team of horses over a wooden culvert and down to the pasture where he had already cut the alfalfa. I was instructed to go around and around the field which was fenced in with barbed wire, manually tripping the rake every once in a while with a metal lever next to the metal seat where I was to sit perched, trying to rake the hay into a straight line so that the baling machine could later gather up and bale the hay.

That seemed an easy enough task, so I climbed up on the round steel seat atop the rake, grabbed the reins, slapped the two nags on their rump and guided them down the well worn path towards the field. Everything went well until we reached a wooden culvert. I could see that there was precious little room on either side and no room for error.

The horses sensed my trepidation as well. They stopped short of the bridge and sort of looked back at me as if to say, "Are we going to do this or not?"

I managed to coax them across the bridge and down to the pasture without incident. Aside from getting the wheels stuck in the fence on the first turn, all went well until the job was done and it was time to go home. I knew it and the horses knew it. Trouble is, they knew what was waiting for them back at the barn. Food, water and rest.

The two old nags suddenly came to life. They put it into high gear and we were off to the races, heading home with the wind blowing through my hair. When I say, 'they put it into high gear', that's exactly what I mean. I had lost all control over the situation. We were heading towards the bridge at a high gallop with the steel wheels of the rake barely touching the ground and me, hanging on for dear life. I could visualize it all. At the rate we were going, we weren't going to make it!

I tried slowing them down, pulling back on the reins as hard as I could. The harder I pulled, the faster they went, as if defying me. I think they call it 'passive-aggressive'.

Approaching the bridge, I was standing up, pulling on the reins with all my might with the horses fighting me every inch of the way. We hit the bridge flying. We probably would have made it had I let the horses have their way, but with me trying to rein them in, and them fighting me, we verged off to the right. The right wheel missed the bridge by a good four inches. Next thing I knew I was flying through the air, ass over tea kettle. I must have gone twenty feet before landing with a thud in the ditch full of water. The rig bounced along for another thirty feet or more and finally came to rest against a large oak tree, none the worse for wear as far as I could tell. The horses continued on down the road and disappeared from sight.

I didn't bother going to the farm house to collect my wages. I figured I had forfeited them and maybe even owed him something extra. I just went to get my bike and rode home, thankful that I was in one piece and vowed never to get within a hundred feet of a horse again.

The next day the farmer showed up at our doorstep with my wages. He explained that he knew the horses had a mind of their own and not to feel bad about the accident. It had happened to him too.

The last job I had every summer was picking watermelons. Eastern Oregon is known for their watermelons. Probably because of the sandy soil. Larry and I went to work for the Walker's, who owned the largest watermelon ranch in the area. Once the melons are ripe, they're all ripe. You don't have to thump them to see if they're ready to be picked or not. You just go down the row and pick them off the vein which by now has gone brown. We'd take turns throwing them up on the truck, one throwing up onto the truck and the other on the truck catching and stacking them. Whenever we got hungry or thirsty, we'd simply drop one on the ground and dig our fingers into the middle and pull

out the heart. That spoiled us for ever eating a watermelon sliced --
seeds and all that jazz.

At the end of watermelon season we had just enough time to go
fishing and swimming in the Columbia River before going back to
school.

Dumped!

As I mentioned previously, my summers were filled with various jobs accumulating enough money to get me through at least part of the upcoming academic year. Since moving to the University of Oregon, I had been going with this girl, Janet that I had mentioned earlier, the one that Dave and Laura had introduced me to. She was a tall, brown eyed, striking brunette with a pageboy hairdo. She stood five-seven and for her summer job, she was a lifeguard. She had a golden tan that accentuated her long legs. In a bathing suit, she attracted a lot of attention, especially being a lifeguard in a public swimming pool. Coincidentally, my roommate Dave, had the same job, but in a different town, of course.

The time between my junior and senior year working, Janet and I corresponded back and forth during that summer and I couldn't wait for school to start so I could get to see her again. We both needed work to augment our education, and somehow we had learned that the freshmen men and women's dormitories were looking for upper classmen to be living-in counselors, offering room and board as compensation. We both applied for the job and were accepted. Her family owned the town newspaper, and I could never figure out why she needed to work. Perhaps it was her father's way of instilling financial independence.

Anyway, after school started, we met again for the first time our senior year at the counselor orientation meeting. After the meeting we left together, holding hands and went out for a coke and a piece of pie. Instead of a lot of 'I missed you', conversation, our time together was filled with small talk. I could tell that something was bothering her. We drove back to her dorm in silence. It wasn't until I had pulled up in front of her dormitory that she informed me that she had seen someone during the summer that had changed the way she felt about me.

My heart sank!

She proceeded to tell me about this guy who had taken her up for an airplane ride over the city and she was shocked, she said, to discover that during the period of time that they were in the air, that she hadn't thought of me. Therefore, she concluded, "I must not love you."

"Was this the first time you had flown in a small plane?" I inquired.

"Yes."

"Well, hell, if I had been invited by someone to go up in a small plane for the first time, I doubt if I would have thought about you either. That doesn't mean that my feelings for you would have changed."

Despite my winning logic, she stood fast in her conviction that her feelings for me were not true and that that was the end of our relationship, as it was. Reluctantly, I accepted my fate and vowed to renew my goal to concentrate on my studies. We dated on and off during the year, but it was never the same. It was the first time that I had ever been dumped by a girl and frankly, it hurt.

Oddly enough, a couple years later, after I had been drafted to serve my country, she managed to track me down while I was still stationed at Fort Ord, California. I met her at some friends of hers house in San Francisco where we had been invite for diner. I was excited about the prospects of seeing her again, because frankly, I hadn't gotten over her. The moment I saw her, everything changed. She looked like a different woman. She had grown thinner and her facial features had changed form a petite, pixie look to something entirely different. We passed the time, having a pleasant dinner with her friends, and when it was over, I was glad that I had seen her again. Any feelings that I had for her had evaporated and we parted, never to see one another again.

Sometime during the second semester of my senior year I went to work at a Volvo dealership, detailing cars. I met this older gentleman who I took an instant liking to. He was just one of those people that you connect with during your travels.

One day I arrived at work, after school, and found him talking to this enchanting young woman with poutie lips, dark set eyes and a fabulous figure. She was about my age. When she left, I inquired who she was.

"My daughter Carol, from Alabama," she said. "She had been out looking for a job. She just came in to tell me that she got hired by the bank yesterday."

"Is she attached?"

"Why? You want to meet her?"

"That would be nice."

"She used to be an airline hostess, you know."

Thirty days later I was living with her, balancing my time between my freshman counseling job and spending time with her. It was an experience that I'll never forget.

Drafted!

I had gotten my first draft notice my senior year at the University of Oregon. As I previously mentioned, at the beginning of the semester, I had been offered the job as a counselor in a freshman dorm, a three story structure overlooking the tennis courts and the football stadium. It offered free room and board. The free room was the typical dorm room. The board part of our agreement consisted of cafeteria food at a common eating hall shared with three other freshmen dormitories. For the past four years I had been cooking Kentucky fried chicken, cooking and serving short orders, parking cars and carving other people's food, so I thought a change in job description would be delightful. Besides, I was tired of working part time and squeezing in school and studies, and my grades showed it, so I took the job. Besides, as I mentioned earlier, Janet had been offered the same job as a women's freshman counselor and had decided to take the position.

After accepting the position of counselor, I thought I would have a room to myself, but was informed I would be sharing a room with a freshman. The freshman turned out to be a kid by the name of Jack who had a farting disorder. He let one go every fifteen minutes or so, twenty-four-seven. This turned out to be a fascination for his schoolmates to the degree that they got to hold contests to see who could light themselves on fire and shoot the flame out of their ass the fartherest. This practice resulted in more than one burnt ass.

When one has traversed through the college ranks and has finally achieved senior status, it ceases to be amusing when pranks such as filling balloons full of water and putting them into the back of the top drawer with thumb tacks scotch-taped to the front so when one opens the drawer, all one sees are these little round objects rolling towards destruction with the obvious result that the rest of your cloths were about to get soaked; or when pails of water which have been positioned over your door just waiting for the next unsuspecting victim to walk in; or dozens of water-filled coke bottles (yes I did say "bottles" - it was that long ago) were stacked under your pull-out bed, waiting to be toppled over with water spilling out of their necks while you frantically try to upright the little critters; or pennies taped to the push-button lock inside of your dorm door so when you venture out into the hall to take a shower, the door locks behind you and nothing, and I mean nothing will open your door except a locksmith; or whatever other pranks their freshman minds with nothing else to do can think of.

No small wonder they house freshmen alone in their own dormitories.

Anyway, I had just begun the first semester of my senior year when a letter arrived from the Selective Service Department, rerouted from my folks' address in Hermiston, Oregon. The only mail I got was an occasional letter from home, keeping in touch, letting me know how the family was doing, so I was surprised when an official letter from the department of defense found its way to my little room on the third floor of the freshman dormitory at Akin Hall. It was a draft notice, informing me that I had thirty days to report to service at the induction center in Portland, Oregon.

I panicked. I knew that my chances of escaping the draft were slim and none. The cut off date for drafting age was twenty-two and one-half years. I was twenty-one. I could avoid the inevitable by getting married which was always a way out, or by having a child which, should I be inclined towards such frivolity, would have to take place within the next thirty days. I resolved myself to the unavoidable fact that I was destined to become one of America's defenders.

I got in touch with the dean of men who assured me that I could get a deferment until I had graduated. He would write a letter as he had many times, and simply explain that I needed time to finish my education, after which I would be available to fulfill my military obligations.

Six weeks passed and I finally received a subsequent letter advising me that I had until mid-August to report. That gave me enough time to complete my degree, which I did in the middle of the year and had then started in the Master's Degree program. In the back of my mind, I secretly hoped that they might forget about me, or at the very least, allow me to continue my education, seeing that I was already in the Master's degree program.

No such luck!

My induction was to take place at Fort Ord, California, September of 1960. I figured I had three courses of action open to me before I began my two year vacation with Uncle Sam. I could take the summer off, something I had never done before, and party my brains out; or continue going to school that summer and get one more semester under my belt before I was swallowed up by the Army. Knowing that I would be the old man of the inductees with most of the recruits ranging in ages between seventeen to nineteen years of age, I decided on the third option, to find the toughest job available that would put me in the best physical shape. I resolved that no eighteen year was going to make me look inferior.

I applied for and was hired by the railroad as a manual laborer. For the next two months I carried rail-road ties, shoveled gravel and hauled twenty foot sections of steel rails up and down the Oregon railroad train track. By the time that the Army took me in, I was in excellent physical condition, ready for anything they could dish out.

At the induction station in Portland, Oregon they piled us onto an old Greyhound bus and fourteen hours later, in the middle of the night, we pulled into Fort Ord, California. We were met by Gestapo-type men whose uniforms had been tailored to fit their bodies like paint on a bowling pin. They wore hard black helmets that glistened under the overhead lights and welded batons which they waived at us like a conductor directing an orchestra, except they were barking instructions left and right. I thought we were in a German concentration camp!

We were loaded onto cattle trucks, and squeezed in like sardines. By this time everyone was tired, cold and scared. First stop, the barber. We were herded in this little building where we were seated in a barber chair for a time span of no longer than thirty seconds, during which time we had our heads shaved, and then were herded back outside to stand in a formation where we were again herded to an old wooden barracks. The guy in charge, a short black man, pointed to several guys, advising them that they had KP. The rest could file into the wooden building and eat. We were given a steel compartmentalized tray onto which they slapped on something they called food. Twenty minutes later, they herded us to another old wooden building where they advised us that this would be our home for the next few days, until we were reassigned to our new unit.

Still in shock, but fed and exhausted, we filed into the large bay area that had bunk beds stacked on either side of the wall. The short, fat, black guy said we had fifteen minutes before lights out. He instructed everyone to stow our personal items, our civilian cloths, etc, in the wall lockers behind the beds. He assured us that they would be safe and further assured us that we wouldn't need them for the next six weeks.

It seemed that we had no sooner fallen asleep than we were rudely awakened by the banging of a night stick on an empty garbage pail. It was still dark outside and we were told that we had fifteen minutes to dress, make our beds and be out side in formation. We were told under no uncertain terms that anyone not complying would curse his mother for being born.

First stop was chow. Second stop, evaluation center. We were given two hours of evaluation tests which were followed by physical tests. It was then that I was glad that I had chosen to be in shape. I knew I would pass. This was the first opportunity that I had to check out my fellow in inductees. They were a lot younger than I imagined, ranging from fat and out of shape to skinny and out of shape. We were supposed to do fifty sit-ups, twenty-five push-ups and at least ten pull-ups along with several other chosen exercises. We were paired off and the physical began. Half of the guys couldn't do the required amount of sit-ups nor the push-ups and the majority of them were lucky if they could get five pull-ups. Some couldn't even get up to the pull-up bar, let alone do a single pull-up.

I was shocked.

I would eventually discover that only one out of ten could keep up on the long runs that they would eventually have.

After the evaluation we were issued an M-1 rifle, and were told to memorize our weapon serial number along with our dog tag serial numbers. We were then assigned permanent barracks. Our group was fortunate enough to be assigned one of the newer two-story brick barracks. For the next six weeks my new address was D-11-3. Our squad was housed in a large bay that held sixty guys. My bunk mate was a black kid from Portland by the name of Jessie. We would become best friends during this six week period.

I knew I was in trouble the first time we were told to fall out into formation. Our platoon sergeant was a little short Philippine dude by the name of Benevente with three stripes on his arm, a buck sergeant. He had the IQ of a stump and spoke broken English so badly that one could only understand every third word. His sergeant was a staff sergeant by the name of ... what else, Jackson. They loved picking on the white boys, and heaven forbid they should discover that you had an education. Then you really were the target of their attention.

Their favorite form of punishment was to have one or everyone do fifty push-ups and if they were in the mood, they'd make the entire company do what they called the dying beetle; which was lying on your back with both your arms and legs fully extended. And if they really wanted to demonstrate their superiority, they had everyone hold themselves in the up position of a push-up and were told to hold it until you drop.

Once, just to be ornery, while the company was being punished by having to take the push-up up-position for the indiscretion of one man for a violation such as talking or not keeping a straight line, I reached back in my pocked and blew my nose. Now, you *know*, I didn't have to blow my nose, but ... have I mentioned that I have a passive-aggressive personality?

"Losness, fifty push-ups!" the sergeant barked.

Now, when you have to do push-ups, the rule is that you have to count them out loud, so everyone can hear you and keep track. That way when they reach twenty and collapse the whole company knows that your next punishment is to run around them with their weapon held over their heads until they drop.

I counted out loud all right. "One, TWO, three, FOUR..." singing out each number as if I were in the shower enjoying myself. When I had finished my fifty and stood back in formation, Sergeant stump said, "Losness! You seemed to enjoy that so much, let's have another fifty!"

"One, TWO, three, FOUR...." After three weeks of harassment (them of me and me of them) they came to the conclusion that they weren't going to break me, and decided to leave me alone.

Basic training went much smoother than I had anticipated. It had to be geared to the average recruit and their abilities or in most cases, inabilities to perform. Every morning before meals we would pass by the chin-up bar and before you could eat, you had to do chin-ups – as many as you could. If the sergeant felt you were malingering or just getting by, he would find another form of punishment such as running you around the compound for an hour or more. I felt sorry for this one fat kid who couldn't even make it up to the bar. Finally, one day the sergeant told two of us to lift him up to the bar. The kid simply hung there like a sack of potatoes, unable to raise his body for even a single pull-up and finally fell to the ground in heap. Every morning he got a terrible tongue lashing. This day was no exception.

After breakfast it was down to the rifle range, a five mile run in the cold, crisp air. Once we arrived at the rifle range which was located a few feet off the ocean, we'd sit in the bleachers, our bodies wet with perspiration, freezing from the cold ocean air. It wasn't long before every guy in the company was coughing and wheezing. They had a name for the coughing and wheezing condition – the Fort Ord crud. I never did get rid of mine. To this day, if I get a chest cold, the Fort Ord crud kicks in and I begin a two month coughing spell.

When I was a kid in Irrigon, we all had .22 rifles and 12 gage shotguns. I could hit a running and darting cottontail rabbit at a hundred paces with my .22, so qualifying on the rifle range was a piece of cake. In the end I earned a metal as an expert marksman. In retrospect, not too smart, because I didn't have any great desire to become an infantryman, hiking up hills and over dales looking to get my ass shot off.

Then came the day when basic training was over and we were assigned to our next duty. Ninety percent of the guys were assigned to the infantry, with some assigned to personnel or the motor pool, driving or working on machinery. Because of my training, I expected to be assigned to the psychiatric division in the hospital. You can imagine the shock on my face when I heard, "Losness: Army Band!"

Turns out that the Army Band has the highest preferential treatment when it comes to assignments, and the fact that I had played a tuba for the past ten years slid me right past the hospital and into the Army band.

Now, normally, band duty is the lightest duty one could ask for. All day long you do nothing more than sit around playing music. You get to eat the best meals, you're invited to play at general's shindigs, and all that. There is no guard duty, no KP, no shit details. But I didn't *want* to play in the band. I had a degree in psychology and was aching to work in my field. I was going to be a psychoanalyst and wanted desperately to get in some practical experience, not play a horn for two years! It was bad enough that my education had been set back two years as it was. I did a little checking and found out that that in my desired MOS, 915, Psychological Technician, there was not a single person available at Fort Ord to fill that space, and the mandate require two people! I was both ecstatic and upset at the same time.

I immediately went to the chief psychiatrist, a major, and offered my services. "Sorry, young man," he replied, "The Army band has first preference. Even though we could use you, I'm afraid you're stuck playing your horn."

Have I mentioned that I have a passive-aggressive personality?

I immediately did what no soldier in his right mind dares to think of doing, let alone do. I disregarded the chain of command and wrote to my congressman. I eloquently penned a seven page letter outlining the Army's mistake; that I had a degree in psychology, and that the army needed someone with my training to fill a position of my qualification and experience, plus, I had mistakenly been assigned to play in the band, and, I explained, I was a terrible tuba player. Not a credit to the fine Army band at all.

Two weeks later I was informed that I was to have a congressional inquisition. I had no idea what that meant, but was sure that my next post was going to be behind bars at the brig. I was told under no uncertain terms to report to a specific room at a specific time and date. When I walked into the room I was met with a table full of Army brass, each with stars, maple leaf clusters and bars on their shoulders, and in front of each of them was a copy of the seven page, prefabricated letter that I had sent to my Congressman.

Oh, shit!

They went through the letter line by line, page by page, asking me questions, and quizzing my abilities. In the end, I got what I wanted. I was reassigned an MOS of 915 and sent to Fort Lewis, Washington.

Why Fort Lewis?

Fort Lewis is what is known as a STRAC command unit. That means that within twenty-four hours notice the fort and everyone therein can be assigned and shipped anywhere in the world. In other words, by being sent to Fort Lewis, the Army made it clear that I was being punished.

The first week after my arrival the fort was divided into two sections and sent off on a six week mock war. As a psychological technician it became clear that I was at the bottom of the pecking order. Those who were real soldiers, the ones that carry rifles, drove tanks and were company clerks, were useful in a war. Psych technicians are not and they made no bones about it. We were assigned, along with the medical group, to be security guards. The kind that stand around outside in the cold weather and guard against enemy attack – with an empty gun, of course.

In this circumstance, they stationed us atop a hill, about a thousand yards from the rest of the fort and told us to dig ourselves a fox hole. It was that foxhole that was to be our home for the next six weeks while the rest of the fort played war games.

We got to go down into the population once a week and shower. Aside from that, we lived and slept in our fatigues. There were two of us per foxhole. Our orders were to stand guard twenty-four-seven. If we saw anyone approach, we were to challenge them. What we did after that, I don't have a clue, and if they ignored us, again I had no clue. Throw a dirt clod at them, I guess.

One day we were sunning ourselves on top of the hill when suddenly this, 'Whoosh' came at us from overhead. We dove for cover and looked up. Some guy in a jet was looking back as us, laughing. He had seen us sunning ourselves and decided to scare the shit out of us. And he did. We didn't even hear him until he was about fifty feet from us. I don't know if he reported us or not, but my guess is not. After all, this was just a play war and he was playing with our heads.

The sergeant in charge of the guards was a crusty old fart that hated anyone in the medical corps in general and psych techs in particular. He spared no measure to let us know just how he felt about us.

"If I ever have to go to war, you're the last guys I would want on my team!" he spouted one day after catching us sunbathing with our shirts off.

"Why is that, sergeant?" I inquired innocently, slapping some more butter cream on my burnt shoulders.

"Because you don't follow orders. If I tell a normal soldier to charge that hill, they do as they're told. If I tell one of you numbskulls to charge that hill, you'll look at me and say, "No way. They're shooting at us!'"

Couldn't argue with him there.

He was always testing us, sneaking up on us day and night, trying to catch us sunbathing or napping so he could belittle us and chew us out. One night he did catch one of the guys sleeping. It was three in the morning and, as usual, nothing was going on. It was cold and the guy on duty had snuggled in his foxhole and had dozed off. The next thing he knew, it was daylight and his rifle was missing. The Sergeant had sneaked up in the middle of the night and had taken his rifle. Boy was he in for it now!

The next thing we knew, the guy was standing before the General facing a court martial. I guess the general had other fish to fry, like winning the war, so he simply assigned the guy to permanent KP and let it go at that. Technically, the guy could have been shot, or at the very least, demoted and thrown in the brig. After all, these were war time conditions.

Once the war was over and we were back to the hospital where we were stationed, I got orders that I was being transferred back to Fort Ord. It seems they needed someone with a 915 MOS status.

Seventy-Nine Dollars and Forty-Six Cents

Back at the hospital, in the clinic, we only had patients for four or five hours in the morning, leaving the balance of the day for reading, playing chess or attending lectures on how to deliver babies in the field, or drive vehicles in war-like situations, or apply bandages to open gunshot wounds. Every first Friday of the month our efforts were awarded by standing in line to receive our monthly pay: seventy-nine dollars and forty-six cents.

Now you would think that seventy-nine dollars and forty-six cents would go a long way when one is stuck on an Army post with nothing to do. The first two weeks I spent my weekends going to Monterey or Carmel and doing the tourist thing, buying junk food, purchasing a few trinkets for the folks back home and seeing some of the sights down on Steinbeck's Cannery Row. It wasn't long before I discovered *California's First Theater*, a small intimate theater located on an obscure street somewhere in Monterey where the audience sat on hard benches ten feet from the stage, ate peanuts and popcorn and booed and hissed at the villain and rooted for the hero. After the theater we would saunter down to the *Hidden Village*, an exotic coffee house with dim lights and original oil paintings from local artists adorning the walls. We would sit on deep cushions on the floor and sip a glass of red wine and eat cheese and crackers and play a game of Chess or Go while listening to classical guitar music. This was a new experience for me and I was loving it!

Life was great! No worries, no stress and no responsibilities. No wonder people make the service a career. It was like having a giant mother figure that gives you everything you need in life and tells you what to do and when to do it. There's no such thing as failure, or working overtime, and the only status symbol that exists is that which you wear on your arm or shoulder. Your rank dictates your pay and prestige at the same time.

Before you know it, the first three weeks of the month have gone by and you're down to a few bucks. There's nothing to be done but cinch in the belt and confine oneself to the base for the rest of the month and wait for the next first Friday to roll around.

The last couple bucks are used to buy soap and stuff at the P.X. Fortunately, the post had a movie theater which one could get into for twenty-five cents. I can't recall if I ever bought popcorn or a soda, because by the end of the month I was scrounging around to dig up the twenty-five cents for admission, so I doubt if I made it to the concession stand.

When I replay this scene to my three house apes, otherwise known as my three sons, who suck up money as if it were peanuts, they roll their eyes and look at one another and laughingly respond, "Sure, and you walked five miles to school in the snow."

"Uphill both ways," another would laugh.

"Without shoes!"

The draft has been abolished now and authoritative discipline had all but disappeared in our public institutions. It's a rare occasion when a young man will voluntarily say, "Yes, sir," to his elders when spoken to. Or, "Thank you." Now days, it's, "The old fart doesn't know what he's talking about. He doesn't understand. Gimme some money for the concert! And while you're at it, throw in a few extra bucks for some suds, too!"

He might say please after the few bucks part.

And get a summer job? You've got to be crazy! Waste all that time that could be spent sleeping in, goin' to the beach, or playing ball and watchin' broads. "Man, this is my youth! I've got to enjoy myself."

"How about saving up for the future?"

"I'll worry about that when I get old. I've got more important things to do with my money. Hey Larz! How about goin' to the concert tonight. We can lie on the lawn and slam down a few brews. Maybe pick up a chick. Can I have a few bucks, pop?"

I don't think anything grates on a father more than a lazy kid. It probably stems from the fact that the majority of us had to scratch and claw our way to where we are now, be it from being educated, and then starting at the bottom of the corporate ladder and working our way up, or starting as an apprentice in some trade like plumbing or carpentry and paying or dues, literally as well as figuratively.

For the simple reason that kids seem to lack the discipline and respect for authority, I'm sorry that they abolished the draft. When I was in college, before being drafted, but sitting on the cusp and knowing it, one of the older students who had been in the service and saw action in the Korean War confided in me by saying that he thought everyone should spend at least two years in the armed forces. That it was good for them.

I damned near decked him, it made me so mad. Now, I know he was right. I know very few kids that wouldn't benefit from time under some five foot-two sergeant screaming orders for them to stand up, keep the line straight, speak only when spoken to and then answer only as requested. And heaven help them if their bed wasn't properly made.

We were forced to not only make our beds, but to make them so tight that if a quarter didn't bounce high enough, when we came home late that day from maneuvers we not only found our beds torn up, but our footlocker upside down as well.

Footlocker?

That was the small space where we neatly stored our *all* personal stuff, like shaving gear, socks and underwear.

Then there was the bay, the place where we slept. Every morning before we fell out for formation, it had to be buffed to a high luster and heaven help the whole platoon if the sergeant found any dust on *anything!* When was the last time your kids rooms looked like that? And then there was the weekly inspection. The floors had to be so clean and polished that you could see your face in it. We accomplished this by literally putting shoe polish on the floor and buffing it to such a sheen that it looked like a mirror. And our footlockers; every sock, pair of shorts and other clothing had to be folded perfectly or it was dumped upside-down on the floor. When is the last time your kids room even resembled being picked up, let alone having each item of clothing in its place, clean and folded. And the bed. Forget it. It's all a matter of discipline. I know kids that are lucky to even be awake by noon, let alone make their beds or …. I'm wasting my breath.

The physical training would do them a world of good too. I saw overweight kids who couldn't even reach the chin-up bar or run a hundred feet in any length of time, turn into svelte, trim young men who were proud of themselves.

Sure they hated it to begin with, but you ask any one of them now, if they had it to do over again, if they would, and to the man (notice I didn't say boy), they would give you a resounding yes. Even for an openly passive-aggressive guy like myself who thought that a two year stint in the Army was the last thing I wanted, I have to admit that it was good for me.

The other side of the coin, of course, is if there is an international conflict. The servicemen and women are in the business of protecting our country. Therein lays the rub. Neither I nor anyone reading these words would willingly send their sons or daughters into harms way, and one must weigh those factors. There are those human beings who volunteer to go into branches of the service such as the Marines, Special Forces, or get Ranger and/or air borne training, where they will undoubtedly be sent into active duty. In short, the probability of your average young man or woman entering the service who does not volunteer for these special fighting skill areas, will be relatively safe. Our current situation in the Near East being the exception.

My Job

Due to my unfortunate run in with the Army brass, i.e. my letter to my congressman, I was always the last one to get promoted. I figured for the five-hundred-and-eight days that I had left in this man's Army, I could stand on my head if I had to. Every day was one less day to go. When you're in the service, anyone can tell you the exact days they have left until they get out, be they a drafted two year man like myself or an enlisted three year man.

At the clinic we were assigned cases in the mornings. My job was to interview the patient, and then write up a summary of my findings and make a recommendation to the psychiatrist. Seventy-five percent of my cases were homosexuals who either wanted to get out of the Army or were gay people who had been discovered and were now caught up in the system. Either way, they were assigned to me first.

The psychiatrist, Dr. Unger, a captain, came to trust my analysis and disposition of each case to the degree that he thought I might be up for a little counseling myself, so he began assigning some of the easier cases to me – marriage counseling, mild depression, things like that. Now, I was really getting my teeth into it and loved it. Forget about playing in the band!

As I said, all our cases were in the morning, leaving most of the afternoons free. We had no patients, and either had classes or simply sat around shooting the bull. It didn't take long for our fertile minds to come up with a scheme to get off base. In the Army, everyone has to be accounted for twice a day, once in the morning and again in the early afternoon. In the afternoon, if we were scheduled to go to class learning about sexual transmitted disease, how to set a broken arm, what to do in case of a pregnancy in the field and birth is eminent, car wrecks, or any one of the hundred other topics that we were constantly being trained for, we and ninety percent of the hospital would cover for each other.

Each class held somewhere between thirty and forty people. The lecturer would call roll and someone would answer, "Here!" for every name called. Sometimes there would only be a dozen or so people in the room, but for the thirty names that were called, thirty times someone responded, "Here!" The person in charge of the lecture could care less. Once roll call had been completed, the film was started, half of those left would leave the room.

My favorite place to go was Lover's Point in Pacific Grove. It's a little stretch of sand where the ocean splashes over large house-sized boulders. For the most part, I usually had the beach to myself, although there was a small contingency of sun worshipers that seemed to filter in from time to time. I recall this one old guy who was a regular. His skin was like leather. Tanned leather, but leather nonetheless. And there wasn't millimeter on his body that didn't have deep crevices caused from lack of skin care and abusive sun exposure.

I would usually bring along a book and read, take a nap, walk on the beach, or climb on the boulders and simple watch the ebb and flow of the sea. It was a great life. What a waste of time, one might say, but as far as I was concerned, being in the Army for twenty-four months was a waste of my time. If I'm going to have to waste time I'd rather do it on a beautiful beach than sitting in some boring office, or listening to a lecture.

One day, while I was sunning myself at Lover's point, there was this couple with a small boy sitting on a blanket. I don't know if they were married or not, but if they were, they were acting like newlyweds. The kid, a boy of about four or five I would guess, apparently got bored and had made his way down to the water.

The water at Lover's point had a gradual drop to it, but the tide was going out and it seemed to be cleaning everything off the beach with it. I noticed that the little boy kept wading out deeper and deeper until he seemed to be bouncing along the bottom. It was then that I realized that the tide had taken him out beyond the point where his feet could no longer touch bottom. He wasn't screaming because every time he bobbed up, his mouth was filled with water. The panic look in his eyes was evident. He was drowning!

His mother glanced up at the boy and I thought that she realized that he might be in trouble, but she made no outward indication that he was doing anything but enjoying himself, so she went back to exploring her friend's tonsils.

There was only one thing to do, and that was to run out and save the kid. It wasn't until I had him in my arms and was wading back to shore that he finally started crying and the mother realized that something was wrong. I'm not sure if she ever realized that her kid was only a moment away from eternity. She snatched the kid out of my arms and gave me such a look that said, 'don't you dare touch me boy'.

*****

The bay in the hospital where I slept held twenty beds, all of which were filled with hospital personnel. It wasn't always the same group of guys, either. You never knew who was going to be sleeping next to you. The cots had been arranged so that we slept head to foot with about three feet between beds. I remember this one guy who moved into our bay, in the bunk next to mine, who snored like a wounded elephant. Being a psychology student, I had learned a thing or two about stimulus-response, i.e. Pavlov's dog. For those of you who are unfamiliar with the experiment, Pavlov used to feed this dog and then simultaneously ring a bell. Of course when the dog knew that he was going to be fed, he would salivate. Pavlov proved that he could condition the dog to salivate by simply ringing the bell and not feed the dog. Stimulus – response.

Well, this one night this guy was snoring so loud that a bomb could have gone off and he wouldn't heave heard it. He was keeping me awake and I decided if I was going to get any sleep, something had to be done. I reared back and smashed him with my pillow as hard as I could, retracting it and then pretending to be asleep while he jerked upright in his bed, and looked around, dazed and confused, wondering what had happened.

Five minutes later he was back asleep again, snoring just as loudly. Again, I reared back and let him have it with my pillow. Again he sat upright, dazed, looking around, wondering what was happening to him. This went on a couple more times until, asleep, he began snoring and suddenly woke himself up. He never snored after that night. Stimulus-response!

Every barracks seems to have a bully and ours was no exception. There was this black kid who took up residency across the bay from me. That in itself was no revelation. But apparently he was gay and everyone seemed to know it. Personally, I could care less, so long as he keeps his hands to himself, but this bully guy found great sport in taunting the poor guy – at all times of the day and night.

This one night in particular, the bully came in to the sleeping bay well oiled after a night on the town, and was hell bent on taunting the gay guy into a fight. The kid was not only much smaller than the bully, but was younger and was clearly no match for him. It was about two a.m. and I and everyone else in the bay were trying to sleep. We were sick and tired of listening to the bully rant and rave, but no one was willing to do anything about it. Suddenly, I found myself standing in the middle of the bay with nothing on but my shorts, shouting, "If it's a fight you want, you got it! Come and get it!"

By the time the words fell out of my mouth, I realized where I was and what I was doing. I quietly asked myself, *What the hell am I doing here?* Something inside of me had apparently snapped and my unconscious had simply taken over. *Well, here I am, may as well make the best of it.*

Fortunately, the bully didn't have a clue what was behind the challenge and had no interest in finding out. The next day after work, I discovered that I had gained a new found fame and everyone was slapping me on the back. The bully had moved out and on. Where to, no one had a clue and no one cared.

When you're in the service your pals are pretty much limited to those guys that you live with on base. I became pals with the Chaplin's assistant, a short, portly fellow that looked much like a penguin when the walked. To top it off when he smoked, which was often, he had this little ivory cigarette holder that he used to hold his cigarette. He looked a lot like a portly gay Mr. Peanut.

We'd go out together to a movie or drinks in Monterey. Periodically, I would notice that people would stare at us and giggle. I wasn't sure if it was due to the Mutt and Jeff combination, the way my buddy walked and looked smoking his cigarette holder, or if they thought that we were a gay couple out on the town. Either way, we got a lot of stares.

I had originally met him one day when he had come to our clinic, depressed. I had seen him around the hospital, usually by himself, but had never spoken to him. As it turned out, he was married and had a child. His marriage had been a joke. He said that they had had sex once, and on that occasion his wife had thrown up after the act. Coincidentally, she had also conceived that night, thus their first and only child was born. Then he got drafted into the Army.

I wrote up my impressions from the interview and handed it over to the psychiatrist who told me in confidence that he was the victim of a deep seeded complex that probably started when he was a child, and that there wasn't sufficient time for him to under go the extensive therapy that he'll need while he was in the Army to get the bottom of his problem. In short, the psychiatrist told him to suck it up and stick it out.

I'm sure that was a great help.

I'm not sure how our friendship started, probably due to the fact that we were both stationed in the same hospital, him at the chapel and me in the wards. I felt sorry for this poor soul that seemed to be so unhappy. We talked about his marriage and I found out that his wife was suing him for divorce, requesting sole custody of his child. He talked about his childhood and how unhappy he had been. He felt that he was an unwanted and unloved child.

During the course of our conversation he learned that I was fascinated with hypnosis and asked if I would consider hypnotizing him. I had actually only hypnotized one person, a girl, Carol, at the University of Oregon, and agreed to give it a try. We agreed to tape everything, so when the session was over, he could listen to what he had said with the thought in mind that it might be therapeutic.

Being a chaplain's assistant, we had access to the one place where no one would disturb us – the chapel. He was an easy subject to work with. Within moments he was under. I immediately regressed him back to his childhood where he talked about his feelings of being an unwanted child, citing several occasions of child abuse. The third session I did something I had always wanted to do. I took him back into another life.

The most interesting part was when I regressed him back into the womb. I counted backwards and as I counted, I instructed him to go deeper into his memory until we finally reached a point when I asked him where he was and he didn't respond. It then occurred to me that maybe he was too young to talk, so I said that even though he might be too young to talk, that he could convey his feelings to me. He said that he didn't know where he was, but that it was very warm and comfortable and dark and cozy.

I immediately thought that I had him in the womb. I asked him to take his hand and run it over his chest. He did. When he got to the middle of his chest he hesitated as if he had bumped into something.

"What is it?" I asked.

"I don't know. It feels rubbery."

"Take your hand and follow it," I suggested.

He wrapped his hand around the imaginary cord and ran it down to his bellybutton and stopped.

"Now go the other way."

He followed the imaginary cord over his shoulder.

I was ecstatic!

"Now, let's go back in time a little further," I suggested, wanting to see how small he might be before all memory was lost. "Where are you now?"

His brow furrowed. "I'm on this table. There are people looking over me. No, that's not me. Yes it is!"

While he continued having this conversation with himself, a cold shiver ran down my back. I figured that I had regressed him into another life and I had caught him in that moment of time when he was dying on the operating table of some hospital. I was on unfamiliar ground, so I quickly instructed him to keep going back in time. I counted backwards and took him even further back in time. It turns out that he was a farmer living somewhere in Sweden. He had a family and loved fishing. He gave me his name, the name of the town where he lived, when he was born and the name of all of his family members. It was fascinating!

When I brought him out we rewound the tape. He listened intently, speechless. He wanted to do it again, but the next time we tried, the Chaplin caught us. I don't know what he thought we were up to, but he told us to get out and never comeback. That was the end of that.

We had fallen into a routine of eating lunch together in the cafeteria and then eventually exploring Monterey at night. We'd go to dances, but the women knew right away that we were dog shit as they considered anyone that was in the service. We'd lie and say that we were graduate students at the Monterey Language School, studying Russian or something, but they knew better. Our haircuts gave us away, if not our clothes.

Then one night I decided to strike out alone. I had this '54 black Mercury two-door coupe that I loved. Best damned car that I ever owned. On weekends I'd wash and wax it until I could see my face in it, but fifteen minutes after it was done, a fine cover of sand and dust would cover the car again. That was the desert for you.

Anyway, this particular night destiny took over and I found myself at a place called the *Mission Ranch Inn* in Carmel. It's out of the way, and how I ended up there, I have no idea. As I said, I never go out alone. I just would rather be with someone. This night was an exception. Destiny would have its hand in the mix and would be stirring the pot.

The Inn had a dining area and a bar just off the dining room. I strolled over to the bar and listened to some blind guy play the piano that I later learned that his name was Jonathon Lee. To this day I have every one of his CD's. If you like a good piano easy listening, check it out. Anyway, as I stood there alone, taking in the sounds, a short dark haired Spanish looking girl strolled into the room and our eyes met. We started a conversation and it turned out that she was from San Jose with three of her girl friends, and had just decided to wander off on her own, something that she never did, she explained.

I didn't know it at the time, but destiny was spinning its web and we were both caught up in it, whether we knew it or not. After twenty minutes one of her girl friends came looking for her and she said that she had to go. I asked if I could call her sometime and she rattled off a seven digit telephone number, and she was gone.

At this point its note worthy to mention that I have a memory like a sieve. Places, events and faces I can remember, but dates and numbers -- forget it! I even have my license plate as my last name, just in case I forget who I am. I frantically looked around for a pencil, but found none. To this day I don't know how I remembered the number, but, as I said, destiny was in charge.

I eventually called her and we set a date to go out. I somehow found her house in San Jose, again, I have no clue how I got there, but it was as if destiny's hand was leading me. I remember the first time I walked into her house. It was a small, single story house on McCreery Street, a Mexican neighborhood. She introduced me to her family, an older sister and two brothers, none of whom seemed particularly pleased to see me. She had me wait on a couch covered with heavy plastic wrapping while the family retreated into the kitchen. I kept hearing this loud, insane sounding voice coming from the kitchen and wondered if they had a mentally retarded person chained to the floor. I later learned that they had a talking parrot.

Thus began a courtship that would end in marriage.

I was into my twenty-first month of Army service with three more months to go when I applied for an early out to go back to college to get my Master's degree. I think the Army wanted to get rid of me anyway, so they consented letting me out early to attend the first semester at San Jose State College where I had applied to and had been accepted to continue my education.

The month that I was scheduled to get out, President Kennedy initiated the blockade against all shipping to Cuba and thus began the Bay of Pigs. All military leaves were cancelled. "I guess you're not getting out after all," my friend chuckled.

I was too upset to be amused. I had been accepted to San Jose State College and had zero interest in staying in the Army. As far as I was concerned, it had been a two year vacation that I didn't ask for. In those two years I could have finished my Master's degree and started on my Doctorial degree. For all intents and purposes, as far as I was concerned, I had wasted two years of my life.

As it turned out the Army thought they could do without one more body and let my exit be complete. On my scheduled date of retirement from the Army I was released from the service at Fort Ord. I drove to San Jose one last time before driving home. I had a few weeks before school started and it had been over a year since I had been home.

The Orphan

After being discharged from Fort Ord, I drove to and stayed in San Jose until two a.m., seeing Estella, the girl that I had met in Carmel at the Mission. I dropped her off home and started out for Oregon. I stopped at an all night pizza joint and bought a large pizza to eat along the way. I figured I had about fifteen hours of driving time ahead of me.

At sunrise I was traveling through southern Oregon when the rays from the morning sun caused a mirage to form in the desert. I had never seen a mirage before and thought this would make a great picture, with the mirage in the foreground and the mountain range in the background. I pulled over and aimed my camera at the scene, but the angle I was standing at didn't allow me to get everything in, so I ran out into the desert until I had the angle that I needed.

In my exuberance I failed to pay attention where I was running until I felt something soft and rubbery beneath my feet. I momentarily stopped to look back and there, sunning himself in the morning sun was the largest rattle snake that had ever seen. He was six feet long if he was an inch. I think he had been just as startled as I had been when I had stepped on him. He looked at me and I looked at him. Then he started crawling towards me.

Did I run?

No.

I looked for a rock and thought; *His rattlers would make a good souvenir!* I found a rock and chucked it rock at him which he artfully dodged as if he had had a lot of practice, and then quickened his pace. I had tried to kill him, now it was his turn.

I ran as fast as I could, thinking, *Where there is one, there are many!* I wondered at the rate that my heart must be beating, how long it would take for the rattler's venom to reach my heart and kill me. Fortunately, I didn't have to find out.

By mid-morning I was in central Oregon, driving through a large stand of redwoods. The sun cause the trees to cast long shadows across the highway when suddenly, without warning, a deer bound out of the trees and in front of my car. I swerved to miss him and in that instant, the thought flashed through my mind, *Where there is one, there are two!*

At that instant I hit another full grown deer with my right fender, throwing him twenty feet in the air, and causing an instant gush of steam to rise out of my now upright, smashed hood. I pulled over and surveyed the damage.

Aside from the bent hood, the front fender was bent into the tire well and had blood smeared all over it. I looked around, but there was no sign of the deer. I surmised that he must have limped off into the forest where I thought that he had been mortally wounded and would probably die. The fender had been bent so that the left front tire couldn't turn and water had formed a puddle on the ground caused by a puncture in the radiator. I looked around. There was no one in sight and I knew there was no town behind me for miles, so my only option was to go forward. I managed to pull the front fender out from the tire far enough to let the tire turn, and then got into the car and slowly started my way north.

Twenty minutes later I entered a small town. There was a vacant lot next to only gas station in town. I pulled into it, my motor steaming like a busted steam engine. I quickly rubbed dirt over the blooded fender. The last thing I needed was someone thinking that I had hit and run over some human and get arrested while they looked for a body.

There was an old guy working on a car in the garage.

"Excuse me. I've had some car trouble and my car is outside on that vacant lot. Would it be okay to leave it there for a while until I can arrange a tow to take it home?"

He didn't even look up from under the hood of the old Pontiac he was working on. "No problem," he said.

"Thanks."

I locked the car. My duffel bag with all my Army clothing was in the trunk, not that I cared if anyone stole them or not, although the steel toed shoes and the fatigue jacket were two items that I would like to have kept. I went out to the highway and held out my thumb. Eight hours later a guy in an old pickup dropped me off on Main Street in Hermiston. It was an easy twenty minute walk home.

I never called the folks to tell them that I was coming home and never told them that I had wrecked the car. I just showed up. That was the way I lived, from minute to minute, letting fate deal with me as it may and going with the flow.

"Hi, Mom!" I said walking in the back door. The front door was always locked and no one ever used it. Even when company came, everyone used the back door. I'm not even sure the front door was real.

She looked at me as if I had just come home from school, and gave me a hug. "Hungry?"

"Starved!"

After I had eaten, I relayed the events of the day, omitting the rattle snake adventure. No use letting them know how dumb I was.

"Can I borrow the orphan?" I asked.

The orphan as it was affectionately called, was the Nash Rambler that my dad had bought one day on a whim. Since its arrival home, everything imaginable has gone wrong with it, thus the term, the orphan.

"You'll need a tow bar," Dad interjected.

"I can rent one from Handy Hank." As you might imagine from the name, Handy Hank is a place where you can find anything that's handy, like a tow bar. Dad tossed the keys of the orphan to me and I turned to Larry, my younger brother. "Want to take a drive?" I asked.

You didn't have to ask Larry twice, even if he was eighteen. It might sound odd, but Larry and I were and have been best buds ever since I can remember. When we were in Irrigon and I was fourteen, I used to go rabbit hunting. I started taking Larry hunting with me, even though he was only seven. I can remember the first time that he shot and killed a rabbit. You would have thought that he had killed his best friend.

Tears welled up in his eyes and I could tell that he felt remorse, even shame of taking the life of a poor innocent creature. It made me feel guilty too, but I got over it, and so did he. Then came pheasant season. I had a twelve gauge shotgun and I managed to borrow one for him as well. Mine had a magazine that held six shells and his was a double barreled shotgun that held two shells in the chamber and that was it.

Whenever we went hunting, we'd always come home with something other than what we went hunting for, except during pheasant season when I don't think we ever got skunked. We never bought a hunting license, but then we never saw a game warden either, except this one time when we were out in the desert goose hunting – Canadian Geese. We were walking through the desert when we spotted the game warden's green truck bearing down on us. We quickly hid our shotguns under a sagebrush and ran like ducks -- low and fast.

When the game warden finally caught up with us, he asked what we were doing out in the desert. "Nothin'. Just walkin'", I said.

He knew better, but didn't see us carrying any guns, so he let us go. Later on that day when dad came home from work, we sent him out into the desert to retrieve our shot guns. How he found them I'll never know.

There was this one time when we went goose hunting in the middle of the winter. It had snowed the night before and the ground was covered with three or four inches of fresh fallen snow. It was before sun up and Larry and I got dressed, and put our shotguns into the car. I grabbed two sheets from the hall closet before mom could stop me and then we drove in the crisp early morning air. I knew where this field was that the geese liked to land for the night. I parked about a mile away and we hiked the rest of the way in under the cover of night.

As we walked, we could hear ducks flying over head, no more than a few feet above our heads. We could have shot blindly in the air and brought down our limit, our limit being as many as we wanted or could carry. We didn't care for the taste of duck though, and besides, we had goose on the brain.

Dawn was breaking in the east, turning the sky bright hues of orange and purple. The geese lay just ahead. We could hear thousands of them, sitting on the snow. One thing you have to understand about Canadian geese. They're smart. While the flock rests or eats, they post sentries around the perimeter, not unlike a general might do in the field of battle. These sentries don't eat, or sit down. Their job is to be a look-out and that's what they do. Their little heads and beady eyes are on the constant lookout for anything unusual; a movement or an unusual sound.

The geese are in a sort of bowl like field with a fence surrounding them. I tell Larry to sneak around the perimeter of the fence while I do the same in the opposite direction. We know that which ever one of us the sentries spot first, they will alert the flock and they'll automatically fly in the opposite direction.

Our guns are loaded and I've given Larry instructions about having the safety on until they fly overhead. He has extra shells in his pocket in the event they fly over him and he gets both barrels off. I estimate that there must be at least a thousand geese here and we're going to bag more game than we've ever bagged before.

We crawl on our bellies on the snow for fifteen or twenty minutes, each of us under a sheet. I can tell by the sound that the flock is getting restless. They must have spotted Larry, because suddenly the sky is filled with geese flying straight overhead. They're so low that I could have jumped up and grabbed them by their feet. Instead I raise my gun and pull the trigger.

Nothing!

The gun has jammed.

I eject a shell and pull the trigger again.

Nothing again!

By the time I ejected all the shells and reloaded, the last of the geese were airborne and were flying a hundred feet over my head. I empty the gun at them, but no one fall to the ground. We had missed our chance.

Larry ran over to me demanding to know what went wrong and I feebly explain that the gun had jammed. To this day, neither of us has forgotten the experience.

While I was still in high school and the folks were working, I thought I would teach Larry how to drive. He was ten at the time, but tall for his age. I wasn't planning on taking him out in traffic or on the freeway you understand, just up and down our street which was unpaved by the way.

I had this '49 Chevy convertible and it had an automatic shift, so it was easy to drive. With Larry at the wheel, we had just driven up the street and had successfully made a U-turn and were heading back to our house which was located on the corner of one of the main streets going out of town.

"Just pull in next to the house," I instructed.

At this point it is advisable to point out that we had a three foot tall white picket fence surrounding the yard. That is until Larry got a little too close and flattened a twenty foot section of it, shearing off the four-by-four posts that had been sunk into the ground to hold it up.

We looked at one another and both visualized dad's face who we knew wouldn't be to pleased having his fence leveled by a ten year old.

Frantically, we tried to prop it back up, but gravity being what it is, wasn't going to allow that to happen. We frantically searched around for some stakes to pound into the ground so we could at least temporarily prop the fence up until we figure something else out. Once we had propped it up as best we could we stood back and surveyed our handy work. Aside from the missing paint, and if you didn't stare at it too long, and my car was parked next to the fence, it might pass inspection until the next strong wind, at which point we'd blame nature for knocking it down.

We found some white paint in the garage and quickly repainted the whole fence. We had just finished when dad drove in from work. Larry stood on one side of the fence (that portion that still had a noticeable list to it), and I on the other, as if we were neighbors chatting across the fence.

"What are you kids up to?" he demanded, knowing that we never stood around on opposite sides of the fence, chatting.

"Oh, nothin'. Just waitin' for you to come home. Want to shoot some baskets?"

We got by with the deception until the week-end. Dad was outside messin' with the septic tank when he noticed that the fence had a perceptual northern list that he hadn't noticed before.

"What's this?" he demanded, shaking the fence.

"Well, I'll be darned. The fence post must be rotten," I observed, putting my foot on the stake that we had driven into the ground to keep it from falling down.

He wasn't buying into that for a single moment.

"Okay, who did this?"

"I didn't want to say anything, but Bobbie Holden drove over the other day and I think the sun musta been in his eyes, 'cause I think he mighta scraped the fence. I didn't want to get him in trouble, so we sort of tried to fix it."

I could see that he wasn't buying that either, but at least it took the heat off of Larry and myself, for the moment anyway.

Now you have a slight flavor of my relationship with my younger brother, Larry. In many respects, even though seven years separate us, we were thick as thieves. Still are.

Anyway, back to the orphan. Dad consented Larry and myself to drive back to central Oregon to retrieve my '54 Mercury. I rented the tow bar from Handy Hank, filled the orphan with gas and we were off.

It was mid-day when we finally arrived at the little spot in the road where the town existed. My car was miraculously still resting where I had left it. The only difference was that it was covered with dust. Still concerned about the blood on the front fender, I looked around for evidence that the sheriff had been around. I think the fact that the car was covered with dust helped save the day. I wiped the dust off the windshield, backed the orphan in front of the Mercury and hooked it up to the tow bar.

Larry offered to ride in the Mercury, to steer it, but I said that that was unnecessary. I knew a shortcut home through back roads that would save us some time. Problem was, it was unpaved gravel for fifty miles. There was no one on the road except us, and it never occurred to me that we might have another breakdown.

It happened two hours from the time we hooked up at the gas station. We were traveling around forty miles per hour when the Mercury began swaying back and forth, spitting up gravel, sending stray rocks everywhere. I figured that something must have gone wrong with the tow bar. I knew that breaking hard would further throw the towed car into a tailspin, so I gently pumped the breaks.

The car continued swaying and then suddenly lurched violently to the right and then again to the left. There was a three foot bank off to the left and the Mercury hit it straight on after snapping the tow bar. I watched in horror as the big black machine rolled along the desert, coming safely to a stop thirty feet from where it had left the road. Thank God it had gone straight over and not sideways, otherwise it certainly would have rolled.

"Now, what do we do?" Larry asked.

"I guess first thing is to assess the damage, then figure a way to get the Merc back on the road.

Aside from the left front fender being bent a little more than it had been when the deer had hit it, the car seemed okay. Fortunately, I had brought along five gallons of water. I poured it into the radiator and then started the car. Thank God it still ran. Larry drove the orphan along the road and I drove the Mercury until we came to a spot where I figured I could climb back up on the road again.

Upon examination the tow hitch had been bent beyond recognition, resembling a corkscrew more than a tow hitch. I had some rope in the trunk of the Mercury so we hitched it as close to the orphan's bumper as possible and started out back home again, hoping that we didn't run into any highway patrol, because the way that we were towing the Mercury was illegal.

We made it home after dark without further mishap or getting a ticket.

Back to School

I started back to school at San Jose State College the summer of '63. The college offered dormitory living in the summer which I took advantage of. It was the cheapest housing around. At the same time the Peace Corps candidates were living in one of the wings. Every day they practiced pole dancing in the lobby. Pole dancing is where they have any number of poles that are held parallel to the floor and clank together while students dance between them, trying not to get their ankles broken.

I only took twelve units that summer, trying to get back in the swing of things, learning how to study all over again. Fortunately, most of the classes were filled with teachers fulfilling their continuing educational requirements. Teachers, I found, ranked in the lowest competitive group of individuals that I have ever met, and they always seem to come out of the woodwork for night and summer classes.

Whereas before, in my undergraduate schooling, I had found it difficult to study and retain information, now, as a graduate student, two years later, everything seemed to make sense and fall into place. In other words, I got straight 'A's. I knew that the proof would be in the pudding when the regular school year started, however.

During those hours when I wasn't in school, I had been able to land a job working with a small construction company, framing triplexes. I found that I thoroughly enjoyed working with my hands, swinging a hammer. To see a wall, then a room and then an entire floor go up before your very eyes was gratifying. I soon learned how to read plans and how to layout a unit from the foundation to the sub-floors to windows and doors, walls and ceiling joists. I began to like the work so much that I really looked forward every day when school was out to start building again.

The summer passed quickly. When the dormitories filled up with undergraduate students, I was forced to find alternative housing. I located an old house that had a room to rent on Twelfth Street for thirty-five dollars a month. There was a common refrigerator and one set of cupboards that were used by the other four guys who lived in the house. Unfortunately, everyone used everyone else's milk and cereal. It was a rare occasion when anyone would actually cook their own meals. I guess they either ate fast-food, or ate cold food in their rooms. I pretty much subsisted on cereal and hand held food – tacos, hamburgers and Togo sandwiches.

By the time the second year came around, I had earned enough money to move up to the second floor and have a larger room that rented for forty dollars a month. School still came easy for me and with the exception of statistics class, I pulled straight 'A's. That is until I ran into Dr. 'T' as she shall become known. The class was Child Development. The students consisted of four teachers; three females and one male, and two male graduate students of which I was one, and of course, Dr. T.

I really loved this class. It consisted of a pre-therapy session whereas the instructor would bring us all together for an hour where we were assigned two or three children each. It was our job to find out what they problem was, and to try to give them therapy in a play room for one hour a week. After that hour, we would then adjourn again to the class and would discuss what had transpired during our hour therapy session, after which we would reduce our findings to notes which were then handed in for further analysis by the instructor. It was our first hands-on therapy since entering graduate school.

This particular day I entered my therapy room. It was roughly a ten–by–twelve foot room with a cabinet containing a sink that occupied the back wall. All the walls were bare with the exception of a mirrored wall which was a one-way mirror to the hallway. We had no way of knowing when the instructor was looking in on us, but there were times when I seemed to feel her eyes burning into my flesh.

This particular day the two children assigned to me, a boy and a girl, aged nine and ten, were already in the room when I entered. Each child was mildly occupied and ignored me as I closed the door.

Kevin was the nine year old. He was of average height and weight with sandy brown hair. He was one of three children in the family. By all outward appearances he appeared to be a completely normal kid. You could tell by his eyes that he is bright. If one were to summarize his problem in a single word, it might be that he was too bright. He was so bright that he analyzed everything everyone said, and took everything that they said literally. If someone told him that he had dog breath, he took it to mean that that person was saying that he not only smelled like a dog, but acted and looked like a dog – the ugliest dog that he could imagine.

I had previously met his parents, before the class semester began, and determined that they were equally intelligent, as far as I could tell. They were well-adjusted and successful. They had brought Kevin to our Child Development class after four psychologists had either given up on him, or couldn't handle his bazaar behavior. "You are our last resort," they had told Dr. T. "Please help us."

Arlene was ten years old. She had dark brown eyes that just seemed to plead for understanding and compassion. The only thing was, she couldn't or wouldn't communicate with anyone directly. In our therapy session, when she wanted to talk, it either had to be on the red plastic telephone that sat on the small table in the corner of the room, or in complete privacy under the sink. Her parents told us that she had become totally unresponsive at public facilities such as school, be it public or private.

"Well, good morning," I said as I enter the room and shut the door.

By their glances they both acknowledge that the door had been shut, but said nothing. Testing the fact that they are locked in is one of the first acts they perform upon entering the facility, each time. One by one, each child went the door to test the knob, only to discover that it had in fact been locked.

I spoke to Arlene first. "And how is my favorite girl this morning?"

She turned her back on me and blushed.

I looked toward the small plastic pink telephone sitting on the table. "I think maybe someone is on the telephone," I said, picking up the telephone. "Hello?" Pause. "Arlene? Why, yes, she's right here. Hold on. It's for you," I tell her, handing her the telephone.

Her eyes sparkled as she tried to suppress a grin. She took the phone and said, "Hello?" in a small voice, barely audible. "Who is this?"

At this point, I picked up the other pink plastic telephone and we began talking. "This is Dr. Howard. I had a few spare moments and just thought I would give you a call."

"That's nice."

"How is your day so far?"

"Fine."

At this point Kevin had had about enough of this idle chit-chat and wanted some attention himself. He walked over to me and tugged at my shirt. "I have a new knife," he announced.

At this point I simply patted him on the head and said "That's nice. Perhaps when I get through talking to Arlene you can tell me about it."

Kevin was not about to be put off. He dug his hands into his pockets and pulled out a large Boy Scout knife.

At this point he has my full attention. "I'll have to call you back," I told Arlene over the phone and hung up.

"Do you mind if I have a look at it?" I inquired, holding out my hand to Kevin who now had my full attention.

Kevin knew he wasn't supposed to bring knives to therapy, but he was one that was always testing the water and pushing fences as far as he could. He opened one of the blades, and held it just out of my reach, showing me.

I fell to one knee, keeping my eye on the knife, for now it wasn't just a knife, it was a weapon. I glanced towards the two way mirror, hoping that Dr. T. wasn't watching.

She was.

The door flew open and Dr. T. rushed in with all the tenacity of a Green Bay Packer lineman with the opposing quarterback directly in his path. All but leaving her feet, she gave little nine year old Kevin a full body tackle, knocking him to the floor.

Still holding onto the knife, Kevin emitted a blood curdling yell that permeated the entire building. Within moments the room was filled with counselors -- first and second year graduate students, all standing with their mouths wide open, looking at two hundred thirty pound Dr. T. wrestling with sixty pound Kevin, who by now was as near to the brink of psychosis as anyone has ever been in such a short period of time.

"Don't just stand there, help me!" Dr. T barked orders, as she laid flat over Kevin, concealing all but the ends of his flaying his arms and legs.

Bill, who was somewhere in the sixty year old plus range, clearly the oldest member of the group, reluctantly grabbed a hold of Kevin's legs from underneath the body of Dr. T. while two of the other graduate students finally grabbed an arm of nine year old Kevin, psychic serial killer. The knife had long since been twisted out of his hands by a skillful Dr. T.

In the meantime, Arlene had been reduced to a shriveling twig and had retreated under the sink and had pulled the door shut behind her. Small whimpering sounds could be heard through the ventilation holes in the cabinet.

Dr. T. finally stood up, holding the knife defiantly in the air like a trophy while she regarded me, about to be ex-graduate student, with all the compassion of Hitler before a mob of dissidents about to be hanged. Not one to be intimidated, I diverted my eyes to Kevin, who by now had been reduced to a pile of sobbing flesh. One by one his captors released their grip on the boy who then crawled towards the nearest corner for safety.

To Kevin, I was the only remaining member of the adult group with a shred of credibility, if in fact I had any at all. I slowly walked over to the boy, knelt down and cradled him in my arms. By this time all the women in the room had moist eyes, and old Bill simply stood by with his head hanging in shame.

"Conference room!" Dr. T. barked. Everyone except me quickly vacated the room, hoping to avert the wrath they know was forthcoming. "You too, Mr. Losness," she said with an icy tone.

The room was now vacant of everyone except for myself who was still holding onto Kevin, and Arlene who was still sobbing behind the closed door under the sink. It was several moments before I finally released Kevin and went over to retrieve Arlene.

Inside the conference room everyone had taken their customary places around the rectangular table, awaiting the entrance of the condemned one -- me. When I finally entered the room, all eyes fall on me. Some with sympathy, some with wonderment of how such a thing could have happened, and one set of eyes boring down on me like a laser gun – Dr. T's.

Before I could take my seat, Dr. T. started in. "Under no circumstances is any patient allowed to bring a weapon into this facility, especially a knife," she spat, tossing the Boy Scout knife, turned machete, on to the table. "Is that clear?" She looked around the table as everyone studied their hands, or the grooving on the table and answered with an inaudible affirmation.

Everyone except me. I'm glaring intently at Dr. T. I had seen enough of her kind in the Army and knew exactly what cloth they had been cut from. She could intimidate them, but not me. I was ready to walk out right then and there, degree or not!

"The children will be confined to their rooms until their parents return to pick them up," she advised everyone who was concerned about their kids. "I think what you have just seen clearly demonstrates the need for complete control when a situation gets out of hand. This could have been an ugly incident that was nipped in the bud." She looked around the room at the faces that dared not challenge her decision. "Discussion?"

Susan MacAfee, kiss-ass second year blonde graduate student-teacher, spoke first. "I commend you, Dr. T. for taking control of the situation and handling it so efficiently."

Dr. T. nodded in the affirmative and held her hand outstretched as she did when she wanted further elaboration. I decided not to give her that opportunity.

"I had everything under control," I said with an icy tone. "I think the situation was handled intolerably." I knew that I had just cut my own throat, but I didn't care.

Dr. T's eyes snapped over to where I sat at the table and then focused on me as if I were an ice cube and she was a laser beam about to reduce my existence to a small puddle of water. "You did nothing to alleviate the situation," she snapped. "The immediate solution to the problem was to disarm the child so he couldn't harm anyone."

"A, he wasn't going to harm anyone and B, if you would have given me two minutes he would have voluntarily given me the knife and none of this would have happened. As it is …."

"A, you have no knowledge that he wasn't going to cut himself, the other child in the room or even you," she retorted with fire in her eyes, "and B, I did the only thing that could have been done, and that was to take charge when clearly you …."

"No one was in danger!" I interrupted, my knuckles turning white as I clinched my fist, an act that was not lost on Dr. T., nor the other members of the group for that matter. "All you did was scare the living shit out of the kid and probably set him back five years worth of therapy."

Dr. T's eyes widened, then narrowed as she was about to shoot off another laser beam. She was ready to pounce on me like a wounded boar when confronted by a hunter, but then probably thought better of it, considering her position as head of the Clinical Psychology Department. "Let's see what the rest of the group has to say," she said, through clinched teeth. She looked to the other members of the class. Her eyes settled on Bill, the only other male in the room. "Bill?"

Bill fiddled with his pencil for a moment, looking at neither Dr. T. nor me. Clearly he didn't appreciate being put in the position of having to take sides. He obviously wasn't going to go against the one person that controlled his grade, and didn't want to alienate the only other male in his class either. He diplomatically chose the middle ground. "I guess I can see Howard's point of view," he said is a small voice, not fitting a man of his size. "I probably would have tried to reason with the boy before getting physical with him. On the other hand, I understand the potential danger that he …."

"There was no potential!" Dr. T. asserted vehemently. "The boy had a weapon!"

From that moment on the rest of the period went from bad to worse. At the end the subject was changed to the other children, but everyone in the room knew that I had just cut my own throat. At the very least, I could kiss any decent grade that I may have gotten, goodbye.

When the class was over, everyone made haste, getting out of the room, exercising every effort not to talk to me, should Dr. T. assume someone might be consolatory towards my plight. They breathed a sigh of relief that it was me and not they who had found his feet firmly implanted in quicksand.

As it turned out, I was the only one in the class to receive a 'B'. Everyone else got an 'A'.

The year finished and so was I. I concentrated on my master's project. I had created a psychological test called the *Object Relation Technique*, ORT. In short, it consisted of several shadowy pictures depicted in various poses that I had drawn that could be interpreted as happy, sad or dramatically tragic, depending upon the subjects personal point of view. I then added colored transparent overlay covers to each picture and then asked each subject what they thought the picture was conveying. The idea being to ascertain the effect that color had on the same picture. The test was somewhat similar to the TAT, the *Thermatic Apperception Test*, wherein the subject is shown a picture and then asked to make up a story of the picture. For example there is one picture of a woman lying half naked on a bed with her arm dangling over the bed. A man is standing over her. Some subjects tell a story of sex and violence, others of illness and others yet of death. The variation of stories are endless, but in the end they all reveal a portion of the subject's personality.

Speaking of tests, one of the classes I took was Psychological Testing. We studied and learned how to give the *TAT*, the *Stanford Benet, the Rorschach, the Gestalt*, and all the others. Towards the end of the semester we were asked to pick a subject and give them a battery of tests, and then write up our analysis of that person, put it all in a report and hand it in.

I chose my mate-to-be.

I already knew her background, the fact that as a child she had been deserted by her father, and then she and her brothers and sister and mother had migrated here from Mexico to this country as a young girl. When she grew up she had worked very hard to put herself through beauty school, thus becoming a beautician.

I had met her father, who her older brother had gone to Mexico and brought back to San Jose in the hopes that their mother and he could have reconciliation, but that was not to be. Without going into the details of her background, I gave her all the tests and subsequently wrote a sixty page report on her. When I got through, I knew more about her than she did.

After handing in our reports, the instructor called me in after one of our classes. "I've read your report," he said. "I trust that this isn't anyone who you are considering marrying." He eyed me conspicuously.

I didn't dare tell him that we were engaged to be married. "No, It's just someone that I know," I replied.

"Good, because this person has some serious issues. Take, for example her response on the Rorschach." He handed me my paper. ""Here," he pointed out. "She says that this is a squashed frog!" He shook his head.

The conclusion that I had written in the paper was equally as bad, but aside from that, I felt that, as a psychologist to be, I could overcome any adverse factors that I had uncovered in her personality. I was to later learn how wrong I was.

The World of Real Estate

I was nearing the conclusion of my degree when I met Bill Henderson of *K and H Construction Company.* He had built and owned, among other things, a motel and restaurant called the *Lamp Lighter Inn* in Sunnyvale. He also built and owned a street full of four-plexes.

In talking to him I came to learn that his motel and restaurant was doing great, but the street full of small apartment buildings that he owned were all fifty-percent vacant. I felt a challenge and asked if he minded if I looked into the matter.

"Help yourself," he said, and gave me the addresses.

The four-plexes all consisted of an owner's three-bedroom unit and three one-bedroom units. They were about ten years old, in good condition and in an excellent area. Each building had a laundry room, a lawn and covered parking. Each unit also had two vacancies. There was one on-site manger that ran all the complexes along with his full time job. To my untrained eye, the solution seemed simple.

"I think I can fill up your buildings, at the very least, cut your vacancies in half the first month," I asserted.

"That would be a savings of several thousand dollars," he said. You've got the job!"

"There is just one thing."

"Yes?"

"Your manger. How well do you know him?"

"He's been a friend for ten years. Why?"

"I'm going to have to fire him."

He studied me for a moment. "You're in charge. Do whatever it takes."

"Do I do it or should you tell him."

He wasn't going to let me off the hook that easily. "It's your baby. If you want to fire him, *you* fire him."

"You wouldn't have a spare office I could use, do you?" His office was in a building that had been designed just like one of his apartments with the reception area on the first floor along with several offices. His office, a conference room and an additional office that he had set aside for his son was upstairs. I could see that only one office was being utilized downstairs.

"Sure. There are offices downstairs. Take your pick."

The office I chose already had a desk and a telephone, so I was in business. Now we'll see if seven years of college has paid off or not. The following day I set up a meeting with the manager, a man in his mid-forties, a construction worker I guessed by the looks of his cloths and hands.

I introduced myself as the new guy on the block in charge of the real estate. "I imagine you put in a full day at work," I inquired, starting out the conversation after we had sat down at the kitchen table over a cup of coffee.

"A full day and then some," he said, lighting a cigarette. "Smoke?" he asked, offering me a cigarette."

"No, thanks." I waited until he took a drag and then I started in. "I noticed that all the lawns need cutting. You do that too, in your spare time?"

"When I get around to it." He blew a smoke ring into the air.

I was beginning to sense a hint of resentment. "And the general maintenance? You do that too?"

"You got it!"

"How about when there is a vacant unit? You do the cleaning, shampoo the carpets, clean the stoves and toilets and paint too?"

"Me and Peg," he said, nodding to his wife who was standing over the stove stirring something in a pot, taking in the whole conversation.

"Sounds like an awful lot of responsibility to me."

He signed and glanced up at his wife. "It is."

"I have an idea." I scooted a little closer and lowered my voice. "What would you say if I were to tell you that all you had to do was just take are of your own building here, and not worry about the other nine buildings? Wouldn't that make your life a lot easier?"

He straightened up as if someone had just knocked a bag of spuds off his shoulder. "Would Henderson go for that?"

"I think I could sell it." I straightened up in my chair. "Of course you'd have to take a pay cut, 'cause now you would be just taking care of four units and not forty."

"Suits me just fine. I've been wanting to get in more fishing and me and Peg have been wanted to go campin' anyway, but these damned apartments …."

"Consider it done."

We stood up and shook hands. I had just fired the man as full-time manager and he was thanking me for it. My training in psychology had paid off after all.

With phase one completed, the next move was to put an ad in the help wanted section of the paper. It read: *Apartment Manager wanted. Discount off rent. No experience necessary. Call Howard.*

I got forty telephone calls the first day. At first I screened them over the phone. If they were too young, or were young and single, or had a family with four kids, I knew that didn't fit the profile that I was looking for. Those that got past the first conversation, I sent up interviews the following day, every half-hour. I requested if they were married, to bring their wife or husband along. If they had kids, I wanted to see them too. By the end of the day I had selected enough potential managers to cancel the ad that I had in the paper.

I had offered them ten dollars off their rent for every unit they managed so a four unit complex manager got forty dollars off their rent. They were ecstatic with the offer.

In order to test their metal, I sent each couple by a pre-assigned building, telling them to assume that they were the managers of that building. I asked them to make a list of the things they would do if they ran the building. How they would take care of the grounds, how they would rent a vacant unit and if a unit became vacant, and how would they fix it up for rent.

Some of the people were magnificent with their suggestions, and others were not creative at all. That wasn't important to me. What was important was their loyalty and ability to run a little four-plex or six-plex.

By the end of the third day I had narrowed the list of potential managers down to fifteen couples. By the end of the week I had hired nine managers and had saved the owner two-hundred dollars in management fees. In one week I had cut his vacancies in half, and had a hundred percent better coverage of not only the buildings, but maintenance as well, and had ten times the security. Henderson was impressed.

I thought, if real estate was this easy, maybe I should look into getting my license. I bought a little green book called the *Real Estate Primer* and read it from cover to cover.

In this same time frame I met an old Italian who bought houses and resold them at a profit for a living. He had just purchased a house off San Carlos Street that had a little one bedroom cottage on its separate lot next to it. He said he had planed on selling the little house.

I asked how much he wanted for the place and he said five thousand dollars.

I didn't have enough money to buy my next meal, let lone a house, but I knew that I wanted this house, so I offered to buy it from him for a thousand more than he was asking with no down payment and told him that I would pay him off within five years. We struck a deal and I bought my first piece of real estate and moved in.

The house was the smallest thing I had ever seen, even smaller than the one we used to live in when we were kids. There was a nice back yard and a long, narrow front yard. The house had to be non-conforming, because there was virtually no side yard. It had a kitchen, a bathroom, a living room and a bedroom. I immediately commenced adding another bedroom and a family room to the front of the house.

I had seen an office wherein the decorator had lined the wall with black walnut paneling with a two inch white strip in between panels. It had looked marvelous, so I decided that that was what I was going to do to my living room. When Inez and Fritz, Dad's brother, the one with TB, remember, came to visit me after the addition had been completed, they smiled and called it my little black house. The name stuck.

Fixing up and adding the rooms had been fun. I looked for another deal. I found it in the form of an eastside house that had been divided into a duplex with a detached mother-in-law quarters. The lot was zoned R-2, indicating that either the in-law quarters or the subdivided house was non-conforming.

Either way, there was no way a lender was going to lend on the property and the seller was into city government, which I think was why he wanted to get the property off his name. We struck a deal with fifteen hundred down and he carried the paper. The price was thirteen thousand dollars.

I immediately proceeded to further compound the non-conforming situation by doubling the size of the in-law quarters.

Now, I had two properties with almost no investment.

I had read the *Real Estate Primer* and knew it from cover to cover, so I decided to apply for my real estate license. The test was given in San Francisco. I passed it on the first try. Now I was a licensed real estate salesman.

I hung my shingle with Bill Henderson and decided that I would specialize in income property. Why start at the bottom selling houses or little buildings, I rationalized? If you're going to sell something, may as well make it something large.

I didn't know my ass from fat meat when it came to income property, so I had to fake it. I'd introduce myself to the owner of a hundred unit apartment building, give him my card, telling him that I had a buyer that was interested in buying his building. I wasn't looking for a listing, I said, just the information so I could present it to my buyer to see if he wanted to take it to the next step.

Sellers liked the idea of not tying up their building, especially to an agent as young as I was. My philosophy was that if I couldn't sell the building in thirty days, I couldn't sell it anyway, and the listing would be unnecessary. As for the commission, I was protected in the purchase contract.

By using this method of using non-listings, I was able to accumulate more buildings for sale than any five agents in the area combined. I threw an ad in the Wall Street journal and the following week that ad resulted in more buyers than I could deal with. I was off and running.

My first sale was the Franciscan Apartment Building in Foster City, a 120 unit apartment complex. The seller was the builder who, coincidently, Henderson knew. The buyer was a cherub looking man in Los Altos by the name of Wayne Miller, who coincidently also owned his own real estate company. He in turn sold it to one of his investors. I would come to find out that this was a fairly common practice – buyers tying up a property and then reselling it to one of their clients for a tidy profit.

Wayne Miller would come to be not only a good friend, but a valuable client. I would later discover that he was also a builder. He built large apartment complexes which he let me have first opportunity to sell for him.

I'm Getting Married

I was thirty years old when Estella and I were married. The wedding took place at St. Martin's church in Sunnyvale, a church that we neither attended nor knew the priest. Estella demanded that we get married and raise our children in the Catholic Church. I wasn't concerned about which church we were married in, so long as they didn't try to convert me to Catholicism. Seated in the church were my mother and father, my sister and her family, her family and approximately a hundred people that we knew, many from my real estate dealings. The wedding had been set for two o'clock in the afternoon. It was two-fifteen and my wife-to-be still hadn't shown up.

I guess it was tradition to have the groom and best man to wait outside of the church until the actual wedding started. This day it was Larry and myself standing outside in the full sun. I knew, down deep in my heart that I was here under mild protest. Larry must have picked up on my hesitancy, because he said, "Sure you wouldn't rather be golfing?"

She finally showed up, thirty minutes late, and the wedding went came off as planned. The reception was held at the *Lamplighter Inn*, courtesy of Bill Henderson. That night we went to the airport and boarded a plane for Acapulco, Mexico. When we landed, the taxi driver inquired which hotel he wanted to take us to. I said that I didn't know, but would take any suggestion that he might have.

He looked at me as if I had just declared insanity. "You don't have a reservation?" he asked, astounded.

"No. Do I need one?"

He simply shook his head. "Maybe I can get you in one of the hotels that I know."

"Thank you."

He pulled in front of a six story hotel called the *Calleta*. The hotel fronted on the ocean and the grounds were filled with lush landscaping, plants thirty feet tall with leaves bigger than me. "Wait here," he instructed us. "I'll see what I can do for you."

By now I was feeling totally stupid for not having had a reservation. The only trip I had ever taken had been on a bus from Oregon to California, complements of Uncle Sam. I was totally ignorant of the requirements of the travel world

The taxi driver came back with a big smile on his face. "They were full, but there was a last minute cancellation. I got you in!" The thought flashed through my mind that somewhere along the way I was being taken for a ride, but at this point, I had no choice. I was grateful to have found a place.

As we got out of the taxi, I was shocked to see that there were piles of debris piled along side of the road, as if someone had just dumped a pickup full of garbage right then and there. I figured I was lucky to have gotten a hotel, and on the beach at that, so I ignored the refuse. The driver helped us up with our luggage, was given a nice tip and then left, but not before giving us his card. "If you want to go anywhere, I'm your guide. I know all the right places. Call me!"

Our room was 626, overlooking the garden at the back of the hotel. The floor had been decorated with a burnt orange colored tile. Everything was tile, with not a stitch of carpet in the place. That made sense. I would have rather had a room overlooking the bay, but at this point, I figured, I should be grateful for what we've got. We decided to leave our luggage and take a tour of the grounds.

I had no preconceived notion of what the bay should look like, but I wasn't impressed with what I saw. The beach was littered with broken coconut shells and discarded branches and leaves from the abundant foliage that grew everywhere. A swimming pool had been built adjoining the beach that flowed directly into the ocean, or visa versa. The water didn't look very inviting as it was filled with ocean debris; discarded ocean life, pieces of plants and a brown sudsy looking substance. I knew right then and there that I wasn't going swimming in the pool.

The next day we ate fruit for breakfast and then headed for the beach. The sea came at us from a semi-circle with a small island rising out of the sea a thousand yards off shore. To the left, the semi-circle ended, extending itself beyond a cliff to a part of the ocean that we couldn't see. She took a rice matt that we had brought with us and lie down in the sun and promptly fell asleep. After a few moments I decided to go for a swim.

I noticed that there weren't many people swimming, but attributed that to the fact that the water wasn't that pristine or inviting. I was hot and I didn't plan on drinking any of the water, so I waded in and slowly paddled out to sea.

Admittedly, I'm not a great swimmer, never have been and never will be, but I can swim, dog paddle, frog kick and float on my back. I figure if push came to shove, one of the four strokes will get me to a point of safety if need be.

I had swam out approximately a hundred feet or more, further than I had anticipated. I turned to look at the beach where my wife lay sleeping. I waived, just in case she was faking it and was looking at me. I got no response so I assumed that she was still snoozing. I glanced off to the left where the beach took a sharp turn, going from sand to a cliff. I could see that a place had been built where swimmers could climb a set of stairs from the sea onto the side of the hill. I figured that it was about a hundred yards or so, and calculated that could make it. A quick glance toward shore let me know that Estella was still sleeping, so I decided to go for it. The current was stronger than I had anticipated, carrying me further out to sea.

I tried not to get myself into a low level of panic, taking easy, long, strong strokes towards the cliff where the stairs were located. By now I could no longer see the shore clearly and if I were in trouble, I didn't think anyone was paying any attention to me anyway. To them I was just a guy out for a long swim.

A good forty minutes later I pulled myself up on the first wrung of the wooden ladder. Exhausted, I hung there for several moments, catching my breath. Eventually, I pulled myself up and climbed the ladder which led to the top of the cliff which led to a dirt road that took me back to the front of the hotel. By the time I walked back to the beach the better part of an hour had elapsed. As I walked back onto the beach I noticed that a crowd had gathered and some hysterical person was shouting instructions.

The closer I got, the more I realized that the voice of the hysterical one was none other than my new wife. She was saying something about someone having been drowned and the lifeguard was saying that if the person had drowned, that there was nothing that he could do about it anyway.

Sounded logical to me.

I strolled up behind her and asked what the commotion was all about. Her eyes went from hysteria to gleeful and back to hysteria again. She began pounding me on the chest as if I had just executed her whole family in front of her very eyes.

I backed up, trying to protect myself, while everyone looked at me in disbelief. During several short assaults that was forthcoming I was to gather that she thought that I had drowned out there in the ocean or something, and now seeing me in front of her, alive and well, she couldn't decide if she should be happy or angry. She chose the latter.

Eventually, everyone disbursed, leaving me to stand there bloody and bruised from my first beating. Eventually, she calmed down and I explained that I had swum out and had several times turned to wave to her, but each time received no response, so I had assumed that she was sleeping, which she was.

Thus ended our first day at the beach and our first day of marriage.

Later that night, after we had eaten our dinner, we were walking the grounds under the bright star-lit night and found ourselves down by the swimming pool. We sat down on the lounge chairs and listened to the ocean. It wasn't long before I noticed something coming in from the ocean and into the swimming pool. It stood about two feet out of the water and moved silently. At first I thought that it was some long necked bird such as a swan, but then realized that what it was, was the dorsal fin of a very large shark, cruising the pool, looking for dessert. I couldn't help but think that I had been swimming in his domain no more than a few hours earlier. I could have been lunch! I never swam in the sea again.

Back Home and in the Grove

As I said previously, my wife was a beautician, so I decided that my first commission should be spent on buying her a new beauty shop. Originally, we thought about buying an existing shop, but the more we looked, the more we were convinced that they were either too small, too tacky, or in the wrong location. I decided to build her one. I negotiated a lease on two thousand square feet of space in a new shopping center that had just been built on the El Camino Real in Sunnyvale. I was determined that we were going to have the most deluxe, dazzling beauty shop in the county.

I designed the shop with a raised Grecian-like blue carpeted platform area for the dryer section with flowing powder blue drapes at each corner. There were separate rooms for shampooing so the ladies weren't on display at their most vulnerable time, appearance wise. I designed the shop with sixteen stations, all powder blue, outlining the perimeter around the dryer section. A showcase of human hair wigs, the finest money could by, were on display up front. We had more human hair merchandise than anyone in the county.

I was ready to have the sign built, but couldn't seem to come up with an appropriate name for the shop. Then one night we were at *Roundtable Pizza* and I was reading the legend of King Arthur when it came to me.

Lady Guinevere!

Original, unique and no one had used it before.

The shop was now finished. Now, all I needed was beauticians. Not just any beautician, but the cream of the crop. I hand picked each and every girl that worked for me, all sixteen of them. If they weren't drop dead gorgeous, they didn't work at *Lady Guinevere.*

I had a glassed in office built at the front corner of the shop where I could close the door and conduct my real estate business and still keep an eye on the shop. The place hummed like a bee hive and we were able to keep our heads above water, even when my wife got pregnant with Larry and eventually had to quit work.

Prior to my getting married, I had been living in a one-bedroom apartment that was part of a twenty unit building owned by Henderson. For rent, I managed the building. My duties were to maintain the grounds which included a fenced in swimming pool, collect the rent and deposit it in his bank account, rent any vacant units and when one became vacant, to clean and paint it. When I got married, I moved from the one-bedroom to a two-bedroom unit and when Larry came along, we moved to a three-bedroom unit. Larry occupied one room, we another, and the third bedroom was for future development.

When she became pregnant with Aaron a little over a year later, it was apparent that my living in an apartment days had come to an end. I needed to find bigger and better accommodations for my family. I needed a house. Problem was, I didn't have any money. What little money we made on the beauty shop seemed to be poured right back into it in the form of supplies, lease payments, insurance and the bare necessities of living.

I was making real estate deals, but a lot of my commissions were in the form of notes and deeds of trust that I held against the property that I sold, giving me a monthly income and a future revenue. Sometimes, I would invest my commission in the property that I had just sold, thus allowing the investment to grow. Our net worth was growing handsomely, but our cash flow just barely kept us out of the poor house.

I found this lovely three bedroom house for sale on the foothills on the eastside, by the country club golf course. The house sat back off the street and down in a gully with a creek running below the structure. It had a large undeveloped basement that I envisioned to be an office while upstairs a full deck ran the perimeter of the back of the house overlooking the creek. There was a very large front lawn and, although the interior was modern, I later learned that where the house had been built, a winery had once stood. Apparently the builder had torn down the winery and had constructed the house with the hundred year old timber that the winery had been built with.

The woman that owned the house lived there by herself. Her developer husband had divorced her to marry his secretary and, adding insult to injury, had built a house for his new bride a mere hundred yards up the hill, in full view from her front window.

She wanted out.

The house was perfect for my family.

She owned the house free and clear and was asking sixty-five thousand dollars, which I was willing to pay, if I had the money. I had a fifteen thousand dollar real estate commission note from an apartment building that I had sold for a dentist in Gilroy. I wrote up an offer for sixty thousand dollars, offering to give her my fifteen thousand dollar note from the dentist, who she said that she knew, and agreed to apply for and obtain a new loan in the amount of forty-five thousand dollars. The cash from the loan would give her the funds to buy a mobile home which is what she wanted and the note, I pointed out, would give her income.

At first she was hesitant, stating that I was buying a house with no money. I pointed out that the fifteen thousand dollar note was money and by obligating myself for the new loan and giving her the loan proceeds, was money.

She considered my thoughts and said that she would get back to me. When I left, I frankly didn't think that I had a snowball's chance in hell of getting the house, but I had tried. Two days later she called and asked if I could come over. She had a counter proposal for me to consider.

When I got there her demeanor was much more receptive than it had been before. She said that she had consulted her ex-husband -- why I don't have a clue, but in retrospect, it was probably because he was familiar with home values and financing. She said that he had told her under no uncertain terms to turn my offer down flat. That I was getting into his house for nothing down and that it was a bad deal for her.

I think it was his advice that turned the deal for me. Just to spite him, she decided to sell me the house, for sixty-two-thousand-five hundred dollars. We went to escrow and we became the proud owners of our first real house.

Aaron was on the way to join our family and we needed some money so I decided one way to get cash was to sell the little black house. I had bought it for six thousand, had doubled it in size, so I figured that it was worth at least double what I had paid for it. I put an ad in the paper and sold it the next day to a mother whose daughter was going to college. After paying off my loan I had eight thousand dollars in the bank, a nice cushion for the family.

Six months after the close of escrow I got a legal document in the mail informing me that the buyer of the little black house was suing me to rescind the deal. I still had her telephone number, so I called her.

"I got your legal papers. What's up?"

"My daughter plugged up the sewer and when they came out to clean it out, they found out that our sewer was connected to the house next door!"

That was a shock to me, but then thinking back on it, with the house being so close to the other house and part of the original ownership, I wasn't surprised.

"Why didn't you just call me?" I inquired. "If you want your money back, just tell me and I'll buy the house back from you. No big deal."

"Oh!"

I returned her money and went out and purchased a pick and shovel. Two days later I had dug a trench from the point where the sewer took off from the house that I owned to the adjoining house. I went down to the local building supply and bought the necessary pipe to connect the service to the street. Now, I needed a plumber to hook up to the sewer. That took about a week.

Once the sewer had been hooked up and was covered, I put the house back on the market. Three days later I sold it for twenty-five thousand dollars. Twice what I had just bought it back from the previous buyer.

Two years after Aaron was born, Christian joined the family. As far as I was concerned, we had a full family and it was time to look to developing the house to accommodate everyone. The first thing I did was to dig a swimming pool in the back yard. It was fifteen by thirty feet with a diving board at the deep end. After the pool was in and the deck made out of cool-deck so the kids little feet wouldn't burn in the heat, I built a six foot wrought iron fence around the perimeter. I didn't want any drowned kids in my family.

They took to water like fish, swimming, diving and playing every day. It was the best investment that I had made. One summer my mother and dad came to visit. I think I have the only picture of dad in existence in a bathing suit. His skin was porcelain white, but he didn't seem to mind, as he dove into his son's swimming pool along with his three grandchildren.

My Sales Technique

I had developed this method of acquiring clients. That is to say, finding building for sale. I would spend every Monday in my car, driving around town, just looking for property. If I was out looking for apartments that day, I would take a section of town, say Branham Lane in west San Jose where there are large apartment buildings. I would then park my car and on foot, go to each building on the street, write down the address, make notes regarding the size and condition of the structure and then take a photo of the building for future reference. Once I had done this, making what I called a profile of the property, I would find the manger's apartment and knock on the door.

Expecting to see a potential tenant, she would of course receive me into the office where I would present her with my business card that announced me as Howard Losness, president of California Investment Company. I had a pad with a preprinted out form with blanks ready to be filled out. Information like the number of units in the complex, the size, i.e. studios, one-bedroom, two-bedroom, etc. and how many and what rent they were getting. And there was a line for the amount of vacancies that they had and if there was a laundry room and if so, was it owned or leased. Once I had this formed filled out, I knew what the annual gross income should be, what the vacancy factor was and in general, how the building was operating and often, what the manager's salary was and what their duties were.

"I'm doing a survey of the neighborhood for an article that our firm is formulating and wonder if I might have a moment of your time?" I would smile and take a seat before she had time to think of an objection.

During the interview, I casually sneak in a question about ownership and once she supplies that to me, I ask, "And in case of an emergency, who do you ask for?"

"Why, Mr. X, of course."

"And his number is ....?"

Usually, by the time I leave, I have enough information about the complex that, using a five percent vacancy, plugging in a laundry income and estimating the expenses at thirty-five to thirty-eight percent of the gross, I can estimate the value of the building pretty closely. I'm now armed with enough information to talk intelligently to the owner, so I get his address from the tax records down at the title company where I spent most of my Tuesdays. Wednesday, I would drop into his office, give the receptionist my business card and state that I would like a moment with Mr. X.

"And this is about?" she would inquire, looking at the young, well dressed man in a business suit standing before her.

"It is regarding his apartment building located at 1234 Branham Street."

She motions towards a coach and then disappears behind pair of double oak doors. Ten minutes later I'm seated before the owner of the two hundred unit apartment building.

Looking at my card that has been printed on rice paper, he inquires what he can do for me.

"I represent a buyer that has expressed an interest in your building and I was wondering if you might be interested in receiving an offer? I'm not asking for a listing," I quickly add, knowing that I had less than a one percent chance of getting the listing if that was my goal. My motivation was to get him to agree to consider an offer. Once I had that understanding, I knew that if I couldn't sell the building within a thirty day period, listing or not, that I couldn't sell it anyway. I had at least three buyers that I represented that I knew would make an offer, and then they in turn would offer it to their clients or partners with a mark-up for themselves, of course. Using this line of doing business, I had more product available than any five commercial brokers in town combined.

One of the clients that I came in contact with lived in San Francisco. He owned a large building in San Jose. It was an eighty unit apartment building that had been built adjacent to the rail road tracks, called the *Metropolitan Apartments.*

"I have decided to retire," he said in our first meeting. "I want you to sell the *Metropolitan Apartments* for me, he stated. He had on his golf clothes and had driven all the way down from San Francisco to play golf at the *Pleasant Hills Golf Course.* We met in my office while his wife waited patiently in the car while we discussed the terms of the sale – the price and my fee. Once we had come to an agreement, it took me two weeks to bring him an acceptable offer.

We closed escrow and then he said, "I have another building that I think you can sell for me, but it has some problems."

I smiled to myself. I loved problems. "What kind of problems?"

"The building is twenty-five percent vacant."

"That surprises me. You can't buy a vacant apartment in this market, the rental market is so tight. The whole town if nearly one hundred percent full."

"Not my building." He sighed. "That isn't the whole story."

I waited.

"It's full of black people."

"They pay rent too," I offered. "Where is this building?"

"East San Jose."

"That's a Mexican-black neighborhood."

"There's more."

I waited.

"No one is paying rent."

"No one?"

"Well, there is a couple that is paying, but there seems to be a rent strike or something. In other words, there is this guy that says he is in charge of the renters group and they pay him the rent and he is keeping it."

I rubbed my chin. "Give me the address and let me go have a look see."

The next day I drove by the building, a three story structure with underground parking and a nice lobby with an elevator. I parked on the street and locked my car and then ascended the steps up into the corridor of the building. For all intents and purposes, it was clean and quiet. The first door that I saw was the manager's apartment off to the right. The elevator was straight ahead. I decided to walk the first floor. There was an interior hallway with apartments on both sides, so that there was no exterior lighting. The only light was a sixty watt bulb every twenty feet or so. In short, it was pretty dark. I walked the whole floor and was surprised to see that it was fairly quiet, save an occasional sound from one of the apartments.

I pushed the button the elevator, and a moment later the doors opened to the elevator cage. I pushed the button to the second floor and the elevator rose, quietly to the second floor.

I walked the whole floor and did the same with the third floor, all the time, not seeing a soul. I took the elevator back down to the first floor again. I decided to see that the mangers u it was like.

At this point, it is necessary to say that one of my favorite tricks when I'm selling a building for a client, or if he is buying a building, is to pose myself as a potential tenant, just to see how they receive and treat me. Sometimes a manger will simply throw you a key and say, "It's the first one down the hall on the right. Lock up when you leave." His life as a manager is short lived if I have anything to say about it.

Anyway, I knock on the door and these two little bald Italian brothers answer the door. They crack the door open just enough to see who it is. "Yes?" the demand, simply.

"I'd like to see one of your units. Me and my wife …"

"We don't have any vacancies," one of the brothers states and then shuts the door in my face.

"Fuck you very much."

I now know what must be done.

I met with the seller the next day at his home off Broadway in San Francisco. He lived two blocks from the entertainment section, *Big Al's, The Hungry i* and all the strip joints featuring everything from nude dancers to gay bars. Even during the daytime, the barkers were on the sidewalk trying to pull customers into their bars.

His house was one of those in San Francisco that had a zero lot line.

In other words, there were no windows on the side of the house as that was the common wall to your neighbor.

"The apartment building is a real mess." I told him. "For starters, the manger has to go." I explained by brief encounter with him. "Why wouldn't he rent to me?" I inquired.

He shrugged his shoulders.

"Well, the building is not marketable the way it is now. A buyer will see exactly what I saw when I went there. The first question they will ask is why there are twenty-six vacant units and the second question is why are all they tenants black?

He raised his hands into the air. "So what do we do? I want to get rid of the building. I'll do whatever you say!"

"Tell you what. I'll run the building for you. I'll fill it up with paying tenants, and make it presentable, but my condition is that I'll need a years listing to do it. This rent strike that you have got going there needs addressing immediately."

"Tell me about it. I don't have enough income from the building to pay debt service, let alone the utility bills."

I wet home and drew up a management contract and a listing agreement for a year. He signed it with no resignations.

The first thing I did was to return to the manager's office. The same two little Italian   brothers answered the door. I explained who I was and said that I was taking over management to the building. "When I came to your door last time, trying to rent an apartment, you said that there were no vacancies. I know for a fact that there are twenty-six vacant units. Why wouldn't you rent to me?"

Expecting a lame answer, the said, "Because you were white."

"Excuse me?"

"You were white. We don't rent to white people."

"And that is, why?"

"All of our tenants are black. If we rented to white people, that would just cause trouble, so we don't."

"You're white," I pointed out the obvious.

"That's different."

I didn't bother asking why. I just said, "You are fired."

I ran an ad in the local paper and hired a middle aged couple from the dozen or so people who inquired to mange the building. I had to explain the problem with the building, including, of course, that half of the tenants were not paying rent and that they were all black.

"No problem," the said.

The next thing I did was to contact the tenant that was in charge of the rent strike. He was a young, single man who came across as arrogant and belligerent. He took an immediate dislike to me and the feeling was neutral. I explained who I was and that I had just taken over the building and inquired as to the nature of the tenant strike.

He informed me that the owner wasn't keeping the building up to the tenant's standards, so until they saw some major improvements, they were not going to give him their rent. When I asked about specifics, he said that he would only tell the owner personally. Not his agent. I said, "If the tenants are paying you their rent , what are you doing with the funds?"

"I have them in escrow," was his lame response.

"How much do you have in that account?"

"None of your business."

The meeting lasted forty-five minutes with no progress on my part. Clearly, this guy was up to no good. I would retreat home to think this through. The next day I went down to the police department and explained the situation to a detective there.

"This guy is extorting money for his own good," he said. "He has no legal right to the owner's rent. If he has a grievance, he should go through legal channels."

"So what do I do?"

"Are you willing to wear a wire?"

"Sure," I said, not really understanding why he had asked that question.

"Tell you what, you call the guy up and set up a meeting."

"Under what pretenses?"

"Say that you are ready to comply with their demands. Meet him in the manger's office. We'll be in the room right next door and when he shows up, I want you to demand that he return the money over to the owner. When he refuses, and he will, we'll enter the room and arrest the bastard."

On the appointed day I went down to the police station where they wired me for sound. An hour later the led the man out of the apartment office in handcuffs. I never did find out what happened to him, but now I had to get everyone to start paying rent. In those days, I thought I could do everything myself. So, I went down to the Municipal Courthouse and in small claims court, filed on twenty of the tenants that had not paid their rent to the manager.

When our court day arrived, the courtroom was filled with angry tenants, all whom knew my face by now. The only white people in the room was me and the judge. One by one they called our cases and one by one, I was awarded a judgment against the tenant. Two hours later, we all filed out of the courtroom. The judge uttered under his breath, "I sure hope you know what you are doing."

The next day the manger called me on the telephone. "Whatever you do, don't come down to the building today!"

"Why?"

"'Cause they're all standing outside, just waiting for you."

As I mentioned, in those days, I worked out of my home, so I grabbed my two year old son, Larry, and together we drove down to the apartment building. Sure enough, there they were, all standing outside of the building, on the sidewalk.

I parked my car right in front, grabbed little Larry, cradled him in my arms and marched straight through the crowd. Everyone starred at me as I didn't have a brain in my head, and that day, I didn't, but no one spoke a word to me as we walked up the stairs and into the lobby and into the manager's office. That day was the turning point in the operation of the building. One by one the delinquent tenants either moved out or started paying rent.

It took me exactly one year to turn that building around where it was one hundred percent full of a good mixture of white, Mexican and black tenants. And yes, I did sell the building.

The Ideal Client

I didn't limit myself to just apartments when I was brokering commercial real estate. Uncle Fritz was once the president of the California Motel Society, and at the time they owned a small 30 unit motel just across the street from Disneyland. That small motel provided them with a job and enough money to raise their family. I thought, here is a commercial vehicle worth checking into, so I started familiarizing myself with motels, eventually specializing in them. The first motel I sold was in Fresno, called Motel Fresno, an 89 unit motel with a bar and restaurant. The structure was a two story building with lush grounds, built in the early twentieth century along a Spanish style. The rooms were small but charming. The owner-operator was an elderly man who had operated it for years and now wanted his freedom back. I talked him into listing it with me for thirty days, thinking, as usual, that if I couldn't sell it in thirty days, I couldn't sell it period.

I ran an ad in the wall street journal and within a week had so many inquires that I didn't have enough packages to send out. A buyer from Los Angles drove up to see the building and left with an accepted offer from the seller.

That was easy, I thought. The next motel I listed and sold was the Merced Holiday Inn. Again, it sold within thirty days. *I think I've found my nitch!*

The Fresno area had loads of motels and seemed to be a fertile ground worthy of my time. They have a street that runs parallel to the freeway called motel row. I started at one end and worked my way down to the other end, talking to managers or owners, telling that I had just sold two motels here in town and that my buyers wanted more. That line got me in the door.

One manager said that if I wanted to talk to the owner I would have to go directly to his office in Orinda, a small town near San Francisco. He gave me his name and telephone number with the promise that I wouldn't tell him how I had gotten the information.

The next day I was sitting in a small office not much bigger than our kitchen. The owner was an elderly man, obviously interested in football, because he had a large silver football on his desk, an Oakland Raider shield on his wall and several pictures of famous Raiders such as Jim Plunket, Kenny Stabler and others.

"You seem to be a Raider fan," I exclaimed after our brief conversation relative to the sale of his motel.

He looked at me sternly and exclaimed, "I *own* the Raiders!" His name was Ed McGaw, Sr., and he was indeed the owner and general manager of the Oakland Raiders. That was before Al Davis became owner and general manger.

The day I got my first offer on the motel, I called his office for an appointment to present to him. "Just come right on over," his secretary had said.

Expecting to find him in his office, I drove up from San Jose to Orinda in my business suit on a hot summer day. "He's at the Black Hawk Country Club golf course," his secretary advised me when I walked in the door. She smiled a sly, impish smile that said volumes. "He said you should go on over there and find him."

I later learned that this was one of his favorite cat and mouse games that he enjoyed playing with me. He would make an appointment, full well knowing that he was going to be out on the course, playing golf. I would then drive out to the exclusive club in my suit and tie, get a golf cart and proceed along the various fairways trying to find him. Once I found him, of course I didn't get to talk to him right away. He had to impress his friends with the game which I'm sure they were up to snuff on, as they would look back at me and snicker while I sat in the golf cart, sweating in my suit and tie while he hit his drive off the tee or putted on the green. Once, after I had located him on the thirteenth tee, he ignored me for a hole or two, and then finally waived me over to sign documents and gave me a few minutes of his time.

Often times I would go to his office only to find him sitting at his desk, on the telephone with a stack of Raider tickets in his hand, calling friends, trying to give them away. I would have given my eye teeth in hell to have had two of those tickets, but never had the nerve to ask him for them. And yes, I did sell his motel for him.

One of my motel owners also owned a convalescent hospital and asked me if I had a client that might be interested in buying it. Of course I replied in the affirmative and was given a listing to sell a two hundred-ten bed unit convalescent facility in Southern California. An ad in the Wall Street Journal yielded several interesting leads, one of which was a broker-operator out of the Los Angles area.

I flew down to Los Angles to meet with him. Over lunch he advised me that he was a real estate broker who was also a motel and convalescent hospital operator. As it turned out, he didn't have the funds to buy anything, but was willing to lease any motel, hotel and/ or convalescent hospital that I found, so long as I had an investor that would put up the money to buy the facility. He offered a 12% triple-net return on their investment. Coincidently, I did have an investor from Silicon Valley, an employee from Lockheed Aero-Space that put together partnerships to invest his coworker's money, so long as he was the general partner. He operated on the OPM principle; Other People's Money. He would raise the money and then take twenty-five percent of the deal. The only catch: he wanted half of my commission.

It took five seconds to figure out the math. Fifty percent of something was fifty percent more than I had before I started. I had just put together a machine that could generate millions of dollars in sales. It also didn't take long to figure out that I was far ahead by hooking up with this gravy train by investing my commission in their transactions.

I began finding hotels and convalescent hospitals for my Silicon Valley investor to purchase, who then leased the project to my Los Angles operator. It got to the point that I would find a deal that I thought filled their investment requirement, would take it to my office and write up the contract and then take it to my Silicon Valley investor for his signature. He trusted me to the point that he would sign the deal without even bothering to read the contract. Nothing could be easier. Only thing is, I was generating partnership equity in real estate ventures and still had no cash for living expenses, so again, we were living close to the vest. On paper, we were worth more than I had dreamed, but in the bank, we were hurting.

My wife would ask me, "Are we rich or poor?"

I said, "Both."

It was about this time that I started to really branch out and started looking for investments beyond the horizon. I thought, here I am in California, putting together hotel deals, why not try selling a hotel in Nevada? Maybe even one with a casino?

I traveled to Carson City, Nevada and went through my usual routine of seeking out the owners of small casino-hotel and came across a 120 unit hotel with a casino on the first floor. After a bit of research I learned that the owner was an elderly gentleman who had not only owned the hotel and ran the casino himself, but that he had in fact built the facility from the ground up. He had amassed his fortune and was looking to retire. To make matters easy, he lived on the premises, in the penthouse suite. I paid him a visit. As luck would have it, I was the first real estate person that had ever contacted him.

After our initial meeting which lasted an hour, more or less, I met with him several other times, gathering the operational numbers for not only the hotel, but the casino as well. That was an education, let me tell you. No wonder Las Vegas has the grandest hotels in the world.

Once I had my sales package together along with glorious pictures of the hotel, restaurant and casino, I flew down to my hotel buyer-operator and submitted the package to him. He met me at the airport, took me to a fancy restaurant where, during lunch, I laid everything out for him. I could tell by the gleam in his eye that I was going to leave with an offer to buy the whole package.

The next day I presented the offer to the seller which was exactly what he had been asking for. He explained that the gaming commission would have to approve the buyer which I assured him would be no problem as he was already a successful owner operator of several hotels and convalescent hospitals in California and as far as I knew, had no criminal record.

We did the physical inspection which was a breeze as the facility was in pristine condition and was operating like a well oiled machine. My buyer removed all of the conditions and we went to escrow. I was in line to earn the single largest commission of my career when the night before escrow was scheduled to close, I got a telephone call from my buyer at ten o'clock that night. Before I could congratulate him on being a new casino owner, he said, "The deal is off!"

I sat back in shock, at first thinking that he was having a joke on me, but the tone of his voice said otherwise. I waited for the other shoe to drop.

"I just had a visitor," he explained. "Two, actually."

I took a deep breath and waited.

"These two guys. They came to my home and when I answered the door, they just barged in and announced that they were my new partners. I have to tell you, Howard, they scared they shit out of me."

"What did you do?"

"It's more what they did. When I told them to get the hell out of my house, the big one reached in his jacket and pulled out the biggest gun I have ever seen, and pointed it at my head. Right between the eyes. Then he cocked the gun and put the barrel to my forehead. I tell you, when I felt the cold steel against my skin, I thought right then and there that I had bought it."

"Then what happened?"

"The big one, the one with the gun. He slapped me across my forehead with the barrel, knocking me down, and then he put his foot on my chest and pointed the gun at my heart. That was it. Then they left. The last thing they said was, 'Remember, we're your new partners. If you want you and your family to stay alive …'. That was all he said before they left. His last words were, 'We'll be in touch.'"

"You have to call the police!" I urged him. "They can't just bust into your home and threaten you like that." Easy for me to say. I could feel him sweating through the phone.

"No. I'm done. These guys. They'll be back. I know that. It isn't worth it." And he hung up.

Despite the loss of my Nevada deal, I was still on a roll with the wind to my back. With my buyer-operator and syndicator, we must have put together thirty deals, all of which I examined carefully before showing each one to my investor-buyer. Then, the inevitable occurred. By a casual slip of the lip I found out that my Silicon Valley investor-buyer and my Los Angles investor-operator had gotten together and had decided to start doing deals without me. *Why pay Losness a commission when we can do deals directly?* Was the logic.

My LA operator had heard that this hotel, a luxury Hilton Hotel in southern California was in trouble and was for sale. He had gotten in touch with the seller, had tied the project up with a purchase contract and had presented the deal to my Silicon Valley buyer. The hotel's operation was reportedly loosing thirty thousand dollars a month, but the operator had convinced the buyer that he could turn that around in nothing flat. Besides, there was a half million dollar commission to be gained, all to themselves.

They came to an agreement, each carving out the delicious fee for themselves at the partners expense, of course and subsequently closed the deal, thus starting their first immediate negative cash flow venture. That purchase was followed by another ill fated purchase of a 200 unit motel in Fresno, which was vacant and was owned by the finance company. My buyer and LA operator built in a million dollar profit for themselves, bought the hotel and resold it to their investment group guaranteeing them their usual twelve percent return, which they anticipated once they got it up and running. Now they owned two alligators that were seriously chomping into the cash flow of the healthy investments that I had sold them.

In less than six months a successful business venture had turned from a cash cow where everyone was enjoying a healthy cash flow into law suits and foreclosures. All because they got greedy and had decided to cut me out. Every investment they acquired after eliminating me went from being a questionable investment to a bad deal. Within a year they lost everything and the IRS was seriously looking into their tax returns. To avoid prosecution, my Silicon Valley investor left the country unexpectedly and hasn't been heard from since, although I heard from his ex-wife that he had snuck back into the country via Mexico to try to get some of his ex-wife's money. The LA investor changed his name and business address, and as far as far as I know, is still bilking people of their money.

The down side – all my investment commission money went down the tubes. The upside – there wasn't one. The obvious moral to the story – don't be greedy.

Then I learned from an associate that there was a major shopping center for sale. A group of local farmers had built a gigantic Shopping Mall, one of the largest shopping malls in the area and they wanted to sell. The price, $215,000,000. As luck would have it, I had just met the acquaintance of a Japanese man who represented a group of investors from Japan and they had a truck load of money to buy investments in America. I acquired a twenty page brochure from my friend that listed all the tenants and the rent they paid and the terms of their lease and then submitted it to the investor group. A week later I had a contract to buy the mall for $210,000,000. This deal could retire me at age 35!

My buddy insisted on presenting the offer, due to the fact that he had originally been the person in contact with the sellers.

No big deal.

I waited with anxious breath to hear from him. The next day I got the call. The farmers had said, "We are not going to sell to the Japanese. We will not sell our mall to any outsiders."

I was devastated, but somehow managed to understand their loyalty to citizens of this country. I had a shot and took it, but apparently it didn't hit the target. A few months went by and then I read headlines in the business section that the mall had been sold to a group of investors from China!

After I regained my composure, I got together with two lawyer friends of mine and we decided to form a partnership whereas, it would be my job to find good viable investments, and then we would raise the money and put together partnerships ourselves whereas we would operate the property acquired. I figured that with two real estate attorneys for partners, what could go wrong?

Things went well until one of the partners, a graduate of Idaho State University in Pocatello, Idaho heard of a 200 unit Holiday Inn for sale in his home town and decided that we should buy it. I guess by now you've figured out the rest of the story as Paul Harvey would say.

The first few months were great until we were inspected by the Holiday Inn reps who periodically visit their hotel franchises to see how the hotels look. They decided that ours could use a makeover; new carpets, drapes, furniture – the whole enchilada. We had to borrow a million bucks from a lender just to satisfy that requirement. The alternative – break the lease and get sued by Holiday Inn. The long and the short of it is, we did the renovations and simultaneously the economy in town declined, taking our gross receipts into the bucket. In short, we never recovered. We sold the hotel at a loss and retired to lick our wounds.

I figured that it was time for me to go on my own.

About this time, our father decided it was time to retire from his job at the paper mill in Longview, Washington where he had been working. I knew from my psychology training that usually when a person retires from their job, that, unless they have a hobby, their interest in life dwindled with the result being that they could pass away sooner rather than later.

To solve this problem, I found a 69 unit apartment building for sale by an investor that I had met in San Jose. He was in financial trouble and had this building with four loans on it and was willing to sell it for a song and a dance and carry the paper. In short, I bought it with nearly one hundred percent loan to value. I knew going in that the building was not operating in the black, but with my background, thought that I could straighten that out.

The building had two washer and dryer locations, so I set my dad up in business, giving him the machines to run and collect the quarters ever week. He was overjoyed at the prospect of owning his own business, plus it got him out of the house.

Everything went well for a few years until the economy in town went into the dumper and the apartment building began having more vacancies that the income could sustain. I was losing serious money. Something had to be done.

I had a plan.

I went to the seller who was carrying a note in fifth place, and said, "Ron, I've had Hillcrest for a little over two years now and the building is loosing money hand over fist. I can't take it any longer. I need to get rid of the building."

Thinking that I was there to get him paid off through a sale, he was overjoyed until I informed him that I was going to Quick Claim the building back to him and walk away from the investment.

"I don't want the building back," he said, holding up his hands, defensively.

"Well, the only way that I can keep the building would be to discount your note dramatically."

"How dramatically?"

"More than you would consider," I said. "Here, just let me Quick Claim it back to you."

"No, no! Tell me what you want!"

I had him. Fifteen minutes later I walked away with a hundred thousand dollar note paid in full for twelve thousand dollars.

The second, third and fourth note holders were once all previous investors in the building and had, by some mathematical equation, decided to split their notes up with each taking their prorated share.

So now, I went to the fourth note holder, a single lady with loads of cash and no interest in complicating her life with a building that was running in the red. It took me all of fifteen minutes of her time to make a deal with a seventy percent discount.

The same went for the third note holder, an elderly couple, also well healed, and the second, a retired doctor in town. He was too busy playing golf, playing poker at the local club and chasing women to be bothered with running a building.

I had now dramatically reduced my debt service. The last victim was the bank, a small, local bank that held the first mortgage. I gave him the same spiel, telling him that the building was running a serious deficit and that I needed to unburden myself with it and was prepared to deed it back to the bank.

He didn't bite, at least not the whole way. "Tell you what," he said, sitting back in his seat and lighting up a cigar. "I can't discount the note, but I can rewrite the loan, re-amortizing it over thirty years and giving you a better interest rate."

When I walked out of that meeting, I now had a building with just one loan, not five, whose payments were miniscule in comparison to those that I originally had.

Through some research, I found out that that same bank had an apartment building on their books. They wanted to get rid of it, and in inspecting the unit, I decided to make them an offer. The bank, now familiar with me, happily accepted my offer. I went to my local

California bank and got a loan on my house and then put a couple of my basketball playing friends along with my family and together we bought the building. I then formed a partnership between me and my brother, Larry, and we went into business together. That's been over twenty years now, and no one has lost a dime, and in fact everyone has at least doubled their money with our investments.

I should have done this to begin with, but sometimes one has to go down the road of hard knocks to discover which fork in the road to take.

Eventually, the partners elected to sell, so, believing in the product, I mortgaged one of my apartment buildings and bought everyone out except brother Larry. To this day we still own and operate the apartments.

Turning a negative
into a positive

We all have periods of adversity, when things don't go our way, when something happens to us and we ask ourselves, "Why me?" My oldest son, Larry, is one person who has certainly had his fill of an ill wind blown his way.

I used to take the kids skiing up at Squaw Valley or Heavenly Valley at South Shore, Lake Tahoe, California. They learned to ski without poles when they were just knee high to a grasshopper at the age of four or five years. They had no fear of falling nor did they know how to turn much. As a result, they would simply head straight down the hill, totally out of control. More than once, I looked down in horror as one of them was heading straight for one of those iron pylons that supported the ski lift, obvious to the disaster that lay ahead. It took every ounce of energy I had to race down the hill and over take them, usually just before kid and pylon meshed into one.

One time after just such a ski trip, Larz was but a lad of twelve. After we arrived home he had begun to complain of a pain in his leg. I thought he had possible strained a muscle, so I rubbed his leg and applied the usual home remedies to minimize the pain and dismissed the matter, thinking that it would be okay in an hour or so.

It wasn't. After a week of continued discomfort, my wife, who was much more prone to taking the children to the doctor with every little scratch, insisted that I take him to the clinic, whereas the kid had to be bleeding to death before I thought medical attention was necessary. A product, no doubt of my upbringing. As a child, the only time I saw a doctor was the time my father had been involved in an automobile accident and I had been thrown through the windshield which had resulted on more than few stitches on the old face, or when the school's athletic program required me to take a physical examination for sports.

We had a very good orthopedic physician not far from our home, a red haired fellow with a cherub face and a big smile. He listened to our complaints, did a cursory examination, took a couple X-rays then put Larry onto the exam table. He rolled his leg back and forth which caused Larry to complain loudly in pain.

"James, come in here for a moment," he said to his fellow doctor as he walked by. "What do you think?" he asked, rolling Larry's leg again with the same painful result.

They looked at one another and then in unison said, "Log roll."

"Legg Perthesis," Our Doc said, confirming their analysis.

"What's Legg Perthesis?" I asked. Sounded harmless enough to me.

"It occurs to one in ten thousand kids. Usually active boys around the age of ten to twelve. We don't know what causes it, but in Legg Perthesis the blood ceases to flow to the femur head, causing the bone to die," he said, pointing out the top of a hanging skeleton's leg bone where it entered the hip.

"The bone will turn to mush, just like ice cream," he explained. "If he continues to walk on it, the bone can splinter or will flatten out. The result is he'll have a painful leg for the rest of his life."

"Is the bone dead, permanently?" I asked, in shock as images of smashed ice-cream cones ran through my mind resulting from a one legged son to one destined to spend the rest of his life on crutches or in a wheel chair or worse yet, dragging it limply behind as he ambled along.

"After about two years time the blood will resume flowing back to the femur head again and it will commence restoring itself," he asserted in his flat monotone voice as if he were ordering a hot dog with onions.

"If he can't walk on the leg, what's to be done in the meantime? Does he walk on crutches for two years?" I was in the beginning stages of a low-level panicked parent.

"Let's put him in traction for ten days and then re-examine him again. We'll know more at that time."

"Does that mean he has to go into the hospital?" I could see Larz eyes betraying his fear as he looked first at me then at the doctor.

"No. You can rent a traction device and keep him home." He gave me the name and address of a couple rental places where I could rent a bed and traction pulley.

We went home in shock. No one spoke. Each of us was having our own private in-brain horror movie. I'm sure that my wife's and mine was the most graphic, but I'm equally certain that Larry's was the most terrifying, although kids have a way of handling things much better than adults, I was to later learn.

We came to the decision to rent a bed and place it in the family room where the family would be most of the time. There, he could have visitors, could study and when he was finished, could watch television. We rented a pair of crutches so he could go to the bathroom without having to under go the embarrassment of using a bed pan. Something neither he nor I looked forward to.

At first the pain was intense as the traction was set up and weights were attached to a pulley which in turn was attached to his foot which pulled the leg away from his hip. After a few days, the pain subsided until he got up to go to the bathroom at which time the femur bone apparently came in contact with the hip, causing him pain again. Apparently, it was like bare bone or raw nerves rubbing against one another.

During those ten days we all remained optimistically certain that his condition would pass. Down deep, both my wife and I felt a continual gnawing pain, wishing we could relieve the discomfort he must be feeling.

We were all in denial. I know that I denied any feelings that he would eventually be anything but better, even if he had to hobble around on crutches for two years. Maybe he would be a fast healer and be off them in six months. The doctors could have made a mistake in diagnosis too.

Eventually, I would get another opinion from another doctor, and another and another, all with the same diagnosis: Legg Perthesis. Larry refused to accept the fact that he would be laid up for any extended period of time. The thought of being on crutches was abhorrent to him. He cried every time the subject came up.

Ten days later, we re-visited the orthopedic office. More X-rays. When the results were in, they were devastating. The doctor recommended immediate surgery on his hip. We went to Mr. Bones again who was still hanging by his skull in the same spot as before. He pointed out the femur bone once more.

"You'll note that the head of the femur isn't totally protected by the hip," he said, pointing his pencil to a portion of the femur head that was outside of the protective cushion of the hip bone. "As you can see, a portion of the bone protrudes out from the hip socket."

We looked at Mr. bones and collectively nodded, not knowing where this was leading. Not sure that we wanted to know.

"What we need to do is operate and tilt the hip bone down like this," he said, using his hand as if it were an extension of the hip bone, his one hand covering the fist of the other. "Then the femur will be totally cradled and protected during the dormant period."

"You say, 'tilt the hip bone'. What exactly do you mean? Do you cut the hip or add a piece to the hip or what?" My mouth was getting dry and it seemed difficult to talk. It was beginning to get scared again.

"We form a wedge in the hip by slicing it here," he said, putting his pen on the bone's hip, "thereby tilting the hip."

"And that protects the femur bone from smashing like you said?"

"I will protect it during the dormant period," he hedged.

I didn't hear the word heal so I pressed on. "So what happens after two years? Has the bone been healed? Is he going to be all right? What happens to the hip bone? Do we re-align it again?"

Lots of questions.

"With any luck, the head of the femur will not have suffered any damage."

More hedging!

"It's difficult to hold an active child down to minimal activity, as you know," he said looking at Larry as if he weren't there, but talking to us. "Especially when he's away to school and seeing the other kids playing ball and stuff. It's entirely possible that there could be some damage during the incubation period. We can only hope for the best."

"How can we be one hundred percent sure?" I was becoming pessimistic about this medical "expert" and was unwilling to take a chance on my child's future. I saw in Larry an image of myself, active in sports. I knew that if I had I been incapacitated and unable to participate in any sporting activity, my entire life would be altered ... for the worse. Coping with life would be very difficult and would subsequently take on a whole new dimension. Exercise is my form of physical escape and mental cleansing process. No reason to think that Larry would be any different.

"By confining him to traction in bed for two years," he offered. "That would give the femur head maximum protection."

Two years in bed, I thought. That's like a jail sentence to an active child. And what about muscle atrophy? I looked at Larry's face where tears were rolling down his cheeks. He was a trooper. He said nothing as he looked up at me with pleading eyes, wanting me to fix it so this ugly thing wasn't happening. It was the first of a multitude of helpless feelings that was to intensify over the next month.

"And if you do the operation," I shuttered, "What happens to the hip after two years? Are we going to be all right?"

"We just leave the hip like it is after the operation. He would probably have a restricted movement on that leg," he stated matter-of-factly, almost off-handedly.

I didn't understand what that meant and wasn't sure I wanted to know. "When does this all take place?" I was thinking that I had a few weeks or a month to think things over, and maybe something would happen that would make everything go away, like a miracle.

"We should book him into the hospital right away." He looked at his calendar. "I could do the operation Thursday," he said, his pen poised, ready to make the appointment.

Beads of perspiration began to pop out of my forehead. "I have to think about this," I said, meekly. My heart rate increased along with my anxiety level. "This is something that will affect his life forever. It's not an easy thing to decide."

"There is no decision," the doctor said flatly. "You can't leave the leg like it is. He'll be crippled for life if you do."

"Unless he stays in traction for the duration," I offered lamely, looking at Larz, buying time to think.

The doctor closed the file briskly, upset with my indecisiveness. "I'll wait to hear from you. See you," he said to Larry, shaking his hand before leaving the room, avoiding my eyes. I was in shock, Larry and his mother simply sat huddled together in each others arms, crying, helplessly.

"I'm going to get another opinion," I offered to them after the doctor had left the room, hoping that this had all been a horrible mistake.

The next day we were at the County hospital, meeting with the head of the orthopedic department. He confirmed the fact that Larz did in fact have Legg Perthesis.

"How do you treat it?" I asked innocently, hoping he would say that you just take two aspirins a day and drink lots orange juice and get a bunch of rest.

"We recommend a combination of treatments to maximize the effectiveness of protecting the head of the femur," he said. Walking over to his Mr. Bones who hung in the corner from an iron coat-hanger affair. He pointed out the femur bone.

"We would do a hip rotation here," he said, using his pen to show where they would slice the hip, "then install a shim from the hip bone to maintain the tilted area. Then we rotate the femur bone by taking a wedge out right here," he said, drawing an imaginary line through the leg bone, "which tilts the femur further into the hip cavity, thus fully protecting the head of the femur bone."

"What happens if you just tilt the hip bone and not the other," I asked, now having a cursory knowledge of the hip rotation philosophy.

"That would still leave the femur exposed to damage. When the blood ceases flowing and the head dies, the bone becomes very soft and has no protection, you see," he said, looking at me as if I had an I.Q. of a fence post.

I thanked him and told him that I would have to talk the matter over with the family and that we would get back to him. We had now had two opinions and three approaches to the problem. I needed another opinion.

I talked to every medical person I could and came to the conclusion that the Children's Hospital at Stanford which was located in Palo Alto must have the best minds in the medical field. Surely, they would have the definitive answer. I made an appointment with the chief of the orthopedic clinic. They were booked solid. The following week was the soonest I could get in.

The Children's Hospital is a one-story, ground level building situated across from Stanford University. As we waited in the waiting room, I was shocked at all the little children that passed by with limbs missing, their hair gone or who had other physical deformities. What equally amazed me was the demeanor of the parents, most of whom were mothers, as the father's were probably working. They portrayed a picture of calmness that I couldn't fathom. I would later come to realize, through my own experience, that time and the sheer numbness of the experience, somehow affords one the protective shield that ones psyche needs to maintain ones sanity.

What really blew my mind was the cheerfulness that the children seemed to possess. It was as if they were normal! Didn't they know that they had cancer, leukemia, was missing an arm or had who knows what affliction? I would come to draw upon their inner strength through the coming months. A strength that only a child can have when his mind isn't cluttered with the rest of the world's perception of normalcy. To them, some of whom would not survive the year, normalcy was laughter and an association with other children who happen to be in the hospital at the same time. Their kind of children.

We met with the senior surgeon. He was a kindly, elderly gentleman who had the demeanor of a grandfather. My wife took an instant liking to him. I was guardedly pessimistic as I had to come to mistrust doctors who couldn't seem to agree on how to handle, what I thought was a major medical problem with my child.

The doctor looked at the X-rays that I had brought with me. He confirmed the fact that my son did indeed have Legg Perthesis. He tested his leg rotation, measured the length of each leg and put him through various stretching paces to test the mobility of the leg as well, taking several angle measurements with a plastic measuring device.

When he was finished, he preceded his comments with the fact that he performed several Legg Perthesis operations a year.

"What sort of operation is required?" I asked, bracing myself for what I had come to expect would be yet another approach to the same problem.

"We take a wedge out of the femur, thus rotating the head of the femur bone under the protective pocket of the hip," he said simply, making motions with his hands as he spoke.

"I've heard that some doctors rotate the hip," I said, authoritatively. "What's the difference between one procedure and the other?"

"Oh! If you have the hip rotation procedure you're just buying a stiff hip," he scoffed, realizing that I had a cursory knowledge of the problem.

"A stiff hip?"

"Guaranteed pain every step of your life," he said, emphatically. "And it'll get worst as he gets older. No," he shook his head, "that's one thing you don't want."

"What's the downside of the leg rotation?"

"We'll, to begin with, one side will be a little shorter than the other. When we take out the wedge, that automatically shortens the leg." He drew a picture of the femur which had about a ten to fifteen degree slant after the wedge was taken out.

"And this stays shorter for the rest of his life?" I asked in amazement, unable to understand how this could be acceptable.

"The growth area of the leg is located in the knee cap area," he said, stroking Larz' knee. "When the patient nears the end of his growth period, we scrape a portion of the good knee, thus slowing the growth of the good leg, allowing the shorter leg to catch up."

"Can you do that accurately?"

"We do it all the time, especially with polio victims. We compute it to the smallest fraction of a millimeter. The legs end up virtually the same length."

I breathed a sigh of relief. At last, a ray of hope at the end of the dismal tunnel. "Does the leg bone just grow back together and become just as strong?" I asked, visualizing a weak bone that could easily break under the strain of an active child.

"We put a pin in the leg with screws that secure both ends of the bone," he said, drawing a picture. "Then, once the femur has healed itself, we remove the pin."

"Doesn't that leave holes in the bone?"

"They heal nicely. Young people heal quickly and, as a rule, there are no after affects." He looked at me impatiently, hoping this was the last of the questions.

I left the children's hospital comforted yet confused. We had been to three doctors, all renowned orthopedic surgeons in their field, who had given us three conflicting approaches to the same disease. I deduced that two of the three opinions must be wrong and maybe even three out of three. It was now the parent's decision to decide what to do with their child's leg. A decision that could very well affect the outcome of his entire life. Needless to say, I felt very uncomfortable.

It was during this time that one of my partners was getting heavily involved with a group of psychic healers in the Philippines. They had heard about them from a local psychic who had been to the Philippines and had seen them perform miracles. The woman had been invited over to their house where she showed them movies of patients being healed without the benefit of surgery. They were fascinated and had subsequently taken numerous trips to the Philippines themselves, filming psychics literally putting their hands into people's bodies and pulling out things like tumors, cancer, bad viruses, poisonous life threatening infection, you name it.

I saw a film of a person I personally knew who claimed to have had a tumor removed from her breast. Another person had the psychic actually put his fingers in a man's eye and pull out some substance, at least that's the way it appeared on the film.

My partner borrowed my video camera and took it to the Philippines. I subsequently saw pictures that was actually taken with my camera! On a return trip, he had taken their father to the Philippines and had a cancerous tumor removed from his body, or so they said, and were now feeling great!

I was hooked! Healing without surgery! I was convinced that I should take my son to the Philippines and give the psychics a try. Anything was better than having his leg butchered and marked for life. My discussion to take him to the Philippines nearly caused an early divorce with my wife fighting me every step of the way. She was convinced that if anyone could do such a thing, they must be the devil's work and was subsequently evil themselves.

After a considerable heated disagreeable discussion, lasting several days, I finally relented, thrashing myself afterwards for not having a stronger constitution. In the end, I nearly took him to the Philippines without her consent, I felt so strongly about the topic. As far as I was concerned, my son's health was more important that marital acceptance.

Although I would have done most anything to save my son the pain of having the operation and subsequent disability, deep in my soul I too feared that anyone who had the powers to perform such feats of removing cancer and the like from a body by simply putting their hands *inside* a body was either endowed with magical powers or was pulling off one hell of a deception.

It was then that I was reminded of a documentary wherein this photographer visited India where it had been acclaimed that a man was able to make a rope rise out of a basket, and then climb it!

We've all heart that story. Right?

As it turned out, he did in fact witness the event while he was standing but a few feet from the event taking place before his very eyes. The man took the lid off the basket, a rope rose into the air whereupon the man climbed the rope! Fortunately, he had it all on video tape, because he knew no one would believe him when he retold the story.

When he arrived home he viewed the tape and was dumbfounded to see that the video recorded a basket with a rope neatly coiled within and a man standing next to it. Period! During the entire duration of the tape neither the man nor the rope moved, yet everyone, in their mind's eye, saw the rope rise and the man ascent the rope.

The answer? Some sort of group hypnosis.

My point being, there used to be a saying that went, "Don't believe anything you hear and only half of what you see." This story proves that you can't even believe everything you see! The psychics performed feats for my partner to video tape, but even that wasn't necessarily to be believed.

Perhaps they are evil, not godly. Was I willing to take that chance? It's amazing what goes through one's mind, how rational or irrational one can become.

In retrospect, I'm glad I didn't take the bait. My partner's father has since died. Other friends I knew who had gone to the Philippines for 'the treatment' have also since died from their medical afflictions. I've subsequently seem documentation on healers who have proven to be frauds, pulling chicken guts from under their hands, or out of cellophane, seemingly coming from a patient.

I read everything I could get my hands on regarding psychic powers and finally came to the conclusion that there is no definitive opinion on the topic. I do believe that there are powers that we neither understand nor can explain. If their powers are good or evil, I don't have a clue. I just know that I don't want to take the chance with my son's life or his soul.

The Operation

After much soul searching, it was decided that the operation would take place at Stanford Hospital, just minutes from the Children's Hospital. I'll never forget the day they wheeled Larry into the operating room. Laying on the gurney, he looked back at me just before they wheeled him through the double swinging doors. "Howard!" He said, his eyes desperately pleading for help. I smiled and said it would be all right, all the time feeling like a traitor.

The next two hours were the longest and worst two hours of my life. My mind conquered up visions of what could happen to him during the operation. What if the anesthesiologist screws up and gives him the wrong mix? I've read about accounts where the simplest of operations had gone wrong and the patient ended up being a cabbage head with the IQ of a stump, simply because the anesthesiologist fell asleep at the wheel. If anything happened to him, I wouldn't be able to live with myself.

When the operation was finally over and the doctor came out to meet with us, I silently thanked God. His words were the usual, "The operation went well. Your son will be delivered back to the Children's Hospital by ambulance. You can see him there."

We thanked him and I said another prayer as we silently walked out of the hospital, each in our own thoughts. It was during this period of time that things weren't going well between my wife and me. Even the trauma of the operation that our son had just endured didn't seem to bridge the gap that had come between us. I've often thought back on those days, wondering what went wrong and why. For the life of me, I can't come up with an answer.

Larry was lying in his bed when we arrived. The blood seemed to have drained from his face and he looked terrible. If I've ever seen the epitome of pain painted on ones face, this was it. He was just coming out of the anesthetic and was in so much pain that he dared not move. Even opening up his eyes or moving his lips seemed a gigantic painful effort.

The following two weeks were the longest two weeks of my life. We stayed in the hospital, by his side, twenty-four hours a day, until he was released. This was during a period of time when doctors didn't believe in fully medicating a patient to relieve his pain. After the operation when the general antiseptic wore off, he writhed in pain from the freshly cut flesh and bone, not to mention the holes that had been drilled into his leg to hold the clamp that held his cut leg bones together.

Tears rolled down his cheeks. He looked at me pleadingly saying, "Howard, it hurts!" I did my best to try to get him to be optimistic, smiling, looking back at him, masking the real feelings that I felt as I held his hand and his mother stroked his face. Words would come to have no effect in relieving the pain.

Somewhere in the distant past, when I was a child, when my mother used to take me to the dentist, I discovered that the after affect of Novocain was worse than the pain endured by drilling on raw nerves. At the age of twelve I decided to discontinue using any anesthetic and tough it out. After all, how long can it last, I rationalized? Ten to fifteen minutes? Surely I could endure a little pain for that short period of time.

I somehow taught myself to take the pain and transfer or convert it into heat. Whenever the dentist hits a nerve, which was most of the time, I simply felt warmth. Later, as an adult, when I had to have a root canal I thought I would try it out. The mere thought of having a root canal without an anesthetic shook the dentist up so much he actually rotor-rooted the wrong tooth! Just as I was looking at the tooth when I got home, the phone rang. It was the dentist.

"I've got some bad news," he said, nervously.

"I know. You did the wrong tooth," I replied coldly.

He was obviously concerned. "If you want, I'll refund your money and you can go to another dentist." There was a silence. "Or you can come back and I'll do the right tooth tomorrow. No charge."

I could read the fear of a law suit in his voice, but that simply wasn't my style. My regular dentist even called me to apologize and explain that accidents do happen. Apparently, he had called her as soon as he found out, pleading for assistance. The long and short of it was, I went back the next day and did it all over again.

"Doctor," the dentist's nurse whined as I made my self relax before he came in. "He won't take any pain killer!"

"It's all right," the dentist replied, inquiring if I was ready.

*****

Larry was given a pain pill every four hours, the effects of which lasted only three hours. That fourth hour I sat by his bed, holding his hand, whispering in his ear, "Think of something pleasant. Turn the pain into heat. Transform the pain. Don't let it get the best of you. Let your mind control the pain. Take my hand and transfer the pain to me."

He was in too much discomfort to even hear my words, although he did squeeze my hand, trying to transform some of it.

I finally succeed in instilling a certain degree of mind control in him, but the intense pain from having his leg bone having been literally cut in two with several pins screwed into it, would have been taxing for anyone. It finally got to the point that, after the third hour, I would slip him a pain pill that I had retrieved from home, to get him through to the next hour.

The worst time seemed to be when the nurse's aids came to change his sheets daily, with Larz still in the bed. They took care in flipping him around the bed as they made first one side then the other, but the pressure put on the leg was simply too much for him to tolerate.

I found myself getting upset at them but they simply explained that they had a job to do and they were doing it. Besides, they were the size of a small Mac truck and could have bounced me off the wall if I continued giving them a bad time. I finally got to the point that I had to leave the room until they were finished.

The first two weeks passed by slowly. There was nothing to do at the hospital but look at magazines and walk the corridors when Larry was sleeping. I figured, once he was over the initial period of recovery, it wasn't necessary for both of us to be there one hundred percent of the time, especially since we were at odds with at one another anyway. She agreed. She went home to do some chores.

It had been two weeks now since the operation and I had stayed in the hospital the whole time with the exception of going home periodically to feed Caesar, our Great Dane, with whom I had left a fifty pound bag of dry dog food for him to eat at his leisure.

It was Friday and I was wired from stress and lack of any physical release, so when I finished taking care of Caesar, I put my tennis racquet and gym clothes in the motor home and called my tennis partner-attorney, Steve, arranging to meet him later that afternoon for a game of tennis and much needed exercise.

When I returned to the hospital, my wife must have been psychic herself, because as soon as I walked into the hospital she left. A few moments later she was back, red-faced and angry. "What do you think you're going to do? Play tennis?" she spat.

"I thought ...."

"Our son is lying on the bed dying and all you can think of is yourself!"

One of her more enduring qualities was exaggeration. Once, when we were at a restaurant with the children, I inadvertently touched the waitresses hand while talking to her, emphasizing a point. When she left, my wife lit into me. "Next you'll be touching her cola (Spanish for one of her private parts)," she spat.

Anyway, to make a long confrontation short, she took the motor home which, of course contained my tennis stuff announcing that she wasn't planning on returning for the rest of the day, and may even not be back until tomorrow, leaving me, of course without any transpiration..

I, of course, had to call Steve, my tennis partner and apologize for canceling. I felt like a mouse whose tail was being held by some sadistic cat, playing with him until he decided to eat him. My partner knew that I was in the hospital with my son and Hot Flashes as I had come to refer to her probably knew all along that I wouldn't be making it to the courts. He knew my wife and had been aware of the brunt of her wrath before.

You may recall, one summer I had orchestrated a tennis tournament with my friends with swimming, burgers and bridge at my house after the tournament. I had provided the tennis balls, made arrangements for the courts to be reserved and had even supplied the trophies. The event was planned far enough in advance to accommodate everyone's schedule and everyone was looking forward to it.

The day of the tournament Hot Flashes got on one of her power trips and announced that all plans of having our friends over was off. Instead of telling her to take a flying leap at a rolling donut, I ate crow and meekly explained to my friends that the afternoon's activities were off. You can well imagine how I felt. Steve, my attorney and tennis partner never forgot that, but had the integrity not to bring it up.

You may ask yourself, why were you such a wimp? Why didn't you simply state, "Hey, I've planed the tournament and the party for the past month! If you don't like it - tough! Don't come!" In retrospect, I ask myself the same question, but I already know the answer. I was trying to soft peddle the situation and not make waves.

Is that being a wimp or what? No comment and put that tomato down!

******

Once we took Larry home, it was painful to see him limp around school on his crutches with a weak smile, while the rest of the boys played sports on the playground. The picture taken at his first communion, standing next to the church's alter, clearly indicates the disguised emotional and physical pain he felt at the time. It still tears my heart out when I look at that picture.

As he neared the end of his growth cycle, we had periodical, annual check-ups with the hospital to keep track of the leg's growth. He couldn't and still can't sit on the floor with his legs crossed Indian style, because of the way the leg was rotated into the hip. He'll be that way for the rest of his life.

When the time came, we returned to Stanford Children's Hospital to see about stunting the growth of the 'good' leg, to allow the other leg to catch up, thus making him walk normal as promised. At this time, one leg was clearly two inches shorter than the other and he was walking with a perceptual limp.

When the doctor didn't bring up the topic of scraping the growth cartilage of the good leg to retard its growth, I inquired about the procedure. "Oh, we don't do that anymore," was the casual comment. "It didn't prove feasible to continue doing that operation so we discontinued it."

Great!

In agreeing to do the leg operation, we relied on the doctor's representation that he would one day correct the deficiency between the two legs. Now, he's destined to not only go through life with the pain that that leg has from the added presser on the hip, but his spine is growing crooked and he has a limp to boot. Of course he can wear an elevated two inch shoe on one side! That will take care of the problem just fine, thank you!

I was angered beyond words. While the wife muttered niceties to the good doctor, I was seething like a boiling pot. My kid was scarred for life! Chalk up another point for the medical profession.

Even when a parent supposedly has all the facts at his disposal, especially when there is disagreement amongst the medical specialists on procedure, it's an awesome responsibility for a parent, a layman, to make a choice of not only which doctor to use but which procedure to let them use on your child. It's often a choice that will undoubtedly affect your child's life ... possibly forever. I certainly don't have a comfort zone when it comes to doctors anymore.

To this day, I still don't know if I made the right choice. If I had it to over, I might pick the choice of having the child suffer through the two years of lying in traction in bed, no matter how hard it was on everyone. I have spoken to patients who had the same disease as Larry as a child and who wore braces that kept their legs at a ninety degree angle for two years – an option that we had but readily dismissed out of hand. In hindsight I still don't know if that would be a consideration. At least now he'd have been in one piece and his legs would balance. The other day I asked Larry what he would have done had I decided to simply put him on crutches for the two year period.

Larry's response was that he would have cheated the moment I was out of sight and would have set them aside and acted like any healthy child, running and playing. So much for hind sight!The result of this experience has altered my opinion of doctor's, dramatically. When they say, "The breast must come off," they really mean, "If we don't remove the whole breast to get that small lump, the cancer might spread and come back to haunt us. Then, we'd get sued, and we can't have that because our insurance premiums would go up. You understand. So off with the breast! What the heck, lets get the muscle tissue while we're at it!"

Now, years after the operation, he's a young man, and he still walks with a perceptual limp. One day, the femur head which is now out of round because the leg operation didn't fully protect the head during that two year period, will wear out and he'll have to have another operation to replace that part of his anatomy.

Another operation. Something to look forward to. I only hope to hell they have a suitable femur substitute by that time!

When Larry questioned why this happened to him, I can only offer the lame comment that there is a reason for everything. We usually don't understand why things happen to us. Perhaps it's to help us grow spiritually. Maybe it's meant to be a lesson for someone else made at your expense, or maybe we're being aided in our spiritual growth to a higher understanding of ourselves that can only be achieved through pain and suffering.

Again?

As if I were walking under a dark cloud, Larry's experience wasn't to be my last. Aaron was born with what is now known as Hyaline Membrane disease that caused him to spend the first days of his life in an incubator. His lungs weren't strong enough and he had to be watched carefully, 24-7. I felt so helpless standing on the other side of the glass, which was as close as they would allow us to be, watching our new son helplessly lay there at God's mercy. Every ounce of spirit that was within my power went out to that little boy. I cried more than once as I stood there with my eyes transfixed on his little body, fighting for every breath of air.

God spared him, but he would grow up with a weakened respiratory condition that to this day would bother him, especially in the spring when the air is filled with fresh cut grass and the trees fill the air with pollen. This particular day he had a head splitting ear ache, I thought probably exacerbated by his sensitivity to pollen in the air. I took him to the Alexian Brothers Hospital emergency room. Our pediatrician's office was just across the street and fortunately, one of the doctors from that office was on call that evening. He wasn't our doctor, but was a partner in the firm, so I had no hesitation in his treating Aaron.

That was all about to change.

It was after hours and Dr. S. who had been home on call entered the room briskly, as if his bowl movement had just been interrupted and he wanted to see the offending party. I thanked him graciously for coming and then explained that my son had a splitting ear ache and needed his attention. He removed a pen light from his lapel and jerked on the offending ear as it to punish it.

It's appropriate at this juncture to point out that Aaron is a trouper and even if his ear was killing him, he kept a stiff upper lip and tried his best not to let it show.

"He's got a boil and it has to be lanced," he said to no one in particular.

Aaron looked at me with fear in his eyes and I winked at him, letting him know that lancing a boil was no big deal. At this point the doctor ordered the orderly to prepare a solution of Novocain to deaden the spot where he was going to lance the boil.

Again he jerked on Aaron's ear which made Aaron scream in pain. All this time I was holding his little hand.

When he screamed the doctor let go of his ear, but not before giving it an angry final jerk, causing Aaron to scream out in pain again.

"Strap him to the board!" the doctor shouted to the assistant.

The assistant brought out a flat board that had been equipped with straps to hold a child's arms and legs. Fear shot through Aaron's eyes and he gripped my arm for protection.

"That won't be necessary," I said, looking sternly at the doctor who, by now I was beginning to lose all of my respect. "I'll hold him for you." I looked into Aaron's eyes with what I hoped would be a reassuring look that I wasn't going to let them strap him down like a common criminal.

"He's going to be strapped!" Dr. S. replied, stoically.

"No, he isn't," I replied, and stood up as if I were going to beat the living tar out of him.

"Fine! I'll get someone else!" he said and departed the room with all haste.

"He's an asshole," the assistant confided when he had left. "You did the right thing."

A moment later another physician entered the room holding the hypodermic needle with one hand and the chart with another. I could tell by his demeanor that he had been sufficiently prepped by Dr. S. as having an uncooperative patient.

Without saying a word, he went to Aaron's ear, grabbed the ear lobe and jammed the needle into it.

By this time Aaron was totally psyched out and fear and mistrust emanated from every pour of his body. The moment that the physician jammed the needle through Aaron's ear, and shot the Novocain, the drug came through the other side, into thin air. I had had enough. I shoved him against the wall, looking him in the eyes with all the hatred that I could muster. "Don't you touch my kid again!" I said through clinched teeth.

Meanwhile the assistant stood in the corner of the room, not knowing what to do.

The physician quickly left the room and the assistant patted me on the back. "Good for you," he said.

About that time a police officer came into the room with his hand on his revolver. I guess he was expecting a serial killer. What he saw was a father holding his sobbing son with the assistant's arm on my shoulder.

"Let's get out of here!" I said to Aaron while the assistant explained what had just transpired to the cop.

We were in the parking lot when the assistant ran up to me with a packet in his hand. "Take these," he said, handing me the packet. "They're pain pills. They'll hold you until you get to a real doctor."

I thanked him and drove out of the parking lot.

The post script to the story is that the following day I got a call from our pediatrician and was informed that our business was no longer welcomed at this office. Dr. S. had apparently blackballed us.

I immediately went down to our doctor's office where I was greeted with a waiting room filled with sick kids and requested a meeting with our pediatrician. Forty-five minutes later I was led into his office. Without waiting for an explanation I launched into a detailed description of the previous night's activities. When I was finished presenting my case I was sure that I had won him over, but his response was that he and his partner, Dr. S. had an agreement that, if anyone was unacceptable by either one of them, that that had to be honored by both parties.

Again I launched into a dissertation about how great of a doctor we all thought he was and that we wanted only him to attend to our children's needs, and why should they be punished for some stupid act that his partner had performed?

The conversation went on for fifteen minutes more. In the end I prevailed with the understanding that under no circumstances should or would Dr. S. ever treat or touch one of my children again. Six months later, Dr. S. was dead of a heart attack.

There is a God after all.

BOOK TWO
Life takes on a dramatic turn

A Little Background

Ever since I can remember, I've been sports minded. I started playing tennis when I was in the fifth grade and played organized sports a soon as I was eligible. Also, ever since I can remember, I've been an independent soul, working since I was in the fifth grade, providing my own way and making decisions regarding the direction my life was going to take. That all changed when I went into the army. There, the army was like one giant mother, telling me what to do and when to do it, taking care of my every need. Like jail, it's easy to understand why people have a hard time adjusting to civilian life once they are released.

Once I had been released from the army and entered graduate school, there was no time for sports. I was consumed with the day to day survival and obsessed with reaching my goal of becoming a psychologist. Then I fell into real estate, got married, had children and bought a house. Still no time for anything except for work, family and just plain survival.

Once I reached the point in my life of getting some breathing room, I had three boys, a mortgage, our beauty shop with sixteen girls working for us and had started my own real estate company. I needed a release from the stress of work and sports was the answer.

I had an occasion to need legal advice from time to time, owning apartments and all. This particular time, I had a tenant that was tearing up one of my apartment units and wasn't paying rent. I went to this law firm that had been referred to me for legal advice. After telling the receptionist what my problem was, she referred me to their newest member of the firm. "Just go down the hall. It's the last room to the left," she said.

I followed her directions and found myself knocking on a door without a name. When no one answered I opened the door and stuck my head inside. There, sitting behind a desk with his feet up on the desk, smoking a pipe with a Sherlock Holms hat on, playing chess with himself was Steve, the guy who was not only going to represent me, but would become one of my best friends.

He was ten years younger than I, but after getting to know one another, we realized that we both had similar likes. He liked to play basketball and tennis as did I. We eventually fell into a routine of playing tennis on Friday afternoons and meeting at his office at least once a week to play chess over lunch which consisted of eating a sandwich and having a can of soda I enjoyed the break in my usual hectic routine and the change of pace plus the challenge that Steve offered was refreshing.

Life was good.

Except for one thing. Well, actually two.

Ever since I met Steve and found a soul mate in the form of an intellectual friend and spots partner, I noticed a subtle change had come over my wife. In a word, she didn't like the fact that I had found someone else that I enjoyed spending time with, albeit, once or twice a week for an hour or so each time.

Then the unthinkable happened, one of her nephews asked me out one Tuesday evening to play basketball with him. Seems that they had a team and were going to be one short that evening and he asked it I played basketball to which I replied, "Do bears go potty in the woods?"

I have always loved basketball and love the competition, not to mention the exercise which is not only good for the body, but clears the stress of the business day out of my head as well. I was getting back in shape and feeling good. Now I was playing tennis for an hour or so on Friday afternoons, and basketball for an hour or so on Tuesday evenings.

I noticed every time that I returned home with set of workout cloths, my hair wet and my face flushed, that my wife gave me the cold shoulder. In other words, she wasn't talking to me. I would sidle up next to her and slip my arm around her shoulder and ask what was wrong. Her answer was a sharp punch in the ribs with a, "Don't talk to me, you cheater!"

Whenever I came home the kids always seem to be around me, wanting a hug and inquiring about me day, so I tried to make it a point to never discuss negative family issues in front of them. I followed her into the next room and ask her to explain herself.

"If you're not with me when you're out having fun," she responded sharply, "you're cheating on me."

"I was playing basketball with your nephew!"

"Same thing!"

So I quickly learned that from her point of view, any activity that I did was off limits as far as she was concerned. "Even when I have a business lunch with my attorney in his office and we play a game of chess?" I asked.

"Same thing!"

"So let me get this straight. You don't want me playing tennis or having lunch with Steve or playing basketball with your nephew? Is that about it?"

Her answer was an icy stare.

"What about when you go out to lunch with one of your ladies? Is that the same, too?"

"That's different."

"And when you take grandma and your sister to Lake Tahoe for three or four days? What does that mean, not that I give a rip."

"That's family."

"At this stage of the game I should mention that from time to time my father gets himself into a pickle, let's say, up in Longview Washington, and everyone once in a while I get a telephone call from my mother asking if I would come up and go out and find him and bring him home. By this time, he may have been missing for over a week. When my mother would tell me this, I would tell her that I would be on the next plane to Portland. I would hang up and then call Alaska Airlines and make reservations for the following morning and then go upstairs to inform my wife that I would be going to Longview on a family emergency.

On this particular occasion she flatly said that I couldn't go and I informed her that I had already made reservations and would be leaving first thing in the morning. "Well, you be back by nightfall," she demanded.

"I'm not going down the block. I'm going to Washington! I'll be back in two days."

She stomped off and I spent the night on the couch.

The next morning I flew into Portland where my brother, Larry, picked me up and drove me to Longview, where we found dad in a local tavern having a good time with his buddies. The moment I walked in, he grabbed me around the shoulder and introduced me to his buddies. "Have a beer!" he said.

"No thanks. Come on, pop's. We're going home."

We got him safely tucked into bed where he slept for two days straight. Mom thanked me profusely and I left home the following day as scheduled. On the way home the airplane encountered a mechanical problem and the pilot informed us that we would be landing in San Francisco instead of San Jose.

Once we were on the ground I called my wife, informing her that the plane had had difficulties and that I was in San Francisco and that she needed to come and pick me up. With an icy tone, she said, "Get yourself home," and hung up.

We didn't speak for a week after that.

Things only got worse. After a while, she moved out of the master bedroom and for the next seven years encased herself in the guest room down at the end of the hall where the only time she emerged was to eat or go to the bathroom.

Who cooked and cleaned?

When we bought the house on Miguelita, the first thing she did was have her brother find a Mexican live-in housekeeper. One day when I returned home for work, there she was. Our new live-in housekeeper, cook and bottle washer had already moved in. I had not been advised that we were even considering such a move, let alone having already hired someone, sight unseen. I protested vehemently, all to no avail.

Her name was Bertha and I was informed that she was here to stray, like it or not.

Life was not pleasant in the Losness household. Those few times that my wife would speak to me, it was with a triple fortissimo tone. In other words, she screamed. That was the way her family communicated. The rule was, whoever screamed the longest and loudest won the argument. And they carried a grudge forever. I recall going to church one Sunday. There was our family and her niece sitting in our pew. The niece said something that irritated my wife and they started an argument right there in church. That little disagreement, what ever it was, lasted four years with one not speaking to the other.

Contrast that to the way that we were brought up. As children we didn't talk back to our parents and never fought amongst ourselves. I can say without fear of contradiction that in our adult years neither my brother nor my sister has spoken to another in harsh tones. And that goes for their families and their children's families as well. When my kids grew up, they never fight with one another, either. It's gotta be in the genes.

Myself and my wife were just cut from different pieces of cloth. In retrospect, we never should have gotten married. I was a Protestant, she was a Catholic. I was a Norwegian, she was Mexican. I spoke English, her family spoke Spanish. I was tall. She was short. I was educated, she was not. I was even tempered, she was hot tempered. Bla bla bla. The only positive outcome of our union was our three boys, Larry, Aaron and Christian.

As a last resort, we agreed to try marriage counseling. Being Catholic, my wife insisted that we attend a counselor of her faith. That was fine with me. Any port in the storm. She found such an animal in Los Altos, a guy by the name of Neery. Having had several years of professional training in the field of psychology, and having a profound respect for the complex workings of the mind, I had hopes that a skilled psychologist would be able extract the unhealthy elements from our marriage like an abscessed tooth, and give us an injection against further blight. He or she would then pat us on our butts, and send us on our way, walking hand in hand, smiling into the sunset, children in tow.

Boy, was I in for a surprise!

The very first words out of out the mouth of our esteemed family counselor, a member of the cloth, I might mention, chosen by my wife was, "In many cases, couples such as yourselves come to counseling only to have their marriage end up in divorce. Don't be too optimistic!"

I thought to myself, what kind of pessimistic talk is this? Divorce has never been a consideration as far as I was concerned. To get divorced was an announcement to the world that we are a complete and utter failure, incapable of holding a family together, the simplest of tasks.

Up to this point, no one in the history of our family had ever failed at their marriages to the degree that they've had to resort to divorce. And, I wasn't about to be the first. The counselor lost ten points right off the bat. He was about to lose a lot more.

In the beginning, we drove to the monastery together, a distance of approximately thirty miles from our home. That scenario eventually deteriorated to the point where we'd take separate cars to the therapist's office. At first it was designed that way. One or the other of us would find an excuse not to be available to go with the other due to appointments, shopping or what ever lame excuse there was. As time went on, we just weren't talking, so it didn't matter. Somehow we would find our own way to the therapist's office, and at the appointed hour, would enter the room, sit in our self assigned seats and start the game that I came to label as, 'Statue'.

Every session was the same. The counselor would enter the room and ask how things went the preceding week. Before I could say anything, my wife would start by spewing all the venom of hatred that had apparently been laying dormant, festering in her soul over the years. Years before I ever knew her, it soon became apparent. When the hour was over, the counselor, who had been silent except for an intermittent brilliant interjection such as, "So you were unhappy because he spent his lunch hour playing chess with his lawyer?" to which she will emphatically say, "Yes", stating that such behavior was considered cheating, or "You were angry with him because he invited his friends over for a swim after playing tennis?" to which she would affirm his question, same reason.

"And I suppose he expected you to do all the cooking and cleaning up as well?"

"Of course!"

Before I could raise my hand to defend myself to his false allegations, she was off to the races, continuing on with the game of Statue.When the session was over he'd say, "Well, we'll see you again next Thursday. I'd pay him a hundred and twenty dollars and we'd leave. I don't know how she felt when we left. Perhaps she continued being angry, or maybe she felt satisfied, because she had been allowed to vent her anger without rebuke. All I know is that I felt drained from spending an hour of being shit on, and being angry at the counselor for letting it happen, and anger at myself for standing for it. On the flip side of things, I rationalized that the well would run dry sometime in the future and we'd go on to more constructive matters.

After two years, the bottom was still not in sight.

To amplify matters, during this 'statue' session, for which I was paying a hundred and twenty dollars an hour, the counselor, in his infinite wisdom, choose not to interrupt her tirade, nor ask for my side of the story, choosing instead to let the constant stream of diarrhea flow, reinforcing the procedure.

At the end of two years, my philosophy had tuned from, "Nothing is going to defeat me and under no circumstances am I going to allow the thought of divorce enter my mind", to "There is obviously so much hatred in this woman and I've been buried with her diarrhea so deep, I just didn't give a damn anymore." In the end, it came to a point that any positive feelings that I had for her were buried so deep that they couldn't find their way to the surface even if they wanted to.

We now had what the experts call a dead marriage. Actually, it was dead before we started playing 'statue' - I just didn't know it, or was unwilling to admit it. Now, there was nothing left but the children.

The children?

Throughout the two years of playing 'statue', I don't seem to recall how they had reacted to the change in the family. It had been seven years since she moved out of the master bedroom and into her own private world, staying there sometimes for days on end, emerging only to go to the bathroom or eat, and then retreat back behind locked doors where Mexican music shook the walls.

The kids must have taken notice of the fact that the hostility had picked up dramatically, or at the very least, had observed that there was less if not no communication between their parents. I made a real conscious effort to try not to have any arguments when they were within earshot. The oldest son, Larry, twelve at that time, asked why we didn't sleep together anymore. I think he was trying to tell me that if we shared a common bedroom everything would be all right. I don't recall what my answer was, but whatever it was, I'm certain it was less than satisfactory.

By the time each session was over, she was riding on an emotional high from sticking it to me and I was so angry for allowing it to happen that neither one of us spoke to the other for days afterwards. It finally got to the point that I wanted to stay as far away from her as I could.

I buried myself in my work and sports. At this stage of the game I didn't really give a damn if she approved of my playing tennis, racquetball or basketball. I did it to maintain what little sanity remained.

This one particular day, after a particular brutal counseling session, I drove over to an office where I had made an appointment with this builder to sell a 237 unit apartment complex that he was in the process of constructing in the city of Visalia, California. We were to drive over to the complex, take pictures, inspect the construction which by now was 90% finished and just generally view the site. When I got to his office, he was still in a meeting with the mayor of Los Altos, so I cooled my heals in the waiting room. The only other person there was his personal secretary, who I had met a time or two before. She had an infectious smile, laughed easily and was great to talk to. We chatted for a while and through a telephone call that she took while I was there, I learned that she was going through a nasty divorce. We shared stories and soon became friends. Little did I know at the time that she was to become my next wife.

"SURPRISE!"

It had been a long hot day, driving back from Sacramento where the summer's temperature had soared to 105 degrees in the shade, resulting in an instant sweat the moment the door of my air conditioned car was opened. As I parked under the only tree I could find, I swear I saw a pair of Mourning Doves frying an egg on the sidewalk.

I had driven to Sacramento to examine the physical premises of a shopping center that our (David Hofmann, Phil Steinbock and I) partnership had just acquired. I wore blue jeans and a light shirt. Little did I know that the heat generated from the flat roof top of the building would be hot enough to burn the enamel off a car, let alone the soles of my shoes. Perspiration rolled down the sides of my face and down the small of my back. Within moments I was drenched.

To add to the unbearable heat of the day, commuter traffic in the early morning can be enough to make a man tear out what remains of his hair. I needed all the strands I had, so I decided to leave later in the morning to avoid both pitfalls. The four hours it took to drive to Sacramento and back coupled with a three hour tour of the complex, talking to tenants and inspecting the building brought me home well after dark.

Tired and glad to be home, I pulled into the darkened driveway, closing the electronic eight-foot wrought-iron gate behind me. Although we lived outside of the city limits where the street lights are

193

all but non-existent. I instantly felt uneasy. Not only were the grounds of our house totally dark, but the house itself was pitch black. When night falls and darkness envelopes the lush landscaped, heavily treed grounds, the premises takes on an eerie presence, even for a healthy male.

Adding to my discomfort was the lack of presence of our Great Dane, Caesar, who always bounded up to great me like a full grown, fawn-colored deer. We leave him to guard the premises when no one is home. Always! Tonight, there is no greeting. No Caesar. Something was definitely amiss.

After a quick check around the house, the anxious, quickened pulse resumes its normal cadence, realizing that the family must be visiting the in-laws. Perhaps Caesar escaped through the slow closing gate when they departed, and is exploring the neighborhood, one of his favorite pastimes. Considering his size, he's been known to lope down the hill, covering miles in a matter of minutes. I'm always amazed how far I have to drive when a stranger calls, telling me that they have our dog. His ID tags have saved his bacon from the pound more than once.

I assumed that the little woman had taken the house apes to visit her mother, so I adjourn to the office which was located downstairs and outside the main house near the pool. There is the day's clean-up paper work to be done while I check the phone messages and thumb through the mail. The quiet time is welcomed, although a quick hug from the kids and a bark from the dog or the wife would have been welcomed. Even Caesar's large feet on my chest would have been comforting. I still had an uneasy feeling as I entered my office, locking the sturdy glass door that led from my office to the outside pool deck behind me.

Consumed by paper work, an unexpected knock on the glass door disturbed my concentration. Looking up, the face of a strange unshaven youth peering at me out the darkness startled me. He was dressed in a plaid hunting jacket, dirty baggy blue jeans and a red baseball cap and was rapping impatiently on the glass door.

My first reaction was fear. I'd heard of robberies and murders happening to country folk, out of hearing range of their neighbors, and here I was, about to become a member of that elite statistic! Knowing that the iron entry gate as well as the electronic gate had been closed and locked, I hesitate rising to meet this stranger who had obviously intruded upon my premises.

Instinctively, I looked for a weapon. Not seeing one, I momentarily felt a little more at ease. At least my knees have stopped knocking. Sizing him up, a thing most males seem to do when sensing a potential confrontation, I deduced that not only was I bigger than he, but I'm familiar with the darkened grounds. If push came to shove, I figured I could get the upper hand. At any rate, he was on my property and his presence needed dealing with.

I slid the glass door open, attempting to fix a look of indignation on the intruder. I sharply inquired, "Are you lost?"

He ignored my caustic tone by asking a question of his own. "Mr. Losness? Howard Losness?"

"Yes," I responded confidently.

"These legal documents are for you," he said, holding out a packet of papers for me to take. "Don't worry, just see your attorney and I'm sure you'll be all right," he offered with a consoling voice, then quickly departed. His words were designed to temporarily catch me off guard so that he isn't beaten to a pulp before I have an opportunity to read the summons. This gives him a chance to retreat to a waiting getaway car, not unlike a Bonnie and Clyde bank robbery.

I recall thinking that here was a young person, probably no more than twenty to twenty- two years old, probably uneducated, certainly in the matter of law, giving me legal advice. Brazen, I thought to myself.

"I wish Caesar was here," I said aloud. Not only would this person not have gotten on the grounds, but when faced with the Great Dane, just encountering his size and vicious bark would have lightened his load five pounds, turning his hair pure white and converting a slow man into an instant world class sprinter, not to mention a high jumper. But, alas, no Caesar.

I followed him up the driveway, trailing a few paces behind just to be safe. I was astonished to see the electronic iron gate was open. I knew I had closed it when I drove in, yet there it was, wide open! As the boy-man drove off with his passenger, I saw a lone figure dart down the darkened road. Cautiously, I approached the gate, closing it with the manual key located on the side of the electric panel. After standing there quietly, listening for a few moments, I made my way slowly back to the office, momentarily disregarding the legal envelope that I held in my hand.

Being a general partner of several limited partnerships, I was not totally unaccustomed to receiving law suits from time to time from disgruntled tenants, vendors or injured parties looking for deep pockets to fill their bank accounts after a purported slip and fall or whatever. Expecting to find a copy of someone's law suit that had been injured on one of the properties, or a tenant serving legal notice to vacate, I was shocked into oblivion as I read the heading, IN THE SUPERIOR COURT OF CALIFORNIA.

Superior Court! *This is heavy duty stuff,* I thought. Certainly, no small claim complaint. I almost fell off my chair when I saw that it was my wife who was the plaintiff and myself as the defendant.

I was being sued for divorce!

I couldn't believe my eyes. I reread the complaint. Not only was my wife of fifteen years canning my ass from the status of husband, but she was kicking me out of my own kingdom on top of it. To top it all, the complaint alleged that I was a physical threat to her well being. Me! The world's greatest proponent to pacifism.

I was instructed to leave the premises within twenty-four hours and not return nor come within a thousand feet of the property, or I'd be in violation of the court order. Additionally, I'm to take nothing from the house. No clothes, no personal property, no business equipment.

Nothing!

Just go!

It didn't say anything about locking up or feeding the dog, wherever he was.

Under the circumstances, her timing couldn't have been better! Just this last weekend I had finished laboring night and day, with the help of my seventy year old father, adding two-thousand-seven-hundred square feet to our little grass shack in the form of three bedrooms on the second level -- one for each son, plus a large bathroom designed and built just for them. The added lower level was to be my office, a family recreation room and a specially built meditation room that I had designed that was to contain an interior strained glass wall and sound proofing.

The last nail had been nailed and the paint was still tacky. My father had returned to rest his weary bones at his home in Washington and put his feet in some well deserved hot water and nurse his blisters - God bless him.

As I said, her timing was perfect. A week earlier and the carpet wouldn't have been installed and the kid's bedroom furniture wouldn't have been delivered.

Unable to think clearly, I sat at my desk staring blankly into the night, stunned, oblivious to the crickets chirping to the beat of a bull frog in the creek below. The night was suddenly still and I felt alone. Very alone.

In time, I came out of the fog. It occurred to me that I had better re-check the house. Thoughts of everyone being done in by the night stalker, or even Hot Flashes as she had become known, crossed my mind.

Cautiously, I walked from room to room, turning on lights. When I was satisfied that the room was safe, I turned them off again and went on into the next room. Old habits are hard to break. I half expected to be jumped by a mad slasher any moment. In the end, no one was home. The house was quiet as a morgue. An air of doom seemed to hang in the air like San Francisco fog. I didn't like the feel of it. I didn't like it at all.

After the first wave of numbness wore off, which was about two hours after my final tour of the house, a slow mounting rage started to emanate from within the bowls of my body, making its way to the top of Mount St. Helens.

How dare anyone try to evict me from my own home! The mere fact that I was not given the time nor consideration to respond to the eviction, or even plead my case for what ever reason caused this drastic action, infuriated me.

The first response was to rush back into the house in a fit of rage looking for retaliation on some inanimate object. I went back to 'her room', hoping to find her there. Logic had temporarily left its place in the brain.

The room where she had resided since she had moved out of the master bedroom seven years ago, was, of course empty. As I stood there staring at the room's contents, there was the feeling that she would return at any moment. The bed was made, her private stereo and television set were all in place as were all of her little nick-knacks and pictures that she had placed on the book case. Mine not being amongst them, of course. A quick check in the closet affirmed the fact that she had left everything, as if expecting to return momentarily. A slow feeling of sadness crept into my consciousness as I realized that an era of family relationship had been shattered like the Jewish wine glass under the heavy foot of a groom, cementing the moment and their lives, forever.

We've all seen the movie where the man rushes into a woman's bedroom, scorned, throwing everything to the floor with a sweep of his arm across the vanity dresser, clearing the surface of its contents. Lamps are smashed and the bed thrown into a heap in the corner along with her cloths. Maybe the cloths are even slashed just to put an exclamation point on the act. Having spent his energy and frustration, the actor departs, leaving the viewer with the feeling that, even though he has taken his revenge on her things, his anger and frustration have not been satisfied.

Having played this scene in my mind, I turn off the light and quietly shut the door, as if not wanting to disturb a sleeping person.

A short revisit of the children's rooms reaffirms that their area is as it always was: beds unmade, shoes and socks strewn about the floor along with jeans, shirts and baseball mitts.

"Baseball mitts!" I said aloud.

The kids wouldn't knowingly go anywhere for more than fifteen minutes without their baseball mitts! That would be like going to Pizza Time Theater without quarters for video games, or going more than fifteen minutes without raiding the fridge. They even took their mitts to the bathroom when they took a bath, laying them next to the tub. You never know when a stray ball might fly by.

A picture begins to jell in my brain. She left the house, thinking it was just a temporarily thing, as the summons clearly states, *"Be out of the house within twenty-four hours"*. That's tomorrow night! Of course when one forcefully leaves, it's expected that one will never darken the doors again. The privilege of paying the mortgage payments, taxes and insurance, utilities, medical and dental bills, food, clothing, gas and repairs, ad nauseam will be retained by the evicted one, of course.

Of course!

The one thing she didn't take into account was the fact that she's dealing with the most passive-aggressive bastard this side of the Mason-Dixon line. If the Army couldn't break me - and God know they tried, - some half-baked attorney sure as hell isn't going to.

Move out in twenty-four hours? Not a chance Charlie. NOT - A - CHANCE! A man is the king of his castle and I'll be damned if some flimsy piece of paper is going to make me move out in twenty-four hours, court decree or not. The vision of being dragged out by a squad of policemen, kicking, scratching and swearing every inch of the way as well as being incarcerated for violation of a court order flashed through my mind.

This husband, or used-to-be as the case seems to be, is going to bend the rules and no woman going through the change of life whose only excitement is an array of hot flashes, unlike the northern lights of Alaska, is going to get the pleasure of seeing me leave with my tail between my legs.

Once again, I walk out into the night, under the blanket of stars. They seem to dwarf my problem, yet, tonight it doesn't matter how small or insignificant one is in the universe, this problem is real and it's mine. Nothing can minimize that.

The only sound to be heard, aside from the constant beat of my heart, are the frogs and crickets, the sound of night that I've come to love. Now, apparently that tranquil, peaceful beat will be exchanged for squealing tires going around busy corners, TV's, stereo and fights from the apartment next door and dogs barking in the night.

Standing in the darkness, my eyes strain towards the road, searching to see the person who I know is out there, hiding somewhere under the cover of night, watching my every move. *She wants to see my reaction, my expression, to gloat over the pain - her victory*, I thought.

You know the one I mean. The one who wants to make my life miserable. The one who will eventually give all the money it took fifteen years to earn, to the lawyers, the blood suckers of our society, the sharks of mankind.

She's out there somewhere. Probably hiding next to the fence, just outside the gate, teeth glowing in the dark, grinning from ear to ear, eyes blazing with delight.

"Gottch ya'!" She's saying to herself. "Suffer!"

One can almost hear her chuckle and see the glow in her eyes. If the crickets and frogs would take a break, one could probably hear her blood rushing through her veins to the beat of her course whispering voice. "Suffer king. Suffer. You're kingdom is now mine. Be gone with thee knave! Darken my doors no more. The mote will be filled with poisonous reptiles and the bridge drawn in your absence. I will see to it that your children will know you no more. Your dog will bite at your heals. Your name will be spoken only in vein. I will see to it that everyone will come to despise you and the ground upon which you tread."

The laughter subsides and the night becomes quiet again, save the frog and cricket concert.

The stars suddenly seem to have lost their luster and the sounds of night falls on deaf ears. Moss has begun to form on Camelot and the walls are crumbling. The king makes his way back to his chambers, looking through misty eyes. He will spend a restless night dealing with dreams gone by and wonder of the unknown path that lies ahead.

"Gottcha"

Fortunately, Nature in her infinite wisdom was good enough to start the next day with a splash of warm sunshine that seemed to somehow minimize the problems of the previous night. Fortunately, my mind has been programmed to work while I sleep, allowing itself to work through the previous day's problems uninterrupted by nonsensical external distractions such at the radio, television, traffic, telephones, screaming kids, barking dogs, etc.

Awaked somewhat rested, with the feeling of helpless despair softened through the night, the decision has been made not to jump from the bridge today - maybe tomorrow. Who knows, this revolution of events may even end up being a blessing in disguise. The last seven of our sixteen years had been anything but marital bliss.

This being Saturday, there wasn't much to be done in the way of seeking legal advice, which is the first thing that enters one's mind after being served and re-reading the complaint several times. A lawyer's job will be to advise me of my "rights" (excuse the word which will become known as the pun of all time).

A few well placed calls from friends who are attorneys, but not divorce lawyers (they seem to run in a pack of their own) are in order. The advice is, "get the best damn lawyer money can buy, because you're going to need him". One friend gave me a list of the best attorney's in town as well as the most expensive, advising that I interview each one

- thus taking them off the availability list as a future opponent. After a moments consideration, I thought better of the idea. Posturing just isn't of any interest at this point. Besides, she obviously already had a mouthpiece. His name was boldly printed on the complaint.

I recalled one of my business acquaintances who had gone through a messy divorce that had been dragged through the courts for years. I called on him for advice. I figured the best advice would be gained from one who had already run the gauntlet. He, of all people, would surely point me in the right direction.

"Come on over and have a cup of coffee," he offered with what sounded like a sinister chuckle. Actually, when I arrived I noticed his eyes were little vacant. Something I hadn't previously noticed. Sad. Yes, they were sad too.

Three cups of coffee and a pack of cigarettes later, I neither drink coffee nor smoke - I drove home with my mind in a fog thicker than ground level at the Golden Gate Bridge. He had showed me a memorialized file which occupied a special place set high in a corner behind his desk, right next to a pair of notched dueling pistols. The file, specially bound in red covering, was more than eighteen inches thick!

"This little baby," he said patting the file with his left hand with a perceptual nervous twitch of his right eye, "cost me in excess of one hundred thirty thousand dollars, and a good share of my sanity." The free hand seemed to automatically reach for one of the pistols as he spoke, but was automatically stopped by the other hand without the owner missing a word of his story.

The nervous tick persisted until he placed the file away out of sight. The experience was obviously painful as he spoke. I admired him for pulling up his socks and walking into the sun again. He had a thriving real estate business, and seemed to have recuperated splendidly, with the exception of that pesky nervous tick over the right eye that seemed to dominate his face every time he came near 'the file'.

Seeing how the experience had obviously changed this man, I vowed to be smarter than he. No woman was going to strip me of all my hard earned money, my share of the assets and certainly not my sanity nor health. I knew I would have to hire an attorney and was prepared to spend maybe five or ten thousand dollars, and that would be under protest.

As I pulled into our driveway - or should I now say 'her' driveway, I instinctively looked for her car, thinking she would have returned to reclaim the house. I had been gone for a while and I'm sure someone was watching the house, so it would naturally follow that when I left, she would have thought that I had abandoned the premises as instructed.

I was pleasantly surprised. No one was home.

I wandered back down to my office, overlooking the pool and the creek. After a few moments of staring blankly into space, I took a deep breath, picked up the telephone and dialed my parents, two states away. It was a call that I dreaded making. The word "divorce" was one word that didn't exist in our family. When I explained what had happened as best I could, they were as shocked as I. They offered to fly down immediately, to help me move they said, but I knew it was for moral support.

"I think I'll be O.K. for a while," I lied, not wanting to add to their burden. "I need to be alone for a while and figure out what to do next."

That old feeling of being totally alone started to give me that golf ball feeling my stomach again. I re-read the legal complaint one more time, then re-read it once again, getting angrier with the passage of each line.

At this stage of my life I have to admit that I'm not too fond of authority, especially someone *telling* me to do something that is contrary to my interest, let alone my welfare, especially when that person or entity automatically assumes a position of authority over my future.

The one and only real employer that I had in my adult life was the United States Army, and as you might recall, that was under protest.

All this is to say that I ain't movin' in twenty-four hours for nobody! Her shark and the court order be damned! I stayed on the premises Saturday, Sunday, Monday, Tuesday, Wednesday, Thursday, Friday and again Saturday.

No one came to visit.

No one called.

No one threatened to kick me out.

By this time I was sick of the boredom of being in a five bedroom house all by myself. It was obvious that my stay here was limited, so I decided it was time to find a place to park my sandals, at least temporarily.

Before embarking on a search for a suitable rental, one I could afford, I set about gathering my personal belongings. I know! I'm not supposed to take anything with me, just the cloths on my back.

Sure!

We had a motor home, so I piled my cloths on the back seat and put my bedroom set in the isle. Since Hot flashes had moved out of the master suite she had her own bedroom and bedroom set so I wasn't taking anything that she would use, unless someone was waiting to take my place, of course and even then I doubt they would use two bedrooms.

Aside from the kitchen table and chairs, a formal dining room set with eight high-back chairs and a gaming table plus its chairs, there were two outdoor patio sets with four chairs each on the exterior deck. I decided to take the smaller set. *I'll need something to eat on*, I rationalized.

Hot Flashes liked buying things in quantity, so when the local food store had a special on table settings, she stored up a supply that would last several generations of five child families, accounting for fifty percent breakage per generation. The entire back wall of our garage was filled with boxes of bland floral patterned dishes. I figured it would pose no great hardship if I helped myself to a serving of four from the stock pile.

I'm a self-taught artist at heart which tells you why I have so many paintings. There wasn't a wall in the house that didn't display my work. I left all but a couple of my favorites, just so I wouldn't feel like a complete recluse in my new surroundings.

Yes, we had no less than four televisions, ranging from the large 25" set in the family room (25" was large in those days) to smaller potables in various rooms. It was one of the latter that I chose to take, along with my personal sound system, one of three in the house including Hot Flashes personal set.

The motor home was now stocked with enough belongings to set up a small one bedroom apartment. I was ready to hit the road and try finding a place to live. I thought of driving the motor home in search of an apartment, then returning home, or post-home, to exchange the motor home for my car once I was unloaded and settled in.

Vacant apartments were somewhat scarce and having no knowledge of where I would end up, it occurred to me that it was ridiculous to negotiate the twenty-six foot beast all over town at the rate of six gallons per mile, looking for a place to live. It's difficult enough to negotiate turns and find parking places under normal circumstances, let along hunting for a needle in a haystack with the Titanic in tow.

Looking for an apartment was an experience I wasn't looking forward to, let alone living in one. The last time I occupied an apartment was sixteen years ago when we were first married and money was scarce as hen's teeth. At the time, as I previously stated, I was able to talk the owner into managing his apartment building and, for my rent, paint and clean the vacant units as well as taking care of the grounds and pool. Three years of people living above you as well as six inches on either side of my unit had filled my life's quota of apartment living, not to mention living in college dorms, the army barracks, rooming houses, etc.

I was still bent out of shape every time I thought of how one person can manage to manipulate another's person's life. What the hell, if she's unhappy, let *her* move out. I have no axe to grind with the present family situation. Granted, our love life was all but non-existent, but when things don't go well, adjust.

Grrr!

I had no idea how hard it would be to find an apartment. I started with the most logical location, closest to home. That way I could be near the kids. I could see them everyday while I continued coaching them in sports, as I had all their young lives.

After six hours of knocking on managers doors I finally found an apartment. ONE! A two bedroom condo which was available for rent.

The rent? Twice the amount of my house payment.

I liked the two bedroom concept however. That gave me another bedroom to put the kids in when they would come to visit me in the future.

Once the financial details were worked out and the paper work signed, I shot home, dodging the evening traffic. My pulse beat faster in quiet anxiety as I thought of moving to a new environment. As the iron gate to what used to be home swung open and I glided down the driveway, it struck me that something was wrong!

What was missing?

The motor home! The motor home is missing. The motor home with all my stuff in it was gone!

Frantically, I drove around the vicinity looking for the darn thing. You'd think a twenty-five foot box on wheels would be easy to spot, but as I increased the circle of my hunt, it was no where to be found.

I drove by Hot Flashes mother's house.

No motor home.

I drove by every relative, friend or hiding place that I could think of.

No motor home.

I looked at every shopping center and public hiding place within a five mile radius where it might be hidden. No luck!

Obviously, Hot Flashes had someone watching the house, and when I left, they struck with a vengeance.

It seemed fitting somehow, that I would be forced to comply with the court order after all, leaving the premises with only the cloths on my back and no more. No personal items, no cloths, no bedding, nothing. Not even a tooth brush.

I had lost the first round.

YOU CAN SEE THE
CHILDREN ... MAYBE

Beaten and dejected, I sulked into my newly rented unit, wearing all of my currently held worldly possessions; a pair of torn tennis shoes, a pair of jeans and a sweatshirt from the University of Oregon appropriately designed with the face of a mad green duck imprinted on the front.

I'm now sandwiched in with three hundred lower-middle class families of all races, creeds and color with their television sets blaring through open windows, dogs barking at every passer-by, old cars with doors that slam into yours, paper and other debris scattered about the grounds, shared dirty laundry rooms and a swimming pool full of kids.

And, I have an attitude.

The time had arrived to reassess my position.

First and foremost I need to find something to sleep on. The floor had been all right when I was a kid, but now - forget it. The flesh is willing, but the bones weld themselves in one position too easily. The lawn might be an option.

Weaving my way through shopping carts and abandoned cars, I forged my way to the local rent-a-bed-couch-table and chairs store where a young salesman in a red checkered sports jacket is at my car window before the ignition is turned off, and my seat belt unbuckled.

After picking out a used bed, hopefully without fleas or flesh eating organisms, a small couch, ditto, a kitchen table and a lamp, it's on to the office to sign a six month lease for a paltry sum of six hundred forty-eight dollars per month, more than my old house payment which, one must not forget, has to be made by, guess who.

Meals? How does breakfast with Ronald McDonald sound. Lunch? Joe's Greasy Diner serves a great gut burger guaranteed to keep his place on your mind for the balance of the day. And Dinner? I don't even want to think about it. This was turning out to be an adventure not to remember.

More sooner than later, all fast food begins to meld into one flavor, somewhere between wood and muskrat feet. The only way to tell one meal from the other is by looking at your watch. Sometimes the color of what you are eating gives you a hint. For example eggs are yellow, which is a strong indication its sometime in the A.M., although that's no guarantee. I discovered that a breakfast jack was just as good for dinner as lunch.

Dinner is a tough one. I found, by trial and error, that a good clue as to which meal I was eating could be how long it's been since I've had a hand-held meal as opposed to one that's actually lying on a plate.

After seven years of college and two years in Uncle Sam's Army I came to the conclusion that it was time to break the pattern of salivating like Pavlov's dog every time the little hand reached a certain point on the dial of a clock. The best way to break this pattern was to stop wearing a watch. In that same time frame I decided to take control of my own life. Along with my watch, I decided to throw all my ties in the garbage can – that is when I get them back, if I ever do. Some guy was in the dumpster looking for souvenirs so I decided to give him my suits too, as soon as they became available. I haven't been the same since.

With my new found freedom, I've been known to actually go fishing on Tuesday and play tennis with my good friend Steve at 2:30 Friday afternoon, and take the kids to the beach during the week. I've slept until 8:00 AM and worked until midnight on a work day if the mood strikes.

That watch can become a real slave driver. First thing you know, you're 65 and retiring, wondering what happened to your youth, let alone your children's youth.

Somewhere between eating the ninety-sixth hand held meal and washing my only pair of jeans for the 18th time, Hot Flashes must have gotten tired of holding my stuff hostage, or couldn't get anything for them at the garage sale. At any rate, through a nephew she informed me that she had decided to unburden herself with my stuff (probably the same nephew that took them in the first place).

Devoting considerable thought to the subject, I reasoned that Hot Flashes sudden change of attitude must have been because my socks and underwear didn't fit anyone in the family and the Salvation Army wasn't into buying used items. On top of that, the motor home was useless while it was still packed with my stuff. It's no fun driving to Reno with all that garbage in the walkway.

You can well imagine my relief when her nephew discreetly arranged a meeting place, the street in front of her house (you notice I didn't say *our* house), to pick up my stuff.

What a refreshing feeling to wear a different pair of pants. I had begun to hate ducks, especially green ones like the one on my sweat shirt. It was nice to have a shirt to change into for once and even have a different pair of shoes. One doesn't realize the luxury of having a change of cloths until someone has taken them from you, or until some entity like the Army has invited you to an extended vacation where they provide you with a khaki green wardrobe for the next two years.

Take it from me, it's tough to find a time, usually in the dead of night, when no one is around, to sneak down to the complex's laundry room, strip and stand around in your skivvies, trying to act casual while your cloths wash and dry. Inevitably, some little house-mouse with insomnia wanders in and there you stand, trying to blend in with the wall paper with a silly grin on your face, glancing nervously at the dryer.

*****

Several months had gone by and Hot Flashes had refused to let me visit my off springs or let them visit me, least I give them a case of malaria or send them home with a case of the green apple quick step as a result of my excellent cooking.

The need and desire to see them grew with the passage of each day, until I finally reached the point of considering kidnapping my own kids.

I'd been a father for a number of years now and the most important ingredient during my marriage, and now post-married life, including my biological family, was my children. Having wife and kids severed at the same time is a fairly traumatic affair, although, as you may well have surmised by now, Hot Flashes and myself hadn't been Bogart and Bacall for quite some time.

The one thought that keeps the mental path somewhat straight is the knowledge that I know that my children not only love their father, but miss him just as much as he misses them. The thought that they must feel, unconsciously if not consciously betrayed, bothered me greatly. Heretofore, they were safe in the comfort and security of a home containing both Mother and Father, irrespective of the inner tension harbored therein. Now, Hot Flashes was playing one-upmanship mind games with them.

In reality, the parents of all children must take some responsible for the pain and suffering that their children experience and will continue to experience if their home life is less than happy. Hopefully they won't harbor guilt feelings thinking that they're responsible for the family's breakdown. Little do they know that a 'dead marriage' is worse than their parents staying together, and that a marriage that is dead is harder on all members of the family in the long run, then living in an environment of constant anger, discourse and confusion. At least this is the philosophy of the psychological experts. In retrospect, looking back after several years of divorce, I'm not sure I fully agree with that concept. I'm certainly healthier, mentally, and I hope the children are, too.

I couldn't help feeling that every divorced child wants to have their parents back together, irrespective of the consequences. I know that would have been my personal feeling, even now, that my parents have departed this earth. I would have hated to see them separated or divorce, even though, because of the proximity of distance, I only saw them a couple times a year. I would have been devastated had they separated, and I'm a grown adult - so you can understand how a child must feel.

Since I've gone through the process of divorce and have witnessed, first hand, the stress and pain that the children go through, I personally feel that the parents of divorced children should be penalized for what they put them through. Parents have an obligation to their children, irrespective of their own failures. If the parents make bad choices, why should the children be the ones to suffer?

Once the decision has been made to break up the family, the father usually goes one way and mother another. Ninety-nine percent of the time the mother raises the children. The result is a division of sort of the family assets. The mother usually gets the lions share: the house, furniture, stocks and bonds, and any available cash. In addition, she's usually awarded child support and in some cases alimony, depending upon the settlement issues that she or her lawyer negotiates.

What do the children get? Grief of loosing their father, massive insecurity because both parents are no longer together and most of all, emotional distress from the constant games that their parents play where, more likely than not, the children are used like pawns in the chess game of parental control.

The children are innocent victims who get nothing but heart aches, neglect and psychological problems. They should be compensated for their loss as well. If there are four members of the family for example, a mother, father and two children, the children should be awarded a portion of the family assets, to be put in an irrevocable trust until they're of age, then released to them to start a life of their own.

Is this a punishment for the parents for failure to make a marriage work? You bet it is! And why not? Ask any divorced child if they've suffered and the answer will be one hundred percent affirmative. Would parental-child property division be a deterrent for some divorces?

Probably not.

I think if a marriage is dead and there's nothing but suffering and anger in the relationship, chances are it's headed for destruction anyway.

If it were up to me, and with the wave of a broom handle, I could mandate a universal child-divorce law, I would award, on a sliding scale, a percentage of the family assets to the children, depending upon their age. There would be a bell curve with the very youngest - say from newborn to two years old to the oldest, say seventeen or eighteen who are about ready to leave home on their own anyway - the lowest percentage of assets. "Why the youngest, the least?" you may ask. The reason is simple. The very young are not only the easiest to adopt to new circumstances, but are also usually the least hurt in a divorce, thus least damaged, especially if the mother remarries.

The middle group would get more of the assets on a sliding scale with a medium age of ten to twelve or so being the top of the bell curve. They're the age group that will end up suffering the most both immediately as well as on the long run. Some will argue that all children, irrespective of their age, should be treated equally and thus, should get equal proportions. Others will argue that they're just children and as such, should receive nothing. They'll make it on their own when the time comes.

In a court of law, every case has allegation of emotional stress and irrevocable psychological damage and the husband is usually labeled with espousal abuse in one form or another. I call this parental child abuse. In my world, when council makes their eloquent plea for damages to be awarded their client, the children should have equal representation and should share in that compensation, irrespective of who is awarded damages.

Visitors

The time finally arrived when I was allowed to have my children visit me. Believe it or not, I felt like an adolescent on his first date. Butterflies fluttered in my stomach and I paced the condo like an expectant father checking my watch every ten minutes, waiting for the time when I could leave to pick them up. What would we talk about, how would we be together, would they like my new place, etc., etc., etc? I knew Hot Flashes had spoken ill of me and I was concerned about their attitude.

As my car approached the iron gate, my eyes scanned the grounds, taking in all the familiar surroundings. A sharp sword-like pain tore through my heart as Caesar, the Great Dane, loped up to the gate greeting me with several loud, "woof, woofs". I couldn't resist getting out of the car and reaching through the gate to scratch him behind his ears and give him a few pats on the head. We had a short man-to-dog chat before the kids ran up the driveway yelling, "Howard! Howard's here!"

I don't know when it first started or why, but ever since they could talk, they've called me by my first name. Most parents are horrified when my kids call me Howard or Howie, but I kinda like it.

They each carried a paper bag containing cloths to wear for the week-end. Although I grinned, delighted to see them, I instinctively search their eyes for a secret sign deceiving their masked friendliness.

All I saw was the warmth and love they felt as they greeted me with, "Hi Howard. How you doin'?"

After a round of hugs, their paper bags were thrown into the trunk and we were off to the condo. Conversation was small and somewhat force at first as they inquired, "How have you been? Was Caesar glad to see you? Do you have a pool at your apartment?" and the proverbial, "How's the office?"

Once we arrive at melting pot USA, I took them on a tour of the grounds. They were impressed with the size of the complex, the swimming pool and were anxious to give the weights and pool table in recreation room a try. They seemed excited even though their house was equipped with these amenities and more.

The weekend was spent swimming in the pool, going out to dinner and taking in a movie. Typical week-end father stuff. Although our time spent together seemed welcomed by both camps, it soon became obvious that an unspoken and probably conscious pack had been formed between the three of them. Somewhere between the time that their mother had gathered them up and swept them off to her mother's house while she had me served, and now, they had formed an invisible bubble around themselves which would seemingly last for years.

It was apparent that they felt the only safe ground was the bond that they had formed between themselves. Anything or anyone else was not to be trusted. And who could blame them? They had been delivered the most vicious slap a child can receive by the two most important people in their lives - their parents. Now, they were like the Three Musketeers, banning together with the backs to each other, facing the world, trusting no one.

It was sad, but certainly predicable. Everyone was an outsider, including their parents. It was a pain that would go unspoken, but obviously cut deep. Only time would tell what the end result will be. In retrospect, nothing can forgive the pain they must have suffered. Only they knew how they must have felt.

We would come together periodically, to temporarily interact like father and sons, I always felt the presence of that invisible shield. One may momentarily, gently penetrate its guarded boundaries, but the shield would keep them safe from emotional attachments and subsequent disappointment, like an umbrella in a rain storm.

As time passed, I felt our times together began to slowly meld back to a greater form of mutual acceptance, considering our respective positions. In the swimming pool Christian would ask me to show him how to dive backwards while Aaron would challenge me to an underwater race. Larry wanted to test his strength by arm wrestling. The relationship seemed to have transformed itself or converted into a big brother - little brother-like outings. We always had a relationship that transcended father-son. Witness the fact that they called me Howie rather than father or dad. But now, our relationship was beginning to take on a different dimension. One that was all but void of my guidance or discipline. I began to more fully understand their confusion.

One night, while we were eating dinner at one of the local steak houses, Aaron and Larry were sitting on one side of the table while Christian sat next to me. We were passing the time with light conversation until our meal arrived. When our food finally arrived, as usually, they began wolfing down their steak like starved children from India. A few moments into the dinner, I felt a tug at my sleeve. I looked down to see Christian's face turning crimson red and his eyes bulging. I heard a slight squeak coming from his mouth. His face had a desperate pleading look painted on it.

Instinctively, I knew what the problem was. Quickly getting up from my seat, I pulled him out after me, turned him around so his back was to me and made a fist with my right hand. I cupped my left hand around the right fist and jerked up and in, hard and up on his stomach.

Nothing!

I repeated the procedure, this time exercising as much force as I felt I could without injuring him. The force of the air trapped in his stomach made the largest piece of meat you have ever seen a nine year old child have in his mouth come shooting out like a missal. Without missing a beat, obviously embarrassed, he returned to his seat and continued eating as if nothing had happened.

His brothers had a look of amazement in their eyes as they asked why I had jerked Christian from his seat and attempted to break him in half in the middle of our meal. Apparently no one in the restaurant, including those at our own table, knew that Christian was within a hare's breath of loosing his life by choking to death.

When the brothers were told what had happened, or more importantly what didn't happen, they fell silent for the rest of the meal, each with their own thoughts. I think Christian tried to minimize the matter more out of embarrassment than anything. Although his habit of wolfing down food never changed, his brothers never let him forget the incident, reminding him, as he jammed a half of a hamburger in his mouth, of the time I saved his life when he ate too fast and too much. To watch him eat, one might get the impression that the cops were after him and that time was precious.

As a footnote, I was to later write this antedate to the Readers Digest, thanking them for their article earlier published on the Himlicker technique. Had I not read that article, I have no doubt that today I may only have two boys, not three.

As a rule, during dinner, conversation would be centered around school and sports, a subject they all loved and participated in, giving each other the business about girls or zits, the way they combed their hair, or just telling jokes. Anytime I gently inquired about how things were at home however, I was given the standard mono-symbolic response, "Fine".

In other words, don't ask. Don't talk about it.

Eventually, the weekend came to an end. The time had come when I had to take my boys home. After a big hug and kiss from each of them, off they went, down the steep driveway to their house, Caesar jumping on their shoulders with his tail whipping them at the same time, leaving me standing at the iron gate, with a heavy heart fighting back a tear.

Each had their own way of letting me know that they cared, however. Christian would always give a cheerful, "See ya later, Howie", as he ran down the hill with his paper bag in tow to meet Caesar. Larry would sometimes give me another hug and/or a kiss before parting with a, "See ya later, How." I knew he was hurting the most, but he managed to keep it inside. Aaron always made it a point to linger a few minutes to talk before giving me a hug and another kiss before walking quietly back to the house. I valued those last few moments more than anything. They would have to last me for the rest of the week.

The drive back to the condo, even though it was only ten minutes away, seemed an eternity. My mind replayed the time we had together, mostly good, at least as good as it could have been under the circumstances. I often wondered what went through their minds as they walked down the driveway back home again, leaving their father alone, standing outside of the gate. A father who by now was rapidly becoming a stranger.

The worst of times was when something went awry during our weekend time together. I recall one time I hollered at one of the kids for something so inconsequential that I can't even remember what it was now. I undoubtedly yelled at him out of stress or frustration. I remember that he cried for probably the same reasons. For the next week, my heart felt like someone had plunged a knife into it, worrying what lasting damage I had done to our relationship.

The reality of the matter is, he probably forgot about it five minutes after he went home. If that same thing would have happened while we were living together at the house, I wouldn't have given it a second thought. I would have just been a father disciplining his child during the normal course of a day. I was rapidly gaining the feeling that my status as a father was slipping into quicksand.

The drive home was bad enough, but walking into the empty apartment, void of the warmth and life, void of my boys who were here only moments previous, was a very sad, lonely feeling. Often, I would be unable to stay in the apartment and would walk aimlessly around the complex's pathways, gazing into the star-lit sky, looking and asking for guidance and strength.

I quickly learned when I called over to the house, wanting to talk to one of the kids – it didn't mater which one, whoever answered the phone - Hot Flashes would invariably get on the telephone, laying a guilt trip on me laced with the finer language of a seaman. It was impossible to carry on a conversation with her and I would invariably hang up in anger and frustration. On those occasions when I did get to talk to the children, I could hear her screaming in the background which invariably resulted in their crying. They were forced to hang up, just to protect their own sanity.

As time passed, they learned to tune her out. It got to the point where they could eventually stand in front of her on one of her eternal lectures designed to inform them of how horrible of a person their father was without hearing a word that was being spoken.

After the weekend, it usually took two or three days to get back to normal before I could go to sleep without the golf ball sized pit in my stomach and a deep feeling of loneliness. Knowing that I couldn't call, I would wait for the telephone to ring, hoping someone would call asking how I was. Once in a while one of them did.

Larry's call was usually in the form of asking for money to go to a concert or to buy a pair of tennis shoes, pants or a shirt. Christian's calls were short and to the point, just saying hi, and then passing the phone to one of the brothers. Aaron was always sensitive beyond his years. He

usually called just to talk about his day or ask how things were going. Rarely did he ask for money or favors and when he did, it was almost apologetically.

Beware Of Sharks

By now, enough time had passed to properly evaluate my legal situation and, short of hiring a hit man from Chicago, I figured that professional legal advice was in order. I'd come to realize that those two terms are actually diametrically opposed to one another. I was on virgin ground here and the only way to get answers was to ask every bright eyed walking, English speaking male that I knew for advice.

Advice ranged from, "Go to the book store and buy yourself a Do it Yourself manual on divorce" to "Hire the best damn high powered legal beagle you can find, and screw the cost because you can bet she's goin' for the jugular on this one".

After hearing advise from everyone from the town drunk to the mayor, I settled on a council (they use this word instead of lawyer because it sounds more sophisticated) that had been recommended by one of their own. After all, who should know these waters better than those that swim in them every day? These excellent breed of legal-beagles are commonly known as *Sharks* outside of their profession.

How can such a name, thus image, be applied to a group of hard working, well educated, smartly dressed, silver tongued bunch of guys as our local crop of Barristers, you ask?

I'm here to enlighten those of you whose only exposure to the world of law has been late night viewing with *Perry Mason , L.A. Law,*

The Practice or *Murder One.* You probably feel you have a modest conception of how the game is played.

Let's say, for the sake of argument, that you and your beloved have lived together in blissful wedlock for the past fifteen years when suddenly, while you're watching the Green Bay Packers have the Jets for lunch while you're enjoying the last of a six pack, you ask honey-bunch for another brewsky, because you're too tired to move the foot stool, plus it's forth and one and Green Bay is going for it.

Instead of a nice cool one, Honey-bunch, coat on and kids in tow, lays a legal document on your chest just as Green Bay crosses the goal line. Now you're torn between asking your honey where she's going, although glad to have her and the kids out of your hair, or read the paper that she just laid on your chest. "Oops, got a little beer on it", you say as you wipe it off with your sleeve while you watch the replay on TV. What the hell, the paper isn't going anywhere. You chuck it on the floor with the empties and peanut shells and return your attention to the game. "Wow, look at that line!"

After the game, while you're in the process of shoving the empties and peanut shells in the corner of the room for the little woman to pick up while you run down to the 7-11 for another six pack before the next game starts, you remember the legal document. After wiping it off on your shirt, what they hell, it needs washing anyway, you're shocked into near soberness when you read the words: IN THE SUPERIOR COURT OF CALIFORNIA, and your name as defendant is clearly typed in a law suit filed by your beloved. "Hold it! The Raiders just kicked off to the Niners. The State of California will keep until half-time."

After the game, according to the document, apparently the little woman wants you ... no, orders you to leave the house and never darken the barn again. It turns out, according to the verbiage set forth by her not-lacking-for-word and forget-the-truth-just-get-the-bastard-out-of-the-house shark, you are a potentially dangerous hombre, and as such, must go. For everyone's protection.

"Bitch!"

Your better half wants a divorce!

"Good for-nothin' no good, ungrateful broad!"

"Divorce?" Your buddy asks as he crushes a can before throwing another empty on the floor.

"She's hired Sam Sharkey downtown to take a bit out of your ass the size of a beer keg, without mercy, and throw you to the wolves."

Put another way, remember all those things you've worked so hard for all these years, getting up at five A.M. and working until six at night, even Saturdays, to put the roof over her and the rug-rats heads, put food on the table and cloths on their backs?

Forgotten!

No one cares.

Don' mention.

Whereas before the legal paper-on-the-chest, everything you had, she had, now it's everything we have, she gets. What you don't know, and she doesn't even know, is that neither one of you are in charge of what's going to happen to you and yours from this moment on.

Who's in charge?

The Sharks!

From here on in, her shark will fight you tooth and nail, bleed you for every cent you own, and then kick your ass in the snow bank without a second thought, but not before he's gotten -- not the lion's share -- but the shark's share of your liquid assets. Better known in layman terms as his money. The difference is, the lion always leaves some for the rest of the pack. The shark doesn't have a pack!

Once reality kicks in and the husband finally realizes that it's over, that he and honey-bunch are really going to split up, he does what any sensible, honest man would do. Makes a list of all the assets and liabilities then divides it in two.

Her half and my half.

You give this well-drawn, equally-split list of assets to your shark, who shares it with her shark over lunch at the bistro which you pay for. There, after a couple of drinks and a fine lunch they light up a stogie and begin figuring out how long they can prolong this little ceremony of splitting up the family at two-hundred-sixty an hour. In the meanwhile, you and honey-bun figure that this can't take more than a few weeks, a month at most, then you can each go your separate way and start a new life.

Simple. Right?

Soon a week turns into a month which turns into six months and you start to get a little irritated.

"Sharkie!" You call, full well knowing that the two-hundred-sixty-dollar-an-hour with a minimum of fifteen minutes which equates to sixty-five dollars per call with the clock ticking. "What the hell's up?"

"Hold on a minute," he says as he goes for a cup of coffee down at the next corner. "Let me pull that file." Minutes and dollars tick by and the sound of footsteps return followed by several sipping noises and then the sound of shuffling papers before he picks up the receiver and says, "I don' know. I call him. He's out. He call's me. I'm out. We keep missing each other."

You ask yourself, *How complicated can this be?* Looking out of Sharkie's pent-house window, you can see the other shark's office across the street. They can wave to each other or at the very least, pass each other paper airplanes or make hand signals. "Well, shit Sharkie!" You advise, "Walk over there and knock on his door. How complicated can that be?"

"Oh no, can't do that. That's not the way it's done." *Might actually get something accomplished.* "I'll write him a letter."

Well that works just fine. Your Shark writes her Shark a letter saying , "I can't get a hold of you. Let's do lunch"!

Her Shark writes back. "Fine, have your secretary call my secretary and set it up".

Well, after your five thousand dollar retainer runs out, the first legal bill comes through the mail. "SEVEN-THOUSAND-FIVE-HUNDRED-FIFTY-DOLLARS - BALANCE DUE!"

The bill is neatly typed, multi paged and chronicled.

Phone call to Sharkie's office, seventy-five dollars.

Received phone call from Sharkie's office, fifty dollars.

There's a couple dozen of these sprinkled with:

"Letter to Sharkie's office, seventy-five-dollars".

Then the heavy hitters come in:

8.5 hours research at two-hundred-sixty-dollars-per hour.

Two-thousand-two-hundred-ten dollars.

Page after page the itemized list goes on: phone calls, missed phone calls, research, letters, more phone calls, more research.

I was always under the impression that when one pays two-hundred-sixty-dollars an hour, one is paying for an educated expert on the subject of law, not two-hundred-sixty-dollars an hour for someone to do their homework on your time and at your expense. Isn't that what law school is for? He's the pro here. Been in the divorce business for the past fifteen years and I still have to pay for research?

Come one now! Give me a second while I brush the hay from my hair and pull my wagon full of pumpkins to the curb.

At these rates and the length of time our case is taking, I could put myself through law school and be my own shark! Then, of course, they never share or disclose what they found during the process of doing their research. If I wanted to educate them at my expense, I would have set up a tax free scholarship fund. It stands to reason that I should be able to back-bill the next client for schooling and recoup some of my losses. Presumably, I'm paying for knowledge to not only educate my shark - thus defend me - but I'm educating him for the next guy and the next guy ... unless he's not really doing research .... Na.

One of the bills stated: *July 26. Research: twenty seven hours.*

How the hell can you get twenty seven hours of anything when we're only allotted twenty- four hours per day, even if you don't sleep, eat, hit the sand box or take a break to shake your leg or fart once in a while. Twenty-four hours is twenty-four hours!

Even the uneducated slob living in tent city can figure that out. We've been had. These guys don't want to settle our case. They want our money. They're not mad at each other. There they are, sitting at the bistro, laughing and banging each other on the back while we pay for their lunch at two-hundred-sixty dollars per. They're making money on us at lunch!. I'll bet dollars to donut holes, they're laughing at how dumb their clients are. "Another round for my fellow barrister! Put it on his clients tab! Har, Har!"

What suckers we are. We give them a list of all our assets, including how much money we have, and they're going to drag this thing out until it's all gone, then miraculously, we'll have a settlement. In the meantime, "Pass the port old boy".

Well, as you might imagine, or perhaps you can't imagine, an entire year goes by to the tune of legal costs in the excess of thirty-thousand dollars - *each*- and we're no closer to resolving the matter than the first day the Packers beat the Jets.

Enough of this stuff! I tell Sharkie to set up a meet with Hot Flashes and her Shark, thinking I'd take a firm hold of things and get everything settled in one fell swoop. Someone has to have a level head here!

It takes two weeks to settle on a time and find an empty courtroom where all combatants can meet. At the appointed day and hour, Sharkie and I patiently wait twenty minutes for the opposition to show.

Finally, the door creaks open. Through the hall light I see a lone figure wearing a top coat with a mink fur collar. The other Shark has arrived!

"Where's Hot Flashes," I inquire angrily?

"Not able to make it," he responds coolly. "We can talk amongst ourselves."

I talk. Both Sharks nod in agreement. After twenty minutes Hot Flashes Shark leaves with the comment, "I hope you feel better now that you've gotten that off your chest."

I just spent two hundred dollars for a therapy session with a shark's skin suit with a fur collar and no results!

By this time the money is nearly extinguished. Two years from the commencement of this exercise, it is decided that maybe another settlement conference would be in order.

The sharks agree on a time and location. I feel like the Mafia meeting the Colombians on a secret drug deal. We find a vacant room and hire a "Rent a Judge" to oversee the proceedings. The judge is retired, but still empowered to make legal decisions. All parties have agreed to be bound by his decision. The two Sharks and the Rent-a-Judge are locked behind closed doors while Hot Flashes sits calmly puffing on a cigarette on one side of the hall and I pace the floor on the other side looking like a man waiting to be hanged.

It occurs to me that there are three men locked behind those closed doors who don't give a rat's ass about us or our welfare. They're in there dividing up our life. What do they know about our needs? The muffled sound of laughter escapes from under the door.

Why aren't the husband and wife in there pushing the pieces around and the sharks sitting outside? After all, it's our assets, what's left of them. The only plausible answer is, after sixty-thousand dollars in legal fees payable to my shark alone and twenty-five months later, why should we have any control now?

I shoot a glance at Hot Flashes. It crosses my mind that after all this time even she must feel a pang of frustration. After all, she's been feeding her Shark all this time too ... hasn't she? I know for a fact he's driving her car, leaving her stranded without transportation. That fact alone makes my blood boil!

Finally, we're called in.

Sharkie rushes over to me with an outstretched hand and a smile on his face. "We have a settlement offer", he announces proudly, handing me a list of our remaining assets split into two parts.

I look it over. Minus the cash in the bank, the list is identical to the one I prepared two years ago! Identical! At this stage of the game, and I underline the work *game*, we're so beat up, tired and broke, that I would have given her everything I owned, just to be done with it. Now I know how the Chinese water torture works. Drop by drop. It's no big deal to begin with, but after two years, it is a big deal. The dripping water has done its job.

My eyes drop to the bottom of the page where a blank line awaits my signature. As I'm about to put pen to paper when something catches my eye. Normally slow to anger, two years of frustration and rage spew from my mouth like a fresh oil well in Texas. I can feel the heat from my face turning beat red.

At the bottom of the list, is Hot Flashes *unpaid* legal fees. I have been asked, no, told, to pay her legal fees!

My Shark has great difficulty in restraining me from knocking Hot Flashes' Shark on his skinny ass. Not only has he successfully manipulated Hot Flashes and myself during this two year period, sucking us both dry of all our liquid assets, he now has the unmitigated gall to ask me to pay his legal bill!

In no uncertain terms, through gritted teeth, I tell him to take his legal bill and stuff it where the sun doesn't shine.

Sharkie, at once sensing the situation, probably because I'm about to have Hot Flash's Shark by his gills, extracting his larynx with my bear hands, takes me to the next room whereby he advises me that it's 'normal procedure' for the beaten and bloodied husband to pay the opponent's Shark bill.

Additionally, if I don't pay her Shark's bill, there will be no settlement and the matter will go before the rent-a-judge. The rent-a-judge, being an ex-shark himself, I quickly deduce that they all swim in the same pond. Rent-a-judge advises me in a quiet, hangman's tone and a fatherly look, "After all, you're a man capable of making more money," he says with a condescending smile. "So it took you fifteen years to accumulate the money you've now spent on legal fees. You can spend the next fifteen years doing it all over again."

Those teeth look awfully familiar.

Thoroughly beaten, dazed, and in a incoherent fog, I find my way back to the courtroom where the beheading is immortalized on record in front of a court reporter who's been sitting near-by, filing her nails.

Future little sharks, not yet full grown, getting ready for the big pond, can now learn how to take a simple matter such as having two people wanting to go their separate ways, and learn how to not only drag it out for two years, but separate the clients from their money, their dignity, their self esteem and last but not least, their sanity.

This has been an education that will set these two people so far back, mentally and economically, that they will never, ever, forget the experience.

One of us will never recover.

Part Three
I Used To Be A Father

Sports again

Spring brings birds, bees, flowers and baseball. It's every father's dream to have his boy play and excel at sports. It's the one socially acceptable pastime that allows grown males to relive ones youth outside of playing the sport as an adult themselves, of course.

I recall during one particular football game where Christian had been attending Archbishop Mitty High as a freshman. They were playing Saint Francis, their arch rival. Any number of father's voices could be heard from one end of the football field to the other, complaining, "What penalty? My kid was held by that kid! Throw him out! Get a new pair of glasses you bum!"

Fortunately for the embarrassed mother who usually sits with other mothers, football is an outdoor sport where the stands are expected to be filled with screaming fathers and students, with cheer leaders with pep bands adding to the noise factor. The embarrassed mother either just grins and shrugs her shoulders to her friends as they stare in disbelief at the outraged father who is standing, screaming at the top of his lungs at the 'zebras' who not only need glasses, but are urged by the father to "Get a real job", or ignores him altogether.

Basketball on the other hand is played in closer quarters. The gymnasium is usually filled to capacity with screaming fathers, mothers and students and the usual array of cheer-leaders and the proverbial pep band. It's socially acceptable, even expected, to shout insults to the refs. "He fouled my kid!" "Walking!" "Get a pair of glasses!" And of course, "Get a real job!" and when the call is against the opposing team it's, "Good call!"

As the game progresses and the spectators get tense, especially if the home team is loosing, the tension picks up a tad with, "You gotta be kidding you blind idiot." I had one especially loud friend whose voice needed no microphone to be heard above the roar of the crowd. His favorite phrase was, "Did you see that?" as he stood, pointing a finger at the offending player on the opposing team. Usually everyone on his side of the gym turned to look at him with a condescending smile.

Baseball is another matter. As a rule, the only people that show up for a game are the player's family, and then only part of the family, if, indeed anyone shows at all. Mother, if she comes, sits quietly in the bleachers under a sun hat or umbrella. Father stands behind the backstop, just a few feet from the plate umpires ear where he can taunt the man in blue. "Strike? You call that a strike? Come on blue, he couldn't have reached that ball with a ten foot pole." The umpire's skin is soon hardened by this abuse and, for the most part, ignores the heat from the bellowing fathers.

Every kind of ball and sporting equipment could be found in our house. All three boys were going to be in the hall of fame of some sport, of that I was sure. They were naturals. I could tell that at once. Can't all fathers? Aaron had a great punch. I can still remember when he was only belt high and had laid me on the floor with one well placed fist. What a kid!

The time soon came for team sports. T-ball was first. The game is simple. Put a soft baseball on top of a stick and let the kid hit away. The ball bounces along the ground as a half-dozen pint-sized kids dragging mitts larger than their head amble to catch the illusive sphere. Mothers and fathers scream as the batter bounces around the bases like a half filled bag of air. Rarely did the ball get past infield.

What a sport! What excitement!

The only thing was, I found myself feeling like I was on the outside, looking in. Every day I brought my pint-sized Hank Aaron to the field only to watch someone else teach my kid how to catch, hit and run. I saw their games on the week ends and aside from taking him to practice and picking him up, there seemed to be a void there somewhere.

I noticed the coaches were, for the most part, just your average Joe. Most of them had no baseball sense, but they were all heart - and they gave of their time freely and willingly. You had to admire that. They had jobs like nailing wood, working in concrete, or selling real estate. They had no special athletic skills nor showed any outstanding aptitude for the game. They were just there. They had volunteered for the job.

As a child, I wasn't fortunate enough to have a father who was able to devote much time to us. He and my mother were too busy keeping the wolves from the door and food on the table. I guess, for that reason alone, I was determined to spend as much time with my children as possible. I recall a Yiddish song entitled "My Little One" wherein a father sings to his sleeping child, a child that he rarely sees during the day due to his work:

I have a son, a little son,
A boy completely fine.
Whenever I see him, it seems to me
That all the world is mine.
But seldom, seldom do I see
My child awake and bright.
I only see him when he sleeps;
I'm only home at night.
It's early when I leave for work;
When I return, it's late.
Unknown to me is my own flesh,
Unknown to me is my child's face.
When I come home so wearily
In the darkness after day,
My pale wife exclaims to me:
"You should have seen our child play."
I stand beside his little bed;
I look and try to hear.
In his dream he moves his lips:
"Why isn't Papa here?"

The next year, I decided to go into the coaching business. When the time came, I applied for a coaching job, without pay, of course. I was interviewed and then hired and thus became a little league coach.

It was great fun. Now I was not only coaching my own kid but seventeen other little runts too. Everyone wanted to pitch, play first or second base. No one wanted to be catcher or out-fielder. A coach always has the privilege of asking his own child what position he wants to play, then assigning the rest of the runts their positions. Somehow, eventually, each kid finds the spot on the team that best suits him, and a good time is had by all. Everyone still wanted to pitch - and they were allowed to try out. Those who could reach the plate were encouraged to continue polishing their technique.

When we finally started playing games against other teams, each coach and their players had learned to work as a cohesive team, all for one and one for all. It didn't seem to matter all that much whether they won or lost, they just liked to play. I soon found that the only one that fretted over mistakes or lost games was the coach. "It's only a game coach," Christian kept reminding me as he wolfed down a pizza after the game while punching a teammate on the arm. Somehow I had a hard time bringing myself around to that philosophy.

It never ceased to amaze me how few parents showed up for a game. Here was thirty kids playing their little hearts out on the field, and no more than a handful of parents showed up. Out of my fifteen to eighteen kids, I probably only knew eight parents to call them by name and *never* saw the parents of five to eight of the kids at either our games or at practice.

It cut deep to feel how the little tykes must have felt, knowing that dad was probably home drinking, or mom was bagging her boy friend while he was out playing his heart out. Every once in a while I would catch the eye of a youngster quickly scanning the bleachers to see if one of them had come, only to turn back to the game in resignation, affirming the knowledge that they weren't there. Didn't they know how important it was to their boy for them to be there and root him on, support him when he needed it? What kind of people were they?

As hard as it was to replace their fathers, I tried to be the father they either didn't have or the father they wished they had. Somehow, I think they knew how I felt and appreciated it. When I think of unwanted children I'm always reminded of the story of a little girl with a cleft palate. The children shunned her because of her unusual facial features and she was generally left alone.

One day, the teacher had each child write on a piece of paper, their most inner-secret desires. She would then have each child come up to her and present her paper after which, the teacher would impart some degree of her wisdom to the boy or girl. Most wished to become great baseball players or dancers, as the case might be. When it came time for the little girl with the cleft palate to come up to the teacher, her paper read: *"I Wish I was beautiful."*

The teacher smiled at the little girl and whispered, "You know what I wish? I wish you were my little girl." That made her day! The little girl's attitude towards herself was brighter from that moment on. It was my fervent wish to make each little boys day special that was on my team.

The time came when my boys were old enough to participate in school sports. Because they attended a private Catholic school, the school had no money to hire professional coaches, so they were sought amongst the families and congregation of the church.

I jumped at the chance and became first a football coach, then the softball coach and finally the basketball coach. Even though, as any volunteer coach will tell you, coaching digs deeply into your work production, I looked foreword to the experience each day.

For several years I coached Larry, Aaron and Christian. Then the big "D" hit.

Being separated from the kids made my coaching time even more valuable. This was solid quality time to not only direct the athletic skills of my own child as well as other children, but set values and examples at the same time.

I was emphatic about discipline - self discipline. I didn't subscribe to the adage that maybe I can't make you do it, but if you don't, I can make you sorry. I wanted them to be self disciplined - to care enough to make a difference. I lectured them the first day of practice. "If I find out that any one of you are drinking or using drugs - I don't care how great of an athlete you are - you're gone! And no swearing. I won't abide foul language or unsportsmanlike conduct. You'll conduct yourselves like young gentlemen at all times."

I couldn't believe the feed-back I got from the parents when their kids relayed my standards to them. People I've never seen before came up to me, shaking my hand, telling me how glad they were that I was their kid's coach. I was just setting the same standards that I set at home.

******

A few months after Hot Flashes filed the big 'D' and sent me packing, I was coaching and our team was in contention for the championship of little league baseball division. Practice was at 3:30, a time when the kids were just out of school, but still energetic enough to give their all.

As I watched each little warrior approach, greeting me with "Hi Coach", or "Hi Howard", or "Hi, Mr. L", as was often the case, I couldn't help wondering where my son was. He was usually the first to arrive on the practice field. For some unknown reason, Hot Flashes forbid me to pick him up at school (probably thought I was going to run to Cuba with him), so she would pick him up and take him directly to the practice field from school.

Maybe he was ill that day or had to stay after school. Maybe his mother was late. I inquired to the other kids who went to the same school and was assured that he was not ill, had not stayed after school and indeed they had seen his mother pick him up.

Practice came and went with me, their coach, having little heart in the practice, periodically looking towards the gate to see if he might come late.

Two more days came and went. No son. Forbidden to visit the house or even be on the street for that matter, I tried calling but the moment she heard my voice she hung up.

I was mad!

I was concerned.

What could have happened?

The fifth day, half way though practice, a lone small figure made his way toward the group. Everyone stopped practicing and ran over to him. After they had all greeted him, he made his way to me slowly, not wanting to look me in the eye.

We sat on the bleachers while the others chased each other and wrestled on the ground. After a few moments, he said that his mother wouldn't let him play anymore so long as I was the coach.

A tear rolled down his face.

While the other kids frolicked like new born colts, I put my arm around his shoulder and he leaned his bushy head against my chest. The pain of the moment was deeply felt by both of us.

"She can't do this," I objected, knowing that not only she could , but she did, irrespective of the cost to her own son. The plan was to get at me through him, and it was working.

I continued coaching for two weeks hoping that the situation would change, but it didn't. He would somehow managed to show up for games, telling Hot Flashes he was going to visit a friend, but his diminished skills showed that he hadn't practiced with the other kids. Not only was it not fair to them, but they were beginning to resent his playing in games while not showing up for practice.

The next game he didn't show at all. I never found out why, but I'll bet a dollar against a donut hole that somehow she found out that he had been coming to the games.

Coaching had lost all its appeal. I was only coaching to be with my son, but with him gone, my heart wasn't in it, and the kids knew it. The next day I went to the staff room and reluctantly resigned.

The following day, my son was back on the team, playing his usual position. My replacement was an unemployed construction worker with the finesse of a cement truck with talent to match. At least the kids had a coach and my son was playing again. That was the important part. It hurt to watch the cement truck take my team to the finish of the season.

I was no longer a coach.

Worse yet, I no longer felt like a father. I had been finessed out of position. I was a stranger standing outside looking in.

I don't want `em.
You can have `em

During the tenure of our sixteen years of living in the same house, the family invariably accumulated an array of trappings. You'll notice I omitted the phrase, *living together* as opposed to *living in the same house*. I figure since Hot Flashes moved out of the congenial bedroom seven years prior to serving the big 'D', occupying the bedroom at the opposite end of the house, the phrase living together was no longer applicable.

She had her own television set and stereo system from which Mexican music shook the door and adjoining walls day and night at triple fortissimo. Eventually, the only time she emerged, leaving Julio et al to catch their breath, was to scurry to the kitchen for life sustaining substance, or to the bathroom down the hall, not speaking to me, in the unlikely event I was within sight.

Eventually, there comes a time in every divorce when one party or the other isn't satisfied with the arrangement, be it financial or dividing up the trappings such as automobiles, furniture, Uncle Fred's pictures, the "good" china, Aunt Martha's silverware, and any surviving wedding gifts.

In my case, I eventually got my bedroom set, and the smallest of two glass patio tables, usually reserved for use for the children's annual

236

birthday parties. A suitable financial arrangement had been agreed upon between Hot Flashes, her attorney and the rent-a-judge who had been hired to decide *our case*. Due to the fact that she got all of the liquid assets, precious metals, precious stones, money, stocks and bonds, the house, car, motor home and the balance of furnishings and household items, her attorney, the rent-a-judge and hot Flashes agreed that there was nothing left but child support that would be forth-coming until the children reached the age of 18.

That made sense, of course. A schedule of monthly payments was set up from which the money sent to her was earmarked as funds to feed and cloth them. The system flowed effortlessly for about a month until she demanded more money. "The kids are starving, they have no food. They need clothes!"

At this early stage of the game, I was afforded the privilege of seeing them every week-end, giving her a reprieve from their energetic activities. While they were in my care we went to movies, ate out and usually went shopping for clothing, be it a pair of tennis shoes, jeans, a shirt or tee shirts. They seemed to have a need of some item of clothing every time I picked then up.

At some point during this time period, the kids got their own telephone. Hot Flashes couldn't stand the sound of my voice and wanted nothing to do with me. Having their own phone line was a sure way to solve that problem. All verbal messages from Hot Flashes were passed from the kids to me and visa versa. They became the conduit through which all information flowed.

It never seemed to fail however, when one of them would call, usually Aaron, she would scream instructions at him to give me an obscene messages through the phone, usually telling the kid to tell me what a "bastard" I was, then demanded more money. The end result always left the poor child being so brow beaten that he was unable to sustain any self composure and ended up in hanging up the telephone in tears.

Within a short period of time, although they had their own phone, they were forbidden to call or speak to me. This system invariably broke down however, whenever she took a nap, which was several hours each day. One of the kids would get on the phone and call, again, it was usually Aaron advising me that if his mother came into the room, he would simply hang up. The routine worked well until she caught on and eventually discontinued the phone line.

Against the wishes and advice of my shark, excuse me - attorney, a short time later I voluntarily increased the monthly child support allocation by fifty percent, and then again increased that amount, thus doubling what the rent-a-judge and the x-wife's shark had originally asked for. I actually felt good about the self imposed increases, feeling that I was not only easing her burden, but helping the situation at home at the same time.

One day, several months after my self imposed increased support payment, I arrived home from work to find a message on my answering machine. The message was from one of the children, emotional and labored. It said, "You don't care enough about us to give us money for food. We're starving to death. You don't love us any more. We have decided that we don't want to see you until you give us enough money to live on. Mom says she needs seven thousand five hundred dollars each month. Until you give us the money, we don't want to see you."

End of message.

I couldn't believe my ears. Back then, seven thousand five-hundred dollars was more money than I made in three months - totally, before any expenses. The request was not only ridiculous, it was impossible to meet. I figured that each kid must be eating sirloin steaks for breakfast, lunch and dinner and Caesar was giving a five pound roast each day, all catered by Paolos Dine and Serve. The only thing I could figure out was that she had made a monthly budget, throwing in everything from redecorating the house to major surgery and then doubled the figure for good measure.

After sitting at my desk, staring into space for several minutes, I decided to get to the bottom of what was going on here. I picked up the phone and dialed their number.

"Hello." It was Larry.

"This is Howard. I got your message, can you tell me ..."

"We don't want to talk to you until you give us the money," he said, coldly.

I could hear Hot Flashes in the background screaming at him, "Tell that son-of-a-bitch of a father of yours that you don't want to see him or talk to him *EVER!*"

"Click."

Dial tone.

So it was, with an ice pick in my heart, the next few months passed without contact, save Aaron's period call when his mother was asleep.

Then, one Friday evening, a knock was heard at my front door. I opened the door to see three faces looking up at me, their arms filled with paper bags containing their cloths. "Mom sent us to live with you. She doesn't want us any more," they said simply, shifting their weight nervously.

Their eyes looked up at me, searching for acceptance. I couldn't believe my eyes. They looked like three homeless children. I stepped aside, letting them in, hugging each one. We were all about to start a new life.

The Glass Menagerie

Having a house full of kids after complete isolation is like feast and famine. They made the transition as if they were in for the week-end. Fortunately, my wife (did I mention that I had just remarried?) and I had anticipated this turn of events and had previously bought a four bedroom home. Each boy was able to have his own bedroom. Life was about to begin a-new for all concerned.

The first transition was to change schools for Christian and Aaron. Larry was already enrolled in a private Catholic high school only blocks from our house, and had been driving himself there every day so there was no need of a change for him. Aaron, however had enrolled in a public high school near his mother's home which was over ten miles away from me. He had gone out for football and wrestling team and had made first string tackle and had made the wrestling team by defeating everyone in his weight class. I now had the decision of what to do with him.

I can recall my parents moving me from one school to another when I was a junior in high school and it was probably the most traumatic moment of my childhood. With that in mind it was difficult to move him, but I decided that it would be in his best interest to enroll him in the local school due to the fact that he had been skipping classes on a regular basis. As much as both myself and the principal had tried to alter his behavior, the problem persisted. I didn't know if it was

240

because he was acting out in defiance of authority or rebelling against his parents or both, but something had to be done. This, coupled with driving him back and forth during peak traffic hours each day, the change seemed logical. The next day he enrolled in our district's high school as a junior, which was only three blocks from home.

Christian was in his last year at an eight year private Catholic school. He was a star athlete, a starter in all the major sports and wasn't about to be uprooted his last year there, so every day I drove him to school then returned home again only to drive back again in the afternoon, where I still coached him and his fellow eighth grade team mates, then back home again after practice. It was a total of over fifty miles of driving each and every day, Sundays excluded. The mileage on my odometer rolled by faster than a space ship on its journey to the Moon.

As I've indicated before, my religious belief plays an important part in my life. I hold firm to the belief that a strong religious conviction as a child gives one the foundation for building character blocks. One evening, while thumbing through the Bible, I came upon Romans 12:9. "Love must be sincere. Hate what is evil; cling to what is good. Be devoted to one another in brotherly love. Honor one another above yourselves. Never be lacking in zeal, but keep your spiritual fervor..."

I remembered a demonstration our pastor gave the children one day, during kid's corner, the few moments spent with the kids at the beginning of Sunday services which is devoted to giving them a lesson in life. The minister gave each of the kids a tube of tooth paste and told them to squeeze it all out on the paper that had been laid out on the floor, which they did with great delight.

Walking down from the pulpit, he approvingly looked at the long line of multi-colored tooth paste, and then said, "Now put it all back in the tubes again." Laughing, they attempted the task in vein. There was no way.

"Imagine the tooth paste as words spoken in haste or anger to a friend or someone in your family," he had said, when they had returned to their seats. "Once the words are out of your mouth, there is no way you can take them back." A good lesson. Put our brain into gear before setting our tongue in motion.

For me, the lesson had another meaning. What was past, was past. What was done, was done and couldn't be undone, no matter who was a fault or who was hurt. I knew everyone was hurting, but the time had come to put that behind us and get on with our lives. From that moment on, I concentrated on the positive, eliminating negativism from my thoughts.

Regrets

As a child, in our small town all the resident's lawns and gardens were watered by irrigation ditches. The price of water was dirt cheep as it was pumped up from the Columbia River which flowed a mere three hundred yards from our house. The period of time when a family received their assigned allotment of water was divided into days which was further subdivided into the hours when the water was expected to reach a particular house and/or garden. Our watering days were Tuesday and Friday at two o'clock in the afternoon.

The drill was as follows: the water would flow down the ditch. The first guy in line would remove the wooden gate that led to his yard or garden and block subsequently block the water, thus diverting it onto his property. Twenty minutes to half-an-hour later, his property would have been flooded. He would then remove the gate from the ditch and replace it at the exit to his property, thus allowing the water to flow onto the next property.

If, for some unknown reason a particular household or farmer was unable to be home to catch the water at their appointed time, such as a death in the family, or a hunting accident like the time Kenny shot his big toe off because he forgot to put on the safety catch before crawling towards a flock of geese, that was just your tough luck. Woe be unto he who would stop the flow of water out of turn. That was grounds for everyone on the route turning out for a tar and feathering session.

Our neighbor, Mr. Smith, was the 'ditch-rider'. It was his job to drive his jeep along all the ditches to see that they weren't blocked up with tumbleweeds or, worse yet, someone opened their flood-gate out of turn. Subsequently, many days and nights, water flowed down the irrigation ditches with the destination of someone down the line.

When we had nothing better to do with our time, my brother and I used to sneak out of the house after dinner, after dark and swipe water melons from Thompson's melon patch up the road a piece. We'd thump the melons until we found one that sounded hollow, then snap the vine and carry our booty to the edge of the trees where we would drop in on the ground, breaking it in two. Then we'd scoop out the heart with our fingers and slurp in up, laughing and thanking old farmer Thompson for his generosity.

With our faces red from water melon hearts, we would sneak back to the patch to find another big, ripe melon. This went on until one Halloween night when farmer Thompson was waiting for us in the middle of the patch, sitting in a little hole that he had dug for himself. It was just deep enough for him not be noticed. In the moonlight his bald head looked just like any other melon.

He waited until a bunch of us hooligans were in the middle of the patch and had picked one of his melons. We thought we would get some refreshments before tippin' over his outhouse. We were giggling as we tiptoed back towards the tree line when we heard this loud bang, kinda like a cannon being fired. It was then that we heard this whipping sound coming through the air. "Bacon rinds," Bobbie Holden yelled, as we dropped the melon and ran for our lives.

Too late. Bobbie let out a loud yell as the bacon rind hit him directly in the seat of his pants, slapping his butt like a leather belt.

"Yeow!" he yelled, as he streaked past us like a jet airplane.

We had heard that some of the farmers had taken to loading bacon rind and rock salt in their twelve gages, but this was the first time that we had first hand experience with the foul, underhanded act. After that, brother and I decided that a more sophisticated technique was needed if we were to continue in our thieving' ways.

We came upon the solution quite naturally as we were swimming in the irrigation ditch after one particularly successful water melon eating session. "Why not let the water steal the melons for us," I suggested.

Brother looked at me like I had one melon too many, but listened to his older brother anyway. "We can just put the melons in the ditch and walk home," I explained, proud of my ingenious criminal mind. "We'll let the irrigation water carry the melon to our house. When it reaches us, we'll pull the irrigation gate and the melons will simple roll down onto our lawn." We agreed gave it a try. The idea worked ingeniously, but it took the fun out of eating them in the watermelon patch.

One day I got caught! Adam Smith was the mayor, town Marshall and fire-chief along with his job of running the general store and gas station. Certain that I would spend the rest of my natural youth behind bars in the jail two towns away, (we had neither formal law enforcement nor jails in our town) I was in a low-level panic.

Our minister, Mel Smith came to my rescue and talked the authorities into letting me be released into his custody. In retrospect, I'm sure that the most I would have gotten was a severe reprimand, or would have had to hoe weeds for the next month, but at the time I didn't know that. I figured I was destined to be a lifer.

I never forgot the kindness and understanding that Mel Smith afforded me. And most of all, there was never a hint of degradation or belittlement in neither his eyes nor his demeanor. I probably didn't hurt that he was close friends of my folks, but at the time, I don't remember appreciating him as much as I do now. This would turn out to be one of those times when a negative turned into a positive, only I wasn't smart enough to realize it at the time. If I hadn't gotten caught and subjected to potential punishment, who knows, I may have escalated to high jacking tractors or robbing' old ladies.

As I mentioned previously, our father used to raise a hundred chickens a year and we raised our own food, including a pig each year. He gave the minister chickens, vegetables and jars of fruit that my mother would put up each year. Maybe his kindness was in return for all the favors we received from him, but whether that's the case or not, I feel a deep sense of gratitude towards the man for the lasting impression that he left on me.

A few years back I asked my mother what ever happened to him. Even though he may not remember the lad of thirty years ago in that small town, I wanted to find him and express my personal gratitude for past favors. I was disheartened when I learned that he had passed away several years previously. I felt a great void for having missed the opportunity to express my gratitude to him, belated as it was.

As I look at my own children, there are selfish regrets that I remember when I think back on them. Things that I'm certain that the children, if asked, wouldn't remember and probably had no impression beyond the moment that it had occurred. But I remember them, and that's what's important to me.

I used to read a story to the kids each night before they went to sleep. I picked out stories that we both enjoyed like *The Adventures of `Ber Rabbit and the Tar Baby* or *Jack in the Bean Stock*. During that the time when the tension was so thick in the household that it could be cut with a knife, I found myself strung out beyond reason. I can recall times when the kids were expecting me to read them a story, but I was so upset that I said, "Not tonight. Go to sleep." In retrospect, I greatly regret those missed moments of intimacy that I foolishly squandered.

The Foundation

I have this good friend, Stephen, (he's the lawyer friend I mentioned previously, and I try not to hold that against him), you'll remember him from earlier paragraphs when I mentioned that we used to played tennis and basketball together. Later on, after the divorce we used to play racquetball on a weekly basis. After an exhilarating three games of flinging our bodies around the court, hitting the blue ball, we would retreat to the stream room, exhausted, where we would have our best conversations.

A favorite approach was often, "What would you do if ....", type propositions. On an occasion he'll bounce a theory off me or we'll discuss a legal problem that he wanted to try on for size which was usually couched in words such as, "What would you do if ....".

He became a father for the first time after entering his forties, so there was a lot of conversation about his new pride and joy: How she picked up on feelings at such an early age, her vocabulary and how cute she was in her mannerisms. It's obvious that she's the apple of his eye, as it should be and would be the case with most fathers. While stretching my legs, trying to work out the tightened muscles, I posed the question: "Let's assume for some unforeseen reason you and your wife knew that you were both destined to part this earth and would be forced to give up your child to another couple to raise until she became an adult. Let's further assume that you could give them only one set of instructions relative to her bringing up, what would that be?"

Not one to quickly respond, a trait no doubt gained from extensive courtroom experience, he thought for a while before responding.

"I don't know. That's a tough one. I would want her to be happy, I suppose."

"That's too general. Everyone wants their loved one's to be happy. Happiness is relative. Does that mean that she has to be given everything she wants to be happy? If she wants a horse or a baby elephant, does that mean that she have to have it in order to be happy, or should she be made to suffer in order to appreciate things then become happy with what she's achieved on her own?"

He looked at me for a moment, not necessarily understanding where I was taking this topic, and, in all probability, wondering if I'd been in the steam room too long.

"I'm looking for a specific response such as, no matter what happens in her life, there is one specific thing that must be taught to her or imparted upon her by her new substitute parents as a condition to their raising your daughter. For example, say above all she must be given voice lessons, because you and your wife have always wanted her to be a performer, or tennis lessons because you had always envisioned her to be a professional tennis player.. See what I mean?"

"Do you know what you would say?" he asked. A good lawyer's response. When on defense, go on the offensive by asking the questions.

"I know exactly what I would require."

"What?"

I knew that he would want to think about his answer before responding, which I appreciated. Steve's that kind of a guy. Introspective, thoughtful and through. I decided to tell him my most important requirement. I was interested in his response, besides, it was getting too hot and I had to get out.

After the steamer, I usually jump in the cold plunge, a six-foot square pool three feet deep filled with cold water. It's not only refreshing, but closes the body pores as well. After the cold plunge, Steve and I sit on the edge of the raised ceramic tile whirlpool and continue our philosophic discussions until we cool down at which time we take a shower and dress.

"Well?" he inquired, looking at me, as I draped myself in a towel.

I look at him for a moment before responding. "You're Jewish," a fact that I'm sure he needed reminding of. "When you were a child, did you and your parents spend much time in the synagogue?"

"Our family wasn't particularly religious, although we do get together with the family and honor the Jewish religious ceremonies such as Rosh Hashanah, Yom Kippur and of course, Hanukah. When I was young I studied Hebrew when I was preparing for my Bar Mitzvah, of course." He became thoughtful for a moment they concluded, "Aside from that, I can't say that our family has been especially religious."

He turned to me for the response that he knew was coming. Without his asking I said, "When I was a child, every Sunday my folks took me to Sunday school then we attended the church services. There was no discussion about wanting to go or not wanting to. As far as I was concerned, that was just the way life was. When I eventually graduated from high school and went on to college, I chose a religious school, Lewis and Clark College in Portland, Oregon, a small Presbyterian College. I went to chapel every Wednesday, prayed before meals and at bedtime, went to church on Sunday and was a God-loving Christian soul.

"Then something happened to me. During my sophomore year, unbeknownst to me or any of the other ninety-eight sophomores who were taking the required History of Civilization and Humanities course something shook our timbers. The time had arrived where our instructors had chosen to methodically tear down our basic religious beliefs. Before we knew what had happened to us, we were all doubting its very existence. You could hear heated discourse emanating from any one of the dorm rooms where two or more had gathered, seeking answers. I took no solace in knowing that I wasn't the only one who had their pillars jerked from underneath them ."

"How did that you make you feel?"

"It scared the shit out of me, to be frank. I didn't realize it at the time, but my faith had always been a significant part of my life, like my hand or a foot or my parents. I just wasn't conscious of the fact. I worried about it so much that I actually got a peptic ulcer!"

"You're kidding?"

"Nope."

"So what happened? Why did the school do that to you?"

"Apparently, their philosophy was to tear down our so-called Sunday-school, childhood faith and rebuild it into a more mature, stable foundation the following year when we took the required religion class."

"And did it?"

"Can't say. After two years at Lewis and Clark I couldn't afford the tuition any longer so I transferred to the University of Oregon."

"And?"

"Three years went by and eventually I was drafted into the army. I don't think it was until then that I actually started to get back on track. It's a frightening thing to have the one stable thing in your life jerked from under you. At least it was for me."

"Can't say that I've ever had that experience."

I replayed my close encounter experience with God to Steve. When I had finished telling him my story, he looked at me for a long moment, not quite knowing what to say. "I've never had a religious experience anything like that or have experience that sort of feeling."

I wasn't sure if he was telling me that religion wasn't that important to him or that he had simply never felt that strong about his faith.

"My wife came from a stoic Catholic background, as you well know. If we were to have kids, a condition of our getting married was that they would have to be raised Catholic, no ifs ands or buts about it and no arguments. I even had to attend classes on Catholicism and sign an agreement that I would raise the kids Catholic."

"How did you feel about that?"

"Actually, it wasn't so important what faith they were raised in so long as they were given a sound religious foundation. Admittedly, being raised as a Lutheran, I've never been a proponent of Catholicism. I don't adhere to their practices of confession, no meat on Fridays which, of course, has since been disposed of, and praying to the Virgin Mary, not to mention giving my money to the wealthiest church in the world, but that's another topic."

"So the kids were raised Catholic. Even after your divorce when you were raising them alone?"

I nodded. "Actually, during the divorce, those days when I had the kids on week-ends, I used to take them to the evening Sunday services at the mission at the University of Santa Clara. There the congregation was made up of mostly college students with a sprinkling of adults. Every week the service was given by a different priest. I liked the fact that they spoke to you on a level as an intelligent person, not as if you had the IQ of a stump like a lot of churches do. It was really intellectually invigorating.

"I remember this one sermon in particular. It was Easter and the priest was describing the crucifixion of Christ. Probably not something that you as a Jew would dwell on," I smiled.

He made no comment.

"He asked for everyone to close their eyes and to concentrate and visualize what he was saying. He wanted us to imagine that we were one of the group of people standing along side of the road when Christ was on his way to be crucified. He invited us to visualize the people who were jeering at him, spitting on him and taunting him as he struggled with the wooden cross. He asked us to imagine a man bold enough to leave the crowd and offer the accused a drink of water.

"He wanted the congregation to examine how we felt, being there and to visualize what we would have done, being in a hostile crowd and all. If we would have been strong enough to be the one who offered the condemned man water. It was very thought provoking."

"So, to answer your own question, you feel that religion is the most single important thing that a child should be taught. Above everything else." He was ready for the shower and wanted to get to the bottom of my hypothetical question.

"If I had but one requirement of someone raising my children, it would be to insure myself that the kids would have a solid, religious upbringing. Not to the point that I'm a fanatic, you understand. To me, when all else fails, friends, job, society or parents, spouse, one can always fall back on their faith."

Steve nodded, and without comment went off to the showers.

No Mirror Images

The kids are all out of the house now, working full time and are, for all intents and purposes, on their own. It's true, I must confess, I did buy them a four-bedroom, two bath fixer-upper. I figured I'd kill several birds with one stone.

First of all, by owning their own place they'd be out of the house for good. There would be none of this, "I can't make it on my own, can I move back in, stuff. I have two acquaintances who have grown children who are twenty-seven and forty-two respectively who have *never* left the nest. When you think about it, they've got it made. Why move? They're provided shelter, food, cooking and laundry. These are people who will obviously never leave home. I'd be willing to bet doughnut holes to dollars that if one of them got married, they'd move their bride in with the folks!

The house that they owned, I say owned because they have since sold the place and have taken the proceeds and – well that' another story - anyway, there had been carpeting on the living room floor. The decision had been made to tear that up and discard it, least it turn to a mud-gray consisting of spilt beer, food and peanut shells textured with whatever their collective thirty friends track in each day, not to mention the two dogs and a stray cat who come and go at will.

I was delighted to find hardwood flooring beneath the carpeting. It was agreed that we would sand the floors, then stain them walnut, the

252

closest color to dirt that there is. Having hardwood floors would make it easier to keep clean. One can shovel the debris off a wooden floor whereas it takes a vacuum cleaner to clean a carpet.

We established the following weekend as a time to start the project. I showed up at ten o'clock armed with an electric sander, paint brushes and stain. Amazingly enough, no one was home. I say amazing because it was still morning at they were gone. Usually I had to throw a bucket of cold water on them to get them up before two p.m.

I started sanding the floors, thinking they would soon show. For two days I sanded until I was finished. Once the floors had been sanded, I applied the stain and then sealant to the surface. I say "I" because, during the time that I was sanding, staining and sealing, they apparently all had job applications to fill out and interviews to attend. Being a dutiful father who wants his kids to get ahead, I concluded that outside employment, thus self sustaining behavior comes first, right after education.

Their list of priorities goes: parties first, then sleep and rest following such exhaustive activity, then studies and last but not least, ugh - a job. So you can see, when they offered to get a job, my mind turned to putty and I dummied up, lack of logic notwithstanding.

For one reason or another, none of them got the job, although the interviews must have been exhaustive, lasting the entire day and then some. I knew that the interviewers allowed them to return home for the evening, because when I returned to the house the next morning to continue the next phase of sanding and staining, I had to be sure the taco and peanut shells were shoveled off the floor before applying the next coat of sealant. I was careful not to cut myself on the broken bottles, however.

I was certain that once the house had been refurbished with a new roof, a new paint job inside and out and landscaping, the value would go up, as all real estate does, and they could reap the benefits from the upside potential, after I recouped my investment, of course. This, I rationalized, would give each of them a nest egg to get started in life, after parties, education, fun and rest and more parties finally got out of their system.

The standard, undeniable, unbreakable rule of real estate is three simple words: location, location, location. You can build a wonderful two-story garden house in a run-down shanty neighborhood and you'll never recoup your investment. But, buy a shanty house in a good neighborhood and paint it, landscape it and make it blend in - in other words, wrap kaka in colorful cellophane, and you've got an investment that will appreciate.

I went one better. Our kaka wasn't a bad house, just the worst looking one on the block. And that was before we bought it. As I said, we painted, re-roofed and landscaped the joint to make it blend in. Aside from the Toyota truck sitting in the driveway whose exterior didn't have a six-inch space without dents, holes or broken windows, and whose bed is filled with twenty bags of garbage, and the lawn has man eating night predators hiding in it from lack of grooming, the place didn't look half-bad.

I grass clothed the kitchen and living room walls, while they painted their individual rooms. One was black, one a dusty brown and the other ... I don't think they have a name for the blend of color yet. Somewhere between algae and mold.

I hired an inmate from one of the local institutions who was temporary on parole, to put ceramic tile around the kitchen sink and cooking area while another able bodied parolee installed new linoleum on the floor. The ceramic tile looked great, except one of the corners came off after someone hit it with the butt of a butcher knife. Killing a fly, I'm told.

When the kids pulled the refrigerator back over the new linoleum, they managed to rip a four foot gash fourteen inches wide right in the middle of the floor. Salvador Dali couldn't have done a better job. It reminded me one of the pictures that he painted years ago portraying bent watches, like melted butter, bending over tables and women with drawers coming out of their chests. At least the grass cloth I put up doesn't show the holes where the darts miss the board.

I used to go over to their house once or twice a week, just to give instructions on cleaning and maintaining the place and yell obscenities at the bodies laying sleeping on the couches whose outstretched hands still held half-filled beer bottles. After I left, I always felt guilty. After all, it was only four o'clock in the afternoon. They were probably still tired from seeking employment the night before. I've yet to find out for sure, because they're never been awake when I'm there.

Oh, I have to take that back. Myself and the wife drove by their place after taking in a movie one night, but I couldn't find a place to park due to all the traffic. On top of it all, you know those cars with the colorful red and blue flashing lights? Well, they were parked two and three deep and uniformed officers were running around, whooping it up with raised night sticks. Some sort of night ritual I've been told. We decided not to impose on their fun.

It seems that every time I went go over there I got so upset that it took me the better part of two days to settle down again. My ulcer would act up so I informed the kids that I wouldn't be coming by anymore. That's when I got a blast in the pants that I hadn't expected.

"Sooner or later you're going to have to realize that we're not three little Howard's running around," my oldest child calmly informed me as he slammed down another brew. "And we never will be. We don't think like you do, we don't have the same values that you do, and we don't have the same goals as you." There was a pause as he let that message sink in. "We appreciate everything you've done for us, but why don't you just accept us as we are and enjoy our company instead of getting upset every time you come over? Watch the dog poo there, pop," he said, as I shifted my weight. "And throw me another brew. There's a good Da."

I had to think long and hard about that one. He's right, you know. We, as a group of fathers, especially those of us from the old school who feel that hard work yields its own rewards, tend to try to mold our offspring's in our own image, especially if we think our image is appropriate. I worked hard all my life, every since I was in the fifth grade, to be exact. I've never asked anyone for anything and what I've got, I worked hard for and I expect my children to be exactly like me, in form, if not substance.

I expect them to work hard and sacrifice to get ahead. But, you know what? They didn't care if they have a nice house or furniture that stands on its own or food in the frig and not on the floor or grass that's actually green or trees that are alive. I say 'didn't', because now that they have grown up, their values have changed.

What did they care about? Friends. And having a good time. Everything else was immaterial, although they did have a propensity for needing cloths, gas and food from time to time.

So, who was right? The older establishment that's worked their fingers to the bone all of their adult life only to retire at sixty-five, or and maybe by that time are too old or broken up to enjoy the finer things that was lost to their youth, or the younger generation that parties their life away without a care in the world? Their only care being getting high, having a good time, getting laid and going to concerts. I think the jury is still on that one. Personally, it would scare the pants off me to think of myself at retirement age and my only income being whatever Uncle Sam sees fit to dole out to me.

One thing I'm sure of, however. If a parent is paying for their kid's way in life, I stand firm on the fact that there are certain expectations that one should be able to depend on. For example, if you're providing housing or money for housing, the least one can expect is that they who are the recipient of same should maintain the place in reasonable cleanliness. That's not too much to ask, is it?

It angers an adult to no end when a kid moves out of an apartment where he, or in this case, I should correctly say I, put up seven-hundred-fifty dollars for a deposit, only to have that garnished when they move out because the place is left in shambles. In addition to garnishing the "cleaning" deposit, the management back-bills the kid an additional two-thousand-seven hundred dollars for additional cleaning, painting, carpeting -- assessed damages that he and his friends did to the place.

I've seen apartments where tenants have lived for six months to a year and then moved out. No normal person would take their life in their hands by venturing in there without first throwing in a dozen bug bombs. The carpeting, whatever color it was prior to their moving in, is now dull grey-brown-black, full of gum, motor oil, ketchup and sand from the beach, all mixed in with peanut shells, taco's, dog poo and who knows what else. The drapes are either hanging from broken rods or lying on the floor, the oven is black on black and the list goes on. The walls are totally painted with skulls, daggers and replications of bottles of their favorite spirits as well as various life forms, both living and dead.

Small wonder they loose their deposits. They couldn't restore that place back to its original status of their life depended on it. When the tenants are kids and they move out, I think the owners just removes the sheetrock, carpeting and all fixtures down to the bare studs and starts over again. After moving from one such apartment into another, one of my off springs asked if I would cosign for him because the landlord wouldn't accept him as being the one solely responsible for subsequent damages. I'll bet you can guess what my answer was.

If you're providing clothing for junior, the least one can expect is that which you had purchased with your hard earned dollars should be taken care of and not found on the floor of one's vehicle, or under the stray dog that is using it for a flea trap. I would like it to be either hung in a closet or stored in a dresser, and to be washed from time to time, so it somehow resembles the color of the original garment.

If you provide food, it should be eaten, not thrown, walked on or worse yet, left to mold in the refrigerator.

If you provide money for their education, it's reasonable to expect that the little darlings should at least devote enough time to their studies to get passing grades with a sprinkling of 'B's. I consider passing grades a 'C' and above. Even though I've been told that a 'D' is passing. It isn't acceptable to my standards. I contend that if they can't achieve this minimal status, they don't have the drive to succeed anyway and may as well join the real world and find a job instead of prolonging the inevitable.

I've told my little treasures that as long as they're in school and are doing acceptable work, I'd help them. They drop out of school and I drop their support.

I can recall one of them advising me as if I had the IQ of a parking meter with questions such as, "I should take automotive so I can learn how to fix my own car, don't you think?" Which is actually a good point because so far, his automotive expertise has been limited to putting gas in the car and inserting the key into the ignition, or, "I should take computer classes so I can understand how to make a program," or, "I should take environmental studies. You know the world is going to hell in a handbag because your generation messed everything up for us."

The best laid plans of mice and men.... Hopefully he'll get tired of wearing the same duds every day and eating chicken pot pies, baked potatoes and corn chips and will someday want a decent mode of transportation.

The question of friends always surfaces, "Now that you've raised three boys, how do you feel about them. They're all good-lookin', nice, young men. You should be proud.

I guess, should the truth be told, a part of me is satisfied that they're healthy, intelligent and are on their own, carrying their own weight.

What does success mean? In my mind, for starters, being totally independent of me and self sustaining. I would like them to eventually be married and have a small family of their own with little grand-Howard's to bounce on my knee. Then, I'll get my revenge!

But then, there I go again. If someone is a duplication of oneself, one of us is unnecessary, and it's probably me. But then, that's what this is all about, isn't it. Raising your child in your image? There's a warm feeling couched inside every father that even if you get a frantic call at midnight saying, "Help! Dad! My car won't work."

It's nice to be needed. But then again, being not needed is when you've done your job right. That's when you can say, "I used to be a father," and feel good about it.

As I said, the boys are now grown up and have matured into fine young men, of which I am immensely proud. They all have graduated from college and have formed their own commercial real estate company, The Losness Group. As of this writing, one of them have been married, Christian, in the year 2008. Congratulations!

I like to think that they have all evolved, in some small manner, into little Howards after all. They all have a great work ethic, have their heads screwed on straight and in their own way, are their own men, just like their father was – is.

I love you guys!

Did I Raise You Right?

Sooner or later, each of our children will take on a bride or husband of their own, God willing and the tide don't rise and they're not gay. Picking a suitable mate is probably the most important decision they'll make in their life. And oddly enough, it's a decision that is packed with emotion and often times not that much thought is given as to the future of their relationship. When I use the word "picking a suitable mate" eyebrows are going to rise.

"You sound like your buying a used car," I've been told.

Well, that's about it. You have to look at it that the full light of the day. Walk around, kick the tires, check out the paint and see what the interior is like. One of my friends had a son who fell in love with everything that walked within grabbing distance. From the age of fourteen he was already picking out his wife. Whomever he marries, I hope I'm wrong, but I'm sure it won't last beyond the next foxy chick that crosses his vision.

You're going to be with this person for the rest of your life, hopefully. You had better look beyond the paint job. "What's her family like?"

"Why should I care? I'm not marrying the family."

"You sure are! Who do you think raised your bride? She's a product of her upbringing. As the twig is bent, so grows the tree." My father once told me, "If you want to know what your wife will look like twenty years from now, look at her mother."

When one has a roommate after leaving home for the first time and lives in a dorm or some other communal living, he is afforded the opportunity to learn a lot about himself. What bugs you about your roommate? Does he make body noises that irritate you? How about when he leaves things lying around the room? Does he snore? Does he have some annoying vocal mannerism that irritates you like clearing his throat, sighing, cracking his fingers or snapping his neck?

These are but a few minor things that are but a drop in a bucket when you pick someone to live with for *life*. I have had roommates for the first five years of college before I was drafted into the army. Then, I lived with a girlfriend two months before actually going into the service. I learned more about myself those two months than I had the previous five years. I was living with a member of the opposite sex, and that in itself is a major adjustment.

I was amazed at how self centered I was. Previously, I hadn't been concerned about anyone but myself. It amazed me how the little things that you share with someone can irritate you. Insignificant nothings! So insignificant that I can't even remember what they were, but I can remember that I was irritated. Take those little irritations for two months and multiply them by fifty years of marriage and let me tell you, you've got some adjustments to consider.

Our minister said that most people think marriage is a fifty-fifty proposition. Don't kid yourself. It's a one-hundred percent proposition. You have to be willing to give one-hundred percent all of the time or you're doomed to failure. Fifty percent doesn't cut it!

During a recent discussion about marriage, one of my boys made a disturbing comment, that send my brain reeling. "I'm not going to have any kids," he announced while we were having our father-son discussion about his future. I was taken aback for a moment, and then inquired what brought on this decision.

"Look at you and mom. And look and so-and-so, and so-and-so, two other couples who have either gotten divorced or who were constantly fighting. I don't want to bring a child into that kind of environment. It wouldn't be fair to either them or me."

"All marriages don't end up in divorce or have ongoing problems. Learn by example. See where others have gone wrong and learn from them. Failure should be our teacher, not our undertaker. Failure is a learning tool, not total defeat. Everyone has made mistakes. They key is to be smart enough to learn from them and become strong because of them."

He didn't look impressed.

"Take me for example. This isn't right on point, but the logic is there. When I first started working in real estate, the first thing I learned was what not to do. And I learned that from watching my fellow associates. When one of them would make a large commission, the first thing they did was go on a vacation, buy a new car or give their wives a fur coat. Next thing you know, they're broke and asking for five bucks to buy lunch!

"And the amazing thing is, they didn't learn from their previous experience! A few months later, they'd earn another commission and out they'd go and celebrate. Pretty soon they're back asking for another five for lunch.

"Whenever I earned a commission, the first thing I did was invest it. I *never* spend my commission frivolously. True, we had to live close to the vest, but my family was always cared for and lacked for nothing. On the other hand, I didn't drive new cars and sport designer duds, but we lived comfortably. During the passage of time I secured my families' future while those other brokers are still out beating the bushes for the next deal."

"Sounds like Arthur Miller's *Death of a Salesman*."

"Exactly! Now can you see what I mean by learning from other peoples mistakes?"

"I'm still not having any kids."

In one sense, off-springs are more important to the man than it is to a woman in that it's important for a man to have a child, preferably a male child, to carry on his name. More than that, if a man or woman doesn't reproduce themselves and have children, their blood line dies with them. To me that's very important. It's our way of living on through our children. It's always sad when I see a couple who either don't want kids, or can't have them for one reason or another. I think their lives are so empty. I've known people who don't have kids but they have dogs or cats. They shower their animals with affection as if they were their children - and they probably are!

I write books and paint pictures and hopefully, my work will succeed me. Call it vanity, but it's a good feeling to know that somewhere down the line, maybe a hundred years from now, a great-grandchild will pick up this book and say, "My great grandfather wrote this", or point to a picture on the wall and say, "My great grandfather painted that picture".

So you can see why I get a little nervous when I hear my healthy male child say that he doesn't plan on having children. I'm sure that he's just pulling my chain. When the time comes and Miss Right enters his life, I'm certain that she'll want to have her own brood of house apes.

A successful marriage is determined on how successful the mates are in treating one another. One needs to treat their mate with consideration as well as with love and affection because when the glow is off the bud and marriage becomes the everyday struggle that inevitably follows, one needs to treat their mate with respect and consideration to keep everything on an even keel.

Children learn by example. If we curse, smoke, lose our temper and put others down all the time, they will feel that this is acceptable behavior. A boy I know uses the 'F' word in nearly every sentence he speaks, and he's a college graduate. One day when he was visiting our house, I took him aside and told him that I didn't appreciate him using the 'F' word in my house and certainly not in the presence of my wife.

He was shocked that I even brought it up, and then apologized. "I didn't know that I was using that word," he said.

"That's the problem with using profanity. You get so used to using those words, you use them without even knowing it. It's similar to a nervous tick like shrugging one's shoulders or wrinkling one's nose. You do it so often; it just becomes part of your natural behavior. In your case, you do yourself a disservice, because, I can assure you, people will view you in a different light once they hear your language."

Humor

I think humor is one of the most important attributes in a marriage. If a husband and wife can laugh at themselves and enjoy life together in a light manner, not to say that they don't take serious things serious, the temperature of the family will certainly be less stressful and you'll find a greater abundance of love between two people.

I'm blessed by being married to a woman who has the greatest sense of humor I have ever known. I can be working at my computer in my office which is in another part of the house, and her infectious laughter will undoubtedly bring a smile to my face. She could be playing with our little Maltese, Tedi, or watching a comedy program on television, or talking to someone on the phone, or reading a book or newspaper and her laughter will ring throughout the house.

Compare this to a home where there is constant bickering, putting one down or continual criticism and you'll find a marriage that's heading for a brick wall. Laughter not only reduces blood pressure, but is actually a form of respiratory exercise. Dr. William Fry once wrote that laughter can be said to give the body a mini-workout that has been compared to stationary jogging.

Our minister related a story of a man and woman going on a vacation that they had planned for months. While on vacation, something occurred that brought tension between the couple and for the balance of the vacation, they were mad at one another. Now, years later, he looks back on that wasted vacation and he can still recall the miserable time they had, but for the life of him, he can't remember why they were angry with each other.

This all goes to point to what I designate as the Losness philosophy. *If it's not important enough to be remembered five years from now, it's not worth wasting the time and energy getting upset over.* How many times has an evening out with friends or family been ruined by worrying over something that you either had no control over or got angry over something trivial? It could have been the lack of consideration of a fellow worker, or your mate forgot to do something as minor as forgetting to set the VCR recorder, or neglected to tell you of a missed telephone call. It's done. That bell has been rung. Let it go, get rid of it. Don't let it hang around your neck like a rock. It'll just ruin your day or worse yet, the day of those around you. And I guarantee you five years from now, it will not have made a whit of difference. Everything passes. The only thing worth getting angry over is something life threatening or future threatening and even then chances are, anger is not the answer. Very few things fall in this category. Why walk around angry, with a chip on your shoulder because some discourteous person cut in front of you, or said something without thinking? Let it go like water off a duck's back. Not only will you be the better for it, but just knowing that you had the insight to walk away from a potential explosive situation will give you a warm feeling. One of my pet peeves is drivers cutting in front of me. They gain seconds at the most and at the least have pissed me off. At the worst, they could have endangered our lives. I've learned to just let it go and back off whereas an acquaintance of mine gets explosive and honks his horn and gives the offending driver the finger. I have a feeling that some day he's going to be looking down wrong end of a gun barrel.

I recall an incident my brother relayed to me once day. He was driving down the highway to visit one of our properties in Longview when he noticed that the car behind his was impatient to get around him. Although he was driving at the designated speed limit, he pulled over to the slow lane, allowing them to pass. The car passed and he was astonished to see to elderly, white-haired ladies giving him the finger as they whizzed by. It was too funny.

I've always taught my kids that if they are confronted with an explosive situation, walk away. Don't lower yourself to their level and get into a confrontation that will only result in someone getting hurt. You may have to eat crow for a moment, but that's better than nursing a broken nose or worse yet, getting shot!

Writing Novels
& Children's books

When I was coaching little league baseball one of Christian's friends had a mother who wanted to be my assistant – to be able to coach her son. They went to school together at Saint John's and were best friends. I needed an assistant so I said, "Sure, why not?"

Come to find out that she was a published author. So, as the season wore on and we became friends, I asked her what kind of books did she write?

"Romance novels," she replied without hesitation.

I had never read a romance novel before, nor any novel for that matter outside of required reading in college. Who had time?

"Do you mind if I read a couple of your books?" I inquired one day after practice while we were picking up after the team.

She shot me a look that I read to say, 'If you want a book of mine, go out and buy one.' But instead, she said, "Sure. I'll bring you a couple next time we met."

The following week she showed up with two pocketbook novels. I thanked her and that night read one of them. I couldn't believe that anyone would write, let alone publish, such trash. I am no critic, but even in my limited experience, I knew I could do better.

That very next day I sat down at my computer and thus began my writing career. It took me a year to write my first novel, including six rewrites. When it was finished, I had three hundred-sixty-two pages typed. My title was, *Once I was Lost.* I knew that I was a novice at writing – duh! – so I set about to find a professional editor to read through the manuscript and make whatever modest changes they might suggest. After all, I had spent a year and had gone over the manuscript with a fine tooth comb six times, and as far as I could tell, it was perfect.

I located a local professional proof reader by surfing the web. I contacted her, agreed on a price, $1.50 per page, and sent her the manuscript. Four months later it was returned by parcel post. My fingers trembled as I removed the document and read her four page letter. In general, it pointed out some format errors that I could correct with my computer and said that she had made several suggestions relative to the plot that I could implement or ignore. My choice. In closing she said that I had potential and that in marketing the manuscript she suggested I hire an agent.

I thought that I could do like I've done with everything else in my life, market the manuscript myself. Then I thumbed through the pages and was shocked to see that *every* page had red marks. If it wasn't spelling or usage of the wrong word, it was punctuation, or a suggestion of how to improve the sentence. In some cases, I had been redundant in the usage of a word or phrase that I hadn't picked up on in my six revisions. I soon became aware that I had the script so memorized that in rereading it for the sixth time that I had simply glossed over obvious errors, not even seeing them. Every page had at least three corrections, and some even six or seven!

I made the appropriate corrections and then went down to Kinko's and instructed them to make ten copies of the manuscript. When I picked them up the next day it was in a cardboard box full of paper. Over three thousand pages! Now, all I had to do was find a publisher. I went down to the local bookstore and purchased a writer's guide to publishing that had the name, address and telephone number of every major publishing company in the country and Canada, plus the name of the person to contact and the type of manuscripts that they liked, i.e. mystery, historical, humors, fact or fiction. It was a plethora of information.

I read the book from cover to cover, over a thousand pages, making marks as to which company I would contact. At the end of each short paragraph describing the publishing company, there was a notation indicating whether or not they accepted manuscripts from writers not represented by an agent. I ignored that footnote and selected ten major publishers to send my masterpiece to.

The postage along was enough to choke a horse, plus every publishing house stated that if you wanted your manuscript returned, that you had to enclose a self addressed, self stamped envelope, SASE, for the returned document. That meant double postage.

I boxed all then manuscripts up along with a dynamite letter stating why they should publish my book, a short synopsis of the story, and a return package with proper postage. I took out a loan on the house and went to the post office where the postal clerk was none too happy to see me. Twenty minutes later I walked out of there whistling. Now all I had to do was wait for the acceptance letters and contracts to come floating back.

A week later the first response came back with a form letter stating that they didn't accept manuscripts submitted without an agent.

They hadn't even looked at it!

Then another came back and another until all ten manuscripts were returned, all with the same notations, *Manuscripts submitted without an agent unaccepted.*

I guess I needed an agent.

I went through the same process all over again, selecting an agency to represent me. I typed out a letter, describing my book, giving a short summary of myself and enclosed a synopsis of *Once I Was Lost*, made a hundred copies and began addressing envelopes. It took two days of typing, but I finally had all hundred envelopes stuffed, stamped and sealed. Now all I had to do was wait.

And wait.

And wait.

Finally, after a month, two letters tricked in, both saying that they would represent me. One was from Deering Literary Agency, Dorthey Deering, president. Her letter sounded most promising, so I signed the commitment letter and fired off the manuscript.

Four months passed and then one day I got a telephone call from the agency stating that they had a publisher, *North West Publishing*

Company out of Salt Lake City, Utah that was willing to publish the book. I was delighted.

A few more months passed and then one day I received the first galley in the mail. The galley was in the form of how the written manuscript would look when published, font and all, including a draft of the cover which depicted a rose with a broken stem, representing the character of the book, I suppose.

I was to read the galley and report any errors or changes that I wanted to submit before the book went into print. It was perfect, so I said, go ahead and publish. Six months went by and then I received a letter from an attorney stating that they represented North West Publishing company in bankruptcy.

Bankruptcy!

The letter went on to indicate that the publisher had printed 10,000 copies of the book and that I was welcome to purchase them from the court if I so desired. They didn't say how much each copy would cost, but the price on the cover was $7.95. What the hell am I going to do with 10,000 copies of my book anyway? Become my own distributor? I would have to think about this.

After a few days I called Steve, my attorney, and asked if he could get in contact with the attorney representing the publisher and ask about the cost of acquiring some of the books. A few days later he got back to me and said that the company had over 500,000 books printed but not yet distributed and that the court had decided to sell them all as one lot. He said that they had received hundreds of phone calls from authors like me wanting to acquire copies of their books. They had made it clear that the court was going to sell all the books as one lot and that there were going to be no exceptions.

After a few months I went on the internet and found a copy of my book for a sale, but when I tried to acquire one, it turned out to be a dead end. To this day, I have never seen a copy of the book and of course have received no compensation for the work.

I don't recall what got me started in writing children's books, but being an artist at heart I recall that I started drawing and painting the pictures while creating the story in my mind. My first book and my favorite was *The Scarecrow and Farmer Rabbit.* To date I've written and illustrated seven children's books, twenty mystery novels and two young adult books and am in the middle of writing my next novel.

I'm getting arthritis in my right hand now so I have to just use one finger on the right hand side of the keyboard while using the whole hand on the left side, making the whole process a little more cumbersome.

Entering a New Phase of Life

When my folks were alive, I went to Longview, Washington as often as I could, but not as often as I should have. I flew into Portland International. My brother, Larry would pick me up at the airport and then drive me to Longview, where my folks lived. The routine was, we'd drive up in the driveway, park the car and go inside to greet everyone. Mom would have prepared a nice lunch for us after which the four of us would go golfing. The folks loved golfing, especially mom. It didn't matter if it was hot, warm or cold, dry or wet, or if there was snow on the ground, we played golf.

Golf ran in the family. Everyone played except my wife, Myrna, my sister's husband, Bob and my oldest son, Larry. One particular nice spring day years ago brother Larry and I were playing when we decided that we should have a family golf tournament. It was agreed that I'd supply the trophy and every year the winner would have their name etched on the trophy. With the exception of me and my kids, everyone lived in the Northwest. It was decided that brother Larry would handicap the field. He was probably the best golfer, so he used himself as the measuring stick and handicapped everyone accordingly.

It was decided that the tournament would be held at Mint Valley Golf Course, just a few hundred yards from where the folks lived. We set a date, made tee times for the whole tribe and ascended upon Mint Valley's first tee in mass. We must have looked like a group of retarded folks, waiting for a buss, with everyone jostling one another, laughing and kidding. All told there were seventeen of us.

After everyone had finished eighteen holes we retired to the folk's house where Larry tallied up the scores, calculated the handicap and announced the winner. The winner was mom! I presented her with the trophy. She was stunned and as giddy as a new bride to have won the first Losness Open. We were all pleased that she had been the first winner.

The barbeque was fired up and several dozen ears of dad's corn freshly picked from his garden patch were cooked and served. It was one of the best days that I can recall, and I recorded it on my little video camera.

In looking through the photo album there were many such days – camping, riding in Uncle Bob's Dunn Buggy, days on the beach where the whole family rented a house and stayed for several days. Mom was a goer. At the drop of a hat, she was ready to go anywhere anytime. Dad on the other hand wasn't that crazy about going any where or doing anything, except golf. He went along because mom wanted to go, but if he had his way, he'd rather have stayed home and let the rest of the tribe do their thing.

I had a motor home and from time to time would drive it up to Portland and a couple times, we drove into Canada with mom and dad and Bob and Janice's family. Usually, while everyone went exploring or shopping, dad would find a shady spot by the side of the road and sit, smoking a cigarette, content to just wait for everyone's return. If we took too long, he'd take a nap in the motor home or car, as the case might be.

We had great times together and our family was as cohesive as they come. We *never* fought or disagreed amongst ourselves. We were a family that stayed together and played together. I often lamented the fact that I had settled down in California, so far from everyone. I missed them whenever I was away, which was ninety-five percent of the time.

Then, things began to change. Little things. We had a condo in Palm Springs and the folks liked to spend a couple of months in the winter there. On one particular visit I recall that the telephone had rang and mom had picked it up.

"Hello?"

No one answered.

"Hello?" She said again in a disturbed voice.

When no one answered, she slammed the phone down and glared at dad. "Can't you tell your girlfriend not to call, even where we're down here!"

Dad would look at me and shrug his shoulders.

"What was that all about?" I asked once mom had stormed off upstairs.

"It's been going on for some time now. Ever since we went to the pizza place and I kidded the waitress. She's under the impression that she's my girlfriend."

"How old is this person."

"Can't be more than twenty."

"How long has this been going on?"

"You mean since she's been accusing me of having a girl friend?"

"Yeah."

"About six months now." He hung his head. "It's been getting worse lately."

"How's that?"

"You know that large plant out on the back porch that Larry gave us?"

"Yeah."

"The other day she accused me of picking a flower from the pot and taking it over to 'my girlfriend'. Then she found a spoon missing. She accused me of taking that over to her too."

Now I know my dad. First of all, because he's smoked all of his life he's confided in me that he's impotent. Secondly, he's eighty something and not about to cheat on his wife. I started to be concerned and wondered if I should say something to my mother. When I brought the topic up, she frowned and accused dad of having a girl friend for some time now and that the very least she could do was not call while they were on vacation.

"How would she know the telephone number?" I inquired. "No one was on the telephone when you answered. Maybe it was just telemarketing. Happens to me all the time."

She gave me a look like I had just fallen off a turnip truck and turned to leave.

Six months later I visited them at their home in Washington where things had apparently not gotten any better. The following morning mom cornered me while I sat at the kitchen table. "I want you to take your father down to the bank and have him deposit those quarters he's been saving," she said.

Dad had a jar full of quarters that he had collected from the laundry coin machine that I had given him at one of our apartments, and I knew that when he was ready to go to the bank, that he would go. He didn't need me interfering with his business. Nonetheless I went into the family room, which was the designated smoking room, as he wasn't allowed to smoke in the house, and spoke to him about it.

He grimaced and said that she had nothing else to worry about than him getting his quarters to the bank. He advised me that he would get around to it when he was damned good and ready. His tone implied that I shouldn't push it, and I didn't.

"Well, what did he say?" she demanded once I had returned to the kitchen.

"I guess he'll get them to the bank when he's ready."

"I want you to take him to the bank today!" she demanded again.

In my most condescending voice, I responded, "It can't hurt to wait a day or two, can it?"

She had a handful of silverware that she was going to set the breakfast table with and she flung them at me, and then stormed out of the house.

I sat there, stunned for several moments with my body covered with silverware, trying to realize what had just happened. I was still sitting there when mom walked back in the door, calm as a cucumber.

"Maybe I should leave," I suggested. "I seem to be causing trouble." I was fishing for an apology, but instead she responded with, "Maybe you should."

Of course, I didn't leave. That was the second time that I had experienced mom's peculiar behavior and it was puzzling. That night I heard mom and dad talking. It was about two a.m. and then I heard them get up, go to the bathroom and then come back to bed. This scenario repeated itself several times. I happen to be up getting a glass of water when dad walked into the kitchen. It was three a.m.

"I can't take this much longer," he said. "Every hour or so she has to either go to the bathroom or demands that I call an ambulance."

"An ambulance?" I was shocked. "Why?"

"She keeps telling me that her back is breaking and she wants to go to the hospital."

"How long has this been going on?"

He took a deep breath. "Too long."

"Hans!" Mom's voice came from the back bedroom.

"There she goes again."

That was the first might that I had any realization of the severity of mom's mental condition.

Passages

It was February when she and our father were on their way to spend two months in Palm Springs, a ritual that they had fallen into every year, to get away from the relentless Washington state rain. As I mentioned earlier, they were both avid golfers. The only way they could get to play in the winter was to escape to a warmer, sunny climate. Palm Springs was warm, and only two and a-half hour flight away. They were going to stay in our condo for two months.

The night before their plane was to depart Portland International Airport, they had stayed at my sister's house. That night mother fell ill and was taken to the hospital with pains that were later diagnosed as a kidney infection. It's uncertain what else happened that night, but it's thought that in addition to the kidney infection, she may have suffered a slight stroke.

The end result was that she was eventually converted from the vibrant person that we all knew and loved into the developing shell of her former self, resulting in the woman that I now see before me. Due to her illness they were forced to postpone their trip a month.

After a month, although it was clear that she wasn't functioning as her old self, my mother and father decided to try to go to Palm Springs again. As a safety valve, my sister accompanied them to our condominium, which fronted on the fifth green of the municipal golf course.

Much to my sister's chagrin, she discovered that not only wasn't mom up to playing golf, neither mentally and definitely not physically, but she seemed to suddenly required constant attention. She rested all day long, sleeping most of the time. At night, now rested and wide awake, she walked the halls of the condo, which included thirteen stairs just off their bedroom -- straight down to the first floor!

Afraid that she might fall and injure herself, my sister and father had to keep a watchful ear for any movement all night long while trying to catch a few winks. As one might expect, they got little sleep. Then during the day, when mom was tired from lack of sleep, she would take long naps. Father and sister felt uneasy about going anywhere and leaving her alone and were afraid to rest their weary eyes, for fear of her wandering off or falling down the stairs.

To add insult to injury, poor mom seemed to be constantly confused and demanded constant medical attention. In the middle of the night, she would shake father awake and demand to be taken to the emergency room. At first, he thought that it was a true emergency and complied by calling an ambulance. At the hospital, she was examined and kept over night for observation -- typical hospital policy -- and released the following day with a clean bill of health. She returned on subsequent occasions, and the hospital came to realize the situation wasn't serious. After a preliminary examination, they would send her back home. Eventually, father came to realize that she wasn't in need of emergency care at all and, when she demanded to be taken to the hospital late at night or first thing in the morning, which was usually the case, he refused to take her. Mom became seriously agitated of course, and turned her aggression towards my father, even resorting to hitting him at times.

When mom demanded someone take her to the emergency room my sister, taking a more subtle, but effective approach, would pat her on the shoulder, take her hand, and in a soothing voice would say, "Let's just go downstairs and have a bite to eat first." Once they were downstairs she would point out what a nice day it was and how nice the flowers looked. She would suggest that maybe they should go sit outside and watch the golfers putt on the fifth green which was directly in front of their condo, or watch the golfers tee off on the adjoining sixth, par three hole. Mom loved golf. If not to play, to watch. She would nod her head, and before you know it she was sitting outside on the patio, sipping coffee and watching the golfers. She had forgotten all about her aches and pains and would say, yes, she was feeling better, thank you.

I told you my sister was a saint!

At night, after she had been in bed for a while the routine would start all over again. She would ask father to help her to the bathroom and would continually complain of various physical elements. If it wasn't her back breaking in two, there was a spur on her spine that was killing her. Then, just when everyone was exhausted and thought she had settled down for the night, she would have to go to the bathroom. Because her back was broken, she needed father to assist her, which he did without complaints.

This behavior continued on for a full month until finally, exhausted and at his wits end, father declared that he couldn't tolerate the situation any longer and made the decision to return home. By this time both sister and father was worn to a frazzle. Mom was constantly on edge, barking at everyone, calling him or her names and verbally abusing them. Like a chameleon lizard, she had changed from a pleasant, loveable wife and mother of three grown children, grandmother of seven and a great grandmother of one into a totally disagreeable personality, seemingly over-night.

When they got back home to Washington my father was worn out. He checked himself into a hospital with symptoms of a heart attack. This would be his third and last hospital visit, the doctors had said. He wouldn't survive another heart attack.

Something had to be done! Somehow, the constant pressure that faced him everyday had to be relieved. Relief came in the form of an acquaintance of my folks. Bill and Lindy, a couple who were unemployed and in need of a job. They had been previous managers of an apartment building that I owned, so we knew and trusted them. When they learned of the mom's condition, they offered to come and live with my parents and take care of her, for a handsome fee, of course.

"Anything," father said. He was to the point that he would have given up golf, food and popcorn and taken up residency in the closet, all for the sake of a good nights sleep. He was becoming irritable and hard to live with himself. Who wouldn't?

The temporary live-ins came and stayed the better part of a month, taking care of mother. They got her up in the morning, dress and fed her, took her for walks out on the back patio that overlooked the back yard and the meadow and mountains beyond. When it was time for her medication, they gave it to her. When it was time for bed, they got her situated and comfy. In short, they catered to her every need. She came to love their constant attentive devotion, all the while verbally abusing father for not fixing her breakfast or being there to give her the medication that she requested, although he did both and was there twenty-four hours a day, under self-imposed house arrest, attempting to cater to her every desire.

The live-in help may have been good for mother, but father was being driven to the brink of disaster. He finally came to the conclusion that either they had to go or he was going to move out himself. His privacy had been severely compromised and the situation had become intolerable. To add insult to injury, his wife of sixty-some years constantly displayed animosity towards him. He no longer felt at ease with another couple occupying his house, depriving him of any privacy. In short, he felt like a prisoner in his own home.

The next day the couple was given their marching orders.

We were back to square one!

Another family meeting was called.

Sister offered to move mom to her house and take her in. The next day, suitcase in hand, mother was moved to her daughter and son-in-law's house in Gresham, Oregon. Although he didn't say so in so many words, father breathed a silent sigh of relief.

Once a week, eighty-two year old father got in his twenty-year old pick-up and drove the distance from Washington to Oregon along the Columbia highway to visit his wife. Every visit was greeted with the same warm reception. "Humph! Where have you been?" she would declare with obvious sarcasm. "Seeing your girl friend? What are *you* dong here?" Usually, after an hour or more, she would calm down and they would have a civil conversation. Then the time came when he would leave. "Humph! He's going back to his girl friend again!" she would hiss.

"Mom! He doesn't have a girl friend! He's just going back home."

"He *is* home. This is my home! I don't know where he's going."

At first sister tried to explain that mother was visiting her at her house, but mom was so confused that she didn't know where she was. She often requested that sister retrieve something from the upstairs bedroom. Neither mom's house nor sister's house had a second story.

Thirty days later, with bags under her eyes, barely able to negotiate her way to the kitchen without falling over, stepping in something or falling asleep, sister was forced to admit defeat. Not only would mom sleep during the day and prowl the house at night, she continued to be abusive, not only to her immediate family, but also to anyone that came in contact with her. She seemed to be especially verbally abusive to our father, even resorting to smacking him one on his shoulder or face periodically, an act that she *never* would have engaged in her previous, normal life. The abuse even extended to her daughter who, as I previously stated, is nudging sainthood for even assuming the task of caring for her under such adverse conditions.

The straw that broke the camel's back came late one night when everyone was sleep. Mom got up in the middle of the night as she usually did and, craving something to drink. She found a bottle of green cleaning fluid under the kitchen sink and made herself a lethal cocktail! She later said she that she thought it had been lemonade.

The next day, battered and weary, barely able to hold her own, sister conceded that even with her boundless love and energy, mom had become too much for her to handle. It was decided that, although none of us wanted to admit it, the time had come to consider an alternative course of action.

The three children, my brother and sister and myself had a meeting. After considerable discussion, it was concluded that we had come to a fork in the road of life. A fork that none of us ever thought we would be forced to face, let alone have to make the decision that was forthcoming.

The decision seemed to be: which parent were we going to save?

On the one hand, if we returned mother back home, to dad, it would only be a matter of time until he had another heart attack. The doctors had said, after his two previous heart attacks, the next one would be his last. He wouldn't survive another. It was that simple.

We concluded that even if we hired a professional live-in nurse to care for mother twenty-four hours a day, at a cost of untold dollars I might add, father would still resent the intrusion. He had already stated that he would not live in the house under such circumstances, so that option was out.

The other solution, the unthinkable, was to put mom away. Put her in an institution with people who couldn't care for themselves. Someplace where she would receive the professional care that she needed yet not be institutionalized, in the strict sense.

Does that sound like double-talk? Well, it should, because that's exactly what it is. We were looking for someplace to house her, someone to take her off our hands and care for her with tender loving hands, so we wouldn't feel guilty about it. Does that sound familiar to anyone you know?

Due to my father's age, it was decided that she be housed in a facility in Washington, close to home where he would be sparred the drive to Oregon under the severe hazardous winter conditions that the northwest had to offer such as black ice, snow and driving rain.

They found a new facility that had just recently been built in his hometown. I'll call it Camelot Gardens!

Being a new facility was a distinct advantage in that it had a vacancy, which most desirable elderly care facilities didn't have. And it was attractively appointed, which most older facilities are not. And they seemed anxious to please!

Refreshing!

The family liked what they saw and signed her in at $2,500 a month!

Have we omitted anything here? Has anyone considered what mom is going to say about this plan of evicting her from her home and our lives and placing her in this well thought out scheme we've hatched?

Let me tell you what a friend of mine did.

Their mother was getting to the point that she also could no longer live by herself. She would cook food then forget to place the uneaten portions in the refrigerator, and then eat it the following day, or maybe the day after. She'd leave the gas stove's burners on and walk away, forgetting their blue flame was still ignited. Then, she started seeing people in her house. I'm told they're called sundowners. She'd summon the police to evict the unwanted intruders. When the police arrived, they'd simply find an empty house, save this frantic, aging woman. In short, she had come to the point in her life where her children thought she could no longer safely care for herself.

Unable or unwilling to take her into their homes, they searched for a place their mother. They settled upon an acceptable residential facility, bargained for her room and board then returned home to get mom.

"How about going for a ride, mom? We'll get some ice cream."

We all know that elderly mothers like ice cream. Or anything for that matter, just so long as they get some attention and are able to get out of the house for a while.

She did get her ice cream. Then, on the way home, they drove around, showing her various sites and neighborhoods, all the while cruising closer to their destination, confusing her a little as to where she actually was. But then, she trusts them. Right? They're family. They'd never lead her astray and, heaven forbid, would never just drop her off somewhere. Right. She's content and secure in their hands.

"What's this? Why are we stopping here?" She asked in a startled voice, looking around as they pull into the driveway of the strange residence.

"I want to show you something, mom. It'll only take a few minutes."

She's a little tentative. "You go. I'm a little tired," she says, sitting back in the seat. "I'll wait here."

"No. They're expecting you. It's important that you come in."

Had she been an untrusting sole, she might have picked up on that strained, sudden authoritative tone, but, being the trusting mother that she is, thought nothing of it.

"Well, if you insist. But just for a moment."

The head caretaker knows they're coming, of course, and is in on the plot. The mother is introduced to the manager. "I'm so glad to meet you Mrs. Small. Please come in. Let me show you around."

Well, you know the rest of the story. Once inside, Mom starts to get nervous. There were other older people, just like her ... but not like her, wandering around, aimlessly.

"I'm as sound as a dollar," she thinks. "These people are -- well -- they're out of it!"

"I'd like to go now," she says, turning to her son, a little nervous.

"Let me show you to your room," the manager says, pointing the way with an obsequious smile.

For the first time, the cat is out of the bag.

The old woman looks to her family with startled, unbelieving eyes. "Wha, what does she mean, *my* room?

Then the dawn of recognition comes over her face. Unbelieving shock that her children would do this to her is replaced with outrage and anger. Terror quickly follows. She tries to escape, but is detained. Physically.

"Mom. This is for your own good! You'll like it here."

Empty words. "I *like it* where I live. Now you take me back home this instant or I'll call a cab or walk there myself!"

A meaningless conversation takes place where son and mother exchange words, one trying to convince the other and neither hearing what the other is saying. Finally, more empty words. "Just try it for a day or two, mom. If you don't like it, I'll take you home."

He looks to the manager who quickly picks up the dialog. "Yes, Mrs. Small. Give it a try for a day or so. I'm sure you'll love it here."

After another vein attempt to convince her son that she should not leave her in this place, the son abruptly turns and departs, leaving the mother in tears, the look of unseen terror in her eyes.

Now it was our turn. We get to be the villains. We get to stuff our unsuspecting mother into an environmental hole with other mindless roommates who stare with vacant eyes, with nonsensical words and reach out for uncompassionate responses.

Actually, it was father who had located the facility. It is what is known as a limited care facility as opposed to immediate care or a full care facility. In order to qualify to live there, one must be able to dress oneself, get oneself down to the dinning room and take care of ones immediate physical needs such as going to the bathroom. If you need assistance in showering, there is staff that will assist you.

Although mom has what has been loosely diagnosed as dementia, the facility is actually an Alzheimer's residence.

The first time I visited my mother there was after she had been there a few weeks. I flew in from California and was picked up at Portland International by brother and sister and then driven to the small town in Washington where my folks lived. I can vividly recall my state of mind, sitting on the airplane as it glided silently through the sky. I had been briefed on her condition and to her state of mind. I was prepared for the worst. I hadn't seen her since their visit to Palm Springs, so a lot of emotional water had flowed under the bridge. This was one trip I wasn't looking forward to.

From what I had gathered, there hadn't been the big resistance of introducing mom into the facility that I had expected. Apparently, she was aware that all wasn't up to par in regard to the upstairs department and she had willing gone into the facility. What her exact thoughts were, I didn't know and probably never will.

When we arrived at Camelot Gardens I requested to go in alone, ahead of the rest of the family, so I could deal with my emotions on a one-to-one basis. I didn't know if I was going to be strong and mask my true emotions or if I would break down like a pile of autumn leaves. Whatever the situation, I needed to deal with it alone.

As I entered the facility, I was immediately impressed with the quality of decorative color coordination, the friendly staff, the newly carpeted and wallpapered common area and the wide hallways. On the surface, it seemed to be a very pleasant facility. After introductions to the administrator, we were admitted through an electronically locked glass door into my mother's wing.

The first person I saw was Pam, an elderly petite immaculately dressed woman cruising around the front of the door, looking for a way out. I smiled and nodded a polite hello. She looked at me as if I wasn't to be trusted, but made no comment and edged towards the door, testing it once it was shut.

The hall leading to the sleeping quarters was approximately eight feet wide with further indentations where the individual rooms were located. A soft blue carpet lined the hall. The walls were decorated with brown and white striped wallpaper. A painted white wooden railing, waist high ran the length of the corridor. *Good planning*, I thought. I liked what I saw.

The common area where everyone congregated during the day was huge, filled with many couches, tables and chairs. A crackling fireplace with a glass enclosure was on one wall and a television situated on the other. A piano sat in a corner and the walls were lined with built-in bookcases filled with homey nick-knacks and books.

The first thing that struck me was that the place was occupied with at least ninety- percent woman. There were two men that I saw. One was situated in front of the television, glancing around nervously, stroking his beard. The look in his eye was one of self-imposed possessiveness, as if to say, "This is my television set. Don't even think about changing the channel or taking my seat." The other man, a smallish fellow wore a baseball hat and a sheepish smile. I noticed that he kept glancing at the women sitting on the couches, eyeing them as if they were candy, and he had some spare change.

Several elderly women either sat on the couches or were wandering about the room aimlessly. When I entered, I could feel all eyes clicking on me. Mom was sitting at one of the small dining tables with her head drooping to one side, her mouth in a catatonic state as if she were breathing her last breath. My worst nightmare flashed in front of my eyes like a freight train.

I knelt down beside her and touched her hand. Without opening her eyes, she spoke my name. "Howard? Is that you?"

"Yes. I'm here, mom." I put my arm around her shoulder and she leaned her head against me. The rush of emotion that came forth can only be described as being as near out of control as I have ever been. I closed my eyes for a moment, trying to steady myself. This was no time to fall apart. I was here for support, not to be supported.

By this time the rest of the family came up to the table and started talking to her. "Hi, Mom. How're you doin' today?"

"You look good. Would you like to take a little walk?"

They were phrases and sentences designed to snap her out the apparent stupor that we found her in. *Was this the way that she was always be*, I asked myself? As a commercial real estate broker who had sold many convalescent hospitals to clients in the past, I was all too aware of the understaffed, overfilled, urine smelling facilities with unattended patients sitting in wheel chairs in hallways with saliva dripping from their mouths. This clearly wasn't that kid of a facility and, as I looked around, mom seemed to be the only person present in this quasi-catatonic state. I was clearly concerned.

"I feel *so* tired," she said, still not opening her eyes.

"How are you doin', honey?" our father asks, putting his arm around her shoulders, kissing her lightly on the lips.

There was little response from her.

"She still looks pretty, doesn't she?" he insisted, stroking her face with his large hands.

For the first time, I realized that tremendous bond of love that was between them. It's always been there, it just hadn't been visible. You envy them, yet admire their devotion and even become a little ashamed at your lack of devotion to those in your own life. This is true, genuine love, reaching a depth that few will ever understand.

It was sister, I would later come to learn, whom not only a knack, but also a genuine gift for turning a negative into a positive. Before long, she was tickling Mom's chin, tugging at her cheeks urging her to open her eyes, which to this point still remained shut.

Within a few moments, mom's eyes opened and she was smiling. The balance of the visit was spent chatting, small talk, her asking me about my family and such things. No one talked about the reason of her being there nor did she bring up the topic.

I had heard that she had been disorganized, and confused at times, but I didn't see any of that displayed on her face. She was still my mother, just located in another place. A place that was foreign to both of us. One that neither of us wanted to be in.

In the past, when I would fly down for a visit, we would usually spend the evening playing pinnacle. She and I always stood father and brother. I looked around and found some pinnacle playing cards. "Want to play a game of pinnacle to pass the time?" I asked her.

Always game, even in her present state, she said, "Sure! Why not? We can teach them a lesson." She smiled.

We settled around the small square dining table and I shuffled and dealt the cards. So far everything was okay. The next five minutes told another story. She had trouble holding her cards, let alone organizing them. Sister, who was watching, helped mom organize her hand, looking at me and slowly shaking her head.

I ignored the head shaking and started the bid. Moments later, it was apparent that mom was so confused that she didn't know what a bid was, or which suit to play, let alone which card. We played out the hand and someone suggested that the sun was shining and we could go outside in the patio and enjoy the weather. We never played cards again.

Guilt City

I sat on the bench in front of the window at the end of the wide hallway next to my mother, the emotions that I felt, but dare not speak, transmitted themselves through my fingers as I gently rubbed her shoulders. She sat there, head bent, relaxed, with her eyes closed. One could but wonder what was going through her mind. I wondered if she felt the message my brain was transmitting through my fingers. Just then the sun momentarily broke through the clouds, shinning through the window, taking the chill from her frail body.

It was December and outside the Alzheimer's unit where my mother had been residing living for the past year (normally I would have used the word *living*, but since she had checked in there, she was doing anything but living), the clouds closed the gap that had momentarily let the sun peek through and rain started to hammer the earth relentlessly. *Typical weather for the state of Washington*, I thought.

My father, brother and sister were seated in chairs in the dining room, one on either side of the table. We spoke in soft tones as if not wanting to disturb any of the other residents, as if they cared. The large dining room that also served as a dayroom was occupied with elderly people, mostly women, who strolled around the room and up the hall aimlessly. Some simply sat or lay around in one of the several couches, ignoring the television that constantly blared in the corner, each locked in their own thoughts. It was nearing lunchtime and, aside from the residents and staff, we were the only non-residents in the room. I wondered how often anyone came to see these people. They were obviously someone's mother or father, someone's sister or brother and in at least one case, someone's daughter and son.

My mother's gray hair needed combing, so I strolled down the hall to her room to get her brush. The sleeping rooms were quite large. On one side was her bed, neatly made, and on the other, her roommates bed. Her roommate was fast asleep; a condition I soon learned was the ideal way to pass time for these poor souls. I found a hairbrush where the name *Lillian* had been boldly imprinted on the handle with fingernail polish by my sister, Janice.

As I departed the room, my attention was diverted to a well dressed, neatly coiffured, elderly lady in her mid-eighties I guessed, slowly strolling up to me. On the surface, she seemed calm, but a quick glance into her eyes told another story. They painted a picture of confusion and fear. Stark fear!

She stepped in front of me, meeting my eyes directly. "Do you know where I'm supposed to go?" she asked with a shaky voice. "What am I supposed to do?" She reached out towards me in desperation as if seeking security.

"You can go to the end of the hall," I offered calmly, pointing the way. "To the dining hall where the rest of the people are."

The look on her face remained unchanged. "I ... I don't know where." Her eyes remained fixed on mine. "Where should I go? Where should I be?"

I reiterated my answer accenting it with an extended arm, pointing to the end of the hall. "There, where that lady is standing," I pointed to Pam who appeared to be desperately trying to get out of a locked exit door.

Her eyes stayed fixed on mine. The look of desperation didn't change. "I don't know. What should I do?" She continued pleading for guidance.

Without hesitation, I took her by the arm and slowly escorted her up to the common meeting-recreation-dining room where the rest of the people were congregated when they weren't in their rooms sleeping or were too busy being confused as to who they were, what they were doing, or trying to figure out what they were supposed to be doing.

She held onto my arm like a vice. Every step of the way, she continued looking into my eyes, pleading for me not to abandon her. "What should I do?" She kept asking. "Where should I go?"

Over the course of the past year I had seen this woman several times, along with the rest of the residents of this facility and, to date, this was the most confused, most frightened state that I had seen her in.

Prior to his time, she had walked the hallways, immaculately dressed, carrying her black purse and a sweater which was neatly draped over her arm as if she were about to be picked up for church or go on a shopping tour.

We reached the dining room, and I noticed several unoccupied couches along with vacant tables that were often used for lounging or playing games when they weren't being used to serve food. Some of the couches were occupied by only one person while others held two people who just sat there, looking out into vacant space. I selected a couch next to the television set where another woman was sitting, studying her hands.

"You can sit here," I explained as I gently guided the woman to the seat.

"What will I do?" She continued asking, the frightened look still plainly painted on her face.

For lack of a better answer, I said, "Wait for lunch." I smiled, and patted her on the shoulder then turned to leave, feeling inadequate and guilty for leaving her there in such a state, but rationalizing that I could sit with her and hold her hand for hours and nothing would change. In the end, she would still be just as confused and just as frightened.

Meanwhile, out in the hallway, Pam was busy pacing. She was very petite, and as usual was well dressed, with her hair neatly combed back in a boyish fashion. She had on a jogging suit and matching tennis shoes. She was one of those people that you have to consciously resist the urge to simply hug every time you meet her. Today, tears were welling up in her eyes.

Unable to resist myself, I stopped to talk to her for a moment. "What's the matter, Pam?" I asked. "Having a bad day?"

She nodded and inched closer to me, eyeing the door to the main lobby, which is always closed and locked.

"I want to go home," she said with a soft voice, fighting back tears.

Having been at the facility several times previous, I already knew her story. The first time I visited my mother along with my brother, sister and father and was about to leave, Pam was standing there with her eyes lowered, but firmly fixed on the exit door. As one of the attendants approached to let us out, Pam quickly melted into our group trying to escape with us. The attendant simply smiled and gently took her by the arm and detained her with, "You're going to stay with us, Pam." We left and the attendant guided Pam back into the dayroom.

After giving us a soulful look, Pam turned back to the common area without resistance. This was not the first time she had tried to escape nor would it be the last.

"You want to go home?" I inquired. Basic Rogerian psychology. "Where do you live?"

She looked into my eyes for a moment, and then with quivering lips said, "I don't know."

Unable to resist, I gave her a hug then returned to the end of the hall where my mother and the rest of my family were still chatting.

As I sat down my mother hissed, "That Pam is a sneak!" she said, looking at Pam who was still standing by the door.

"Why do you say that?" I asked, surprised at her reaction. She had always been such a forgiving, tolerant person. To hear such a condemning tone come from her lips frankly shocked me.

"She's always snooping into other people's business and gossiping," she offered, with down turned lips.

"I think she's a nice lady, mom," my sister offered, looking at me with a knowing smile.

"Huh! You don't know. My remote control is missing and it's my bet she took it!"

"You shouldn't accuse someone if you don't have proof," brother said.

"And you always said, if you can't say something nice about someone, don't say anything at all," sister added with a smile.

"Humph!"

It was clearly time to change the subject. "How about going for a little walk down the hall. It's almost lunch time," my sister offered.

"Okay."

Dad slid her walker towards her and with great effort she pulled her eighty-six year-old body to a stand-up position, leaning on the walker. She rested there for a moment, then looked towards her destination, and then started the slow shuffle down the hallway. Her steps were obviously labored as she took one baby step after another, toe to heel.

"You won't get so tired if you take bigger steps, mom," I offered.

She responded without comment by taking larger steps.

As I looked at her, frail and listless, it was nearly impossible to imagine that this little bent over woman shuffling down the hall was my mother. The same woman, less than a year ago, was a vibrant, energetic woman, playing nine holes of golf several times a week, walking a good deal of the time, and was an active leader of her church Bible study circle.

When our visit was over and we all left mom, I paused for a moment to look back. She was still there, alone, looking at us depart through the locked, glass door. One can but wonder what went through her mind. We were going and she was staying.

I know what was going through my mind. I instantly flashed on our society as a whole and, as if comparative analysis, flashed on the same situation in an oriental society. We live in a Chinese neighborhood, as a matter of fact, we're the only white people on our block. We've seen how they treat their elderly. They take them in and care for them. Americans have become a race of mice, racing through our respective, self-appointed mazes of life, rounding each bend at neck-break speed, looking for the next obstacle, barely noting our environment.

Our goal? Not unlike our smaller rodent counter-part that knows there's cheese or some similar reward at the end of the maze, we see nice automobiles, houses in the suburbs, designer cloths, luxurious jewelry, and future education for the kids and above all prestige among our peers. Where do the elderly fit in this picture?

Answer: Visits during Christmas and/or Thanksgiving. Maybe a few days during a summer vacation, providing it doesn't interfere with camping in Yosemite or fishing in Alaska or golf and gaming at Las Vegas.

When we were young, our parents fed us, clothed us, housed us and took care of our every medical, physical and emotional every need.

That's as it should be. They're our parents. They brought us into this world and that was their responsibility. But, hey, now that we're grown up, we don't need them any more! We have our own needs. We have our own families. Our own goals.

Somewhere, back in the caverns of our brain, we always knew that some day they would grow old. It just never occurred to us that one day they might become ill and need support and care. We just thought they would live long, prosperous lives and, in their old age, enjoy life on the Golden Pond, then, one night, when they were very old, while they were sleeping, God would take them home to the hereafter.

Reality check!

We've all seen pictures of older people sitting in wheel chairs, parked in a corner of some institution, they heads hanging to one side, their eyes listless, staring into space, seeing nothing. But, that was old people. Other old people. Our parents would never suffer that lot. Their genes were too good. They lived too rich of a life to ever have that happen to them.

But it does.

It did!

The question is, now that one of them has fallen by the way side, what do we do about it?

Well, we certainly can't stop the race, get out of our well designed maze and put everything on hold while we care for them, now can we? All of a sudden, like an auto accident in the next lane, we're detached from the situation. It's like, they're someone else. The confusion part is, we still know them.

We'd like to take them in, but then, who would take care of them? I mean, there's no room. And who'd administer to their needs? I've got my job. I certainly can't quit that! Who'd pay the bills. And the wife has tennis every Thursday and club meetings on Tuesday and church goings on and she has to cook and clean and care for the house apes. She barely has time to care for al of that.

Then there is the time that the house apes need attention too. Going to their games, picking them up everyday after practice. Monitoring their school work.

All this would suffer if we had to take in our aging parents. No. It wouldn't work. Maybe Brother Mark or Sister Sue can take them in. Yeah! They can do their part. Let them do it.

Do we see a pattern developing here? A bit of selfishness? Some of that old ostrich mentality -- if I don't see it, maybe it'll go away. If I ignore it, the problem will solve itself.

Yeah, excuse me, I hear the telephone. Gee, look at the time. Gotta go!

*****

As we drove back to my father's home, I sat in the back seat, lost in my own world. There were no words to express how I felt about seeing my own mother, helpless, alone and all but abandoned.

I know, we visited her, but then we left. She stayed behind. By herself. I had a lot of emotions to work through, not the least of which was guilt.

As one may well imagine, seeing one's mother in an institution, no matter how nice and cozy it is on the surface, it's still an institution and she's still there.

We go back the next day, hoping that she's better and maybe we can take her home, but we know better and the moment you walk through those doors, you know nothing has changed. Try as you may, you can't get that stabbing pain out of your heart. You cry, but no one notices. This is not about you.

Then, finally it's time to get back on that airplane and go back home. In one sense, you're glad you get to leave, and then you think about the rest of the family that isn't leaving. Your father who will visit her every day and slowly watch her deteriorate in front of his eyes.

The Major Decision

The last time I visited mom, she was in the hospital. She had wasted away to under a hundred pounds, was unable to feed herself, walk or otherwise communicate. The doctor, a German fellow with a thick accent, said that the time had come to make a decision. We could put her on life sustaining fluids, but he assured us that she wouldn't get any better.

I told him to leave us alone for a while, to discuss the matter between ourselves.

He said that he would be on the floor when we had made our decision. There were just the three of us, Janice, Larry and myself. Dad had elected to stay home. He was both physically and mentally drained. We talked about what mom had wanted to do under the circumstances. She had previously executed a Living Will, stating that in the event she ever deteriorated to this state of affairs, that it was her wish not to be kept alive, just for the sake of sustaining unproductive life.

I went to her side, held her hand and whispered in her ear. "If you can hear me, squeeze my hand."

She did.

Her eyes were closed. I asked, "Can you see the bright light?"

A slight squeeze.

"Can you see your brother and sister, your mother and dad there, waiting for you?"

Another slight squeeze.

"Go to them. It's all right. They're waiting for you. Go." It was all I could do to keep from breaking down and Janice and Larry were having a difficult time maintaining their composure as well.

We talked and decided that it was in the best interest of our mother not to keep her lingering on, holding onto life's thread when she wasn't going to get any better. It wasn't an issue of money, because we would have paid anything to get her well. It was a matter of fulfilling her wishes.

"We need to consult with dad," I said. "In the end, it's really his choice."

Dad didn't hesitate. He agreed that it was time to let her go.

Again, we had two choices. Put her into an intensive care home where they would do everything to sustain life or put her into a Hospice and let her go peacefully. We decided on the latter.

That day she was transferred to the Hospice.

It was a nice unit, fairly new, with professional looking help.

I wanted to make it clear that I didn't want her to suffer and was given the understanding that she would be given everything she needed to be comfortable. She even indicated that there had been people admitted that had gotten better and had been returned to their families.

A ray of hope.

I left for home with the feeling that mom would die peacefully and her that soul would soon be returned back to God's arms.

Janice, as usual, was the pillar of strength, staying on with dad to visit her everyday while I flew home and Larry returned to his duties in Portland. I called every day to see how she was doing. And with each passing day, I was amazed how she kept holding on and holding on, refusing to leave her emaciated body. I was certain that her soul had long since gone home, but why was she still hanging on?

For ten long days she held on. I later learned that she had survived that long period of time without food or water. In short, she had literally been starved to death! When I learned this I was furious, not only with the Hospice where I had been given the assurance that she would not suffer, but with myself for allowing this to happen. Now, whenever I say, "I'm hungry. I haven't eaten since ...." I think back on mom and how she must have suffered.

Whenever I hear someone thinking of putting a loved one in a Hospice, I tell them to think twice about it.

*****

A memorial service was held in the Lutheran church in Longview where she and dad had been members. We, the family, were kept in an isolated room until the service was about to start, then we were led up into the first pews where the grieving family sat. Why we were isolated I have no idea.

Janice and Larry had compiled an array of pictures depicting happy times camping, vacationing, golfing and family get-togethers. A 16 x 20 colored oil portrait of her that I had painted stood on an easel in front of the church. The painting had been coped from a black and white photograph taken on the day of her graduation from beauty school. She had this little impish smirk on her lips that hinted of a secret that only she knew. Tried as I may, I wasn't able to capture that look.

The photos that were on display mapped out many of the good times that we had as a family, on trips, family gatherings, golf and camping outings, but there was one picture that was missing that meant more to me than all the others, and I have no clue where it is today, and even if I had possession of it at the time, it wouldn't have made it to the picture board. It was a four by four black and white picture taken with my brownie camera when I was a sophomore in high school. The folks had just arrived home from work that evening and were exhausted. They were sleeping on the couch, wrapped in one another's arms, still dressed in their work clothes.

To me, that single, simple picture depicted everything they represented in their marriage and in my life. Their love and devotion to each other and the sacrifices that they were making to the family.

I loved that picture.

The minister got up and said a few words and then indicated that some of the family members could get up and speak. Larry and I were designated with me going first.

Knowing that I was supposed to get up in front of the congregation and talk, I wrestled with my thoughts, wondering what to say. When the time came for me to get up, I stood at the podium and looked over the large congregation that had come to wish her a farewell. I saw faces of people that I had no idea who they were, but who probably knew me, people who were her church members, prayer groups, friends and some who I was surprised to see sitting there such as Dale Hackett whose wife, Carol, used to be one of my apartment mangers and had since passed away.

I thanked everyone for coming to celebrate our mother's life, saying that mom would not have wanted this to be a solemn occasion, but a celebration of her life.

Janice had found a book of poems in mom's bedroom. It had a page marked. This is what it read:

When I must Leave You

When I must leave you
for a little while,
Please do not grieve
and shed wild tears
And hug your sorrow
to you through the years,
But start out bravely
with a gallant smile;
And for my sake
and in my name
Live on and do
all things the same,
Feed not your loneliness
on empty days,
But fill each waking hour
in useful ways,
Reach out your hand
in comfort and in cheer
And I in turn will comfort you
and hold you near;
And never, never
be afraid to die,
For I am waiting
for you in the sky!

God, I miss that woman!

Mom? Is That You?

It had been several months now since mom had passed away and I thought about her everyday, often lamenting her final days. I just couldn't seem to let it go. I finally concluded that I needed a change in scenery.

"What do you say about taking a trip to Palm Springs for a few days?" I asked Myrna one day. She agreed.

After driving for seven hours, we arrived at the condo three o'clock. The weather was a balmy ninety-five degrees. After unpacking and walking our toy poodle, Brandi, around the complex, we decided to hit the pool. The complex has seven swimming pools and at any given time, you can almost always find a pool all to yourself. The water was just perfect and we swam for a while and then sat in the pool for a while before getting out and retiring to one of the several lounges that had been placed around the deck.

While my wife rested under the shade of a tree with her eyes closed, I sat in the sun, near the flowers and mediated. I couldn't get my mind off mom. More to myself than anything, I said, "If you're okay, and can let me know, I'd appreciate it."

At that exact moment a small bird flew down and landed on one of the flowers that had been planted a few feet from me. It was the smallest thing I had ever seen, perfectly formed, about one-quarter the size of a humming bird, but formed like a sparrow, except more colorful.

The bird sat on this slight flower stem looking at me and I looked back, amazed at how tiny it was, yet perfectly formed. It seemed almost friendly. I don't know what possessed me, but I slid the lounge chair over next to the flower, making a loud scraping noise as I did so, but the bird didn't falter. It sat perfectly still, her eyes transfixed on me. I say her because she didn't seem to have the colorful markings that a male bird might have.

Again, I don't know what possessed me to do so, but I reached out and cupped the little creature in my open hands. The bird didn't fly away or even seen concerned for that matter. It just continued sitting there in my open hands, looking at me.

I got up and went over to my wife, still holding the bird in my cupped hands, and said, "Look! This little bird just flew down and lit on the flowers over there. She let me pick her up. I can't believe it! She doesn't even seem to be frightened."

Myrna reached out and stroked the little creature's head with her forefinger and we both sat there amazed, studying the little wonder.

"Why do you suppose she flew down here to you?" she asked.

I thought back to when I had been meditating on mom, and at that very moment, realized what was happening. The moment that I realized what was going on, the little bird took off from my hands and flew straight up into the sky.

We watched as it disappeared and then we simply looked at one another.

"Have you ever seen anything so small and perfectly formed?" I asked.

We both knew that the answer to that question was that it was mom's spirit, letting me know that, yes, she was okay. She had answered by prayer – to let me know.

Pop Decides To Go

It had been several months now since mom had passed away. Dad said that he missed her every day and seemed to be taking a lot more naps than usual. Then, he started giving everything away, pictures, furniture, odds and ends. We were all concerned, but just chalked it up to his generosity. He would have given you the shirt off his back if you asked.

He had been having a little trouble with his stomach and hadn't had a bowl movement on this particular night and had checked himself into the hospital. They ran their usual battery of tests and discovered that he had signs of blood in his stool. He had hemorrhoids so bleeding from one of them was no mystery. Nonetheless, they decided to make him fast for twenty-four hours so they could run tests to see if he had colon cancer.

He hadn't eaten the previous night and was hungry. He asked the nurse for a sandwich or a bowl of soup, both of which was denied him because of the test they wanted to run the following day. Subsequently, he went two days without food and by the time they ran his tests and got around to deciding what to do with him, he was fed up with the hospital and simply got out of bed and gave notice that he was checking out, like it or not. He called Bill and Lindy and told them to come and get him, which they did.

Back home, Bill reports that he could get dad to eat a few spoons of soup, but for all intents and purposes, he had apparently given up the will to live.

Then, one night Bill and Lindy had changed his bedding after an accident that dad had. When he got back in bed he smiled and told them, "I'll be seeing you."

Those were his last words.

As a post script, I had visited Dad a few months earlier and was sleeping in the room next door as I always did. It was around midnight and I hadn't gotten to sleep yet when I heard him say, "Why didn't you wait for me?"

You can draw your own conclusions to what was happening, I know I have.

I never fully appreciated the depth of the love that he had for our mother until I saw him with her at the convalescent hospital. He was very attentive, stroking her hand, gently kissing her when he arrived as well as when he left, and spoke about her in none other than loving and affectionate terms.

I think the reason none of us saw this behavior when we were young is because they were both working full time just to keep a roof over our heads and food on the table. When they came home, they were bone tired, yet they fixed meals for us and saw to our every need. We were poor as church mice, but none of us knew it, and could have cared less.

Then when they were older and retired, they played golf together several times a week, had friends over for dinner and played cards, and of course, mom was heavily involved in the church. I never got the impression that dad was much on going to church, although after mom had been committed, he did attend church alone every Sunday for a while until the minister who he liked greatly had been transferred to another church.

I talk to my brother and sister frequently and the topic of our folks always comes up. I think about them every day, and I know they do as well.

Grandchildren?

As of this writing, I'm seventy-three years of age with three healthy young sons. With the exception of Christian's recent marriage to Erica-Ann, they are all single, healthy, young, men. What am I harping about, you might ask? They are all handsome, able bodied, healthy, successful young men, about to enter into middle age and I still don't have any grandchildren.

I played tennis with a man several years younger than I yesterday and he was bragging that his granddaughter was about to graduate from college.

College!

I said, "I'll be happy just to live long enough to *have* a grandchild, let alone see one graduate from college."

Then he rubbed in by saying that this was his third grandchild to graduate from college.

We're no longer friends.

A number of years back, Aaron was at the doorstep of marital bliss. I believe he was less than two weeks from tying the knot. I had already been fitted for my monkey suit, but had not yet picked it up when I noticed my three sons standing on the lawn next to the tennis courts where I was getting in my weekly Monday tennis game. After the set was over, I walked over to where they had gathered, kinda like in a huddle.

"What's up, guys?" I asked casually. I could tell instantly that something was wrong, just by the way that they were standing. It was Aaron who spoke up, first.

"I guess you won't be needing that tux, pops," he said, choking out the words.

I looked first at him and then at his brothers.

"The wedding is off," he said quietly, chocking back his emotions.

I was astonished, because I knew that everything had been set from the time, place and who was going to attend the happy event down to the last detail, including pictures and the place of the reception.

"What happened?" I asked.

He proceeded to tell me the circumstances under which he came to be informed that there was not going to be a wedding, at least not now, not with his intended. Without going into the details of the reason for the break-up, needless to say, everyone was shocked, most of all, Aaron.

Not that that event, or non-event carried any importance when it came to my having or not having any grandchildren, it was an obvious setback.

Grandchildren?

I may have to be satisfied with nieces, nephews and their children. Do pets count?

Family Pets

A recent study disclosed that sixty percent of us own a pet. From my experience that should read that sixty percent of us are *owned* by a pet. That is to say that we are allowed to house, feed and take care of their needs while in reality, it is they, the pets, who are really in charge. I mean, really, who picks up after them when they poop, and who feeds them on demand, and who is in charge of grooming, walking, taking them to the vet and are on twenty-four hour call when they bark, meow or make other demanding noises that says, *I need food,* or *I need to go outside* or *hey, how about giving me some attention?*

I would surmise that the majority of us who are pet owners have either a cat or a dog, while others prefer birds, lizards, toads, turtles or even snakes and spiders. To me, if it doesn't have fur, and you can't take it for a walk, I don't want it.

I got my first pet when we moved it Irrigon, somewhere around the fifth grade. It was a mixed breed. I named him Sparky. At the time, I think Sparky was the most common name that anyone could give to a dog. Not too imaginative, but it worked. He was an outside dog that was never allowed in the house. How he spent his day, I don't have a clue, but we lived on the Columbia River and there were jackrabbits galore just across the street, so I imagine that he and they became fast friends. All I know is that he came when I called his name. He met his demise under the tires of the local oil delivery truck one day while I was at school. Although I was sad about loosing Sparky, I don't recall being all that shook up about his demise.

When the folks moved to Hermiston, we got another dog, an Irish Setter named Skippy. Again, not to original of a name. He had a beautiful red coat and was smart as a whip. I don't recall spending all that much time with him as most of my spare time was spend on sports. All I can remember is that he was still alive when I went to college, but I have no memory of what happened to him after I left the household.

After high school I went to college for five years and then the Army got me for a couple of years and then it was back to college again for two more years and then I got married. During that time there was no time for pets. My next pet, after I got married and had bought a house, was another Iris Setter. I had it in my mind that Skippy had been such a great pet that I wanted a repeat.

"What are you going to name him?" my wife inquired when I brought him home to meet the family.

"Skippy!"

After getting the, *try something more imaginable, fool*, look, I decided that a creative name depicting the business that I was in, namely commercial real estate, would be in order. I settled on Trust Deed. I'll bet you've never heard a dog named after a legal document, have you? Word got around that I had named my Irish Setter after a legal document and I even made the *Sacramento Bee* business section of how far a man would go to bring his dog into the business.

I can remember when the kids were small, I brought home an angora guinea pig. That's a hairy rat for the uninformed. He had the run of the house and didn't eat much, just a small pellet once in a while and his poop was so small, we never did find that. It didn't take long to learn that he had a sweet tooth for lettuce however. Whenever we opened the refrigerator, he would make a mad dash to the kitchen making a high pitched, *weeee*, sound.

At this point I should mention that when I bought the house on Miguelita out on the far east side of town, one of the first things I did was to construct a five foot tall fence around the property to keep kids and animals in and others out. It worked fine until Trust Deed grew into adulthood and began hurdling the fence and took to exploring the eastside on his own, until I either got a call from an irritated neighbor, telling me to come and get him, or I found him in the dog pound three days later, or he returned home on his own. Eventually he left home, never to return.

My next pet was a Great Dane named Caesar. He was a great animal to have. I had never had a dog that was bigger than me. Standing on his hind legs, he was clearly taller than six feet- two inches! While he was still a pup and in his developmental years, we had his ears boxed, which is to say that during his formative development, his ears had been taped to stand straight up. When the taped rack had been removed, he looked handsome. And fierce. Whenever anyone came to the gate or even walked by, he would bound up to the gate and give a ferocious bark that would scare any normal person.

I liked to take a run every morning, before work, so when Caesar matured into a full grown dog, I took to taking him on my morning runs. I soon came to the realization that my run was only up to par with his normal walk. So I tried taking him for a run while I rode my bicycle. It took only the first squirrel to cross the road and run down the ravine to realize the error of my ways. After picking myself off the ground at the bottom of the ravine, picking the burrs out of my hair and spitting out the gravel that I had ingested, I realized that there must be another solution to taking him on a 'run'.

You should have seen the looks that I got from passer-buyers – some in utter amazement, others - outright disgust – when they saw him running besides my Mercedes with me holding onto his leash from the driver's side.

Can't say that I blame 'em.

Caesar did have one bad experience as a pup under our ownership. The next door neighbor had a dog – what breed I have no clue – but somewhat akin to a pit bull. We had had Caesar for only a short time when one day both he and the neighbor's dog got free from their confinements and had met on the street at the apex of both of our properties. Their dog, named Sport, being much larger and mature, attacked Caesar and beat him up pretty good that day. Why he attacked him, I have no clue. Maybe to demonstrate his dominance, or to mark his territory. At any rate, apparently Caesar never forgot that incident. Every time we passed the neighbor's house, he would snarl and make a break for the house, all the while the other dog, now chained, would make similar aggressive moves toward Caesar.

Then, one day, several years later, Sister Joan Marie, a teacher from the boy's school, happen to come by for a home visit. Caesar of course was roaming the grounds, freely, and when the gate opened up, he came to greet our visitor – in a friendly manner, you understand.

When the sister Joan Marie saw the size of Caesar, she felt fearful, to which I responded, "Oh, he's okay. He wouldn't hurt a flea."

As fate would have it, at that exact moment Sport had managed to get free and came charging up after Caesar who by now was full grown and had a memory like an elephant. It took only two seconds for Caesar to have Sport by the neck and was calmly marching down the hill of our driveway with his prey helplessly hanging between his teeth. I can only imagine what was going through his head, but it must have been something like this: *I'm going to take him where no one will be a witness, and rip his head off his ugly body!*

After making apologies to Sister Joan Marie I raced down to release Sport from Caesar's mouth, apologizing to him for taking away his revenge, but not being able to justify to Sister Joan Marie nor the neighbor about the dog's eminent demise, so when I let Sport go, he ran up the hill and was never heard from again.

Caesar was too large to take on periodic trips that we took to Oregon to visit my parents. Usually for a week or more, so when I left, I left him and Muffin our cat, a sixty pound bag of dried dog food (Muffin had a ten pound bag of cat food where Caesar couldn't get it) and running clean water and the run of the land until we got back. He took care of the house very well in our absence, thank you.

Up to that point in time, Caesar was clearly the best and greatest dog that I had ever known. Sometime after the period when I had been evicted from the house, he apparently died. Cancer of the mouth, I was told. He was a great and magnificent dog. And I feel privileged to have owned him. Or was it I that had been owned by him?

During this same time period when I owned Caesar, I happened to be playing tennis with my friend Steve down at the city park tennis courts off Tenth Street in San Jose. I noticed this young German Shepard nervously wandering around the park, as if he were looking for something or someone. It was a hot day and when we took a break,

I filled the tennis can with water and gave it to him. He was skittish at first, but then hesitatingly accepted my offer, allowing me to pet him once before backing off, with his fangs showing.

We resumed our game. I noticed that after giving him the water that he wasn't so skittish and was hanging around the court where we were playing. Once our match was over, Steve took off in his little BMW and I walked toward my car, a little Javelin that I owned at the time. Much to my surprise, the German Shepard followed me and when I opened the door, he jumped in, as if he had done it a thousand times.

Deducing that he was either an abandoned dog or lost, I took him home. He immediately took to the family, including Caesar who seemed to welcome a fellow dog to play with. The only problem was, when the kids went swimming in the pool, which they did almost every day, Skippy, as we called him, (I know, not too original.) apparently thinking that the kid's screaming and splashing indicated that they were in trouble, would jump in and grab hold of their bathing suits and drag them to the side of the pool.

During this period of time, Christian and I were riding in my car down on Stockton Street one day when we saw this young chicken running lose. I knew it was only a matter of time until it go hit by a car and run over, so we stopped the car and caught it and took it home. We had no pen to keep it in, so we simply let it have the run of the grounds, like the dogs. I don't know why, but the dogs took a liking to the bird, adopting him as one of their own.

The chicken grew into a full grown hen, and began laying a brown egg every day. She had no nest, so she simply laid the egg wherever she seemed to be at the time that the egg was due to come out. Then one day, she accidentally let it drop on the sidewalk where it broke. One of the dogs found it and ate it. From that day on, it was a race between dog and man to see who got to the newly laid egg first.

Skippy and the chicken became close friends. I was amazed at how close they had become. One day I caught them in the act of playing a game. Skippy would chase the chicken, catch it in his mouth and then walk around with the chicken just handing between his jaws as if it were dead. Then, Skippy would set it down, at which time the race was on again, dog chasing the chicken. Not once did he ever hurt or injure the chicken.

Whenever I arrived home after going out on an appointment, the dogs – and chicken – would race up the driveway to greet me. Whenever the dogs were fed, usually in the evening, out of one large dish, dogs and chicken would eat together. I've got to say, that that chicken was the strangest pet we've ever had.

Once I was divorced, I didn't have another dog until nearly twenty years later. This friend that I play tennis with had a wife that bread and sold toy poodles. One day he told me that they had a litter and asked if I would like to come over and see them. On a lark and nothing more, Myrna and I went over to see the puppies and to visit with him and his wife.

We notice right away that there was this little runt of a poodle that was being intimidated by the other larger dogs and was hiding under the chair, probably out of self preservation, more than anything else. Myrna picked her up and that began a fourteen year love relationship with Brandie, as we called her, mostly because her fur color was brandy colored.

We took her everywhere. We drove to Palm Springs, 7 hours. She sat on our lap the whole way, looking out the window between cat naps. We drove to Oregon. 12 hours. Same thing. She was one of the family and we loved her almost more than any human being that we knew. If you have pet, you can identify with what I am saying. She was an integral part of our lives.

The thing about pets is they give you so much joy; they become part of the family. When they get old and you have to depart with them -- when they pass away, they leave this baseball sized hole in the pit of your stomach that refuses to go away.

We were in Palm Springs. It was Sunday, Mother' day, 2008, when Brandi passed away. The previous night, she had trouble breathing, so I got up and held her in my arms the whole night, comforting her when she became agitated. The next morning she died in my arms. We cried like babies at the loss.

Our neighbor had a Toy Poodle and, like Brandi, one day had suddenly passed away. Like us, they grieved and swore never to get another dog. The following day they went out and bought a replacement dog. That was their recommendation to us, go out and get a new dog right away. We thought about it for about two minutes and decided that to go out an immediately get a replacement dog would be an insult to Brandi's memory. It would be like your spouse dying and then the next day, go out and find a replacement. No thanks. We did think that we might wait until the following year and then maybe go out and look, but not before then.

The following November I was working on my computer when I saw the picture of a little Maltese that was for sale by a breeder. I knew instantly, that this was to be our next pet. We drove to Union City where we located the address of the breeder. She had four puppies for sale. We watched them run and play, picked them up one-by-one and then chose one. "This is the one," I said, handing it to Myrna.

Thus began our relationship with the newest member of the family, Tedi. I think, considering our age, Tedi will be our last pet. Who will outlast who, is up for grabs.

*****

Well, that's about it. As of today that's my journey in a thimble. I tried living my life, staying within the guidelines as set forth by faith and my fellow man. In the process, I have had a wonderful family, I produced three great young men, have a fantastic wife, have had the companionship of great pets, made a few friends along the way, didn't embarrass myself too much along the journey and, as of today, I still remember my name, although I have it written on my auto license just in case, and the names of my significant others, and am still able to walk and chew gum at the same time.

How about you?

How is your life?